"COME OUT!" SHE CRIED IMPULSIVELY. "COME OUT AND GET IT OVER WITH!"

She glared at the open door. When he sauntered through it, he *looked* real—even younger in the daylight, more hopeful somehow.

"Are you here or are you not?" she demanded. "If I'm crazy, then tell me and I'll go back to New Hampshire and my people will take care of me."

He shrugged. "Ye seem all right to me. A little prickly maybe."

What am I doing? I'm asking my hallucination if I'm hallucinating! "Look, O'Malley, if you're real—really a ghost—then prove it. Make something levitate. Tell me something about myself no one else knows."

"Can't do either one, as it happens." He rubbed his chin. "Ah, I've got it." He glanced around the room. Then his gaze settled on the stripped pine dresser that was her grandmother's. He stared at it intently, and the room began to fill with blinding, hurting light.

"Not that, not that!" she cried, shielding her eyes.

"Ye want the bloody proof or not?" he answered, annoyed, but the light subsided.

When Emily opened her eyes again, she saw, burned into the top drawer of the honey-colored pine, the name Fergus O'Malley in a childish, scrawling signature. Stunned, Emily put a finger to the deeply scorched drawer. It was hot to the touch. Her nostrils filled with the smell of charred wood. From behind her she heard O'Malley's voice, irritated and impatient once more, say, "Now. Can we get to work?"

"Highly original and emotionally rich reading . . . *Emily's Ghost* is pure and unadulterated reading pleasure." —*Romantic Times*

"An engaging heroine, a sexy senator, and a rapscallion ghost make *Emily's Ghost* an irresistible read." —Susan Elizabeth Phillips

Also by Antoinette Stockenberg

Embers
Beloved
Time After Time

Emily's Ghost

ANTOINETTE
STOCKENBERG

A Dell Book

Published by
Dell Publishing
a division of
Bantam Doubleday Dell Publishing Group, Inc.
1540 Broadway
New York, New York 10036

ISBN: 0-440-21002-X

Printed in the United States of America

Published simultaneously in Canada

May 1992

10 9 8 7 6 5 4 3

OPM

For Mom,
in Memory

1

Emily Bowditch threw down her notes in disgust.

"Can you believe this? The United States is three trillion dollars in debt, and Senator Arthur Lee Alden the Third wants funding for intergalactic communication. Can you *believe* this?"

No one in the newsroom paid any attention to her; everyone was on deadline. Emily turned her computer on and began setting up a new file.

"Not to worry, E.T.," she muttered to no one in particular. "If the senator gets his funding, pretty soon you *will* be able to phone home."

The minutes ticked by. Her hands flew over the keyboard; her muttering became more indignant. "Of all the hopeless wastes of taxpayers' money . . . of all the liberal spendthrifts . . . of all the misdirected . . . whimsical . . . irrational . . . downright weird . . ."

Stan Cooper looked up annoyed from his computer screen. "What *are* you going on about?" He swiveled his chair to face Emily and reached for his coffee mug. "Tell me now and get it over with, for God's sake, so I can get back to work."

The irritation in his voice didn't bother Emily at all. She assumed that all forty-eight-year-old bachelor newsmen came that way. "It's Senator Alden."

Stan's eyelids flickered. "Yeah? What about him?"

"I've just got hold of a letter he wrote urging the National Science Foundation to fund a heck of a lot more psychic research than they've been doing. I didn't know they were doing *any*," she said through gritted teeth. "And now they're going to do *more*."

"How much more?" Stan asked. His voice was low and still, the way it got whenever he talked about Senator Alden.

She shook her head. "It doesn't say." She fished her copy of the letter from a school of papers on her desk and read from it aloud. " 'We urge you'—blah, blah, here it is—'to allocate substantially greater sums for psychic research, which, among other benefits, can have far-reaching ramifications for both our domestic and foreign intelligence.' "

Stan's laugh was short and derisive. "FBI. CIA. Yeah. Rumors have been going around for years that they've been fooling around with psi." Stan drained the dregs of his coffee and made a wry face. "So how you gonna handle the story?"

Emily sighed. "I'm sure the chief'll want me to play it straight; he respects the senator too much to feel any moral outrage here."

"No problem," Stan said with a deadly smile. "Between you and me we have more than enough."

"Well, it *is* outrageous," she insisted defensively.

"I agree."

"I mean it, Stan. Our government is out of control, absolutely out of control. Our bridges are falling down, our sewers are disintegrating, our schools need overhauling, and this guy calls for psychic research! Who needs psychic research? We need concrete; pipes; schoolrooms."

Stan swiveled slowly around to face his computer, effectively ending the coffee break. "What an innocent you are," he said in a tired voice. "I suppose it comes from living and working in New Hampshire."

Emily flushed. She'd met Stanley Cooper when he was on assignment in Manchester seven years earlier. She was a junior reporter then, really just a gofer, and she'd been thoroughly awed by the hard-boiled political reporter from the *Boston Journal.* He liked what little she *had* written, though, and when she took a job in New Bedford covering municipal affairs for the local paper, his name was on her list of references.

Then, six months ago, she sent her résumé to the *Boston Journal.* Stanley Cooper interviewed her in depth, recommended her, and put her through her paces after she was hired. Later she learned the exact wording of his recommendation: "She'll be a royal pain in the butt. We need her."

At twenty-eight Emily Bowditch was as much in awe of Stan Cooper as ever. She didn't think much of him as a man—he drank, smoked, gambled, detested kids, and didn't keep house—but as a political writer he was without parallel. She'd do just about anything to impress him. Whenever he cut her down to size (and that was often), she took it hard.

She studied his profile as he hunched over his keyboard, pecking fitfully. His clothes were shabby. His face was lined, unshaven, unhappy. He was thin, almost bony; he was suspicious of everything, probably including food. But he was brilliant, and Emily wanted desperately to make her mark with him.

"Stan?" she ventured, risking his wrath. "I've been

mulling over an idea for a story. I think it could be pretty good."

"Hmm."

"Maybe even sensational."

"Hmm."

"Do you want to hear about it?"

"No. Just do it."

That was it, the permission she wanted—more or less. She grabbed her tweed jacket and said, "I'll be at the library for the next couple of hours." But as she sprinted down the steps of the bland brick building that housed the *Boston Journal*, the thought occurred to her that her idea was cockamamy at best and a pretty good reason for getting fired at worst.

Emily spent the rest of the afternoon in the Boston Public Library, plowing through old copies of *Etheric*, a magazine devoted exclusively to psychic phenomena, a magazine that until that morning she had never known existed. She was working strictly on a hunch, and she wasn't sure what she'd find.

When she'd called Senator Alden's office earlier in the day to confirm the existence of his letter to the National Science Foundation, she was put through to his aide, Jim Whitewood. In the process some signals had obviously been crossed. Mr. Whitewood had come on the line and, before she could say boo, said in a very sharp voice, "How did you get hold of the letter? Are you from *Etheric*?"

"What's *Etheric*?" Emily had asked, a little stupidly.

"Who is this?" Mr. Whitewood had demanded.

That's when she made the first of a series of snap judgments that later came back to haunt her. She had said in response, "Hello? Hello? Oh, darn, something's wrong with this phone," and hung up. She needed time, time to track down *Etheric* and see what or who had made Mr. Whitewood so press-shy.

And so, with the bright May sun shining through the ceiling-high windows, warming the back of her neck under her straight dark hair, Emily thumbed drowsily through dozens of back issues of the fascinating and bizarre periodical, stopping every now and then to peruse an article that caught her fancy. At five-thirty she sat up straight.

"Bingo," she whispered softly to herself.

In the "Newsworthy" column of a two-year-old issue of *Etheric* was a photo of Senator Alden shaking the hand of his new aide, Jim Whitewood. Mr. Whitewood, who claimed "only modestly psychic powers," promised to "keep the lines of communication open between Senator Alden and those with genuine psychic ability."

Only modestly psychic. That was like saying someone was only modestly out of his mind.

Emily hugged herself with joy. Her original plan suddenly got a little more cockamamy.

Armed with a photocopy of the *Etheric* photo and caption, Emily cornered Stan Cooper alone in the *Journal*'s smoking lounge the next morning. "Stan, I really need your input on this." She handed him the photo she'd found and watched him break into a contemptuous smile. "The magazine folded soon after this issue came out," she said. "It had no circulation at all, so I doubt if your average voter even knows about this."

With a flick of his wrist Stan let the sheet of paper float down to the floor. "Your average voter couldn't care less," he said. "Your average voter is female and madly in love with Senator Alden."

Emily scooped up the sheet and tucked it in her bag. "Says who?"

"Ask anyone at a shopping mall. Lee Alden was a devoted husband for ten years. When his wife died in a car accident a couple of years ago, there was talk he might not run again, that's how devastated he was. For a while he refused to appear socially at all." Stan lit a new cigarette from the stub of his last one, took a deep drag, and let it out through his nose. "Lately he's begun to show up at an occasional charity function, but he arrives alone and early and leaves in an hour. Every socialite in Massachusetts has tried to land him. Every female shopper in the state nourishes her own silly, secret hope."

The measured tone in his voice had gradually turned bitter, so much so that Emily averted her eyes from the coldness she saw in his face. For the first time it occurred to her that Stan might not be objective when it came to Senator Arthur Lee Alden III. She couldn't imagine why.

"Well, I think women are as well informed and conscientious about who they vote for as anyone," she said firmly. "But they have to have the information out in front where they can see it. They have to know this guy's a flake."

"Oh, Christ, Emily, the man could get thrown in jail for life and they'd vote for him." He snubbed out his cigarette in irritation and stood up to leave. But at the door he turned suddenly and said, "What're you up to?"

"Okay," she said, taking the plunge. "Originally I planned to call and say I was looking for a good medium—channeler, I guess I mean—and ask if the senator could recommend anyone. Then I found Whitewood's open invitation in *Etheric* and I thought, why don't *I* just show up and say I have psychic powers. How far could I get?"

"You're insane, Emily," Stan said calmly.

But Emily could see in his face that he was intrigued by the possibilities. "No, really, Stan. I mean, I *do* have certain . . . intuitions. I'm very *good* at . . . intuition. I've called my friend Cara several times at the exact moment when she's picked up the phone at the other end—"

"—which probably means it's your friend Cara who is telepathic," Stan said dryly.

"Whatever. But I've been reading up on this stuff. A lot of it is just plain old common sense and shrewdness—"

"—both of which you possess in abundance, I can tell."

There was a sneer in his voice, but it was a kindly sneer. Emily took hope from it and said, "So you think it might fly?"

Stan looked at her intently for a long, withering moment. Then he said, "This conversation never happened," and walked out.

Emily was left puzzling over his parting shot. Did he mean, "Lucky for you I'm not a snitch"? Or did he mean, "Don't tell me until it's over"? She threw herself into a battered Naugahyde lounge chair and remained there, deep in indecision, for some time. But the sound of voices in the hall got her moving again. Yes. There *was* a story there, dammit. And the taxpayers of Massachusetts had the right to know it.

The security guard had to throw Emily out of the library that night; when she left, her book bag was full. For the rest of the week she crammed herself full of facts—well, they were hardly *facts*—on the paranormal and learned all she could about Senator Alden. Jim Whitewood, the senator's aide, was due back in Boston on Monday. By Sunday afternoon Emily felt ready for him. She felt sure that she could seem as mystical and vague as the next guy. She'd be just fine, as long as he didn't ask her to bend a spoon or anything.

The only thing bothering Emily was what always bothers women in new situations: what to wear. How did a channeler dress for a job interview? She'd seen one or two people who claimed to be mediums on talk shows, but they were men. She'd never seen a woman channeler; all she had to go on were a couple of book jackets from the seventies in which the women mediums had posed for their autobiographies.

So she did the best she could. She rummaged through her closet and came up with a Ralph Lauren skirt from his peasant period, and a frilly white blouse, and a large straw hat with turquoise flowers. The outfit flattered her dark eyes and hair; she was even tall enough to carry off the hat. She looked exciting; she looked exotic; she looked ready for lunch under a palm tree in Barbados, which is where she'd bought all the clothes in the first place.

But the JFK Federal Office Building in downtown Boston?

Emily turned slowly around in her full-length mirror, trying to gauge the effect she'd have on Jim Whitewood. One thing was sure: She'd stand out from the pack. She smiled. The crazy lady in the straw hat smiled back, her dark eyes dancing with mystery. For an instant Emily believed she really was a psychic.

Whoa. Maybe I've been reading too much of this stuff. It's catching. In a kind of panic she snatched off her hat and threw it on her bed; she pulled off the blouse and skirt and tossed them in a heap on top of an old steamer trunk. After that she slipped into her softest cotton nightgown, made herself a cup of hot tea, and fished out the financial section of the Sunday *New York Times.* It was just the dose of reality she needed. In twenty minutes she was fast asleep.

The next morning found Emily, hat in lap, sitting on the Boston "T" and bound for the senator's downtown offices. She tried hard to focus on the otherworldly, but it wasn't easy; everyone around her was dressed in a three-piece business suit. She tried hard to be inconspicuous, but that wasn't easy either. When the lawyer type next to her jumped up for his stop, he took off with her hat, which had got caught in the zipper of his open attaché case.

If I believed in omens, I would not be comforted by this, she thought grimly, tucking the remaining flowers back into the hatband.

Still, by the time she found herself face-to-face with the senator's secretary, she'd got back her sense of outrage and with it, her confidence. It seemed completely clear to her that both the senator *and* his aide were gullible at best and unfit for their jobs at worst.

The secretary—a nice, normal, middle-aged woman dressed sensibly in a linen suit—was kind but firm. "Miss, ah, Bowditch, is it? I'm sorry, do you have an appointment with Mr. Whitewood?"

This was the tricky part: getting in. "No, I don't," Emily replied candidly, "but I feel *absolutely certain* that he'll want to hear me." Emily gave the secretary a significant look.

The secretary gave her a significant look back. "Can you tell me the nature of your visit?"

"No-o-o, I'm afraid I can't," Emily answered meaningfully.

"I see. Well, Mr. Whitewood hasn't come in yet. Perhaps if you take a seat . . . I'll see what I can do.

But I believe Mr. Whitewood is full up with meetings today."

Emily moved away to the reception area. The secretary took down a black binder and began scanning the page. Emily was set to spend the whole day waiting if she had to, but she hoped that the secretary was finding a blank slot in the calendar before noon. After about twenty minutes Jim Whitewood came in; Emily recognized him instantly from the photo in *Etheric*. He was impeccably groomed, a little slick, maybe even opportunistic, she thought. He looked more Wall Street than Federal Office Building.

She gave him a mysterious smile as he hurried past her into his office. The secretary followed. In less than a minute Emily was being ushered in, and it wasn't even nine o'clock.

Whitewood introduced himself and offered Emily a seat. "I understand you have something to tell me?"

"Well, not *tell*, exactly. It's more something I have to . . . offer you."

Whitewood gave her the briefest of glances, taking in the rounded curve of her shoulders; the cut of her bodice; the hat.

"Really."

Emily blushed deeply. "I mean, not *offer*, exactly. That was probably the wrong word." *Ah, what the hell*, she thought. *In for a penny, in for a buck*. She stood up, swept her hat from her head, and glided across the room, coming to rest near an enormous potted schefflera. She was going to play this for all it was worth.

She turned to face the senator's aide and said in a throaty voice, "I understand that you extend a welcome to those with . . . extraordinary perceptions."

"And you are such a person?" he asked noncommittally.

"I am."

"How do you know?"

She lifted one bare shoulder. "How does one ever know? There are only so many events that can be attributed to coincidence, only so many dreams that turn out to be prophetic—"

"You're a channeler then?"

"Yes." *Oh, boy. No turning back now.*

"Physical or mental?"

"Physical. No, mental."

"I see."

"Thoughts . . . words . . . images. *Feelings."* Emily had twisted a flower loose from her hatband and was pulling at it absentmindedly; a soft rain of turquoise petals began fluttering to the floor.

"Full trance?"

"Light."

"I see."

He spun his chair toward an impressive view of downtown Boston, then slowly spun it back again. "You've worked with a teacher?"

"To be honest," she said, feeling her way carefully, "I was hoping *you* could recommend someone. Someone with experience in training channelers, someone you know and trust—"

"Please wait here, Miss Bowditch," the aide said suddenly.

He left the office and Emily dropped onto a pillowed settee. *So far so good.* It amazed her that absolutely anyone could come in off the street, ask to spend time with an aide to a United States senator, and then talk utter nonsense with him. What a waste of a national budget. Where had he gone off to, anyway? To consult his Ouija board?

She looked around the beautifully appointed office. More tax dollars. Those were real oils, not prints, on the walls. That Sheraton desk was no reproduction. The carpet was richly woven, palest cream—what must it cost to keep it clean, for God's sake? The wing chairs opposite her—Portuguese crewelwork, or she wasn't from New England. It was all wonderfully understated, all shockingly priced.

Her eyes widened. *Oh, Lord.*

From where she sat she could see a dozen giant turquoise flower petals—fallen soldiers in her battle of wits with the senator's aide—lying in a heap on the pale carpet. She jumped up, ran across the room, and was on her hands and knees plucking petals when Senator Arthur Lee Alden III walked in.

2

"Whoops. Well! Senator!" Emily scrambled to her feet and extended her hand to him, but her hand was full of silk petals. She hurled them into her bag; half of them fell back to the floor. "I'm Emily Bowditch."

He took her hand in a warm and easy grip. "Lee Alden; pleased to meet you," he said in an electric baritone. "Jim Whitewood tells me you're looking for some information; suppose you tell me about it."

The senator. Himself. She'd never seen him up close before. On CNN and local news, sure. In the papers and in the magazines, lots of times. It was quite well documented: Senator Alden was a heart-throb. Six two, blue eyes, square jaw, thick hair, great bloodline, lots of money—a man *made* for the media. But the media came nowhere near capturing his sheer, knockdown *presence.*

"You have a fabulous aura, Senator," Emily blurted, much to her own astonishment.

The senator grinned. "Is that a professional evaluation? Jim says you have psychic ability. Please. Have a seat."

He dropped into one of the wing chairs; Emily sat in the other.

"I'd like to find out whether I have it or not," she murmured, but her voice suddenly lacked conviction. It was one thing to take on a con man that she felt instinctively superior to; it was another thing altogether to take on a demigod. Her confidence was slipping fast.

"You're not in Washington," she added with something like reproach.

"No. There was a family emergency last night—thank God, a false alarm. I'm only passing through the office this morning on my way back to the Senate. My time *is* a little short . . ." he said, glancing first at his watch and then at her expectantly.

"I understand *completely*. Well, I won't keep you, Senator," she said, lifting from her chair like a dove in flight. Suddenly she wanted out.

If he was surprised by her change of heart, he didn't show it, needless to say; politicians were a cool and collected lot.

"Miss Bowditch, this power you claim to have—" He stood up, towering over her, and slid his hands into the pockets of his Brooks Brothers suit. "We're talking about the power of the press, are we not?"

"Press?" she repeated in a very small voice, fastening her gaze on his wing-tip shoes.

"Press. As in *Boston Journal*."

She winced. "You know?"

"That you're an investigative reporter for the *Journal*? Yes. We know."

She raised her dark eyes to meet his look. "How did you recognize my name? I haven't been with the paper long enough to rate a by-line."

"My secretary looked you up in the Media Directory. You were behaving a little . . . oddly. She guessed you might be from the press." His expression was bland, but his eyes were dancing.

That got her dander up. That, and the thought of the three of them having a good laugh over her. *"I* was behaving a little oddly! Has it occurred to you, Senator, that people who believe that other people can levitate, bend spoons, and talk to aliens through the fillings in their teeth—that *those* people are the ones who are a wee bit odd?" She didn't bother hiding the contempt in her voice.

The senator was rocking a little on his feet; she might have been a pesky lobbyist bending his ear. His expression was still bland, but the light in his eyes seemed to have gone out.

"That, I take it, is the gist of the exposé you'd like to write about me?"

"Do you deny that you wrote the NSF a letter urging that it spend more on interstellar communication and psychic research?" She whipped out her steno pad, ready to take down his "No comment."

Instead he said quietly, "Do you really believe that a silver filling and the Arecibo radiotelescope are on a par with each other?"

"Yes or no, Senator. *Did* you send the letter?" she demanded crisply, Bic pen poised.

"Oh, for—" He shook his head, exasperated, and said, "This palmist getup and so-called search for a master to teach you—is this all with your paper's sanction?"

Her eyes lowered slightly. "Yes."

"I don't believe it."

"Well, they didn't tell me *not* to do it."

"Ah." He glanced at his watch again and made an impatient sound. "Look, I've got a plane to catch. If you wanted to know how I feel about psi, why didn't you just ask me?" He waved his hand up and down, looking at her clothes. "Why put yourself through all this embarrassment?"

"I am *not* embarrassed," she said, embarrassed. "But I do know one thing: Among all the cabinet members, congressmen, senators, and ambassadors who fervently believe in psychic phenomena, only a handful have come out of the closet. And you're not one of them," she said, not quite truthfully.

"I've never tried to hide my beliefs; they're a matter of public record."

"Public record! Every once in a while you throw a bone to some obscure little magazine like *Etheric*, and that's supposed to update the voters. Why not come clean in the *Journal*, Senator? That's what real people read around here."

What am I doing? she thought wildly. *I'm standing here trading punches with a United States senator!* In her seven years as a reporter Emily had gone after landlords and lawyers, developers and diet centers, but never had she taken on someone with so much power, so much prestige.

"All right," the senator said after a moment.

"Pardon me?"

"I said, 'all right,' Miss Bowditch. You have your wish. See Mrs. Cusack and she'll set up a time. I'm afraid it can't be right away."

"Pardon me?"

He flashed her a sudden, good-natured grin—and a heck of a vote getter it was—and said, "There's an old Chinese curse: 'May your most fervent wish come true.' " Then he glanced at his Rolex again and said, "My car's waiting; I have to run. You have a good day, Miss Bowditch."

He left Emily in a state bordering on shock.

So. The way to land an exclusive interview with an important man on a controversial subject is to wear a dumb hat. A slow, wicked, utterly jubilant smile transformed her face.

"*I* knew that."

When Emily popped out of the senator's office, it was still only midmorning; the day, which Emily had asked to take as a vacation day, was still very much her own. She was in a jump-for-joy mood and wanted to share it with someone, so she called her friend Cara.

Cara Miles was the Pisces to her Virgo, a woman she'd met one summer in New Hampshire, where Cara had retreated to do some painting—"and/or," she'd said, "get in touch with my inner self." In every way they were cheerful opposites. Emily was a small-town girl from a big blue-collar family; Cara was a Boston-bred only child whose forebears apparently owned the *Mayflower.* Emily had worked nights and weekends to put herself through community college; Cara was a Vassar girl. Emily had scrimped and saved for years and only just managed to close on a one-bedroom condo in an iffy neighborhood of Boston; Cara owned—free and clear—a four-level town house in the Back Bay. Emily paid her taxes; Cara paid her accountant. Emily favored shirts and jeans. Cara draped herself in hand-printed silk. Emily trekked. Cara flowed.

But they both loved New Hampshire and to shop. Emily had taken Cara around to every antiques shop in the Manchester area and to a few attics that weren't in the yellow pages. Cara had reciprocated when Emily moved to Boston. To Emily the secret to their friendship was obvious: They'd never yet desired the same antique. They came close once—an oak pharmaceutical cabinet for seventy-four dollars—but after a few minutes Emily gave up wanting it. She had no place to put it. Anyway, she didn't believe in bric-a-brac; what would she have kept in it?

When Cara arrived at the small Spanish café tucked in one of the step-downs on Newbury Street, Emily was waiting for her. She was still dressed like a frilly peasant Gypsy, and Cara nearly passed her by.

"Emily!" she said, doing a double take. "I *love* you in that. It's a whole new look."

"But the same old me; don't get your hopes up," Emily said, laughing.

"Well, you ought to give in to that side of yourself more often; you'd meet more men. So. What's the occasion?"

"I was on a job assignment, and it turned out well. I'm celebrating," she said, holding up a glass of sangria. "Can you join me?"

"Ooh, that could be dangerous—antiquing under the influence." Cara slid into the chair opposite the tiny table and tossed back a mane of softly curled brown hair. "I don't dare buy anything more—I've been sending things off to Sotheby's for auction as it is. I'm trying to clear space for a studio." She motioned for a waiter.

"Cara! You've gone back to painting."

"N-no-o, not painting. Painting didn't really express . . . wasn't really the . . . couldn't . . . well, I've taken up sculpture. It's so much more . . . *essential* as an art form."

While she was ordering, Emily thought, *I know why I wanted to be with her right now. She's forever struggling with the mystical essences of things.*

Not for the first time, Emily wondered why she herself was not. Life seemed to Emily a pretty straightforward affair. In general her mother was right: You were born, you worked, and then you died. If you were lucky, you fell in love with a great guy and had a couple of kids. So far she hadn't been so lucky.

Which brought her back to her original view: You were born, you worked, and then you died. It was very important to be kind and fair, it was almost an obsession with Emily. But for the life of her, she could not understand why some people had to have a mystical experience every time they ate a cheese sandwich.

"So tell me about your assignment," Cara said as she plucked a peach slice out of her sangria. "What poor crook have you set your sights on this time?"

"He's not exactly a crook," Emily answered with a wry smile. "He's just hopelessly misguided—and *you* wouldn't even think he was that."

"Something to do with the astral plane?"

Cara had tossed the question off casually as she eyed the plate of crispy shrimp rissoles that was being placed between them. But she'd hit a bull's-eye, and Emily was extremely impressed. Stan Cooper was right: Cara probably *was* the telepathic one.

"Not even close," Emily lied, a little shaken. "Anyway, I can't talk about it until after the interview in a couple of weeks."

"Fine with me." Cara bit into the hot fried appetizer and went into a swoon of pleasure. "These are out of this *world,*" she cried, and then: "Okay, let's talk about men. You first. Find any?"

Emily's mouth was full. She shook her head.

"I did. A doozy." Cara rolled her eyes and tossed off the rest of her sangria. "I met him at one of Daddy's bank things. From across the room I thought he was the most handsome man I'd ever seen. From a foot away he was even better. Snappy dresser; sexy drawl; bluer eyes than mine. There was only one little hitch. . . ."

"He was married?"

"He was investigating Daddy's bank." Cara dropped her head into her hands, then looked up with a hopeless, tragic smile and motioned for a refill on her wine.

By the time they left two hours later, Emily and Cara both were convinced that for a tragic situation, Cara's dilemma was pretty darn funny. Feeling mellow and amused, they wandered aimlessly and contentedly through the lineup of exquisite shops on Newbury Street. They paused to stroke a fine Italian handbag here, an Inuit soapstone carving there. They stared in the window of a florist for a full ten minutes, choosing the flowers for their wedding bouquets, just in case. Cara tried on an Australian outback coat and a pair of lizard boots, bought them, and arranged to have them delivered. The bill came to $3,137.40. She wrote a check.

Emily didn't mind. She figured that in Boston she could get along pretty well without either an outback coat or lizard boots. In general she felt pretty immune to impulse buying. She tried on a handmade sweater from Ireland, for example, but convinced herself that it was too scratchy. She picked up a stoneware mug from Scotland and walked around with it for a while, but then she put it back on its shelf. It wasn't hard; in every shop, thoughts of her mortgage hovered tauntingly overhead.

Until she ambled up to the window of a shop called, with charming understatement, Something Old. The shop specialized in estate jewelry, and the window display was enchanting. Scattered on a bed of deep maroon velvet were a dozen pieces of antique jewelry, mostly of diamonds and pearls. Their owners were there, too, in sepia photographs whose edges were curled with age: grand ladies in *fin de siècle* ball gowns, their throats ringed in thick chokers of pearls, their tiny waists encircled with diamonds. There were tools of their trade as well: a mother-of-pearl hairbrush and a silver comb, and an intricate, hand-painted fan of ebony. In every fold of velvet a random treasure lay partly hidden: a ruby hatpin; a set of pearl teardrop earrings; a tortoiseshell buttonhook.

Emily was charmed by all of it, from the tiara to the buttonhook. But it was a necklace of pale pink stone that cast a spell over her and held her fast. It was not a magnificent piece or even an elegant piece. It was an odd piece. The big rectangular stone, set in delicate gold filigree but hung on an extremely heavy chain, was like nothing else in the window. Emily couldn't imagine a woman of either taste or wealth having adorned herself with it, yet it was undeniably old. Something about it—the way the track lighting bounced off its facets or the Gypsy look of it—made her want to know more.

From over her shoulder she heard Cara say, "What a funky piece. I like it."

The words struck dread in Emily's heart. Until this moment she had not known she wanted the necklace. "I like it, too," she said, a little fiercely.

"Let's go in and try it on then," said Cara, oblivious to the fact that there were two of *them* and only one of *it*. She looped her arm through Emily's and tugged. "Maybe it's some rare and exotic stone."

"You mean rare and expensive stone," Emily said wryly. *This is going to be it,* she thought. *The thing that finally does in this screwy, illogical friendship.* But she went in with Cara anyway, trying desperately not to resent her money.

The saleswoman, a Coco Chanel look-alike, passed

immediately over Emily to focus on the Possible Sale. "May I help you?" she asked Cara in a cultivated voice.

"Yes, that funny pink-stone necklace in the window," said Cara. "We'd like to see it."

The saleswoman wasn't quick enough to hide her surprise and—Emily thought—disappointment. "Oh. That one. Certainly."

By the time she laid it out carefully on a swatch of black velvet, though, the woman was back in business. "It's a charming little trinket, don't you think? It's turned quite a few heads. Very unusual."

Cara lifted it from it from the velvet and said, "Heavy; is the chain solid gold?"

Emily's hopes sank.

"Oh dear, no," said the saleswoman, releasing a tiny smile. "Some sort of plating. The stone is possibly rose quartz, or maybe pink tourmaline. It's costume, which is why the price is so reasonable."

Emily's hopes rose.

Cara turned over the tiny white stringed tag. "Five hundred dollars?"

Emily's hopes sank.

"It really *is* just costume then," Cara said, disappointed.

Emily's hopes rose.

Why, why, why, you dopey fool! You don't keep five hundred dollars in your sugar bowl; Cara does.

Cara held the necklace up around her throat and gazed at herself in a gilded mirror on the wall. "Pretty," she said musingly.

"Your color sets it off well," said Ms. Chanel, tilting her head and touching one red fingernail to her chin.

Emily thought she might possibly explode. "May I?" she asked through clenched teeth. Never had she wanted to possess the way she was wanting to now.

Cara smiled and handed it over with an "I can't decide, I really can't." Clearly she did not consider that Emily was in competition for the purchase.

Emily felt the sheer weight of the necklace in her hand, held it up before her, stared at the odd shafts of light in the pinkish crystal. Her hand was trembling.

"Oh, look, the stone is chipped!" cried Cara. "On the back. How really too bad!"

"Well, of course, it isn't a *diamond*. And it's old," said the saleswoman, a little irritated. "But if you were really interested," she said to Cara, still pitching to her alone, "I suppose I could—"

"I want it," Emily said suddenly. "I want the necklace."

"You *do!* Oh, I'm so glad," Cara said, breaking into a surprised and beautiful smile. "It suits what you're wearing so well."

"Cara, these are *not* my normal—" Emily began, and then gave it up. It didn't matter to her whether the necklace suited or not. It didn't matter whether it was chipped or not. It almost didn't matter whether it cost five hundred dollars or not. It only mattered that when she held it in her hand, she felt completely, bizarrely satisfied.

"And how will you be paying for that?" asked the saleswoman politely. She had dropped all mention of what she could or could not do, seeing as it was chipped and all, but Emily did not even want to renegotiate the price.

"VISA," she answered faintly, handing over her card.

"Let's put it on you," said Cara excitedly as the clerk wrote up the sale.

She undid the heavy clasp and lifted the chain over Emily's head. Emily watched the big pink stone pass in front of her and come to rest on her breastbone.

The necklace felt heavy and icy cold; she caught her breath—she *couldn't* breathe—and let out a sharp, frightened cry.

"Oh, sorry; did I catch your hair?" asked Cara off-handedly as she struggled to close the lock. "This clasp is a wicked thing to work."

"No . . . no, it surprised me . . . with its weight, that's all."

"Okay, turn around and let's see what we've got," said Cara, ready to be amused. Emily did so, and Cara said in an altogether different voice, *"Emily.* It's wonderful on you—strange, and overwrought, and . . . wonderful. I can't get over the change it makes in you," she said thoughtfully. "It makes your cheeks glow, your eyes shine—"

"Embarrassment is making my cheeks glow, Cara; stop it," Emily said in a hush as she eyed the saleswoman approaching with a tissue slip for signing. "It's just a piece of jewelry. Nothing more. Nothing less."

When Emily was finished, they stood outside on the brick-lined sidewalk in the warm late sun, deciding what to do.

"I'm shopped out; how about you?" Cara asked. "Maybe a cup of coffee before we split up?"

Emily, suddenly exhausted, agreed. "I think I'm having an attack of buyer's remorse," she admitted. But even as she said it, she brought her hand up to the rose-colored stone and was comforted by its being there.

Her ambivalent mood lasted through coffee with Cara, and on the subway ride home to Charlestown, and all through supper and an evening of dull summer reruns. The facts were undeniable: Five hundred dollars would've paid for a toaster oven, a new muffler for the Corolla, a year of cable TV, a whale-watching trip in Provincetown and, say, half a dozen seafood dinners at the No-Name restaurant. Instead she'd blown it on—what? A chipped crystal and a lead-heavy chain.

So why did it feel so *good* to have it? Was it because for once in her life she'd bought with her heart instead of her mind? And got one big treat, instead of a dozen little ones? Was it because she'd thumbed her nose at Miss Coco Chanel? Or was it just because—she desperately hoped not—it felt so satisfying to behave like a rich girl instead of a working one.

She stared down at the rose crystal that she'd been idly rubbing. Emily did not care for jewelry very much, but she cared for this. There was something soothing about the feel of its clean-cut facets, and the filigree work really was quite intricate and very pretty. In the soft light of her deco lamp the stone gleamed more amber than pink. She gazed at it in half-dreamy pleasure. She'd once had a cat with eyes that shade of amber. She could almost hear him purring in her lap as she rubbed his chin, feel his silky fur as she stroked his back. Spooky had been gone for fifteen years, but, oh, Spooky was here with her now.

3

At eight o'clock the next morning Emily placed a jelly doughnut and a large black coffee from Dunkin' Donuts side by side on Stanley Cooper's desk. "For you," she said. "Because life is good."

"Meaning you actually got somewhere with the senator yesterday." Stan wasn't surprised.

But Emily was. "How did *you* know I met with the senator yesterday?"

Stan popped the lid on his coffee. "For one thing, I heard that Lee Alden's mother had some kind of attack. Alden's brother was away on business in Czechoslovakia and couldn't get a flight over. That left the senator to fly back up. They thought it was her heart, turned out it was her stomach.

"And for another thing," he said, sipping the hot stuff gingerly, "you took a vacation day, out of guilt, because you were about to do a nutty thing. So. You really nailed down the interview?"

Emily busied herself with unfolding the wrapping from her croissant. "What d'you do, read tea leaves?"

It was vastly annoying that Stan had gone to bed last night knowing more about the senator than she did.

Stan shrugged. "I observe." He took a monstrous bite out of his jelly doughnut; a blob of bright red filling oozed out and landed on his knee.

"Ah, hell," he said from under a powdered-sugar mustache. He dabbed uselessly at his pants leg and said in irritation, "I mean, why else would you have bought that absurd bauble you're wearing around your neck, unless you were feeling mighty pleased with yourself over something?"

Automatically Emily's hand went to the crystal necklace. She hadn't taken it off since she bought it, nor was she about to. "Tsk, tsk, you're taking out your jelly on my jewelry, Stan."

Stan was heading with a napkin for the water cooler, still muttering, when the phone on Emily's desk rang. She picked up the receiver. It was Jim Whitewood, the senator's aide, wanting to know whether she'd be available for a twelve-thirty call from the senator. "Of course," Emily answered, and he rang off.

Emily considered whether to brag to Stan about her continuing contact with the senator and then thought better of it. Maybe Senator Alden was canceling. In any case, she didn't want Stan sitting eight feet away with one ear hanging over her desk at lunchtime.

Luckily it was a slow news day; at twelve-thirty the newsroom was pretty empty. When the phone rang promptly at the half hour, Emily lunged for it, aware of a kind of first-date giddiness. If she were, oh, a hall monitor, then Arthur Lee Alden III was the high school quarterback.

"Miss Bowditch?"

"Yes, sir."

"Ah. You're in." It was his voice all right. But something was wrong.

Canceling, dammit. She saw her Pulitzer prize going straight down the tubes. "Senator? You sound very . . . tentative," she hazarded. "Are you having second thoughts?" She closed her eyes and grimaced. *Dummy! Give him an opening, why don't you?*

His laugh was low and rueful. "I'm having second thoughts, third, maybe even fourth. Not about the interview, though, but over what I'm about to suggest."

"Sa-a-y," she said, trying to lighten the mood, "this wouldn't be nothin' illegal, would it?"

"Obviously not," he answered, a little testily. "But I'm putting myself very much on the line, something no elected official likes to do. Look, this conversation is off the record. Agreed?"

"Sure." She said it without thinking, then wished she hadn't.

Because his next question set the hair on the back of her neck on end.

"Have you ever been in the presence of a 'sensitive'?"

Emily chose her answer very, very carefully. "No-o-o," she said, "I have not." She felt obliged to add, "I don't believe in 'sensitives.' "

There was a pause. "So you've never been in a position to judge whether a psychic is a fraud or genuine? Because you've never seen one?"

"That's right, Senator," Emily responded. "Wait, I'm a liar. Once I went with two of my friends to see a palmist, on a lark. The palmist was *definitely* a fraud."

You will struggle between life and death, child, the psychic had said. *In the end you will have what you want.* The others had got nice, cheery, tall-dark-and-handsome type readings, but *her?* No such luck. The palmist had practically shoved her out the door. No doubt she knew an investigative reporter when she saw one.

Emily shook off the unpleasant remembrance and said, "Why do you ask?"

"I ask because I'm seriously considering doing something impolitic: inviting you to a séance."

"Get outta here," Emily said, grinning. *A séance!*

His voice became suddenly reserved, almost cold. "You're right. Dumb idea."

"No—no, it's not," she said quickly. "I've never been to a séance because, well, I guess no one's ever asked me before. I mean, how do you find out about these things? It must be word of mouth. It can't be in the yellow pages. What would you look under? Recycling? If you wanted a mere palmist, that's easy enough. They advertise; they're available for parties. But let's face it, a person who channels spirits, well, that's pretty heavy stuff. I wish you *would* consider asking me, Senator," she pleaded, at a loss at how to seem more like a believer to him. She could feel the story slipping through her fingers, and it horrified her.

When he said nothing she added, "I hope I haven't offended you, Senator. "I suppose I *am* what you people would call a goat, but—"

"No, no, that's no problem," he interrupted, still thoughtful. "I've been to a few of these things, and nothing's ever happened. But people whose opinions I very much respect have talked about this particular girl—she's just a girl, eighteen or nineteen—in a way that intrigues me. Unsettles me, even. Apparently she has power, undeniable power—"

"Oh, Senator, *please* let me come." Emily was prostrate with desire.

There was another long, unbearable pause. She

forced herself to remain silent, to wait him out. When at last he spoke, he said, "Let me give you a time and place—"

"I appreciate this *so* much, Senator."

"Naturally the séance, like this telephone conversation, is off the record."

"What?"

"It has to be. I'm sorry."

She absorbed the blow well, all things considered. "I understand, Senator," she answered calmly. It didn't matter. Somehow, some way, she'd finagle some kind of qualified permission from him. Or she'd imply what she needed to say. Or she'd work through third-party quotes. But the story of "The Senator and the Séance" *would* be told. There wasn't a doubt in her mind.

The senator arranged to meet Emily on the following Saturday in Westford, Massachusetts, and gave her simple, clear directions for getting there. He said very little about the nature of the sitting, only that there would be some attempt to communicate beyond the living. The sitting was scheduled to take place just outside the town, in a farmhouse with a reputation for hauntings—frosting on the cake, as far as Emily was concerned.

The week sped by. Emily was as good as her word and said nothing to Stan about either the phone call or the upcoming séance. Part of her, a big part, wanted to one-up Stanley Cooper once and for all. And unless her phone had been tapped by him the other day, that's exactly what she would do.

When Saturday came, Emily was very careful to dress and behave exactly as she always did. That meant a plain white shirt, a casual jacket, and stone-washed jeans. That meant showing up early, eating lunch at her desk, and exchanging sharp-edged banter with the boys all day. The only break in routine—it couldn't be helped—came when she announced she was ducking out early.

"Where to?" asked Stan.

"Library," she said briefly, pulling a vinyl cover over her computer screen.

Stan gave her a sharp look. "Where's your book bag?"

"In the car."

"You brought your car? The library's a block away."

"Not for that. I'm meeting someone—Cara. For supper." She locked her desk.

But Stan was feeling suddenly expansive. "Hey, how's Cara doing? God, it's been a while," he said, leaning back in his chair and stretching.

Stan had met Cara exactly once, in the newsroom. At the time he'd called her a silver spooner. Now all of a sudden he was talking as if they'd been raised in the same orphanage. *He knows I'm up to something,* she thought, dismayed. *How does he do it?*

"I'll tell her you said hi," Emily said with a tight smile, and fled.

She shrugged off the thought of Stan Cooper the way she would a wet sweater. He could guess all he wanted, but he'd never *know,* not before she was good and ready to let him know.

By the time she'd grabbed a hamburger and shifted the Corolla into fifth gear on Route 128, her mind was focused completely on the evening ahead of her. It seemed to her an extraordinary thing that a U.S. senator was willing to risk looking like a jerk a week before a scheduled interview. Where was the angle here? He couldn't be hoping to impress her with his sincerity. Being a sincere believer in ghosts wasn't exactly a character asset.

Was he hoping to make *her* a believer? Impossible. He must know that. Unless . . . A wildly irrational fear seized her. What if he belonged to some kind of cult, and they were going to brainwash her, and she'd come out of the haunted house some kind of, whatever, some kind of zombie or something?

Get a grip, girl. He's a senator. You're a journalist. You're not driving into the Twilight Zone; you're headed for Westford, Mass., a no doubt nice little bedroom community to a bunch of yuppies from Boston.

Still, a person couldn't underestimate the hypnotizing power of sheer personality. The senator had it to spare. And more. *What a charismatic man,* she thought, a little depressed. So that's what people really vote for: the smile, the voice, the low chuckle. He'd certainly caught *her* off guard once. Well, twice. But he wouldn't get away with it a third time. She was ready for him tonight.

That led her to another possibility. What if the evening was set up as an elaborate hoax—screens and rapping tables and flying trumpets, that kind of thing? Obviously some of these people were really good; too many otherwise intelligent observers had been sucked in by them. She smiled grimly to herself. *Try pulling a fast one, Senator, and our gentleman's agreement is null and void.*

She played around with various scenarios in her head, and by the time she turned off Route 495 onto the road to Westford, she was actually hoping for something outrageous to happen. A haunted house and a debutante medium—they gave whole new meaning to the phrase *coming out.*

Emily found Easton Lane, which was unmarked, but had an awful time finding the house. She traveled the mile of potholed road up and then back down again before she noticed a car turn into a driveway that was all but hidden by overgrown shrubs. The car was a BMW. The senator had said he'd be in one. She turned in after it, sidled around a huge exposed rock in the center of the winding drive, rolled up her window to keep out the scratchy branches that were poking their way in, and fetched up in a kind of clearing, in the middle of which stood a slate-roofed farmhouse made of stone.

The house was at least two hundred years old. At both ends huge crumbling chimneys, cast in silhouette by the setting sun, stood like brooding sentinels. A towering pine loomed over the heavy Dutch door entry to the house, throwing it into premature darkness. Massive shutters, their black panels peeling, hung unused and uncared for. The only light was lurid light—streaks of red sunset, cutting across the tattered, overgrown scene. From high overhead a purple finch warbled notes of piercing sweetness, a single song of renewal amid continuing decay.

Emily tried hard to resist being affected by it all, but it wasn't easy; the atmosphere of foreboding was overwhelming her. She touched her hand to the crystal she wore—she'd begun to regard it as a good-luck charm—and looked around for the BMW. It must have gone alongside the house, because suddenly the senator emerged from there with a smile and a wave. Her heart lifted unreasonably in her breast.

A human being, she thought gratefully. "I *am* glad to see you, Senator," she said, her spirits rising. "I could never have found this place on my own."

The senator, dressed in khakis and blazer, seemed grateful that she had come. "I was here once before," he said, taking her hand in a warm grip. "The house was just as shabby then, but the owner was keeping the grounds up. The woman was an avid gardener right up until the time she died, at ninety-six."

"Is *she* the one who's supposed to be haunting the place?" asked Emily with a giggle. The truth was, she was feeling very nervous and ill at ease.

"You continue to be amused," the senator answered in the deepening twilight. "I suppose I can't blame you. No, it was the old woman herself who complained about the hauntings. At first no one took her seriously. She was in her seventies at the time, and people sometimes get a little paranoid at that age. She was living here with her grandson. The grandson was twelve when he moved in with her, after his mother died of pneumonia. The hauntings apparently began two years later."

Emily glanced at the door to the house. It did not open for them, and the senator seemed in no hurry to approach it. So she said, "Maybe the boy resented being stuck out here and was just trying to frighten his grandmother."

"That's the obvious conclusion. The boy really was angry and resentful, about a lot of things—the death first of his father, then his mother; having to leave Boston and his pals. That's a tough age, anyway," the senator added, sounding as if he remembered it well.

"But," he continued, "credible witnesses said they were in the house when objects flew off shelves, pictures fell from walls of their own volition, windows blew out from their frames—"

"A poltergeist?" She tried to look scientific.

The senator shrugged. "Some say that. There's another theory going around: that any so-called poltergeist is really a manifestation of a kind of nervous energy in a disturbed child. Either way, it's intriguing, don't you think?"

He was baiting her. He couldn't be serious. And when were they going in to the damned séance anyway? The bugs had turned fierce. Suddenly Emily was annoyed. "So you're saying a disturbed kid either attracts destructive energy or projects it from his subconscious. Fine. What happens when the kid grows up? What happened when *this* kid grew up?"

The senator was leaning against her Corolla, perfectly at ease, as if he'd chanced upon her at a Washington soiree. "The hauntings stopped."

"There you are," Emily said triumphantly. "Can we go in now?"

"They'll let us know," he answered, and went back to his train of thought. "Trouble is, there've been new disturbances since the old woman's death two years ago. A young Boston couple bought this place with all its furnishings, intending to renovate it. Two weeks later they moved out. The place is for sale and there are no takers."

"The market's flat all over," she said, just to be perverse. "Is that why we're here tonight? To identify the ghost?"

Again he shrugged. Only by now it was dark, so that Emily had a sensation of broad shoulders shifting, but that was all. It really was eerie, and she did not like it. She saw thin slits of dim light through slightly parted drapes. It all was obvious now: First the senator would frighten her out of her wits; then they'd pull her inside for some stunt. Maybe the senator thought it would be funny. Maybe it was all a practical joke. Maybe Stan Cooper was inside. Ha-ha-ha. Very amusing.

Suddenly the door to the stone house opened wide, and Emily jumped. A stout middle-aged woman, perfectly pleasant, appeared in the doorway and said with a friendly wave, "Hello. I hope we haven't kept you waiting, Senator."

Emily and the senator approached her, and she held out her hand. "I'm Mrs. Lividus. You must be

Emily Bowditch. I'm so glad you agreed to come. Come along, and I'll introduce you to our Kimberly."

She led the way. Emily turned to the senator with eyebrows raised. "A psychic named *Kimberly*?" she whispered.

The senator whispered back, "Her mother's from Long Beach."

"Oh, that explains it," she murmured dryly.

She looked around curiously at the darkly ornate Victorian furnishings, half expecting to see Vincent Price tucked in a wing chair somewhere. But when they reached the sitting room, they found only a young, very pretty girl and two gentlemen. Emily learned that the man with the beard was a professor of philosophy at Harvard. The other—from San Francisco—was a publisher and editor of New Age books. It was impressive company—if they were who they said they were.

As for the girl, she looked exactly like a Kimberly. She had fair skin, straight blond hair, and long legs set off by a shirtwaist dress of emerald silk.

Emily had been expecting a Gypsy, someone called Allana or Sabrina, with dark hair and eyes. "*I* look more like a medium than she does," she managed in an aside to the senator as they approached the girl for introductions. She stole a sideways glance at her companion and saw him frown. It occurred to her for the first time that she could push the skeptic thing too far with this man.

Kimberly turned out to be as sweet as her name. She was remarkably attractive. She wore little makeup, only some pale lip liner. Her porcelain skin and pale green eyes gave the impression of openness and naïveté, and nothing in her brief exchange with Emily changed that impression.

"What a pretty necklace," said Kimberly, singling

out the pinkish crystal that Emily wore. Her hand reached out, as Emily's had so often in the past week, to stroke the crystal.

"Thank you," Emily said. "I bought it on a whim. I shouldn't have. I'm not at all the type for it, but you know how it is: feeling like you just ought to get *something,* and—"

Emily felt a slight pressure from the senator's elbow and stopped in mid-babble. What was she doing? No one in the room wanted to hear about her shopping spree.

Except maybe Kimberly. "Oh, I know what you mean," she said in her gentle, childlike voice. "Sometimes I do that and I get home and I wonder what I was thinking of. Once I bought a live parrot—"

"Kimberly, should we begin, dear, do you think?" It was Mrs. Lividus, moving things along with a brusque but not unkindly push.

"Oh, okay, Aunt Lois. Should I sit in the big chair again?"

"Why don't you, dear?"

The girl nestled into an overstuffed armchair that had its back to an enormous brick fireplace. Emily and the senator sat side by side on a painfully hard horsehair sofa opposite. Mrs. Lividus stood behind them for the moment, while the two others sat on each side of Kimberly in oak spindle chairs. There was no table to rap, no trumpet to speak through. The professor from Harvard produced a writing tablet, the publisher a yellow pad. Emily jerked her head around to the senator, hoping for permission also to take notes, but he frowned again and shook his head imperceptibly.

Disappointed, Emily turned her attention back to the girl. She had no idea what to expect. The senator had said that Kimberly was a trance medium, that disembodied voices might speak through a spirit "control" that would take possession of her. Assuming the poltergeist felt like talking, would it speak through Kimberly directly, Emily mused, or did it have to speak through a control?

Probably there's a certain protocol, she thought wryly.

Kimberly laid her head back against the dark green armchair and became quiet. She let her half-closed eyes fall on Emily's rose crystal and murmured, "Pretty." Then her eyelids fluttered shut. Mrs. Lividus dimmed the lights, putting Emily instantly on the alert. Kimberly began to yawn repeatedly. Soon her body fell into a slump. Her breathing became heavy and even; she seemed to be asleep. Emily had an impression, nothing more, that a trickle of tears flowed down the girl's pale cheek.

The lights dimmed even more. Emily strained to see. As soon as her eyes adjusted to the darker room, the lights were turned down yet again, forcing her to adjust again. It was distracting—and worse, disorienting. She felt drugged, but she'd taken no refreshment. She tried to focus on something, anything—the paisley pattern of the Oriental carpet. But it was no use; the paisley spiraled madly beneath her, a Persian maelstrom pulling her down, down into its depths.

What saved her at last was a sound she knew well: the scratching of pencils on tablets. *Yes, yes, notes! They are taking notes! Two men—educated men, rational men—are taking notes! They are watching a girl take a nap and calmly recording their observations.* She clung to the sound of the pencils as a drowning sailor would to a floating log, miserably grateful for its existence.

And then the pencil scratching suddenly stopped, as a low moan came from the girl, followed by a voice

—a shockingly male and angry voice—that said, *"I'll damn well go where I please and do what I damn well want!"* There was a pause, and then the man's voice again, now melancholy: "Merciful God . . . *I cannot stand it* anymore." And then a cry—a piercing, blood-curdling cry that ripped through the hushed and darkened parlor. Kimberly shuddered and awoke.

Immediately Mrs. Lividus turned up the lights and went to her niece. She pressed her cheek to the dazed and tear-stained face of the girl and murmured reassurances. The New Age publisher let out his breath in a rush, as if he'd been holding it all night. The Harvard professor nodded quietly to himself and resumed his note taking. The senator was leaning forward with furrowed brows and his elbows resting on his knees, the fingers of his hands tented together, forefingers pressed against his lips, as he studied Kimberly in the arms of her aunt.

And Emily? She saw everything in incredible detail. She missed none of it, from Aunt Lois's apparent distress at her niece's pain to the chip on the majolica plate that stood on the mantel behind them. It gave her mind something to do while her body remained all too frozen to the horsehair sofa. The temperature in the parlor seemed to have fallen thirty degrees; she had goose bumps on her arms.

I don't like this, she thought. *This is sick and unkind, to the girl if nothing else. She's obviously deeply disturbed.*

Mrs. Lividus had whipped out an enormous hankie and was handing it to the girl to blow her nose. She placed her substantial bulk between her niece and the audience, and that broke the spell for Emily. She turned her attention back to the senator, who seemed still entranced, and wondered: *Why does he bother with this stuff? He's not old; he's not suffering from terminal disease. He doesn't lead a dull and hopeless life.* He continued to amaze her. Here was a man with looks, brains, charm, money, and power, who still needed to believe that after death we'd all truck merrily along in some slightly altered astral form.

The senator turned just then and gave her an ironic and utterly charming smile. Her heart fell to the floor and when she picked it up again, she thought it might be broken. She listened for the beat. Ta-thump ta-thump ta-thump. Nope. Everything was still okay. But the incident gave her a fresh new slant: *Of course,* he'd want himself to go on; how could he bear to see himself end?

The senator grabbed both his knees and did a cat-like stretch. He stood up and turned to Emily. "I've seen enough. Have you?"

4

Emily glanced back at the small group. Kimberly was pretty much out of her trance; the men were packing up their things. The séance was over.

"Will there be tea and cookies?" she asked the senator with an innocent smile. She wasn't *about* to let him know that she'd been shaken by the event.

His grimace was reasonably good-humored. "Don't be a snot. C'mon. Let's say good night to our hostess." He took Emily by the arm—she was very aware that it was the first time he'd ever touched her—and guided her toward Mrs. Lividus.

The girl's aunt was upset or acting that way. Her brow was furrowed, and she seemed distracted. "Oh, yes, Senator, well, it was good of you to come," she said, almost mumbling the words. "I—could I see you for just one moment, Senator?" she added in an earnest voice.

The senator acquiesced, and after she took him aside, the two spoke in quiet undertones. Emily was left to create small talk with Kimberly. What could you say to someone who'd just been taken over by a demon, inner *or* outer? "At least it wasn't for long"?

The Harvard professor and the New Age publisher were making no attempt to join them. Maybe they all were going out afterward to a late supper. Maybe they were Kimberly's handlers or agents or whatever. Maybe they were afraid of the girl; Emily was.

So she treaded water while she waited for the senator. Afterward she remembered saying inane things like: "I hope this wasn't too much of an imposition." And: "Have you been doing this for very long?" And worst of all: "I had a really interesting time."

To everything that Emily said, Kimberly just shook her head in sad silence. At the end she fixed her pale green, tear-stained eyes on Emily and said only, "I'm sorry."

Puzzled and flat out of chitchat, Emily decided to wait in silence for the senator. She saw him put his hand on Mrs. Lividus's shoulder and saw the elderly woman impulsively take his other hand in both of hers, clinging to it and murmuring emotional good-byes.

Yep. He's got her vote. And probably a campaign contribution as well. These guys ran for office from one end of the year to the other. She wondered if there was a Political Action Committee for Psychics and if he'd ever taken an honorarium from it for a speech. An interesting angle for a story.

Mrs. Lividus let the two of them out with a warm smile and a friendly good-bye, and despite everything, Emily found herself liking the woman. She said so to the senator as he walked her in near darkness to her Corolla.

"Lois Lividus isn't actually Kimberly's aunt," he explained, "but a second or third cousin by marriage. She's Hungarian, and in her village she was considered something of a psychic healer. She was the first to recognize Kimberly's so-called abilities. When she came back East from her visit with Kimberly's family in California, the girl came with her."

"Kimberly's parents didn't mind?" asked Emily, incredulous.

"They minded," the senator answered cryptically. "Watch your step here," he warned.

Almost as soon as he said it, Emily tripped on a rock and fell forward. The senator grabbed her and kept her from going head over heels; she ended up more or less in his arms. Emily had considered a dozen different endings to the séance, but she hadn't considered this one. She was blushing furiously—because of her clumsiness and his nearness—but in the light of the two-watt bulb that bleared over the entry door it was impossible to read the senator's face.

"All in one piece?" he asked in a whisper that she thought was more polite than husky.

"Sure. Sorry. Dumb." *So. I no longer can form sentences.* This was interesting. Was it Kimberly who'd addled her brain, or the rock?

He released her. She hated herself for feeling disappointment when he did. "Now comes the real trickery—getting out of here," she quipped, mostly for something to say.

"Just fall in behind me; I've done battle with this driveway before. And look, can we have coffee somewhere? You're looking shaky on your pins, and you've got a long ride home. An evening like this can be a little unsettling."

"In every way," she admitted, and then instantly regretted it.

"Yes. Well." The silence, like the darkness, loomed between them. "There's a coffee shop not far from here," he said at last, in a softer, lower voice. "Will you follow me to it?"

"Thanks," she answered in a voice as soft, as low. "I will."

Emily got in the Corolla and bumped and bounced her way out of the drive behind the senator's BMW, all the while thinking, *What just went on here? Anything?* Yes. No. Or maybe; it was the kind of night when anything was possible. She had to smile. In sixty minutes she'd gone from fearing abduction into a cult to wondering if one of the most eligible bachelors in America was coming on to her.

"In your dreams, girl," she said aloud, with a laugh. She was letting herself get tangled in the house's cobwebs. By the time the senator pulled his car onto the dirt-and-gravel parking lot of the Time Out Café, she'd vowed ten times over to resist the man's spell and to come down hard on him. She owed it to the taxpayer.

The Time Out was one of those little diners with vinyl tablecloths and polyester lace curtains that always seem to be located next to a John Deere dealer. It was clean, cozy, and empty. With less than an hour to go before closing, the owner was refilling the ketchup bottles and packing Sweet'n Low into the pressed-glass sugar bowls that were standard issue at every table. They took the table farthest from the counter, which wasn't very far, and the senator held up two fingers. The owner nodded and brought them two coffees. Emily wondered if the senator had been here before.

"Well, what did you think?" the senator asked as soon as they were left alone. "Self-hypnosis? Delusion? Hallucination?"

"Mine or hers?" asked Emily, peeling away the top of a creamer packet.

He looked impressed that she'd done her homework. "Touché," he said with a smile. "But no, I don't think I'd ever consider you the type to have a fantasy-prone personality."

"You probably don't mean that as a compliment," she countered with an even look.

"I do and I don't. I was hoping you'd walk in to the séance with a really open mind—"

"I *did!*"

"Do you think so? I watched you as we went through the house. You were like a kid at a carnival. Nothing would've pleased you more than to have had a table levitate. You'd have been all over it, looking for cables."

"I consider myself a reasonable skeptic," she replied with dignity.

He sighed. "I suppose it's a sign of the times," he added, sitting back in his chair. "A hundred years ago people would've run from a haunted house. Now everybody wants to spend the night."

"Blame it on Stephen King," she answered, laughing. "He's made fans of us all." She was liking the senator a lot just now. For a believer, he was awfully tolerant of her mocking ways.

She was liking the senator for another reason as well: He was looking at her over the rim of his coffee cup with eyes so crystal blue that it made her ache to have to look away. But she couldn't just gawk at him like some political groupie. So she looked away.

"I have another possible explanation of the girl's behavior for you," she said, making a process of adding a sixteenth of a teaspoon more cream to her coffee. "Couldn't she have been telepathizing what was going on in one of the men's minds, yours or the others? Couldn't one of you—say it was you—have felt stuck at the séance and been in a hurry and been thinking the things that Kimberly then picked up and said, in that—that voice?"

"You believe in telepathy?" the senator asked, surprised.

She shrugged. "A limited form of it, sure. One of my brothers always knew exactly when I was mad, and why. Another one of them never had a clue. The others fell somewhere in between. It's my opinion that telepathy is all a matter of degree."

"How many brothers do you have?"

"Four. All registered to vote in New Hampshire, so don't be getting any ideas." Despite herself, she favored him with her most winning smile. He was so hard not to favor.

"Do I dare ask how many sisters you have?"

"Zip," she said, careful to keep it just as light. "My mother and I used to have to huddle together a lot."

"But you don't anymore?" He guessed the answer even as he tried to stop the question.

"Can't. She's not around anymore." Emily sounded coldhearted and flippant—anything but how she felt, which was devastated, even now, two years after her mother's death. Her mother had been her best friend and ally in the world, and her mother was no more. If ever there were a reason for believing in ghosts, it would be Agnes Bowditch.

"I'm sorry," he said quietly. "It was stupid of me to press."

"Oh, that's all right," she answered in her breezy way, trying to cover her hurt. "I'm not going to vote for you for completely other reasons."

He winced at that. *The best defense is a good offense,* she told herself; but it brought her no comfort.

There was a very awkward lull; she took it as her responsibility to fill it. "*I* saw a mildly telepathic girl sitting in a chair tonight," she said. "What did *you* see?"

He made a funny here-goes-nothing face that she kind of liked and began in a roundabout way to explain why he was a flake.

"You have to understand that the nature of channeling has been very consistent across all cultures throughout recorded history. And you have to accept that there is a strong desire in all of us for the irrational to triumph."

"I'm not sure about *all* of us," she felt obliged to argue.

"Trust me," he said. "Even you. In the broadest sense, channeling involves any form of focusing creative energy. Artists channel. Poets channel. Physicists channel. Rocket scientists channel."

"And California dreamers named Kimberly channel." Emily was losing interest in the discussion. She hated vague, mystical talk. *Who, what, why, where, when*—that's what she was after. Facts. That's what she'd been taught in journalism school.

"Okay, so my plumber channels. Senator, why did you go there tonight? Why do you *care* about this channeler, or any other channeler?"

He pushed his chair back from the table, balancing it on its hind legs. Emily knew a thing or two about body language, and she didn't care for the distance he was suddenly putting between them. *He's not going to tell me a damned thing about himself,* she thought, disheartened.

"You want a story," he said at last. "Okay. Here's a story." He looked away, staring over the café curtains into the night beyond.

"Once upon a time there was a young couple very much in love and with everything to live for. He was a rising force in politics. She was a beautiful and accomplished pianist. No one thought the marriage would last, yet for ten short years the two were incredibly happy. They lacked only one thing, a child, and in the tenth year the woman became pregnant. Now they lacked nothing.

"But in the tenth year as well something in the heavens fell out of alignment," he said in a baffled, wondering voice. "The man came down with a stupid attack of appendicitis. He was rushed to the hospital for an emergency appendectomy. It was no big deal. But the wife didn't believe that. All she knew was that she had to be at her husband's side. So she canceled a concert appearance in Denver, and on her way to the airport she was killed in a car accident." He continued to stare out the café window. "She was so fiercely determined to come," he said softly.

Emily had seen the facts of his life on microfiche, but they had not torn her heart the way he had just now. "I'm so *sorry,* Senator—"

He turned to her and smiled bleakly. "The story isn't finished. The man was lying in the hospital, heavily sedated and unaware that half a country away his wife had just slid off an icy highway into an embankment, when he had a sudden sense of almost euphoric joy. The room seemed to fill with a kind of whiteness . . . a whitish light . . . an awesome brightness . . . and he was filled with just . . . so much joy. Later, when he was clear of the sedation, he thought it must have been the drug. That's when he learned that his wife had died, and when."

"Ah." It came out of Emily in a whisper, and there was nothing of triumph in it. But suddenly she understood the who, the what, the why, the where, the when. She understood it all perfectly. And in fairness she couldn't blame the senator for trying to track down the source of that white light ever since. It was an extraordinary coincidence. Of course it was the sedative. But still.

"So when you go to these sittings, you're"—she was almost afraid to ask it—"hoping to establish contact with your wife?"

"Always, always hoping," he said with a sad shake of his head. "And always, always disappointed."

Emily had to admit that wherever the voice that had taken over Kimberly had come from, it hadn't come from a beautiful concert pianist. "There'll be other sittings," she said softly, and amazed herself. So much for coming down hard on him. So much for the downtrodden taxpayer.

She could see, even as she groped for the right thing to say, that he was forcing himself out of his condition of pain. He turned to her with that dazzling smile and those clear blue eyes and ran his fingers through that shock of thick brown hair.

"This is the part where you accuse me of having had a hypnagogic hallucination," he suggested with a boyish grin.

How did he do it? It was like turning on a charm spigot.

"I didn't say that," she said, hedging, though she was thinking it.

"You're supposed to tell me that ghosts are always spotted right after people go to bed or when they wake up."

"Apparently you already know that," she said, still hedging.

"Ah, what's the use?" he said suddenly, signaling for the check. "I've gone only to the best, and the best can't give me Nicole. I don't know why I continue to try."

Because you loved her with a love that most women would kill for, thought Emily, and she was filled with a wistful envy for this Nicole, this fiercely determined wife and concert pianist. Emily had never loved that way, and she was absolutely certain she'd never *be* loved that way. She cared too much about her job, and her job demanded that she be clear-eyed and hard-edged. A clear-eyed woman saw all too many flaws in a man, and a hard-edged one turned most men off. If she'd wanted high romance in her life, she should've been a concert pianist. And, of course, rich.

The senator had stood up to get Emily's chair for her. It was a charming—or political—bit of chivalry, and it flustered her ever so slightly. She bobbed up suddenly, and her face ended up very near his.

"Freckles," he said, focusing on the bridge of her nose. "For such dark eyes and hair, you have very fair skin."

"I guess." Were freckles good or bad with these people? Bad, she suspected.

"Skin that I think is having an allergic reaction to the chain on your necklace." He traced a feather-light but sizzling line across her collarbone, alongside the heavy chain. "There's a bit of a rash here."

"Really?" she said, reaching up automatically to the spot. If there was a rash, it was impossible to separate it from the trail of heat he'd left behind. "I can't tell," she said with perfect honesty.

"I'm not sure you want to keep on wearing that," he cautioned as he held the door open for her.

"Keep up this kindness, and I'll be forced to vote for you after all," she quipped. The fact was, she was feeling very vulnerable. Obviously the evening was taking some kind of emotional toll. The rational thing to do was to head home with all due speed.

Still she dallied, there in the clear May night. "Senator—"

"We've been through our first vocal trance together; call me Lee."

"Senator," she said again, ignoring the bantering request. "You didn't have to tell me all that you did tonight. I know that." She braced herself and threw out the next observation: "I guess I'm wondering why you did."

"Why?" He sounded less puzzled than incredulous. "Is that the only word you know? *Why?*"

She'd never heard his how-dare-you tone before. Not that she wasn't familiar with it; most of the people she investigated eventually hauled it out and batted her over the head with it. But somehow she wanted Arthur Lee Alden III to be different. Somehow she was wrong.

"What I mean is, you can't have told any but your most trusted friends and associates about your—your vision, or I would've read about it somewhere. Why did you tell *me,* of all people?" Simple question; she thought it deserved a simple answer.

He just stared at her, so she answered the question for him. "It's not just because tonight is off the record. I think it's because you were hoping to make me so sympathetic to your plight, so moved by it, that I'd back off investigating this side of your character. After all, I'm a woman; that's what women do—sympathize. You took a big risk, Senator. You'd never have tried this with a man."

"Jeez, you're paranoid," he said at last.

"No, sir. *Not* paranoid," she answered, throwing an index finger up in the air. "I just want to know why you told me."

"Fine," he growled, his hand on the door of his BMW. "You want to know why?" He threw the door open. "I'll tell you why." He got in and slammed the door. He rolled down the window. "I don't know why. That's why."

He turned the key, the engine jumped to life, and he roared off, leaving Emily alone with the strength of her convictions. Her chin was set, her breathing coming hard and fast. She'd just reduced a United States senator to gibberish; it should've been a moment of triumph.

But it wasn't, and all the way home she tried to fathom why. Eventually it all came down to this: She thought more of him for having the courage to face her laughter than she thought of herself for having the courage to laugh at him.

It wasn't fair. Lee Alden had it all, including a good-old-boy understanding with the press not to expose his fanciful side. Even Stan Cooper left him alone. Yet not all politicians were immune to scrutiny. She thought of Gary Hart; she thought of John Tower. Somewhere someone had stood up and said, "Enough is enough." So why was there this reluctance to go after Lee Alden? Was it because when you did go up against him, you felt rotten about it? The way she was feeling now?

Too bad, kiddo, she told herself with grim determination. *You're gonna have to learn to live with it.*

By the time she'd squeezed her car into the lone space left on her street, Emily was bleary-eyed with exhaustion. It was well after midnight, but that wasn't the reason she was having to force one foot up the stairs past the other. She'd just spent a most unconventional evening, and she considered herself a very conventional girl. This kind of thing was more of a strain on her system than it was for Shirley MacLaine.

She was whimpering with longing for her bed by the time she slipped her key into the dead bolt of her door. Muddled and impatient for sleep as she was, after she turned the key to the left and right, she wasn't sure whether she'd even locked the door before dashing out that morning. Most likely not; it wouldn't have been the first time. She flicked a switch on the living-room wall. As always, her little condo looked perfectly happy to be what it was: a little condo. Everything was neat and tidy because everything had no choice.

Emily ran the place like a ship, which is why she noticed, even half asleep, that one of the silver candlesticks on a small writing table was knocked over. Automatically she stood it back up; she must've hit it when she dumped her book bag on the table that morning. She pulled open a louvered door to a tiny hall closet to hang her jacket inside and wrinkled her nose. Tobacco. She stuck her face in the sleeve of her jacket, but now the smell eluded her. *The Harvard professor*, she remembered. *A pipe smoker*. The two were practically synonymous.

Still, somewhere in the deepest part of her brain she was toting up the irregularities as she found them. She had long ago decided that messy people lacked a certain gene, which is what enabled them to live long and happy lives. Neat people, on the other hand, were always noticing things and worrying about them, just as she was doing now.

When Emily went into her bathroom, she suddenly got a lot more worried.

She was reaching for her nightgown behind the bathroom door when she saw that the jewelry box she kept on the top of a small bureau—the little inlaid wooden jewelry box her brother had sent her from Korea when he was stationed there—had been thrown open and its three drawers pulled out and left that way. Short of fleeing an earthquake, Emily was incapable of having left that kind of mess behind. Shocked, she went through the box quickly and inventoried the few things she kept there. Coins, earrings, broken watches, her mother's wedding rings, an old charm bracelet—all present. Frightened and relieved and very much awake, she thought: *They took one look and decided it wasn't worth it.*

Mere bravado. Exactly four seconds after that thought, Emily had another: that they—or he—didn't actually finish the burglary. She ran back to her living room. The VCR was still there. The TV. The stereo. *Oh, God. Oh, no.* If they hadn't finished, where were they now? Had they been scared off by a neighbor in the hall? Were they trying to find a parking place for their van? *Oh, God.* They weren't in the kitchen. The kitchen opened out into the living room. She could see the kitchen. They weren't in the kitchen.

She looked across to the bedroom, the dark, unlit bedroom. The bedroom with no wall switch, where the nearest light was a lamp on a dresser located exactly six and a half steps to the left of the door. The bedroom where to date the only phone was plugged into the only jack. She cursed the lamp, the phone, the darkness. She would not go in there.

She would go to a neighbor instead—Mr. Olafson, who had to get up at five-thirty for the commute to New Hampshire—and bang on his door and beg him to come to her apartment to find the burglar for her. He would ask if her door had been open. She would not be sure. He would ask what they took. She would say, "Nothing." He would ask why he, Mr. Olafson, was standing in the hall instead of lying in his bed.

No, she could not go to Mr. Olafson.

If this were a boardinghouse, we'd have a pay phone at the end of the hall and I could call the police, she realized, furious with the management. But *would* she call the police?

Mace! I have Mace! Her brother the policeman had given her a big, unwieldly can that she kept next to the Raid under the bathroom sink. She crept back into the bathroom, her heart hammering wildly and erratically in her breast, and took out the can of Mace. She had practiced it a thousand times, grabbing the can so that the button fired away from her. But she grabbed it backward anyway, dropped it in her panic, picked it up again, backward again, finally got it with the right side facing out, and marched out of the bathroom with it at arm's length, just in case she hadn't got it right after all.

She stood in the lighted living room at the threshold to the bedroom, clutching her Mace, her eyes failing completely to adjust to the darkness within. She took one step inside, then another. The air flowing from the bedroom was ocean cold and damp; it wrapped itself around her like a Nantucket fog. A new and utterly horrifying sensation took hold of her. Inside her bedroom there was no burglar lying in wait. There wasn't even someone as comforting as a Boston Strangler. There was something else. Something more. Something worse. Her heart became absolutely still in her breast. She took one step back.

The lamp was six and a half feet to the left, but she saw—she was certain she saw—a shadow move in the emerging dimness to the right. She aimed recklessly and fired; the wet hiss of Mace managed to go somewhere other than her face. She saw someone leap away, heard a startled oath. Petrified, she fired again, this time sweeping the area. Again the figure leaped away, unaffected by it.

"Jesus, woman! Put that thing away!"

She knew the voice. Oh, God, she knew the voice.

"Kimberly," she whispered, frozen in terror.

"Kimberly, my ass! I'm Fergus. Fergus O'Malley."

5

For an eternity or two Emily stood silent and still.

Then: "I don't believe . . . I know . . . an O'Malley," she managed to whisper.

"Ye do now." The voice was low, almost a snarl. "Get in here, girl. Let's see what we have."

"Ayyy . . . don't think so," Emily said faintly, taking another step back. Her knees were rubbery; she was close to collapse. The can of Mace fell from her hand to the floor with a sharp rap.

Once again the figure started in the shadows. "What in bloody hell *is* that?"

"I . . . it's . . . Mace," she answered in stupefied obedience.

"Mace? A spice that can hiss like a snake?"

"What?" Her head was reeling.

"Girl, are ye deaf? Never mind, then. Come here, I say. Why do ye dress in trousers, like a cowboy? *Come here, damn ye.*"

Emily began to sway; she grabbed the top of her dresser to steady herself and tried desperately to rally her wits. In a low and terrible voice of her own, she warned, "Get out of here right now—or I'll start screaming."

It happened instantaneously. The shadowy figure seemed to increase in size and hover over her, around her, through her. It was all done in thundering silence. Emily felt powerless, consumed. She shrank beneath the possession, shutting out the terror of it all. It was an unbelievable nightmare; she *had* to wake herself up from it.

So she fainted.

When Emily came to, she was on the floor, and every lamp in every room was ablaze. There were not that many watts in her light bulbs; this light was fantastic, blinding. Warding off the brightness with her hand and squinting as if she were looking into the sun, she peered into the corner where the figure had been lurking and begged, "Please . . . the light . . . it's hurting me. . . ."

At once the lights in the other rooms returned to normal, and the bedroom became dark once more.

Oh, hell, Emily thought, *this is where I came in.* She staggered to her feet and stood there, woozy and unsure what to do. "Mr. O'Malley—" she hazarded in the darkness.

"Plain O'Malley to ye," the voice answered roughly. "We ain't exactly on formal terms."

"O-O'Malley, then. Can you just . . . stay wherever you are? Until *I* turn on the lamp?" If he permeated her again—it was the only word that could describe how she'd felt—she would probably burn out and die. He had a power that no man still on earth could ever hope to possess. She had to keep him—it —whatever, at a distance.

"Light the bloody lamp, then, and let's get on with it."

"Get on with what, Mist—O'Malley?" she temporized, creeping the six and a half steps to the right. If she could just reach the phone; if she could just dial 911 . . . *Then what?*

The voice was muttering, "Gawd. So ye're the best I could do. A female no less." The figure seemed to be talking almost to itself.

Emily picked up the lighted Princess phone—it was an old and beloved rotary, her mother's, though she was cursing its slowness now—and dialed the 9. The rapid clicking sound set off the figure in the shadows again.

"What's this?" the voice demanded in an angry roar. "More bloody *Mace?"*

"Nothing! It's nothing!" Emily cried, slamming down the phone. "I'm turning the light on. Please . . ." she begged, near tears. "Don't do anything rash."

The voice made an impatient sound. "Turn up the lamp," it threatened, "or so help me, I'll turn it up once and for all."

She did as she was told, and when she turned around, she saw the thing that claimed to be Fergus O'Malley, boots and all, standing on her bed.

He was a young man—as nearly as she could tell. Because although he was there, somehow he wasn't quite there. At first it was nothing she could pin down. She saw his image in extreme clarity: He was no more than thirty, attractive and slender and of medium height, with reddish brown hair and green eyes and very fair skin. His hands were resting on his hips, and his mouth, finely cut, was curled in an expression of amused contempt. He was wearing a full-cut muslin shirt under a vest of brown corduroy that had four flaps on the front. His pants were dark gray, woven of some coarse material; the pockets lay flat and empty. His boots looked like work boots, with a high shin piece and low heels, the kind of boots a farmhand might wear. Except for the fact that he was standing on Emily's bed, he might have looked perfectly normal, if old-fashioned.

But there was one tiny other thing: His boots left no imprint in the bedding. Fergus O'Malley was not standing *on* the bed so much as standing *over* it. Emily had the proof—not that she wanted it—that the threat that faced her was anything but physical.

"Oh, shit," she whispered, awestruck, as she lowered herself into a caned chair without taking her eyes from the apparition.

He scowled. "Not only do ye dress like a cowboy but ye talk like one."

"I talk like everyone else nowadays," she said, defending herself.

"And what days are 'nowadays'?" The image descended—it wouldn't be fair to say he stepped down —to the floor and stood before Emily, hands still on his hips. "The newspaper in yer privy is dated a hundred years later than the last one I picked up. Is it possible?"

Emily looked up at him, her mouth agape, and said, "You're asking *me* what's possible? Who are you? Where are you from? Why are you here? Who *are* you?"

"Hey now!" he said suddenly, with a sharp chopping movement of his arm. Emily cringed in her chair, and he said in a voice rich with anger, "Ay, ye'd be the press all right. Ye bring to mind the rest of 'em in full cry—hounding me like a pack o' wolves all the way to the scaffold. Well, all that's over. Now it's

Fergus O'Malley can hound a man easily to his death. So *back off, girl!*"

"I'm sorry," she said humbly. "I meant no disrespect." Her knees had begun to shake uncontrollably. To be taken hostage was one of Emily's great fears in life, and now here she was. What should she do? She'd read that in a hijacked plane it was best not to be in first class or in an aisle seat or on a technical mission. She hadn't read a thing about ghosts in bedrooms.

She thought of Lee Alden, longingly. He'd know what to do. No doubt there was an incantation for times like these. But Lee Alden was nowhere near, so Emily smiled nervously and didn't make a move.

"That's better," the visitor said, appeased. "All right, then, ye're going to need a certain amount of history about me for the investigation. I'm goin' to tell ye things I wouldn't have told me own mother, which I suppose can't be helped. Ye need to know."

"Investigation?"

"Into my wrongful death by hanging."

"You were hanged?"

"Haven't I told ye that twice now?" he snapped. "Do ye need to see the mark of the rope?"

Automatically her glance went to his neck. She saw nothing, but he saw that she was looking for marks and reddened. That surprised her; she had no idea that a ghost could be embarrassed.

In a solemn voice he continued, "I was hanged by the neck until dead in front of seventy-six townsmen, one o' which was my eleven-year-old brother, in the year of Our Lord 1887, for the crime of murdering a young lady of station in her bedchamber."

Not just a ghost; a murderous ghost. "How did you murder her?" Emily whispered, dreading the answer.

"Goddammit, I did not murder her! Do ye hear *anything* I say?"

"Yes, of course; no, I understand perfectly," Emily said quickly. "I only meant, how . . . was she murdered?"

"Strangled," he replied with something like distaste. "A vicious job, with no thought behind it."

A thoughtful, murderous ghost. Emily heaved a sigh of utter exhaustion. It was obvious that the night was never going to end.

"She was wearing a medallion of pale rose crystal. It hung on a heavy plated chain, which ended up bein' the weapon," he added calmly.

Emily went very still. Her hand reached up to the locket that she'd wanted so fiercely; she remembered the paroxysm she'd felt when Cara fastened it around her neck. She shook her head, unwilling to accept the connection.

"Ay, it's the very one," said Fergus O'Malley with an ironic look, pointing a ghostly finger at her throat.

She tried to unfasten it and hurl it away from her. But the clasp seemed sealed shut, or else her fingers were fumbling too much.

"And ye were obliging enough to wear it someplace that mattered to someone like me. I don't mind tellin' ye, I began to despair of ever being able to straighten this mess away."

She wasn't understanding him at all. "Please . . . I'm so . . . tired," she pleaded, letting her hands drop helplessly into her lap. She wondered if she was going to faint again.

"Don't tell me ye're tired!" he shouted, snapping her awake once more. "Ye've gone an hour or two without sleep; I've waited a hundred-odd years to get on with the rest of my eternity. So who's more tired, hey?"

He crouched down in front of Emily and seemed to grab the arms of her chair, terrifying her. He was close enough for her to see a mole on his right temple; she would have bet her life he was absolutely real.

"Understand me once, and understand me good," he said in a voice thick with emotion. "That necklace showing up at that séance was my ticket back across the veil. I may not get a chance to prove my innocence for another hundred years, or a thousand. I had no idea who'd be wearin' the jewel, who it was I'd have to use as my instrument on this side. I was prayin' it wouldn't be some addle-headed whore, which is all I figured would wear a cheap trinket like that. When I learned ye was with the press, I was glad; some of them that covered my trial was sharp as tacks. But now, lookin' at ye, I'm not so sure. Ye're a fearful little thing. I might've done better with the whore."

"I resent that," Emily flashed, fully awake now.

"Resent what?"

"All of it, dammit! I mean, what do you expect? You drop into my condo, scare me to death, nearly blind me, order me to investigate something or other—"

"*Not* 'something or other'! A murder!"

"A hundred-year-old murder! I'm not a detective; I'm an investigative reporter. I thresh out slumlords, and they're usually alive when I do it."

They were eyeball to eyeball, she sitting, he crouching. She wanted to swing at him for half a dozen valid reasons, but the thought that her hand would pass right through him was more intimidating than if he'd had a gun pointed at her head. She contented herself with a sullen "Besides, do you know how cold a hundred-year-old trail can be?"

"I know exactly how cold a hundred years can be," he answered quietly, not moving his eyes from hers.

Emily stared into those green depths and looked away. There was too much pain there, too much knowledge for a young man to have. "I don't understand," she said, almost shyly. "Where have you been staying for the past hundred years? I guess, not in—heaven?" *Heaven. Here I am, asking a ghost if he's been hanging out in heaven.*

"No, not in heaven," he answered wearily. He stood up and rubbed the back of his neck; it made Emily wonder if he felt chronic pain there. He seemed to read her thoughts and drew his hand away instantly. Annoyed, he added, "And not in hell either. Not anywhere. And frankly by now I don't much care where I go, as long as it's somewhere."

"You can't mean that! No one wants to spend an eternity in hell."

"No one wants to spend it nowhere either."

"Are there others in this . . . limbo, with you? Did you ever meet anyone named Jimmy Hoffa?"

He waved her question away and fell into a room-long pace. That intrigued Emily; obviously he could've marched through the walls if he'd wanted to. She was becoming a little used to him. He didn't seem quite as terrifying as he had at first.

Maybe the nightmare is winding down, she thought. *Maybe it's almost morning and the alarm is getting ready to go off.*

He stopped in mid-pace and turned to her. "Have ye ever tried to understand nothingness? To imagine yerself *not being?* No; why should ye? Ye're too busy living. I was the same when I was alive . . . always thinking about the next job, always planning the break, the entry—"

"Then you *are* a criminal!" she blurted.

"A thief, not a murderer, ye dimwit. There's a difference."

"I know that," she answered, offended. "And I wish you would address me with some civility. We don't treat women like servants anymore," she lied. "In any case, I thought you said you were innocent."

"Not of all the charges. I admitted to the court that I broke into the place. I admitted I stole the silver—excellent pieces, mostly by Paul Revere but some Viennese stuff of real value. By the by, the candlesticks in yer parlor ain't worth a hell of a lot. Plate, and not very heavy at that."

"They have sentimental value, thank you," Emily said crisply.

"But I never touched the girl, never even bothered with the bedrooms, because I knew they kept their jewelry in a safe. It was the silver I was after; the old man was a keen collector before he passed on. Trouble was, the son had no interest in it; he was startin' to sell it off. I had no choice."

O'Malley was sitting on—above—the bed now, looking rueful. " 'Twas me own fault, rushin' the job. I was sloppy. Someone saw me. They nabbed me before I had a chance to unload any of the goods." He clenched his fists. "But *I didn't strangle her.*"

"Who was she?" Emily asked in a cautious way.

He shrugged. "The millowner's daughter. She was a flighty, silly thing, I'd always heard; her head was full of cotton wool. But she was real kind, others said, and generous. Loved animals, loved children. There was talk of a spurned suitor, but no one bothered to prove it. There was talk of a secret affair, but no one would believe it. They were in too much of an all-fired hurry to get someone, and the someone they got was me. Oh, they all hated me, all right. Her brother come at me a couple of times during the trial, screaming I'd murdered his sister and I'd burn in hell for it."

He made a wry face and stood up. "I guess I showed him."

Emily had been listening to his story with quiet fascination. "Have you, you know, kept track of all these people where you are?"

"Christ, woman, I told ye, I don't see no one, I don't hear no one, I don't know anything. I don't know who's been made President, or if we're at war, or if the British are running the country again. All I know is what I just read in yer privy: that there are ten traits a *Cosmo* woman should run from in a man, and that some kind of savings and loan crisis ye're having is going to last into the next century."

She allowed herself the luxury of a broad grin. The ghost continued to look baffled and she thought, *If I have to die, let it be now, in a moment of nonterror, my first of the night.*

Still, when the ghost began to scowl again, Emily quickly wiped the grin from her face. "I know I seem unsympathetic to you, but I'm not," she said, careful not to anger him. "It's just that you've made me realize that you never lived to see the worst war the world has ever known or the invention of the atom bomb—"

"What do I care about wars and Adam bombs!" he cried, whirling around on her. "I never lived to fall in love, or have a son, or teach him to work with his hands. He might've become something—a silversmith maybe. He might've made me damn proud." His eyes burned with a century of indignation.

For one incoherent second she imagined herself being the wife of Fergus O'Malley in 1887. She banished the thought as instantly as it formed. "But you can't turn back the clock," she said almost gently.

"No. I can't. But I can get in line for another try at life, *if* I can get the bloody hell out of this—"

"Limbo? Is that the name for it?"

He snorted with impatience. "There is no bloody name for it. Limbo is someplace else."

Emily threw up her hands in confusion and slumped back in her chair. "I don't get it. Are you telling me that anyone falsely accused of murder just sits around indefinitely in a state of oblivion?"

"Right. When ye die a wrongful death, ye're trapped. I spent enough energy to move any mountain ye can name on earth. I ranted. I railed. I called on every dead relation and every saint I could think of. It mattered not."

His eyes glittered with angry emotion; when he resumed his pacing his steps had a driven, purposeful rhythm. He seemed to be talking to himself, reliving his hundred years of frustration.

"All that resolve, all that fury—useless! Because it all comes down to blind circumstance: to whether or not there happens to be someone on this side who'll make it possible to come over."

In a tiny, sinking voice Emily said, "Me?"

The ghost stopped in his tracks. The look he gave her was half threatening, half ironic. "Ye."

Emily swallowed hard and tried to rally her spirits. "*Well*. It seems like a pretty dumb system to *me*. I was right in the first place: It's horribly unfair."

He laughed at her, a laugh filled with contempt and pain. "Who ever told ye death was fair?"

She didn't know what to say to that, so she said nothing.

After a pause Fergus O'Malley said, "Well? Will ye get started?"

"Now? It's nearly dawn!" she wailed.

"No better time. Get a pencil and paper."

She'd been sitting in the hard-backed chair for what seemed like half the night. One of her feet was asleep, her rear end was numb, and her eyes hung heavy as andirons. She glanced at her spindle bed with its downy comforter and beckoning pillows and said, "I can't, Mr. O'Malley. I just can't. In the morning, okay? Just . . . an hour of sleep. One hour. Then I'll do whatever you want."

He flushed angrily at being opposed, and she thought, *I don't care. Let him kill me, let him blind me. But let me sleep.* She let her eyelids droop and stay closed for one exquisite moment, like an exhausted driver on a dark country road, and when she forced them open again, he was gone.

Without questioning why or where, Emily threw back the comforter and collapsed, fully clothed, onto her bed. She fell like a stone into a deep and dreamless sleep, and when she finally stirred and opened one eye, the sun was neither in the east nor in the south window; it was two o'clock in the afternoon. At first she remembered nothing. Then, slowly, bits and pieces of the previous day came back to her, floating at the edges of her consciousness like dried leaves on a pond. Kimberly, and Mrs. Lividus, and the senator—had they all happened only yesterday?

And then she remembered—obviously she'd been trying not to remember—Fergus O'Malley. Her eyes opened wide, and her heart took a flying leap out of her chest. The ghost! She had dreamed of a terrible, endless, bizarrely realistic encounter with a ghost. She sat bolt upright and looked around the room, her breathing coming short and fast. No ghost. She looked for signs of the Mace she dreamed she'd sprayed all over. No Mace. Her bedroom was absolutely quiet. From somewhere outside she heard children playing their Sunday games, and that was all.

It was several moments before she dared feel reassured. Never again would she deny the power of the subconscious mind to produce a terrifying reality of its own. She had wandered into the realm of the mentally disturbed yesterday, and she hadn't got out again without one hell of a scare. Someday, but not now, she'd analyze the symbolism of her spin-off dream of Fergus O'Malley. What a naïf she'd been to skip off blithely to a séance expecting only a little innocent foolery.

She swung her legs groggily over the side of the bed and realized for the first time that she was wearing jeans and a shirt. God, she *was* exhausted last night. Automatically she tried to slip her feet into the slippers that hadn't been placed neatly by the bed before she turned in. Instead, she kicked a can, which went rolling off to the side.

A can of Mace.

Oh, good God. I can't go through this again, she thought, free-falling into hysteria.

"Come out!" she cried impulsively. "Come out and get it over with!"

She was standing now, and her head was splitting as if she'd been on the beach in the sun all day. She actually stamped her foot. The pain in her head doubled. *"Fergus O'Malley!"* she screamed, even though she felt extremely silly doing it. She glared at the open door.

When he sauntered through it, her first thought was, *I am making this hallucination happen. This is the first step in the descent into madness.*

He spoke. "What's the hue and cry?" he asked, surprised. "I was letting ye sleep as ye implored me, and now ye sound like I've gone and stole yer horse."

He *looked* real—even younger in the daylight, more hopeful somehow.

"Are you here or are you not?" she demanded. "If I'm crazy, then tell me and I'll go back to New Hampshire and my people will take care of me." She gave him a lofty look, fully expecting an answer to that.

He shrugged. "Ye seem all right to me. A little prickly maybe."

What am I doing? I'm asking my hallucination if I'm hallucinating! "Look, O'Malley, if you're real—really a ghost—then prove it. Make something levitate. Tell me something about myself no one else knows."

"Can't do either one, as it happens." He rubbed his chin as if he were due for a shave, then said, "Ah, I've got it." He glanced around the room. Then his gaze settled on the stripped pine dresser that was her grandmother's. He stared at it intently, and the room began to fill with the blinding, hurting light of the night before.

"Not that, not that!" she cried, shielding her eyes.

"Ye want the bloody proof or not?" he answered, annoyed, but the light subsided.

When Emily opened her eyes again, she saw, burned into the top drawer of the honey-colored pine, the name Fergus O'Malley in a childish, scrawling signature.

"I never went but to fifth grade," O'Malley explained self-consciously.

Stunned, Emily approached her grandmother's bureau and put a finger to the deeply scorched drawer. It was hot to the touch. Her nostrils filled with the smell of charred wood. From behind her she heard O'Malley's voice, irritated and impatient once more, say, "Now. Can we get to work?"

6

"Well, well, designer furniture," Emily quipped. But all the while she was thinking, *That drawer front could just as well have been my thigh.* The thought sent her spinning.

"That bureau was my grandmother's." Her voice came out high and shrill and full of crazy indignation. "Erase it, please."

O'Malley's surprised chuckle gave her courage.

"I mean it! We have to have some rules."

The ghost continued to be amused. "Such as?"

"Such as, you may not harm me, or anything of mine—or anyone of mine."

"Or else?"

"This investigation will *not* go forward."

She watched the muscles in his clenched jaw grind her impulsive threat into dust. At last he spoke. "So ye think ye cannot be replaced?"

She seized the chance to protect herself from his wrath once and for all. "That's right. Even if it were possible for you to get someone else to take over the job, who would do it? Not a lawyer—no one's going to do *pro bono* work for a ghost, not when he can be pulling down two hundred dollars an hour."

"An *hour?* When I didn't earn that much in a year?"

"Yeah, well, different dollars. A doctor won't do it either. They save bodies, not souls. Librarian? Too meek. A man of the cloth? Maybe, but most of 'em would balk at wearing the necklace. No, I'm the one you need."

"Ye didn't think so last night," the ghost said sullenly.

"I was tired last night. What about it, O'Malley? Deal? No harm to me or mine? Whether I succeed or not, as long as I do my best?"

"I can't undo the dresser drawer," he said scrupulously. "Ye should have told me it had value for ye. In my day pine was a poor man's wood."

Suddenly relieved, Emily said, "Never mind. I'll sand it out. Look, I need to bathe. I'm going to go in there, to the . . . bathroom," she said, pointing. "And you'll stay . . . *here,* won't you?" she added, making a swirling motion with her hands as if she were speaking in a foreign tongue.

O'Malley shrugged, and Emily opened the charred drawer and discreetly took out some clean underthings. She walked over to the closet and began groping mindlessly, conscious that the ghost was positioned over her right shoulder. Annoyed, she turned on him. "I'm sorry. I need more breathing room than this."

"I do not take up much space," the ghost said with mild irony.

"You know what I mean. I need privacy. I'm used to living alone."

"I lived with eleven sisters and brothers in a flat half the size of this."

"That was then. This is now. We live alone more nowadays." *And we like it less,* she thought, but it was nothing he needed to know.

The ghost frowned. "Where *do* ye want me, then?"

Emily resisted the obvious retort and snapped, "Out of sight."

"So be it."

He vanished.

"Oh, for—" Hands on hips, she said to thin air, "Do you have to take it so *literally?*"

There was no answer. "Have it your way," she murmured, and hauled herself off to the shower to rinse away twenty-four hours of psychic shock waves. She closed and locked the bathroom door, then let out a short and bitter laugh. *As if it really matters.*

But somehow it did matter. The closed door let her get as far as peeling off her jeans and shirt. After that things skidded to a halt. Emily sat on the edge of the tub in her underthings, feeling reluctant, feeling stupid. Am *I insane?* The thought hovered in the air around her like thick fog. It was as if she could not see the horizon; she had no idea anymore which way was up.

"If you're in the bathroom, please tell me," she whispered humbly. There was no reply, so Emily decided, very arbitrarily, that she was alone. She took a deep breath, stripped, and stepped quickly into the shower, yanking the curtain closed with something approaching hysteria.

Another thought occurred to her. "Are you in the *tub?*" she demanded.

Again there was no answer. She turned on the water, hot, torrential, cleansing. Maybe she could wash his spirit down the drain. She stood under the spray for a long time, waiting to be clean. *I feel exploited,* she thought. *I feel violated. It doesn't matter whether he's right here or not. He might be. I have no way of knowing. Can he read my thoughts? Does he know how much I detest this? I'm a prisoner in my own home. He's like having a television camera in every room.*

She soaped up her neck; her fingers caught in the chain of the necklace. *And all because of this misera-ble, godforsaken . . .* She clutched the necklace with soapy hands, trying to unfasten the complicated clasp. No luck. It infuriated her. She threw open the shower curtain, stepped in front of the mirror and wiped away the steam with her hands, straining to see the mechanism reflected there. Impossible. She pulled at the chain with both hands until her neck burned and ached. She swore; she moaned; she whimpered with frustration. But she remained be-jeweled.

"Hey, now!" came the call from the other side of the door. "Do ye plan to be hosin' down all blessed day?"

"None of your business!" she snapped. She leaned back into the door, tears of frustration welling. Then it hit her that the ghost seemed to be honoring the closed door between them. It was a small gesture. But it was something.

She emerged dressed and with a towel wrapped around her hair. The ghost was sitting on the small, deeply cushioned love seat. Emily sat down at her desk, smiled primly, and took out a yellow pad. "Okay, let's get started. Tell me all you know about the woman you . . . who . . . the victim."

"She was twenty-six and her name was Hessiah Talbot," the ghost said in a burst. "She was tall and thin, with pale skin and hair; she had the look of a cornstalk in October, if ye know what I mean. Faded, like, and scraggly."

"You did know her then?" Emily asked sharply.

He looked surprised, and then he looked away. "No."

She watched the by now familiar flush creep over his clear-cut profile. He was lying. "Look here, O'Malley, you have to tell me the truth, or we can't get anywhere. *Did you know Hessiah Talbot?*"

"Our paths crossed once," he said with extreme reluctance.

Emily waited, and after a pause he went on. "One day . . . she finds me a little in my cups, on a side street. She's free to step over me, o' course, like everyone else. But no, she has to call her driver over to haul me off to the mission to get cleaned up and fed. Like a stray dog," he added bitterly.

"And you resented the kindness?"

"Kindness, hell. I offended her sense of order," he said. "I was a piece of trash that tumbled into her view."

She was impressed by his fierce if misplaced pride. She wondered how deep it ran.

"Hessiah Talbot was a bitch, plain and simple."

Emily placed her pen down deliberately. "It sounds very much like you despised her. Why should I believe that you didn't kill her?"

He returned her cool stare. "Because I haven't killed *ye.*"

She compressed her lips. "Hokay, that's logical," she answered faintly. "Well, let's continue, then."

Her knees had begun to shake again. It occurred to her that she would never, ever feel safe around him. If she had to believe in his existence at all, she'd have preferred to think of him as a friendly ghost. Naturally that was absurd; he was an entity from another plane, driven by another set of rules from hers.

Unless, of course, she *was* hallucinating. The thought that she was simply schizophrenic, projecting demons from her own psyche, was looking more and more attractive to her. After all, nowadays there was hope for the mentally ill; Fergus O'Malley might be nothing a good dose of medication couldn't cure.

But until she could visit a shrink she decided to sit quietly and take down every word spoken by this ghost who called himself O'Malley. Just in case. As the afternoon wore on, her yellow pad filled up. Dates, names, places—the ghost knew them all. With precise detail he laid out the 1887 mill town of Newarth, Massachusetts, street by street: from the Talbot mansion at the top of the hill to the Irish shanties hard by the river that powered the mill. He trotted out a goodly number of its citizens, from the ambitious, hobnobbing mayor who played cards with the victim's brother at the mansion every Thursday night, to the Gypsy peddler who sharpened the Talbots' knives. And he recounted a great many details of the trial itself, including the color of the lining of the cape the mayor's wife, seated in the front row, wore on the day he was sentenced to be hanged: red.

All through the day Emily had been sustaining herself from cracker boxes and fueling up at her Mr. Coffee machine, but by eight o'clock she needed something more substantial. "I can't keep going," she pleaded, pushing away the yellow pad. "Let's send out for Chinese."

The ghost stopped in mid-pace. "What? Will they sit and take yer notes for ye?"

Her smile was weary. "Chinese *food*, not people. But on second thought, I'm hungrier than that. I'll order a pizza."

"Peet-sa?"

"It's a kind of dough and tomato thing, with cheese and toppings. You'll like—" She stopped herself. "Well, anyway, give me a minute," she said, heading off for her Princess phone.

The ghost tagged absently along, still deep in thought. But when Emily picked up the phone and began to dial, he snapped out of his reverie. The room began to become painfully bright again with his damnable light; it was a reflex reaction with him, like a porcupine erecting its quills. "Stop!" she cried. "I'm only getting food!"

The light subsided; the ghost mumbled an apology, then watched suspiciously while she ordered a large pepperoni, half mushrooms, half onion, extra cheese. "I have to eat, you know," she told him in injured tones after she hung up. "I have to sleep. I have to bathe. *I have a job.* I can't stop living so that you can—" She was at a loss. Die? Live?

"That's true. Ye'll have to leave yer employ," he said, rubbing his chin thoughtfully. "It goes without sayin'."

"*What?* Absolutely not. Who knows how long this may take?"

"Who knows how long I've *got?*"

"And I have to see a . . . physician soon," she said suddenly, veering away from the confrontation. "I think I may have something . . . wrong with me. I'm going to try to get an appointment tomorrow."

She was stunned by the transformation in his face. His eyebrows tilted, his lips compressed in sympathy. " 'Tisn't serious?"

"It's . . . internal," she hedged, vaguely stroking her right temple. "But I do need to see a doctor." She smiled uneasily, aware that she was very possibly asking herself for permission to find out if she was crazy.

"Agh, I'm sure ye're fine; ye look the picture of bloomin' health to me." His voice was filled with gruff conviction.

"Thanks for the reassurance," she answered stiffly. *As if he really cared.*

They worked a little more on what she'd begun to think of as the "chronicle," when the shrill brrrring of the doorbell went off. The ghost jumped, and so did Emily. "Hide!" she said without thinking. She ran to the door and opened it to find a lanky, gawky kid from Domino's, balancing a steaming cardboard box on the palm of his hand.

"Oh, my wallet," she said, her thoughts in disarray. "Wait there a sec."

She turned and found herself face-to-face with the ghost, who smiled amiably and said, "This is it? This is a peetsa?"

"My God, what are you standing here for?" she cried.

"You told me to wait here," the Domino's boy said, confused.

"Don't move," she commanded the boy. *"Into the bedroom. Now,"* she practically shouted to the ghost.

She turned back to the delivery boy, who was pop-eyed with wonder. "My mom told me this would happen," he said in a cracking voice. "Wow."

"Not you. Him," she answered, jerking her head over her shoulder as she rifled through her purse. She tracked down fifteen dollars and threw it at the delivery boy, who barely had the chance to say, "Who?" before she said, "Beat it," and slammed the door in his face.

Heart thundering, cheeks on fire, she leaned her

forehead against the door and whispere
he didn't see him."

She waited a moment, drawing a deep b
two. The aroma of tomato sauce and onions w
up from the pizza box she held. Ghost or no gh
she had to eat. She dropped the box on the tiny oa
dining table; then, still standing, she slithered a slice of pizza away from the rest of the pie and with both hands lifted it for that first satisfying triangular bite. She polished off the slice, then wandered over to the fridge, took out a Bud Light, popped the top, and took a long, thirsty pull of beer. *This has been one heck of a hell of a day.* She heaved a sigh; it came out a burp.

"Would that be beer?"

"Yikes!" There he was, perched on her Formica counter and looking wistful. Where he'd come from she hadn't a clue. "You know, it's very unnerving when you evaporate and reappear like that. And yes, it's beer," she added, annoyed that he'd caught her in a burp.

"In cans; fancy that." The ghost shook his head, bemused. "Beer. There be few joys in life more profound than a cold stein on a hot day. I do miss it," he said softly.

He was making her feel guilty, which annoyed her still more. Out of sheer spite—and forever after, she was sorry she did this—she walked over to the sink and poured the rest of the can down the drain. "It makes my thinking fuzzy," was the excuse she offered him. "I'll stick to coffee."

He looked almost hurt; she chose not to see it. Hostages sometimes developed a bizarre sympathy for their abductors; everybody knew that. But Emily would not become a Patty Hearst for him or anyone else.

that way?" she demanded.
o feel bad because you can't
the big deal about a glass of

of emotions on his face—
d thought, *He can't hide his*

in this pitiable age like ye? Cold, and defensive, and so eager for battle?" he said, giving angry voice to the feelings she had just seen play across his face.

"I am not!" she cried, stung. "You don't know anything about me. How can you? You haven't let me get a word in edgewise."

"I didn't come all this way just for ye to get a word in edgewise!" he answered hotly. "Yer job is to find out who killed Hessiah Talbot—"

"Nothing to it!"

"—and then make known the murderer! That's all!"

"And how am I supposed to do that? We don't have town criers anymore."

"It's news, ain't it? Ye'll print it in yer newspaper."

"Are you *crazy?* I'd be the laughingstock of Boston!"

"As near as I can tell, a little laughter'd do ye good."

"Out of the question."

"Ye have no choice."

"Don't I?" Her anger goaded her. "Listen to me, O'Malley. I'm making you up. You don't exist. My mind can create you; my mind can take you away. *The pizza boy didn't see you at all,*" she added triumphantly.

He snorted. "And the writing on the drawer?"

"That doesn't exist either!" she cried, working herself into a frenzy of denial. "I could have done it myself, in my sleep. Yes! *I* put it there, and now *I'll* take it away." She rushed to a low kitchen drawer crammed with odds and ends and pulled out a sheet of sandpaper and a screwdriver. Then she ran into the bedroom, pulled out the drawer, and dumped its contents on the bed. She removed the knobs and began furiously to sand away the scorch marks, muttering bits and pieces of incoherence all the while.

"It's stress, of course . . . working too much . . . the séance . . . suggestible . . . or worse . . . in the family . . . Uncle Jerry . . . oh, God, after Vietnam . . . lost it . . . his demons . . . I forgot . . . look at me . . . what's happening? . . . out, out . . . please . . . go . . . hold on, hold on . . . later . . . funny . . . tell them . . . Lee . . . laugh . . ."

Exhausted and in pain, her tears falling in dark, wet stains on the freshly sanded wood, Emily ran, at last, out of steam. Her fingertips were on fire. She turned her hand over slowly, dumbly, and stared. Her fingers were scraped and raw. She'd sanded through her skin.

"What am I doing?" she mumbled, letting her head drop to her chest, no longer fighting the waves of sobs that rolled over her. "What am I doing? What am I doing? . . ."

When she woke up it was blackest night, and a driving, vindictive rain was pitching itself through her open window. The wind was bending the tops of the maples outside her third-floor bedroom; their heavy, wet branches clawed at the side of the shingled house, pressing, insisting. Emily sat up in bed. Her right hand buckled with pain. Wincing and groggy, she staggered to the open double-hung window and tried to pull down the lower part. It stuck—

it always stuck—and was impossible to lower with only one hand.

She tried a combination of forearm and good hand, but still the window resisted. With a moan of despair Emily crawled back into bed and pulled the quilt up to her chin. The rain pounded and bounced and made flying leaps from the windowsill to her cheek, where it mingled with an occasional tear. She'd never felt as alone and helpless in her life as she was feeling now.

The room became suffused with soft light—no more than forty watts' worth—and O'Malley was there, sitting at the foot of her bed. He seemed less real to her now, more shadowy. In her tired and fanciful state she wondered whether some of his essence had been absorbed by the storm or it was just that her madness was subsiding.

"Feeling better?" he asked in a kindly voice.

She rolled her head away. "Not especially." *He sounds as real as ever,* she thought, dispirited.

"Yer thoughts seemed far away."

"I was wondering," she said to herself more than to him, "who will take care of me if I am mad. All four of my brothers are married; all of them have wives . . . and kids. . . ."

"Never fear, Emily. Ye're not mad."

"I suppose I'll find out tomorrow."

"When ye go off to Newarth? Ye'll see I'm right."

"I don't want you to come along," she said dully, thinking about the psychiatrist she planned to see. "Not at first."

"What? Ye'll need my help—" he argued, jumping up.

"Not at first," she repeated. She pulled the quilt up over her shoulder and burrowed into her pillow, signaling an end to the discussion. Reality or delusion, she wanted him to go away.

For a moment the only sound was of the rain drumming on the roof. Finally O'Malley spoke, in a voice of chilling calm. "All right. Since ye seem to think I'll be a hindrance, I'll stay out of it for the present. But hear me good: We made a bargain. *I trust ye to keep it.*"

When Emily dared open her eyes again, it was blackest night.

7

Monday morning was nothing like Sunday night. With a bright, warm sun to give her courage, Emily marched defiantly out of her condo, determined to take her problem and lay it at the feet of the man who had started it all: Senator Arthur Lee Alden III. Forget the psychiatrist. Forget the library. What she wanted was something more along the line of Ghostbusters, and it was the senator who came closest to fitting the bill.

She slipped her key into the door of her parked Corolla and glanced up at her third-floor window, half expecting to see a shadowy figure move away from the shutters. But there was no sign of Fergus O'Malley, nor had there been all morning. It didn't matter. Hallucination or abomination, shortly he was going to be someone else's problem. Emily wasn't too proud to admit that she needed help on this one.

She drove directly to the senator's office building in downtown Boston. Lee Alden would be in Washington, but his secretary would know his schedule, and his aide would be able to add to it. She found Mrs. Cusack behind her desk, looking as sensible as ever. The secretary let her know that the senator wasn't due back until the end of the week. Was there, she asked Emily pleasantly, a problem with the upcoming interview?

Emily answered just as pleasantly, "Not at all. But it's rather important that I speak with him, even if only by phone."

As if on cue Jim Whitewood popped his head out of his office and said, "Millie, I've got the senator on the horn, and I can't find the day-care file. Is it on your desk?"

"No. I'll help you look." She stood up, and Jim Whitewood withdrew without a glance at Emily. The secretary paused and reconsidered, then pressed the blinking button on her phone line. "Senator? I have Emily Bowditch next to me. She needs to speak with you. Do you have a moment, while we look for the file? Good."

With a smile that might have meant anything she handed the phone to a dumbstruck Emily and went off in pursuit of the aide.

"Emily?" Lee Alden's voice, deep and assured, rocketed through her. "What's up?"

Oh, sure, let's talk ghosts, Emily thought wildly. She kept a watchful eye through the open door on the distracted pair and said in a whisper, "Look, Senator, there's been a complication. It has to do with the séance." Only then did she remember that Lee Alden had left her in a huff afterward. It seemed a hundred years ago.

Yet he sounded friendly enough—even glad to be talking with her. "If you tell me you've sold your story to the *National Enquirer,* I'll be disappointed," he said dryly.

"Nothing like that," she answered, intensely preoccupied. The other two could return any second. "But that night I think something got . . . loose."

"You mean, like a parakeet?"

"No. Not a parakeet." Mrs. Cusack, who'd stuck her head around the corner to see if Emily was still on the phone, gave her a curious look.

"Emily, this may not be the appropriate forum for Twenty Questions," the senator suggested at the other end. "Tell me what it is that got loose at the séance."

Emily turned her body away from the open door and cupped her hand over the mouthpiece. "A goddamned *ghost*, that's what."

There was no response. Then she heard Jim Whitewood's voice on an extension: "Hello? Hello, Senator?"

The senator's voice came in at last, cool and detached: "Thanks for the tip, Miss Bowditch. I'll take it under advisement."

Emily hung up and got out of there before Jim Whitewood had the chance to tell her what a nitwit she was—if he'd heard her. On the other hand, if anybody'd believe her, presumably he was the one. Unless he was a fraud and opportunist. Or unless he thought she was making it all up to—who knows?—get in bed with Lee Alden. Any way she looked at it, it was a mortifying thought.

When she got to work the first thing Stanley Cooper said was, "What happened to your hand?"

Apparently she'd been favoring it; she cursed Stan's relentless powers of observation and said, "Burned it." She slung her purse over the back of her chair and that's when she saw the telephone message written, thank God, not in Stan's handwriting: "Concerning the parakeet, call at noon."

"Getting a new pet?"

It was asked oh-so-casually.

She avoided looking at Stan. "No. Yes. Why not?"

Stan shrugged and turned back to his computer screen. "It's just that you've always made a big deal about being footloose and fancy-free."

"A parakeet is not a farm animal," she said in a strained voice.

"Still needs to be fed. Watered. Paper changed."

He knows something's up. Why do I try? "You're right, Stan. There's no room in my life for a parakeet. I'll call the guy and tell him that."

Stan gave her a sharp look and then backed off. But for how long? Emily wasn't sure where Jim Whitewood really stood on the paranormal, but she knew *exactly* how Stanley Cooper felt. One little complaint from her about a haunted condo, and her career was history. Her only possible ally right now was a man she was fond of calling a flake.

At noon Emily slipped away from her desk and found a quiet phone. She was put directly through to the senator.

"Is this line, you know, safe?" she asked naïvely.

He assured her it was.

There wasn't much point to beating around the bush, so she said, "There's this guy, Fergus, who showed up after the séance. Actually he showed up *at* the séance. You heard him; he's the one who said he couldn't stand it anymore. What he meant was, he couldn't stand being left between heaven and hell, if that's what they're called, because that means he can't come back until . . . well, he's an astral being, or he *would* be, if he could be vindicated of a crime he didn't commit. Well, he did commit the burglary, but not the murder—he says he didn't, and I believe him." She paused for breath.

"Are we on *Candid Camera*?"

"*No,* we're not on *Candid Camera.* I'm not kidding. There's a ghost in my condo. Kimberly let him out, and I can't figure out how to get him back in . . . wherever. He says if I solve the murder, he'll be able to get on with . . . whatever. That's where he thinks I am now, in the library, working on the case."

"In the library?"

"Well, it happened a hundred-odd years ago. Where else am I supposed to go?"

"Are we on *Candid Camera?*"

Her voice began to rise in her throat. "Listen, Senator, if it weren't for you, I wouldn't be in this mess. Ever since Kimberly, my life has been chaos. You started it; now you do something about it." She hadn't realized what an emotional wreck she'd become; her next words made it clear. "Please, Senator," she begged, her voice dropping to a hoarse whisper. "I need you here . . . I—" She broke down and began sobbing. She hated herself for every sniffle, but she couldn't help it.

"My God, Emily . . . all right." His voice sounded alarmed but firm. "I'll be at your place tonight. Expect me late. Give me the address."

She did, in a halting voice, and they hung up. Instantly she felt like a fool. She tried not to think about it for the rest of the day and instead forced herself to go through the motions of her next assignment for the *Boston Journal:* a dull little exposé of a defaulting builder who'd submitted false bond securities to the city for a playground he'd never built. Luckily the builder had an ego as big as the Prudential Building; he was more than willing to talk in a phone interview, so half the story wrote itself. Nonetheless, Emily worked late, not because the piece was giving her trouble but because she couldn't face Fergus O'Malley alone.

And she wasn't sure why. She was basically terrified of him, that went without saying. And she was weirdly sorry to disappoint him by coming home empty-handed. But mostly her pride was smarting because she'd been forced to call in the marines. She stalled a little longer by eating dinner out, and then at about nine o'clock she headed home to what was bound to be a no-win night. Tired and preoccupied, she had to park her car well up the street and then force herself to stay alert for muggers.

She made it in one piece and saw the senator's BMW parked squarely in front of the rambling Victorian of which she was making payments on such a very small part. He was here! The question was—since there was no lobby—where? She let herself in and found him sitting on the top stair outside her apartment, looking rumpled but at ease.

"Senator! I'm sorry! You said you'd be late!"

"I meant don't hold dinner, that's all." His smile was captivating. It bowled her over, that ability to be almost intimately reassuring and yet not quite pushy.

"How did you get in?" she asked. "Wait, don't tell me; the outside door wasn't locked. Darn college kids. They're renting the first-floor condo, and they treat the whole building like a dormitory. Just about anybody could get in here."

The senator nodded toward her apartment and then turned back to her. "Apparently just about anybody *did*," he said, without humor.

She'd been fumbling with her keys. Now she dropped them. "I can't begin to imagine what you must think of me," she mumbled, stooping to pick them up. "A nut case, right?"

But the senator was there before her. Scooping the keys up in his hand, he stood as she straightened up.

They were very close, very tentative. "An *intriguing* case maybe," he murmured, "but not a nut case."

He was near enough that she felt the sweep of his breath across her cheek. There was something about him so warm, so vital—so completely in contrast with Fergus O'Malley—that she lifted her face to him, as a daisy orients itself to the sun. The senator touched his finger to the tip of her nose and said, "Now. Shall we see what's behind that locked door of yours?"

He selected a key, the right key, from her ring and slid it into the lock. Immediately Emily had misgivings.

"He could do something, could hurt you," she whispered suddenly. "He has a horrible temper. He threatened me last night."

The senator threw her a glance of real concern and turned the key. He pushed the door open, then paused at the threshold.

Emily grabbed his arm and said, "*No.* You shouldn't have come."

"Too late now," the senator said, and flipped on the light just inside the door.

Emily was right behind him. The condo looked the way she'd left it—a mess. There were yellow pads everywhere and loose sheets of paper littering the room. Clothes were left where they had fallen, the pizza box lay open on the dining table, and empty cracker boxes were sprouting like mushrooms from the floor. Juice cans, Coke cans, a saucer piled high with dried brown tea bags—the place had the look of a dorm room after an all-night cram. And the television was on! Had she left it on after catching some morning news? She stared at the baseball game, trying to remember.

The senator was glancing around the room, taking it all in.

Emily sprang into action. "This isn't normal," she said, grabbing up litter by the armful. "I'm much neater than this, really, but he was dictating so fast—"

"Don't worry about it," the senator said, walking up to the television. His hand paused on the off button as the announcer intoned, "So at the end of the fourth inning it's the Boston Red Sox three, the Yankees one." A half-smile flitted briefly over his face. He turned off the set.

Emily was watching him. "You don't believe me," she said, stopping dead in her tracks. Her arms were full of damp towels and empty cartons; her eyes were burning with indignation. "You're more interested in the game!"

"I turned it off," he protested.

"Eventually!"

"Emily, trust me on this one: I really can walk and chew gum at the same time. Whether the Red Sox win or lose will not affect my ability to help you."

"You're right; I'm sorry. I'm just on edge, that's all." She dropped the armload, crumbs and all, into a side chair and said helplessly, "He might be anywhere."

"They're said always to appear in the same place," the senator ventured.

Emily pointed to her darkened bedroom. "He was in there the night of the séance." She felt a ridiculous, intense surge of disloyalty. She flashed back to the third grade, when someone told the teacher that she was hiding in the cloakroom, eating a stolen candy bar. *Snitch!* she'd cried to the girl later. Snitch, snitch, snitch!

But this was different. "Please be careful. He filled me with light, a great . . . burning light. It was terrifying. . . ."

Part of her was convinced that the ghost wouldn't dare attack a United States senator, and part of her shut her eyes tightly in self-defense. She waited. When she opened her eyes again, the senator was standing in the doorway of the bedroom, watching her thoughtfully. "Nothing?" she asked in a small voice.

"Nothing obvious," he answered. "I've brought a pocket tape recorder with me." He set it up on the desk at which she was sitting. "I want you to tell me about this light."

She did, running through the sequence of events in great detail, trying to convey her terror. "I've always read about knees that knocked," she said, "and the accounts always seemed melodramatic. Now I know better." She studied her hands, folded and locked in her lap, aware that she sounded like a patient spilling her guts to a psychiatrist. Yet she *was* feeling relieved, finally talking about it with someone.

The senator had let her run on, almost in a monologue, before he spoke. "Do you think he's here now?" he asked from his seat on the sofa. His voice was very calm, a therapist's voice.

Too calm; it annoyed her. "Of course I do," she answered. She'd been trying so hard not to make Fergus sound like a hallucination. All things considered, she preferred that Fergus be real and that she be not insane. "You're probably sitting on him right now," she added, a little evilly.

The senator didn't flinch; his handsome face remained impassive. "Do you think he'll show himself to me?"

Emily pushed her locked hands away from her in a stretch to relieve her tension. "I dunno. Maybe you have to be wearing the necklace. Want to try it?" she challenged, reaching up behind her as if to undo the clasp.

"No, not now," the senator answered quickly. "We can always try that later. After all, he's not appearing to you either at the moment."

He rose to his feet and began taking in the measure of the apartment, stopping now and then to pick up some object or look at a framed print. It was as if he were trying to know her through her things. He seemed to Emily much too big for her place, larger than life somehow. He belonged in a suit of armor and on a horse—not easing himself between a TV stand and a shelf of paperback books to get a better look at a poster print she'd bought from the Harvard Coop. Emily thought of her friend Cara Miles. Cara's town house would be grand enough to suit him, and *her* Picassos—both of them—were genuine.

The senator's little tour didn't last long. He came back to the tape recorder and turned it off. Emily noticed, not for the first time, how big his hands were: strong and well formed, with prominent veins. If it were a question of manual combat, she had no doubt who'd prevail. But it wasn't. The senator picked up some of her notes and glanced through them while she kept one eye on the table lamp, watching for changes in wattage, and one ear cocked for ghost sounds.

"Am I missing something?" the senator asked lightly, looking up from the yellow pad of notes. "This is an impressive amount of information, by the way," he added. He turned the tape recorder back on. "Have you ever been to Newarth?"

She shook her head. "He's not going to show," she said, drumming her fingers nervously. "I knew he wouldn't. I just knew it."

"You last saw the apparition last night?"

She nodded. "It was raining; I was very depressed. He came into the bedroom, I think almost to comfort me. We ended up arguing about whether he was coming with me on the investigation. I told him not to tag along, and he got mad." Emily slumped in her chair a little at the recollection; her hair slid forward over one cheek.

The senator caught the wayward lock in a feather's touch and slid it back behind her ear. "Emily," he said in a voice that was at once reassuring and infinitely sympathetic, "do you know what you're saying?"

She felt simultaneously patronized and electrified. It threw her off completely, so she retreated to her usual defense, sarcasm.

"Yeah. We argued. He walked out. The usual thing." She closed her eyes, wanting more than anything that he touch her hair again.

"I mean, how incredible all this sounds to someone?"

He *wasn't* going to touch her hair again—for whatever reason. Stung, she pushed her chair back and stood up. "I've told you *exactly* what he said. I remember every word."

"People do hear voices—"

"Stop right there! Don't you dare call me a paranoid schizophrenic!"

"I haven't called you anything. But documented apparitions tend to describe vague, mostly featureless, almost transparent forms that don't last long. Whereas you know this man down to his brass buttons. You mimic his accent; you claim to have seen his face flush, for God's sake. Think about it, Emily. A flush is a rush of blood under the skin. *How can a dead man flush, Emily?*"

"I don't know and I don't care! He flushed! Repeatedly! How can you not believe me? Look, look here! I'll show you!" She dragged him into her bedroom and pulled her top drawer half open. A jumble of underwear exploded brazenly from it; she didn't care. "See this drawer? See it? That's where I sanded the name out!" she cried. "And then I waxed it!"

"It looks like every other drawer," he said cautiously.

"Of course!" she cried, absurdly pleased by the compliment. And then she comprehended what she'd done. "Oh." She bit her lower lip, amazed at her stupidity in destroying the evidence. "Well, it *was* there. 'Fergus O'Malley.' In a child's scrawl."

The senator slid the drawer closed and said gently, "That doesn't prove it was a ghost who scrawled the name."

"*What?* Do you think *I*— What *is* this? *I'm* the skeptic. You're supposed to be the *believer.*"

They both were hovering over the bureau, like opposing attorneys wrangling over a piece of evidence. She began to have a sick feeling in her stomach. If Lee Alden, Rhodes scholar and spirit connoisseur, didn't believe her, maybe she didn't have a case.

She made a last-ditch effort to force him to believe. "I saw him there, I tell you, in the corner. And standing on my bed. And sitting on it. And in the living room. And in the kitchen; he wanted a beer. My God, why would I make him up?" she cried.

"Stress?"

"Stress, oh, that's it! When anything goes weird nowadays, blame stress! I haven't been under any stress!"

"You lost your mother, Emily; that's a stressful event," the senator suggested quietly.

The arrow hit home. She herself had been wondering if there was a connection. She sat on the edge of her bed and said in a careful voice, "People lose their mothers all the time. But they don't make up ghosts to take their place.

"Besides," she added, jumping back up, "Fergus O'Malley is *nothing* like my mother. He's desperate to come back again and start over. He's full of ambition and unfulfilled dreams, and he wants beer, pizza, the works. He wants it all. My mother just . . . didn't."

She thought of her mother as she lay dying. She had said so little, just now and then a sigh, waiting to be done with it. No matter how hard Emily had tried, she could not make her mother want to stay. And now she was gone.

"I don't know," Emily said, sighing heavily, "maybe you're right. Maybe Fergus has something to do with my mother . . . some kind of wish fulfillment . . . I don't know. . . ." Her voice trailed off as she struggled with the concept, her gaze drifting aimlessly around the bedroom, watching automatically for signs of Fergus. He'd been so real. Right down to the mole on his right temple.

"No!" she said, shaking her head vehemently. "I did see him! I admit I thought I might have been hallucinating, but I wasn't. He's here! Somewhere!" She dropped down to her knees on the Virginia carpet and pulled up the dust ruffle of her bed. "Fergus! Damn you, show yourself!" She jumped back to her feet and threw open the trunk that held spare blankets. "Come out!" She ran to the living room, stopped, listened, ran into the kitchen area, opened the fridge, left the door agape, checked the oven, left that door hanging, flew from one cupboard to the next, opening each door in succession, whirled around once, twice, and finally came to rest, drained by her own hysteria.

She managed, somehow, to come out of her daze

and recognize the senator standing not six feet from her. "Lee," she said in a desolate voice, "I'm losing it." In a gesture of supplication, she held out her arms to him.

Suddenly he was there for her, enfolding her in his warmth and rock-solid embrace, making up in every way for the phantom that was eluding her. "Shh," he whispered through her tears, rocking her gently against his chest as he would a child. "Don't talk like that . . . shh, shh." She felt his hand weave through her hair and pull her close as he murmured little words and half phrases of reassurance. "Emily . . . Emily . . . it will get better . . . it will."

Somehow, she believed him. She let herself feel for one exquisite moment that she was safe from harm. Being in his arms, listening to his voice, was more comforting than sleep, more soothing than a soft lullaby. She needed so much to be able to let her guard down, and Lee Alden was making that so easy. Gradually her breathing slowed and her tears dried. She drew in an enormous breath, held it, and let it out.

"Attagirl," he murmured close to her ear. He continued to hold her.

She lifted her face, tight with fear, to meet his gaze. "What should I do, Lee?"

A look of consternation, almost of pain, passed over his face as he beheld hers. He stroked her cheek with the back of his fingertips; began to say something; stopped. After a moment he said, almost stiffly, "I'll stay on your sofa tonight."

Though she hadn't dared to hope for his protection, it was exactly what Emily needed to hear. She'd been right in the first place: Lee Alden was the only man alive she could trust to see this thing through with her. Yet with the relief came guilt. The senator was a public figure, a man of reputation. He was taking a considerable risk for her sake. She should turn down his suggestion, but she wasn't feeling brave enough.

"I shouldn't be doing this to you," she admitted sorrowfully.

"No, dear heart . . . you should not."

His voice was rueful, but there was something ambiguous in it that sent a ripple of heat through her. She was in his arms, and his blue eyes were intense, and the moment was no longer about comforting. Worse, Emily no longer really wanted comforting. Suddenly it wasn't enough, wasn't nearly enough. It seemed incredible to her that her mood could change so abruptly, yet here she was: cheeks on fire, heart thundering in her breast, every nerve ending aroused.

The senator was cradling her head in his hands and was lowering his mouth to hers. Her eyes were partly closed, and her mouth had parted for the kiss that was to come—when he stopped.

"Oh, boy, out of bounds," he said in a husky voice, bringing himself back under control. He took her by her shoulders and held her away at arm's length. "Definitely out of bounds." His breath came with an effort.

Confused and disappointed, Emily swayed dizzily and murmured, "No, you're not."

But the senator smiled bleakly and shook his head. "Oh, Emily . . . believe me when I say this is not the time."

"Because there might be a ghost in the house?" she asked, with a heartbroken attempt at humor.

He hesitated. "Because there might not be."

"Ah." The word, bittersweet, hung in the air between them. But one word didn't seem enough, so she added two more. "I see." She dropped her gaze from his and concentrated instead on the third button of his shirt. It was all too clear: Lee Alden did not make love to crazy women.

"You're way too vulnerable right now," he was saying. "And as irresistible as you may be, it wouldn't be right, wouldn't be fair to you." He let go of her as if she were too hot to hold.

Emily's chin came up. "You talk as if you'd be stealing the kiss," she said, hurt and offended. "It would have been freely given."

"It's been a long time since I've been with a woman," he explained, sidestepping the pain in her voice. "It wouldn't have ended with one kiss."

"You're *so* sure!"

"I could be wrong," he admitted with infuriating modesty. He went deliberately over to the sofa and sat on one arm of it, widening the gap between them, further offending her.

He was in complete control of the situation. Emily had known confident men before, but Lee Alden was in a class by himself. The worst part of it was he had every right to be. Who could resist him? Who of sound body or mind would want to? Was it his fault that women kept throwing themselves at him? That they ran to him for help all week long? Heck, it was his job.

"You've been in this situation before," she said dryly, trying not to sound reproachful.

He grinned good-naturedly. That was another one of those charming things about him she couldn't stand: He had a sense of humor about himself.

"I've been in a lot of situations, Emily, but not in this one. Not even close."

She was becoming angrier, irrationally so, but she didn't mind it a bit. Anger sometimes made her fearless; if this was one of those times, she'd make it through the ordeal without him. "I think you ought to go," she said coldly. "I'll be fine."

"Do you have a spare pillow?" he asked, ignoring her bravado.

Her eyelids lowered dangerously. "You're not listening."

"Yes, I am. You'd rather I left. I'd rather I stayed. I did fly up from D.C.," he reminded her. "You owe it to me to let me feel helpful. What are politicians for anyway?" He tried an engaging grin.

When she didn't respond, his mood became more serious. "Look, Emily, something—anything at all—could happen tonight. I've brought a briefcase filled with work. I'll catch up on my reading, and if nothing happens, I'll take the six o'clock back in the morning." He undid the knot to his loosened tie and tossed it aside. "I spend half my nights on my Senate sofa anyhow."

Hands on her hips, Emily glanced at the maroon silk tie draped over her sofa. It looked so decisive. *Well. That's that. Whether I want him or not.* She glanced at the tie again. *I do want him here,* she decided. *Just for tonight.*

The senator said, "My briefcase is in my car; I'll be right back," and headed for the door.

But she intercepted him and held out her hand. "Give me your keys," she said gruffly. "I'll get it for you." She couldn't offer him much in hospitality; the least she could offer him was anonymity.

He understood her perfectly and was grateful. "Thanks."

Emily skipped down the stairs far happier than she had a right to be. This was not the answer, having a man she considered a handsome flake conclude that she was an irresistible flake. She smiled at the thought and shrugged cheerfully. *What the heck, it's a start*. God, she must be punchy. She tried to keep things in perspective. The senator was there on business, and his business was the paranormal—or, as those people liked to call it, "human potential."

She noted with gratitude that his BMW hadn't been stolen, opened the trunk, and took out his briefcase. That there was no overnight bag said good things for the senator's integrity but left her feeling a little stab of disappointment. Still, her mood on the whole was upbeat. Nearly twenty-four hours without a trace of Fergus O'Malley, and a big, strong senator to make sure he never came back. Things were definitely looking up.

Emily stood aside on the landing while a group of seven or eight rowdy college kids pushed their way past her, laughing and hooting. She went in, then paused at the foot of the stairs of the ornate Victorian hall, trying to remember if she'd locked the trunk. Yes. She started up the stairs.

Suddenly a shaft of cold pierced her body. It was so cold, so unexpected, so fiercely painful, that she staggered under the blow and grabbed the balustrade to steady herself. The shaft of cold seemed to dissolve into a mass inside her, then expand and wrap itself around her, constricting her chest, stealing her breath, numbing all thought. She thought it must be her heart, but her heart knew better.

Fergus O'Malley.

8

The moment passed as quickly as it had come. Emily waited for the adrenaline to subside, then fled up the stairs. She found the senator at the front window, staring out into the street. He turned, took one look, and said, "Good God, Emily, you look as if you've seen—"

"I haven't seen a thing, Senator," she said quickly.

"Baloney. What happened out there?" he demanded, moving closer to her. He took her by the shoulders again, tilting his head to meet her downcast look.

Tired of seeming the hysteric, Emily lied outright. "I ran into the kids from the first-floor condo. They were loud; they were drunk; they were rude. That's all."

"Emily—"

"That really is all," she said, lifting her head and forcing a smile. "I think I'll turn in if it's all right with you. The sofa folds out; the bed's already made up. I'll get you a pillow. There's a new toothbrush under the sink. If you'd like a nightcap, well, there's beer. There's milk."

She slipped gracefully out of his hold somehow, leaving him to stare after her as she went into the bedroom for a pillow. *Why don't I just tell him what happened downstairs? He came here to help. Why won't I let him?*

But when she returned, she still hadn't figured out why she'd refused to tell him. "Here you go," she said lightly, tossing him the pillow on her way to wash up for the night.

When she came out of the bathroom she saw that the lights had been turned off except for the one at her desk, where the senator sat reading a bound document and making notes. She took in every detail: the light from the brass lamp, dancing on his thick, unruly hair; the left hand, shading his brow, which still bore a wedding band, no doubt to ward off female molesters; the shirtsleeves rolled up over solid forearms. He looked so right. He looked so at home. It made something inside her begin to ache.

And then she saw that his open briefcase was sitting smack on top of her yellow pads. So he hadn't bothered to delve further into her notes. The realization was a crushing blow.

He looked up, preoccupied, and smiled. "How're *you* doing?" he asked her in a comfortable, sleepy way.

"Doing great. Good night, Senator," she said stiffly. "And thank you."

For nothing, she thought bitterly as she closed the door to her bedroom. *He's never going to believe me.* It was incredibly insulting, that a believer in ghosts didn't believe in her ghost. She changed into a white cotton nightgown threaded through with a yellow ribbon and climbed into bed.

But who could sleep, with him in the next room? All at once she realized why she hadn't been able to tell him about her hideous moment downstairs: because she didn't want him to believe she was either crazy *or* haunted. Suddenly it had become imperative that Lee Alden regard her as one of his more normal constituents. And why? Because he'd almost kissed her—and would have, if it hadn't been for Fergus. Because she wanted that kiss so badly that still, here, alone, she could taste it. Great. Her only option now was to deny the existence of Fergus on any level, real or imagined. Great. A knight in shining armor had come charging in to be of service and she, the fair but possibly nutty damsel, was being forced to decline. All because of an almost kiss.

Great.

For the next hour or so Emily tried valiantly to sleep. A toss, a sigh, a kicked-off cover—she went through the motions a hundred times. But all her senses were on red alert. Every little thing hindered sleep. Her hair tickled. The bed squeaked. Her toe itched. The pillow was too hard. Her gown was twisted. The pillow was too soft. Nothing seemed right; something was missing. And Emily Bowditch, twenty-eight, never married, not very experienced, was having trouble figuring out what it was.

Sometime after two in the morning, when her mind was drifting in a feathery float between sleep and awareness, she heard the door to her bedroom open. She opened her eyes just enough to see the senator's form silhouetted by the dim light of the living room. He stood there for a moment, watching, and then he closed the door very quietly and left her in darkness. Her heart lightened immeasurably, and soon after that she fell into a deep and peaceful sleep.

* * *

But then the dream came, a brutal nightmare that left her clutching her throat and snatching at a rope that wasn't there. She dreamed that she was one of the crowd at Fergus O'Malley's execution. At first she hung back and let the gawkers and the curious push their way past her for a closer look at the gallows. She had the sense that someone in the crowd was completely evil, and she was afraid of him. Still, as the prisoner was led up the scaffold she found herself pressing forward, straining to make sure it was Fergus O'Malley. It was. But instead of being dressed in coarse trousers, a muslin shirt, and a corduroy vest, he was wearing gray suit pants and a maroon tie, with his shirtsleeves rolled up.

The executioner, who looked like Jim Whitewood in a plain black suit, pulled a dark hood over Fergus O'Malley's head and slipped the rough hemp noose over his neck. She watched as the executioner stepped back, then grabbed hold of a rusty lever with both hands. She had her hands over her mouth, certain that she was going to be sick, when a bizarre diversion occurred. A small boy with only one arm somehow slipped past the guard and ran up to the top of the platform. Before anyone could stop him, he butted the executioner in the stomach with his head and swung at him with his one good arm. The boy was grabbed and carried off; he never said a word.

Emily thought that the hanging would be stopped. But no, the executioner pulled the lever, the floor fell away, and Fergus O'Malley dropped dangling into the hole. It happened so fast she had no time to scream, much less to prevent it.

And then she bolted awake, choking and gasping for breath, fully convinced that she was being hanged. The door to her bedroom flew open and Lee Alden was suddenly at her side, holding her.

"Emily, what's wrong? Are you all right?"

She tried to talk, couldn't, cleared her throat, tried again. "It was horrible . . . he was hanged . . . but it was me all along. . . ."

"It was a dream," the senator reassured her, cradling her in his arms. "A dream, and it's over. It's over."

"But it wasn't a dream . . . I was there, really there . . . in Newarth . . . a hundred years ago . . . with Fergus," she insisted, only half conscious.

The senator laid her gently back onto her pillow. "Shh, back to sleep . . ."

She shot back up. "No! Stay by me, oh, please, Lee. . . ." She was trembling violently.

"I'm right here," he whispered, pulling up the comforter that had slipped off the bed. He wrapped it around her shivering torso, but it made Emily feel entombed, and she threw it off.

Yet she was ice cold; her teeth were chattering. She crossed her arms, huddling, trembling, desolate. "I'm fine, I'm sorry, I'm fine," she babbled, remembering that she'd wanted above all to seem unpossessed to him.

He gathered her back up in his arms. "Emily, Emily . . . I can't stand to see you like this," he said, holding her tight.

Something in his voice, something stricken and tender and sympathetic, filled her with an almost aching sense of relief. She opened her arms to him, still shivering, and said, "W-wouldn't you know, I c-can't bear to b-be this way either," and pressed her cheek close to his heartbeat, doing exactly what she swore she'd never do: cling to someone with every cell of her being.

He was nuzzling the top of her head with his chin, murmuring reassurances, soothing her, calming her.

Her trembling subsided and her emotions, flash-frozen by the nightmare, began to thaw. The bedroom was very warm, and she was in a man's arms, and she was wearing very little. She had an almost hypnotic feeling that she was having an erotic dream, an antidote to the nightmare that had preceded it. She shifted her position against the senator, wanting instinctively to draw still closer to him. Through the thin fabric of her nightgown she felt him shudder.

"Emily . . . don't," he said in a taut voice.

"No?" She whispered the word, the tiny word, with a humility born of the nights and days of insanity she'd just lived through. She simply had no idea anymore whether she was in or out of bounds. "No," she repeated to herself with infinite melancholy.

"Oh, Christ . . ."

She heard his resolve snap, exactly as if he'd broken a branch over his knee, and then suddenly he brought his mouth down hard on hers in a kiss of electrifying passion, holding her breathless, kissing her again and again, each kiss more overpowering than the one that went before it, reducing her to rubble. None of the men in her life had prepared her for this, for the driving, physical hunger, the raw ache of passion, that Lee Alden was bringing to her. The others were nothing, mere boys having fun on a Saturday night; she saw that now.

This was new, and this was real.

She returned his kisses with a kind of dangerous fierceness, aware that they were dancing on the edge of a cliff and reveling in the sensation. His lips were bruising hers, trailing hot kisses on her cheek, her ear, the curve of her neck. She caught his face in her hands and dragged him back to her, to kiss him again, to taste his tongue. A low cry of hunger tore from his throat; the sound of his passion thrilled her, driving her own desire to new levels.

He dropped fierce, tonguing kisses between the curves of her breasts. "God forgive me . . . I want you so much," he said hoarsely.

"Then have me, Lee . . . have me." She lay back on her pillow in the semidarkness, signaling her complete willingness. In a heart's beat he had shed his clothes and slipped her gown over her head. And then he was kissing her again and again, fanning her desire with love words, breaking away for random forays over her nakedness, creating flash points where once there were none. He was leaving her breathless and gasping for air, turning her nightmare inside out with the skill of a sorcerer. Emily was not prepared for this, for the reckless, consuming power of sexual desire; she was amazed to realize that she knew nothing about sex—nothing at all.

Then they came together and continued to dance to the same frenzied, primal rhythm, until they got too near the edge of the cliff and tumbled over it in a free fall into nothingness. Her nightmare came full circle because now, falling, she was completely content, completely without fear. It was the first time since Fergus showed up—the first time in her life—that she'd felt like this. She was falling down, down, down, detached and serene, safely beyond the reach of any force, in this world or in any other.

And when she landed it was on a downy pillow, with her knight, glistening from his heroics, lying next to her. Lee had rolled a little to one side, his legs still wrapped in hers, and was idly raking out the tangles in her hair with his fingers. When she opened her eyes, heavy with spent passion, she saw that his rugged good looks were softened by the same secret smile she knew was on her face.

"Is it always like this?" she asked him in quiet wonder.

He traced the outline of her kiss-stung lips and said, "You're asking the wrong fella. But if I had to guess, I'd say no; we'd all be dead of heart attacks."

She chuckled softly but persisted. "Then why was *this* like this?"

"Dunno," Lee answered, lowering his mouth to hers in a feathery kiss. "Chemistry. Privation. Could be the devil made us do it."

"I've never . . . this was so . . . I mean, I'm *experienced,* don't get me wrong, but . . . wow." She blushed, thinking she might have put a tad too much emphasis on the word *experienced.* And was it necessary to sound so enthusiastic?

He was listening to her, looking more and more thoughtful as she rambled on, trying to express herself. When she trailed off, all he said was: " 'Wow' is about right."

Because he sounded almost depressed about it, Emily instantly surmised that he must have been fantasizing about his deceased wife, the beautiful and adored concert pianist, all along. "Were you thinking about . . . someone else when you made love to me?" she asked softly. She remembered that he'd never once used her name in passion. She considered it proof conclusive.

He'd been idly stroking the chain of her necklace, but now he stopped. "Someone else?"

Instantly Emily was sorry she'd brought it up. She felt him shift his weight and move off to one side. In the near darkness she was glad she couldn't see his face. "You've said how much you loved your wife," she ventured, swallowing hard, stepping over the new ground carefully. "And that you were still hoping to, you know, establish contact with her—"

"—making you some kind of proxy for Nicole? Is that it?" He looked genuinely shocked. "How many ghosts do you think are flying around this bedroom anyway?"

Whether or not he'd meant to wound her, he succeeded. Emily switched on the bedside light and sat up, yanking the sheet over her breasts. "All right," she said testily, "maybe that's not it. Maybc I'm just trying to figure out what went on here. Whatever we had, it wasn't just six-pack sex." She brushed a lock of hair away from her eyes; her mouth was a thin, firm line.

He was leaning on his right elbow, looking up at her. His eyes—so intensely blue, so intensely sincere—lingered on the white knuckles that held her bed sheet in place. "Yup. Big mistake."

"What!"

"I'm the world's biggest horse's ass," he said, shaking his head slowly. He smiled bleakly, then reached up to touch her face; instinctively she drew back. He sat up alongside her, pulling his legs up and circling his shins with his forearms. "This was a dumb thing for me to do," he said quietly, focusing on his knees.

"Excuse me," she said, amazed by his arrogance, "but I was there, too."

He turned and looked at her, and his expression blurred and softened for an instant. "I remember."

"Then why do you act as if it were all *your* idea?"

"Because I was the one with the runaway testosterone. You asked me for help, Emily. I betrayed your trust."

Her eyes slanted suspiciously. Having been satisfied, suddenly he was talking sorry. Surprise, surprise. Now she *was* feeling betrayed. "You're not my psychiatrist," she said, just to be perverse. "You didn't breech any code of ethics."

"Speaking of which—"

Her eyes widened. "I don't believe it!" she cried, jumping out of the bed, wrapping the sheet around her. "You've slept with me, and you still don't believe me about Fergus! Do you! You want me to see a *shrink!* Don't you!"

In reply he blew air out of puffed-up cheeks, got out of bed, and began to dress. Neither of them spoke. Emily stood clinging to her sheet, a Statue of Liberty minus the torch, and fumed over this newcomer to her shores.

After he had finished tucking in his shirt and buckling his belt, he took Emily's tattered pink chenille robe from the back of a chair and wrapped it around her and her J. C. Penney sheet. "Come into the living room, fully clothed, and we'll talk," he said with a heart-wrenching smile. "I guarantee I cannot be trusted under any other conditions. I don't know if I believe in Fergus or not. But I do believe in you." He kissed her on her cheek, then went into the living room to wait.

Left alone, Emily became rational once more. The facts were pretty straightforward: She had summoned him, she had seduced him, and she had picked the fight. Apparently it was the newswoman in her. She'd always treated every man she ever knew like a guest on *Face the Nation*. Once the men had got her number, most of them had backed away from her politely. A few had bolted outright. Maybe because Lee Alden was a bona fide politician, he seemed to be able to hang in there better than most.

Or could it be that he really wanted to believe in Fergus? If there was a Fergus, then there would be a Nicole. Somewhere.

Emily dressed quickly in a pair of jeans and a cotton sweater of pale apricot, then went out to talk. All things considered, she decided it was best not to mention the sex. She needed time to sort that whole thing out.

Lee was staring at his bound document, but he didn't seem to be concentrating. Emily curled up in a side chair and wrapped her arms around a chintz throw pillow, propping her chin on it. "I'm glad you didn't run out on me," she confessed. "I wouldn't blame you if you had."

Lee tossed his Bic pen down on the document and leaned back in his chair, locking his hands behind his head in an isometric stretch. "And miss all the fun? Never," he said with a half-smile.

"I don't have a clue how I can prove he exists," she said, cutting straight to the heart of the matter.

"I've been thinking about that. For starters, maybe you ought to give *me* the necklace."

She hesitated. "I don't think I should, Lee. What if that breaks the contact and forces him back to the other side of the veil?"

"Would that bother you?"

She thought about it for a moment. "Yeah," she confessed, "it would. Fergus O'Malley deserves a break."

"It doesn't sound like he's giving *you* much of one."

She gave him an ironic smile. "You've heard only my side of the story so far."

"Sure, but journalists are supposed to be impartial."

She nodded absently, a little taken aback by the answers she heard herself giving him.

Lee got up, walked the few feet over to the kitchen area, and poured himself a glass of water. "Not to put too fine a point on all this, but you could have declined to give me the necklace on other grounds. You could've just said, 'Fergus doesn't exist, so what's the point?' "

She looked at him blankly for a moment while his remark sank in. "You're right," she agreed, stunned. "But that possibility no longer occurs to me. You're *right,*" she repeated, impressed with his fine logic. "I'm talking about Fergus the way I would a man unjustly held in prison: He's there; it's wrong; let's get him the heck out. That's all there is to it."

"Then there's no longer any ambiguity in your mind. Fergus O'Malley is real."

"For better or worse," Emily answered with a grim smile. Aware that she'd just put their relationship, such as it was, on the line, she watched Lee's reaction. By denying that her problem was psychological, she was offering him a good excuse to bolt and run.

He walked over to the window and stared into the deserted street below. "Hoo-eee," he murmured without turning around. "The evening is not going quite the way I pictured."

"How did you picture it would go?" she asked, curious.

He shrugged. "I guess I thought I'd find the loose wire that was making your lights blink or trap the squirrel in your attic that was sounding like a dead body being dragged across the floor. Or fix whatever innocent thing was going on here. And then I thought we'd laugh about it, and share a bottle of wine, and—"

He turned around and lifted his glass of water to her in a toast that was only half ironic. "Come to think of it, maybe I *did* have a pretty fair picture."

Emily winced. She had vowed not to bring up their torrid liaison, and here was Lee Alden, already happily reminiscing. How did men do it? No remorse, no guilt, no second-guessing. Clearly it was chromosomal.

She was about to open her mouth to say so when Lee pressed a forefinger to her lips. "Just kidding. But I would like to know where we go from here."

She wasn't self-centered enough to assume that he was referring to the two of them. "I guess I try to solve the crime," she said simply.

"You don't need me for that."

She thought he sounded disappointed, but who could tell? "Don't be too sure," she quipped. "I may need a sponsor for a presidential pardon for this guy."

He laughed his easy, intimate laugh, and Emily realized that she was becoming addicted to the sound. It was painfully obvious why the man was on everyone's favorite-singles list. She couldn't help wondering who would finally win him. Surely the only fair thing would be to hold a lottery.

In the meantime, she was trying very hard to ignore the fact that she'd just become another notch in his gun handle.

He trailed a finger along the line of her chin. "One last time: Are you sure you don't want me to take the necklace?"

"Sure as shootin'," she said with a brave smile. "I don't think the darn thing comes off anyway."

"I'd like to look at it," he said suddenly, and when she didn't object, he stepped behind her and lifted the clasped ends from her neck for a closer look.

Emily held her hair up out of the way while he puzzled over the intricate lock. After a bit her hands began to tremble. Everything about him seemed to set her on fire: his voice; his touch; his warm breath on the back of her neck.

"There doesn't seem to be a way to open this," he

said, stymied. "It looks like a typical barrel mechanism where one half should screw into the other. But these two halves make up a seamless whole. It's as if they were fused together. Did you just slip this over your head when you bought it?"

"No, my friend Cara Miles fastened it."

"Your friend Cara has a genius IQ in that case. Would she like a job as a campaign strategist?" he asked lightly.

The idea filled Emily with quick cold panic. *Jealousy? Is that what this is?* She let out a gay laugh; it sounded horrible and false in her ears. Cara would be *perfect* for Senator Arthur Lee Alden III: sophisticated, clever, rich, wellborn, and a dilettante. The perfect politician's wife. It would only be a matter of time before they merged dynasties. She could picture Cara's calling card in discreet raised lettering: Cara Miles-Alden.

"Cara lacks the killer instinct," she said, clenching her jaw.

"To be a campaign strategist? Isn't that a little cynical, ma'am—even for a journalist?" He released the necklace, and Emily felt the familiar weight on her neck again.

"I don't think I'm being cynical," she protested. "It's the campaign strategists who're behind all the mud that's been flying so thick and fast—and the primaries are still months away. I don't mean your campaign," she said grudgingly. "You'll take the high road; everyone knows you always do.

"But then," she couldn't help adding, "you have an eighty percent approval rating and a challenger with all the charisma of a pencil sharpener. You can afford to take the high road."

"I take him very seriously," Lee answered somberly. "He has more PAC money than I do."

"Lee, I'm *serious*. Political campaigns have become dirty little mudslinging contests. I'm sure I speak for voters everywhere when I say—"

Emily stopped in mid-sentence. She sounded desperately prim. And hostile. Where was it all coming from? After all the emotional highs and lows of the night, was it really going to end up in a boring political harangue?

It was the sex. The sex was just too good. Why hadn't he asked her to move in with him immediately? Wasn't that why she was in a snit?

"When you say what?" Lee asked at last, his eyes alight with good-natured curiosity.

"When—when I say it's three in the morning and the last thing you need is a filibuster. You've got a plane to catch in a couple of hours, Senator. You should try to get some sleep." She padded barefoot back toward her bedroom, then paused at the door. "You don't have to worry about me anymore, Lee," she said softly. "I'm going to be all right."

He had his hands in his pockets and a bemused smile on his face. "I'm sure you will," he agreed. As she turned away she heard him say, "It's Fergus O'Malley I'm worried about."

9

When she woke up the senator was gone. There was no sign that he'd pulled out the sleep sofa or curled up for a quick nap in the easy chair. Emily had to assume that he'd read until dawn, preparing for the upcoming Senate vote on day care. The television was on, but that was no surprise to her; all politicians were news junkies. Emily wolfed down a bowl of Cheerios while she watched Joan Lunden interview Patrick Swayze on *Good Morning America,* then picked up the phone and called the *Boston Journal.* She left the message that she wouldn't be in until later because she was tracking down a lead on a great new story.

Even for Emily, it was brazen bluffing. If she was wrong—if someone named Hessiah Talbot had never been murdered and someone named Fergus O'Malley never been hanged for the crime—then she'd better have some other great new story lined up to present to her boss. But despite the fact that Fergus was still nowhere in sight, Emily was filled with confidence, the result somehow of the incredible time she'd spent with Lee Alden. It was impossible to sort out the connection; she needed quiet and serenity and a pot of tea to do that. Right now she had to find the Newarth Library. Any other thoughts—they were all of Lee Alden—she pushed resolutely from her mind.

After an hour's drive she found herself on the main street of Newarth, a mill town that had seen better days. Emily was vaguely familiar with Newarth's history. The town had peaked in the late nineteenth century and then languished until the late twentieth, when the long-empty textile mills were converted one by one into discount outlets that attracted busloads of tourists. But there ended up being too many outlets and not enough busloads, and lately Newarth had begun, once again, to languish.

Emily drove through block after block of triple-decker tenements once filled with millworkers, searching for the downtown district. What she found was a mile of shabby, anonymous storefronts erected in the 1950s, no doubt replacing much more charming Victorian shops. She wondered whether she'd find any historical records at all; Newarth did not seem much in love with its past.

The sun had been in a fitful mood during the drive from Boston, but it decided to come out for good just as Emily pulled up at the Newarth Library, a block or so off the downtown path. She blinked in the sun's brilliance and stared. The library was an architectural gem, a small Gothic fantasy of turrets and slate and diamond-paned windows. The building was almost hidden behind lavender rhododendrons and flowering cherry trees that dropped their pink petals onto a tiny pond on which two white swans floated, serenely unaware that they were the highlight of a vision too pure to be true.

A narrow brick path ended at a varnished door that opened into a chapel-like interior filled to the rafters with the sweet, musty smell of books. Emily was surprised and oddly distressed to see that except for an elderly man nodding over his morning paper, the library was deserted. Even the checkout desk was unattended. A door behind the desk was left open to the outside; Emily went up to it and spied a stocky old woman on her hands and knees, weeding a tulip bed.

"Good morning," Emily called out pleasantly. "Can you tell me where I'll find the librarian?"

The woman raised herself slowly, one knee at a time, and smiled through a wince of arthritic pain. "That'd be me, dear," she answered, brushing her hands clear of soil. She reached into the pocket of her denim apron and pulled out a rag to finish the cleanup.

She was short and very stout. The flesh hung heavy and loose on her liver-spotted arms, and her legs sagged into a bow shape under her weight. Her gray hair had probably started the day tied back in a bun, but it wasn't there now. "How may I help you?" she asked pleasantly.

"You manage all of this by yourself?" Emily remarked, impressed. "The library and the grounds?"

" 'Tisn't much to manage, dear," the old woman said as she pulled her apron over her head and dropped it on a hook inside the door. "Everything in here was published before the war—that'd be the Great War, dear—and I'm sorry to say there isn't much demand for any of it. A few years ago I began whiling away the hours outside. It started with a little weeding, and now I've turned into a maniac. I'm Mrs. Gibbs," she added.

Emily introduced herself and said, "It's all perfectly lovely. But . . . Newarth has no books printed after 1917?"

The librarian smiled. "Sure we do; they're in the Newarth *Public* Library. You're not from around here, I suppose."

Emily shook her head, feeling stupid. It hadn't occurred to her to scan past "Newarth Library" in the white pages of the phone book.

"This library was built by John Talbot. He was the owner of the biggest mill in town and a philanthropist, of course—they all were back then. Very concerned with the welfare of their towns. Still, things would be less confusing if he'd named this the Talbot Library. Anyway, the endowment dried to a trickle, the acquisitions stopped, and now we get by on a wing and a prayer. . . ."

Emily wasn't hearing her any longer. The certainty that she'd been feeling all morning rushed in to overwhelm her. If there'd been a millowner named John Talbot, then he'd had a daughter named Hessiah Talbot. Who'd been murdered.

"*So,*" the librarian was saying, "let me give you directions to the Newarth Public Library—"

"No, no, I've come to the right place, I really have," Emily answered feverishly. "Do you have copies of the *Newarth Sentinel* in your archives?"

"Oh, dear me, yes, almost every issue from 1868 to 1917."

"On microfiche?"

The librarian laughed out loud; the old gentleman awoke from his doze, harrumphed, and snapped his morning paper back into position.

"My dear, we have the crumbling originals. You'll have to help me get them out; the bindings are very heavy. *Microfiche?*" She laughed again.

Emily spent the next two hours in the large, dry

cellar of the Newarth Library, poring over yellowed and brittle newsprint. She'd gone directly to the first issue to be printed after the day of the murder on August 12, 1887, and confirmed what she already knew: that she was not insane. There it all was, in old-fashioned black and white. SHOCKING MURDER OF TEXTILE HEIRESS. ROBBERY THE MOTIVE.

Ah, well, she thought with a jittery sigh, *at least I've saved myself the cost of a shrink.*

She read through the next few issues. Every detail was there, just as Fergus O'Malley had described it: the frenzied hunt, door to door, for the murderer; the discovery of a silver spoon emblazoned with a *T* near the front door of O'Malley's flat; his sensational arrest and parade past jeering, rock-throwing citizens. After that, the trial itself—swift and, by all accounts, impartial. Soon after came the sentencing and finally, the hanging.

The hanging. It came like a blow to the stomach, knocking away the fascination she'd been feeling and leaving her dizzy with nausea. She was thrown back bodily into her nightmare as she read the account. "The murderer, bound and blindfolded, lashed out with his legs twice, and then he was still. Justice has been done, and a terrorized town will sleep more safely tonight."

She stopped reading for a little while, then brought herself under control and forced herself to continue, taking constant notes.

At the bottom of page four she found a postscript to the hanging: An eleven-year-old crippled boy had tried to attack the hangman and was bound over to a home for wayward youths just outside Newarth. The boy refused to give his name to the authorities, and so far no one had come forward to identify him.

"Ah, Fergus," Emily murmured, overcome with sadness, "your little brother really did love you."

She closed her eyes, reflecting on it all. Then it occurred to her that Fergus had never said a thing about his brother's being crippled; she'd only dreamed it.

So how did she know? Had Fergus somehow been able to penetrate her nightmare? *Oh, God,* she thought wearily. *Can it possibly get any worse?* She folded her arms across the pile of *Sentinel*s and buried her head there.

After a while she sighed and lifted her head—and there he was, with his arms folded against his chest, leaning on a file cabinet marked "Retired—A to H." Same clothes, same arrogance, same glint in his eye.

She felt a kind of triumphant shock at the apparition. "Fergus! What are you doing here?"

"Reliving old times," he said dryly.

He looked as incredibly real as ever.

"You shouldn't be here," she said testily. "You said you'd let me do the research on my own."

"And so I planned. But there seems to be a limit to how far apart we can be." He pointed to the crystal that hung around her neck and added, "About the time ye hit the shopping district, I found myself being yanked out of yer place. Which is just as well. Ye'll be needing me help."

In a barely controlled voice she said, "Are you telling me we cannot get farther than forty-five miles apart without your popping up?"

He shrugged. "It appears."

"I will not be joined at the hip to you, Fergus!" she cried, exploding with frustration. "You can't be here, dammit! Someone is bound to find out!"

"Keep up the shoutin' and—"

Right on cue the librarian called down, "Is everything all right down there?"

"Ah . . . yes, ma'am," Emily called back. "I was just reading aloud."

She heard the librarian murmur to someone, "What a strange young thing she is," and then walk away from the stairwell. Emily lowered her voice to a whisper. "Where have you *been*, anyway?"

"Watchin' ye make a bloody fool of yerself—when I wasn't watchin' yer picture box."

"*What!* You were in my condo all the time?"

"Not *all* the time. The folks below ye was havin' a shindig, and I slipped in to see what the noise was about. They are fond of their drink, them university types. And the language. Migod."

"*What did you see, Fergus?*"

"Not much," he answered with a shrug. "A lot of backslappin' and belchin'. One of 'em juggled three beer bottles. Then two young ladies—"

"Not down there, you jerk! *In my apartment!*"

"Oh. There." He blushed a deep, deep red. "Nothing."

Emily was absolutely scandalized. "You saw us *together,*" she whispered, devastated. "I can't believe this." A vivid mental picture presented itself of Lee Alden and her, locked in passion. She looked away, then shook her head. Tears stung her eyes. "Have you no sense of shame?"

"Have *I* no sense of shame? I like that!" Fergus answered, turning indignant. "Do ye have any idea what yer behavior seems like to a man like me? In my day a woman—even the poorest woman—would never live alone, much less invite a man in alone, much less throw herself at 'im the way ye did. Not unless she was the worst kind of tramp."

"But this *isn't* your day, is it?" she said, seething.

"Men don't fool around with the town tramp and then propose to virgins anymore. There are no virgins anymore—"

"The devil there aren't!"

"Believe it, Fergus. The double standard has gone the way of the buggy whip. Society permits men and women to come together as equals—"

"But what do they come together *for,* if not to marry?"

She blinked. "Well—for pleasure."

"But that's what *tramps* are for!"

"I *told* you, Fergus, there are no tramps anymore. Well, that's not exactly true. I suppose there are, but —oh, skip it. The point is, what the *hell* were you doing spying on me?"

"What did ye expect?" he asked with dignity. "I'm a male."

"You see?" she asked, throwing her hands up in the air. "That's my point about you. A female—ghost or alive—would never spy. She would have allowed us our . . . moment of privacy."

"I thought ye said men and women were equal. Ye talk as if the female is the superior sex today."

"Not at all," Emily replied coolly. "I would expect a modern male to behave in exactly the same way." But a little voice inside her said, *Sure, right. Name one example.*

"I see," said Fergus. "Well, then, accept me apology. I'll try to behave in the manner of a modern male. It's the least I can do." He watched her curiously. "Will ye be marryin' the man, then?"

"Of course not!" she snapped. "He's a United States senator."

Fergus nodded sagely. "I understand. Above yer station."

"No, that's not it," she said irritably. "We don't

marry according to station anymore. Anyone can marry anyone."

"Ah. He doesn't love ye, then."

"I didn't say that! I . . . have no way of knowing," she added in an overly casual voice.

"Sometimes men don't say," he agreed in a helpful way. "But ye told him ye loved *him,* of course."

"I don't have the faintest idea whether I love him!"

"Ye didn't do it for money, surely?" Fergus asked, shocked.

"Of course not!"

"Then—"

"That doesn't mean I'm a tramp!" she shouted, slamming her hand on the table. "This is different! These are the nineties!"

"If ye say so," he said, rubbing the back of his neck. "No doubt it'll come clearer to me."

Suddenly his head jerked up in the direction of the stairs. He began to more or less vaporize in front of her. In a panic she hissed, "Wait, don't disappear!" then turned in time to beam reassuringly at the approaching librarian.

"I heard a crash," the old woman said, looking around.

"That was me, stomping a bug," Emily improvised. "The shouting was me, too," she added. "Spiders terrify me."

"They oughtn't to," the librarian said crisply. "They're *quite* helpful in the garden. Have you found what you need?"

"Oh, yes. Actually, I'm doing a kind of historical piece on the murder of Hessiah Talbot. It's covered in great detail by the *Sentinel.*"

"You're interested in the Hessiah Talbot murder! How wonderful!" the librarian cried, clapping her hands together. Instantly she thawed and became friendly again. "Then you know that the publisher of the *Sentinel* was a good friend of John Talbot's, one reason for the thorough coverage."

Mrs. Gibbs lowered her battered weight into a chair opposite Emily at the long oak table and settled in for a chat. "It was an absolutely shocking event at the time. And of immense historical importance to the area.

"The Talbots had been the dominant force in Newarth for four generations," Mrs. Gibbs continued. "But after Hessiah Talbot was murdered, her family sold the mill and moved to California, setting the mill on a downhill course. Talbot Manor was allowed to fall into near ruin as well, part of the curse that fell on Newarth and is with us still."

"Not a curse, surely," Emily couldn't help saying. "Just simple economics. Historical trends were already threatening the success of smaller textile mills. Concentration of labor, foreign competition—"

"All irrelevant," the librarian snapped. "This town lies under a pall, plain and simple. The sad thing is," she said, leaning across the table in a confidential whisper, "if it had been a more sensational crime, we could at least be making some money from it. Look at Fall River. Fall River has the legend of Lizzie Borden, and that makes all the difference."

Mrs. Gibbs bounced her knuckles off the table in a gesture of supreme confidence. "A female axe murderer is a number one draw, take my word for it: 'Lizzie Borden took an axe / And gave her mother forty whacks.' That's what we don't have: a simple, effective marketing device. The strangling of an heiress by a common burglar just can't compare," she said, sighing heavily.

Emily stared at the sweet old librarian—digger of tulips and friend of spiders—and suppressed a scandalized smile. "I see your point. The Talbot Manor could have been a tourist attraction and the library a museum."

"Exactly. But instead, Talbot Manor struggles as a bed and breakfast, and the library needs a new roof. It's all so tragic," the librarian said, shaking her head over the injustice.

"The manor is operating as a B and B? Do you suppose they'd let me have a look around?"

"I don't see why not," Mrs. Gibbs said, hauling her battered weight out of the creaking chair with an effort. "I'll call Maria Salva and let her know you'll be over. You won't learn much from Maria, though. Her husband bought the place in spite of its history, because it was dirt-cheap. I've told her she's missing a bet not promoting the crime; people love that kind of thing. She could host Murder-at-the-Manor weekends and do a booming business on Halloween if nothing else. She'd be willing, I know, but her husband is not adventurous. He's a plumber. Most of the rooms have individual baths now," Mrs. Gibbs added with a shrug, "but they're still empty."

"It sounds like *you* should be running the manor," Emily said, impressed with the woman's entrepreneurial spirit.

"Probably," said Mrs. Gibbs, brushing a clump of earth from the hem of her dress. "But this place needs me more. Which reminds me. Someone just donated two dozen half-sprouted Asian lilies to the garden; if I don't get them in the ground, the poor things are going to consume themselves. We may not have the biggest library in town, but we do have the prettiest garden. Come look at it, dear, before you set off."

* * *

Talbot Manor was easy to find. Presiding over the highest hill in Newarth, the house was an imposing structure built in 1876 to replace a smaller one, put there by John Talbot's grandfather, which had burned to the ground the year before. The new manor had a granite—and fireproof—tower on its southeast corner where John Talbot had made his family sleep. The inside doors of the tower were lined with the highest-grade asbestos, and fire escapes from every room were cut into the outside granite walls. This much Emily had learned from Mrs. Gibbs during their tour of the library garden.

Emily parked her car at the bottom of the hill on a street called Stepstone Lane, because she wanted to get a better feel for the manor's environs. Stepstone Lane wasn't the main access to the manor—Talbot Street was—but Emily trekked up the winding, narrow lane anyway, drawn by its tattered charm. Once there had been cobblestones; she could see the edges of the stones peeping out through the asphalt every once in a while. The lane was a shabby little block, a hodgepodge of tiny cottages with peeling shingles and broken shutters shoehorned into impossibly narrow lots—a kind of Nantucket in the rough.

Emily didn't need a degree in sociology to recognize the pattern: A grand house falls down on its luck, the grounds are sold off, and humbler houses pop up like weeds all around it. When times get tough—and in Newarth they were very tough indeed—the big house and all its weedy neighbors slide into ruin together. It seemed impossible that Talbot Manor could ever succeed, murder weekends or no, until the local economy turned around.

Emily, a property owner now, was completely engrossed in such pragmatic thoughts when she suddenly stopped, held fast by a sharp sense of déjà vu. *I know this place,* she thought, looking around. She was in front of what had to be the oldest house on the block, a down-and-out shingled charmer with a crumbling brick chimney on its north side and the collapsed frame of a greenhouse still attached to its south side. Unlike the others, this house was set back from the street enough for an ancient apple tree, mauled and distorted from repeated pruning, to be almost able to fit.

It was the gardener's cottage for the original Talbot Manor, Emily was sure of it. All the land around it must once have been cultivated—herb, vegetable, and cutting gardens, and obviously an orchard. She drew nearer to the apple tree, the last remnant of an affluent time. Half of its few remaining limbs were not in leaf; it was very near the end of its life. She was wondering whether there was any way to save it when she saw a shadowy form at the base of the tree gradually assume the shape and depth of Fergus O'Malley. He was deep in sleep, his mouth slack, snoring noisily. He was, she realized, dead drunk.

"Fergus! How could you!" she cried, shocked.

Immediately he opened his eyes and grinned. "Well, that's just it; I can't anymore, can I?" He scrambled to his feet and fell in alongside her. "Still, I thought I'd show ye what Hessiah Talbot was up against the day she run into me."

"I don't blame her for shipping you off to the mission," Emily said, annoyed. "You make a disgusting drunk."

"Wasn't me fault. I dropped by at harvest, innocently looking for work. Turned out I knew the gardener, who invited me in to sample the cider. He spiced it with a wee bit o' something, and before long his wife is shooing me out the door with a broom. I got as far as the apple tree."

Emily remarked, "Nothing is ever your fault, have you noticed?" But her mind was puzzling over the déjà vu business. Fergus had told her of the incident with Hessiah Talbot, but not the details. How had she known to stop at the apple tree?

" 'I love what ye do for me!' " Fergus shouted with sudden glee.

"What?"

"Toyota," he answered with an elfin grin, pointing to a Corolla parked in the lane. "I saw it in yer picture box." Then he did the Toyota leap—about twenty feet into the air.

"Oh, for—look, Fergus, number one, we call that picture box a television, a TV. And number two, you can't just be out here in broad daylight shouting ad slogans and jumping up and down."

"Yes, I can. Ye're the only one who knows I'm here."

"What are you saying? That believing is seeing?"

For an answer he pointed silently and somberly to her necklace—or to her heart. Either way it meant that she'd never be able to parade Fergus past Lee Alden in the flesh, so to speak. She wanted to ask Fergus what would happen if she took off the necklace, but she had a real dread of alarming him, so she let it go. "Don't watch so much TV," she said instead. "It's bad for you."

"TV is wonderful. Ye have a Sony. And that's no baloney," he said happily.

"Stop it. Stop making me react. Either disappear, or walk alongside in silence."

They were approaching a frail, elderly man trimming his hedges with an electric shears. Fergus watched in amazement as the old man flat-topped the sprouting bushes in one clean sweep. Emily saw that Fergus was aching to comment, but he held his tongue as they walked by. His silence lasted until they came to a souped-up red Camaro parked in the middle of the lane with its engine growling through dual exhausts. Fergus stopped in his tracks—or whatever they were—and walked slowly around the car.

" 'The heartbeat of America,' " he said with awe. " 'Today's Chevrolet.' "

"Fergus, for Pete's sake; the owner could come out any second—"

"You got a problem with it, lady?" the owner himself asked from behind her. She turned to see a menacing-looking youth dangling a cigarette from his lips.

"Hi!" she said all too brightly. "I was just thinking out loud that—that your car had begun to roll down the hill! Look! There it goes!"

She watched bemused as the Camaro took off at a pretty good clip, with its owner in hot pursuit. Fergus rejoined her, smiling beatifically. He was loving every minute of every step of his little stroll.

"How did you do that?" she asked under her breath.

"Ain't really sure," he said. "Should we try another one?" He looked around, spied a little blue Escort, and said, " 'Have ye driven a Ford—lately?' " He rubbed his hands together.

"No! That isn't what they mean. You're supposed to get *behind the wheel.*"

Emily looked up to see a middle-aged woman who'd been shaking out a dust mop from the second-floor window yank the mop back in and slam the window shut, then peer down suspiciously at her. *Perfect. I'm terrorizing the whole neighborhood.*

She resolved not to be provoked again; Fergus was too dangerously exuberant, too uncontainable. But a minute later they passed a parked Oldsmobile, and she saw his eyes light up.

"Fergus! 'This is *not,*' " she said wryly, " 'your father's Oldsmobile.' "

He threw his head back in a hearty laugh. "What a world! What wealth! Everyone has a car! When I think what me life could've been . . . But a motorized carriage was a fantasy then. There was talk in Finchie's Tavern of a man, a German, who was said to be designing a horseless carriage in the year before I was tried—but who knew? Daimler! That was his name."

"Today that name has a long and venerable history, Fergus," Emily said, smiling despite herself. He reminded her of her brother Gerry, an automotive nut who'd spent his puberty under a car chassis and now had his own thriving mechanic's shop back home.

She sneaked a look at Fergus in profile, so animated, so raring to go. *O'Malley's Auto.* Yes. It had a ring to it. If she could, she'd cosign a loan for him.

They were at the top of the hill now, at the entrance to a circular drive leading to Talbot Manor. The manor gates, pitted and rusted in their hinges, were swung open in a permanent position. "Hush, now," she commanded Fergus. "Not a word."

"Just one," the irrepressible ghost begged. "Look at this rose," he said, pausing before an enormous bush buried in rose-pink blossoms. "I remember it well. It's a Bourbon—Madame Isaac Perrierre—and there is no finer-smelling rose in all the world. The gardener had half a dozen of 'em out back in Talbot's rose garden. Only do this one thing," he said in a voice gone heavy with emotion. "Smell the blossom for me, would ye?"

"You want me to smell the roses?" she murmured. "That's pretty funny." But she said it in a shy and thoughtful way, and when she leaned her face into the petals of a huge cabbagy blossom, it took her breath away. It was heavenly, glorious, and, until Fergus O'Malley made her stick her nose in it, just another pink flower.

When she straightened up again, Fergus smiled and nodded forlornly. "I thought so."

They walked up the flagstone walk in companionable silence, but as they got nearer to the house, the ghost began to hang back. Emily slowed her pace to his, thinking he was enthusiastic over something or other, but his steps dragged, and finally he stopped.

"I cannot go in there," he said in a choking voice. His voice was breathless, his eyes wide with alarm; his arms were raised against the looming presence of the huge house as if he were warding it off.

And then he disappeared, leaving Emily standing alone on the threshold of a set of huge oak-paneled double doors swung wide in greeting.

10

The woman who greeted Emily had the kind of beauty instantly recognizable as Mediterranean: glossy blue-black hair; dark brown eyes ringed by thick black lashes; olive-skinned cheeks setting off a straight nose and white teeth. Her smile was not so much reserved as it was otherworldly: Maria Salva knew things that other people could only begin to guess at. When she took Emily's hand in her own, Emily had to resist an urge to fall on one knee and kiss her ring.

And yet Maria was a young woman. As they exchanged pleasantries about Mrs. Gibbs, Emily tried to pin down the essence of Maria's spirituality. Maybe it was her voice, soft and low and breathless. Maybe it was her size: She was thin and fragile and dressed in flowing challis. Or maybe it was something as basic as the look in her eyes, which was unfocused and vague.

"Have you owned the manor for long?" Emily asked as they walked through an entry hall of gleaming paneled walnut. She could see that the restoration work was first-rate, right down to the electrified verdigris chandelier that hung a dozen feet above the slate floor.

"We've had it for two years," Maria said in her strangely faraway voice. "We bought it from a man who'd spent the previous five years working on the main floor restoring the entry hall and living rooms. He ran out of money and, perhaps, out of heart. Later he bought a condo."

She stopped and gestured rather vaguely around her, while Emily took in the sheer magnificence of the place. From the central core where they were standing she looked up at soaring, open arches, trimmed in serpentine carving, that supported the third story. The effect was of a Gothic cathedral. Emily slid her fingers over the sensuous, gleaming wood paneling.

"All the wood was stripped of paint, sanded, oiled, and hand-rubbed by the owner," Maria said with a sigh, as if she were reciting a very difficult lesson.

Somehow she made Emily feel reluctant to ask questions. The phone rang, Maria went over to a small reception desk to answer it, and Emily was left alone to apply what bits and pieces of history she'd been able to gather on her own.

She knew that John Talbot, the millowner who'd built the new manor, had had two children: his daughter Hessiah and a son, Stewart, who was four years older than his sister. The house apparently was built to please Talbot's wife Celeste, a Frenchwoman who was homesick for the grand cathedrals of her country. Celeste scarcely had time to enjoy the house; she died in a riding accident. John Talbot never remarried. Emily had no idea who'd brought up the two children; from the accounts of the trial she deduced that a series of wet nurses, governesses, and housekeepers had come and gone. She wondered why the turnover was so high. Did the problem lie with the master, his children, or the help?

While Emily was peeking into the open door of the drawing room, Maria returned and said in her trancelike voice, "All the antiques were left by the previous owner, who furnished each of the downstairs rooms as soon as he finished it. The brocade love seats, and the inlaid gaming table actually belonged to John Talbot. Most of the other pieces were bought locally."

Emily said, "And you have eight guest rooms?"

"Yes. When my husband is finished, we'll have twelve, not counting the tower."

"Would it be possible to see any of them? I'm very interested in the history of Talbot Manor, as Mrs. Gibbs mentioned on the phone. I'm, ah, doing a piece on historic houses in Newarth."

"How nice," Maria said vaguely. "But there isn't much history, except for someone being killed once in a burglary. In the early seventies it passed on to someone who rented it out to some sort of religious commune, and then one winter all the pipes froze and there was a lot of damage, and after that the man we bought it from began but never finished his restoration. But if you're curious . . ." she said, inviting Emily to precede her up the beautiful curved staircase.

It seemed intensely ironic to Emily that Maria Salva was so uninterested in the house's original inhabitants. *She* saw Talbots, old and young, everywhere: sliding down the curved ebony banister; playing a good rubber of long whist on Thursday nights; curled up with a Pekingese on the velvet-tufted window seat that looked out on the morning sunrise;

brooding over a meerschaum pipe in the library; decorating the staircase with garlands for the annual Christmas ball; flirting in a discreet corner of the drawing room.

But then they reached the second floor, and it was as if the Talbots and their Victorian life-style had been suddenly drywalled from view. Frank Salva had converted the entire floor into a warren of dull square rooms, each neatly papered with the same beige print, each fitted out with an identical reproduction bed, bureau, horse print, and brass-plated lamp. Each floor was covered, like the hall, in industrial-strength beige carpet, and each window hidden under beige miniblinds and brown drapes. Every room —it was true—had been provided with its own bath. No one had to share. It was all very clean, very neat, very . . .

"Is the third floor the same?" asked Emily, depressed. It would be impossible to learn anything about Hessiah Talbot here.

"Half of it is. The other half is gutted. My husband works nights and weekends on it, but it's slow going, as you can imagine."

"And the tower?"

The dreamy look on Maria Salva's face turned wary. "The tower is just as we found it. My husband says it will be very expensive to plumb because of the asbestos everywhere that has to be removed first. It's too far from the flow of traffic, and it's very cold in winter. What we do with the tower depends on how successful we are at renting rooms in the rest of the house. At the moment the first two floors of the tower are empty. The third is pretty much as we found it, a storage place for discarded furniture." She looked exhausted, as though she wished the conversation to be at an end.

"May I see it?" Emily asked in a cheerfully oblivious voice.

Maria smiled faintly. "There isn't much to see."

"I'd *love* to mention it in the article."

"Very well," Maria said with one of her breathless sighs. She took Emily up to the third floor. "The tower had its own stairs from the lower rooms, but they're in disrepair and unusable. For now this is the only route," she explained, leading Emily through a newly installed door that opened directly into the top floor of the tower.

The inside of the tower was much larger than it appeared from the shaded glimpse Emily had caught from the street. A worn and faded Persian rug that curled up against the walls and a four-poster bed, still draped in torn velvet, dominated the room. The walls were papered in a Venetian water scene that was peeling off in long, shredded strips. Evidence of water damage was everywhere. A jumble of broken furniture—three-legged chairs, small warped tables, drawerless bed stands, and a set of carved Oriental screens—made walking around difficult. From where they stood, the view once must have been wonderful. But today they looked out at a sea of black rooftops and utility poles and, beyond them, eight lanes of east-west highway traffic.

Maria flipped on the light; a single bulb flickered and went out. It didn't matter; the room was bright with sunshine. Emily made ooh-and-ah chitchat about the furniture, edging her way deliberately toward an enormous, battered slant-top desk buried under piles of papers. *Talbot papers?* She lined herself up behind the Oriental screens and said, "What a striking view," while she scanned one or two of the piles. Nothing. Just utility bills made out to people she didn't know and old typewritten theses on subjects she didn't care about. It was all too recent to be of use. But the desk had three large, half-open drawers bursting with papers, and she wasn't leaving without a peek.

She was in the process of sliding out the top drawer when Maria Salva suddenly said, "I think we ought to go now." Her voice was anxious, almost angry.

"I'm sorry. I'm holding you up," Emily said, and promptly crawled out from behind the piled-high furniture. "Was this John Talbot's room?" she asked casually.

"I doubt it. His must have been on the first floor. Perhaps this was the nursery." Maria surveyed the room and added, "When we first bought the place, we found some small . . . bones . . . in this room, and strange, ritualistic objects. It seemed . . . ungodly."

"Maybe the religious group that rented the place was really a witches' coven," Emily said, peering out the casement window at the grounds below. "Well, Maria, thank you for the tour. For goodness' sake, there's Mrs. Gibbs, turning away from the front door!" Emily swung open the window and greeted the librarian. "We're coming right down!"

Mrs. Gibbs looked up and waved, and in a moment they were all together in the drawing room and Mrs. Gibbs was saying, "I phoned, but no one answered, so it seemed just as easy to pop over. Won't you both come to dinner tonight? Emily got me started thinking about an idea for Talbot Manor, Maria. Frank—even old Frank—will like this one."

Maria smiled her vague smile and said, "Frank is away tonight, Mrs. Gibbs. I have to be here at the desk."

"Oh, dear. And I have such a wonderful stew in the

Crockpot—all right, here's what to do. I'll bring it over here!" the librarian said. "What do you think of that?"

Probably not much, Emily thought.

But Maria smiled limply and agreed to let herself be drafted as hostess. She was so very passive. Emily had a sudden flash of Fergus's being forced to work with Maria Salva instead of with her. It'd serve the chauvinist right.

The thought made her smile, until she remembered Fergus's faintheartedness at the front door. Of all the ones to get weak-kneed at the scene of a crime, she wouldn't have expected it of him. If she looked at it another way, she could make the case for Fergus's looking pretty darn guilty as he fled. It was a troubling thought.

Dinner was a success. Maria set a lovely table in the ornately paneled dining room, with lace and candlelight. One or two of the guests peeked brazenly around the corner, but for the most part Maria, Emily, and Mrs. Gibbs were left in peace to enjoy the librarian's Crockpot of Secret Stew. They finished one bottle of burgundy, then opened another.

The talk during dinner had focused mostly on the hard times Newarth was having. Mrs. Gibbs had very precise opinions on how to turn around the Massachusetts economy. "As for Talbot Manor, there's an obvious way to double your business," she was insisting to Maria. "Cut your price in half!"

Maria went off into gales of tipsy laughter, and Mrs. Gibbs said, "No, my dear, it's not as wild as it sounds. Lots of B and B customers are repeat customers, so it's money well spent if you introduce them to Talbot Manor with two-for-one weeknights. You won't have any more laundry than for one night, and an extra doughnut and coffee are no big thing. You must do whatever it takes to get them in here," she said, rapping her knuckles emphatically on the dining table.

Maria rested her cheek on her hand and twisted the stem of her glass dreamily. "Oh, *I* know what it takes to get them in here," she murmured, staring into the rich red liquid. "You think I don't, but I do. I could get them here tomorrow. With just one . . . little . . . word."

Emily felt the hair on the back of her neck stand up. She leaned on her forearms confidentially and stared into the bottomless depths of Maria's dark eyes. "What little word is that, Maria?"

Maria shook her head so vehemently that her long black hair whipped around the front of her face. "So that you can print it?" she demanded, throwing her head back and laughing. "Oh, no. *My* secret. Mine alone. Not even Frank, dear . . . old . . . Frank . . ."

Mrs. Gibbs topped off Maria's glass. "Maria, if you have a brilliant idea, share it with us. It may need tweaking."

But Maria shook her head again and laughed. She stood up abruptly. "Time to tear the clable—clear the table," she corrected with a puzzled frown. And then she laughed again, nervously this time, as if she no longer knew or trusted herself. She reached for her wineglass but knocked it down instead, sending burgundy flying across the lace tablecloth and into Emily's lap. "Oh, no!" Maria cried, horrified. "Your silk blouse!"

"Not silk at all," Emily said reassuringly. "Plain old wash-and-wear."

"Let me wash it for you, then," Maria begged.

Emily demurred, but Maria was so distressed that

finally she gave in. Maria went off to find her something to wear, and Mrs. Gibbs murmured, "Poor child. I don't think she's used to spirits."

"I wonder," Emily said dryly.

Her own mind had become a little dulled by wine, but not enough to stop an idea from bubbling up in the last few minutes: She must stay the night. It was the only way to look at the three drawers in the slant-top desk. Frank Salva was away, and Maria obviously would sleep soundly after the wine. There were very few guests; the third-floor rooms were empty. The coast was as clear as it was going to get.

It would, of course, be simpler to come right out and ask Maria for permission to rummage through the desk. But whenever Emily brought up either the Talbots or the tower that afternoon, Maria had turned her resolutely aside. The subjects were off limits. Emily wanted to know why.

By the time Maria returned, Emily and Mrs. Gibbs had cleared the table and were loading the dishwasher. Maria handed Emily a crisp linen blouse much finer than the one she'd stained and directed Emily to her bedroom, which lay just beyond the receiving room.

The circular layout of the ground floor really was ideal for an owner-occupied bed and breakfast, Emily decided. She made her way to what was once a music or morning room, as exquisitely fitted out as every other room downstairs. Emily couldn't help wondering how long it would be before Frank nailed drywall over the tapestried paneling. After changing she hurried out, then noticed a carpenter's wooden toolbox in the hall with a small flashlight tucked neatly between the hammer and the cordless drill. She picked up the minilight and slipped it in the pocket of her mid-length skirt.

Emily's blouse and the wine-stained tablecloth were soon sloshing side by side in the front-loading washer, exchanging tales of woe. Mrs. Gibbs poured coffee, and Maria set out a tray of petits fours. The last course took place in the drawing room, where the women perched gingerly on horsehair-cushioned chairs. "We have a small sitting room off our bedroom, which we prefer," Maria admitted. "Frank finds this room gloomy. Even our guests seem to avoid it."

"It *is* a somber room," Mrs. Gibbs agreed. "But then the Victorians weren't exactly party animals," she added dryly.

Emily was thinking about the effect a room like this would have on a courtship. "I wonder," she mused aloud, "if Hessiah Talbot was ever kissed here."

It was a thought best left unspoken. Maria dropped her cup on its saucer with a crash and began to choke. It was a ghastly sound; her eyes were wide as she leaped up from the love seat and began to flail ineffectually at her chest. Emily was at her side instantly, prepared to perform the Heimlich maneuver, when Maria suddenly waved her away, swallowed hard once or twice, and took a sip of coffee. She sat back down, and so did Emily.

Mrs. Gibbs said mildly, "Went down the wrong pipe, I expect." And that was that.

But the incident added to Emily's sense that Maria was connected to the Talbots in some way other than shared real estate. She wondered why the outspoken Mrs. Gibbs hadn't brought up Hessiah Talbot once during dinner. Perhaps she'd given up on the subject long ago. And now the evening was clearly winding down and any opportunity fading.

"Dear me," Mrs. Gibbs said after a few minutes, "I should be running along before the sun goes down. I don't like to drive after dark. Thank heavens for June twilights."

Emily rolled out her plan. "As for me, I've had altogether too much wine to drive in the light *or* dark. I think I'll book a room here for the night."

"Here?" Maria repeated, stunned. "But . . . have you packed anything?"

"Nope," Emily answered cheerfully. "I'll have to wing it."

"Not me, thank you," said Mrs. Gibbs. "I need my Serta. Besides, I'm sober as a judge. The problem with you two," she added with a wink and a pinch of her ample waist, "is you don't have the weight to offset the wine."

Mrs. Gibbs packed up her Crockpot and bade them both good night. "You will let me know how your little article turns out, won't you?" she asked Emily with a deliberately bland look. She'd guessed that Emily was up to something; obviously she was a very shrewd old lady.

That left only Emily and Maria.

Emily said no to another cup of coffee, protesting that she was keeping Maria from her duties. Maria replied that she had no duties, and Emily suspected she wasn't just being polite; the place really did seem to run itself. She wondered whether Maria had any domestic help. Somehow she felt sure she did.

"It really is a grand old house," Emily said. She decided to drag up the Talbots one last time. "Have you ever been visited by descendants of John Talbot? You know, great-great-grandchildren passing through on their way to Disney World, that sort of thing?"

"There are no direct descendants," Maria said sharply. "None." She let out a little gasp, as though she'd been indiscreet again. "That's what I've heard anyway. No . . . I'm sure someone would have said."

"Oh. I'm sorry to hear that," Emily said carefully. "It's always sad when a line dies out." She tried to chat away the moment. "There's no danger of that happening in *my* family. I have four brothers—four Bowditches—and every one of them is married with children." She sighed heavily. "And I suppose I will be the spinster Bowditch."

It was the most irrelevant little confession; Emily had no idea why she'd made it. It had to be the wine.

"I don't think there's anything wrong with never having married," Maria admitted in her sad, dreamy voice. "Nothing at all."

A thought occurred to Emily. *So that's where the faraway comes from. She's unhappy with dear old Frank.* She wondered just how old Frank was. A young and beautiful wife, a steady turnover of male visitors, and a plumber-husband working all the time —it didn't look promising.

Still, it was none of Emily's business. She stood up and said, "Is there any chance that you sell toothbrush kits from that charming reception desk?"

"I do, but not to you," Maria said with a pretty wave of dismissal. "Come, and I'll give you one as well as your key. You'll want to freshen up. Room six is very quiet."

"Can I be on the third floor, above an empty room instead?" Emily asked quickly. "I have an exercise routine in the morning. Nothing that your plaster can't handle, but I'd hate to disturb anyone."

Maria started to say something, then stopped. "If you prefer," she said at last.

They parted with polite phrases, and Emily made her way up the elegant staircase to the inelegant third floor. The finished half was neatly separated by a sheet of plastic from the unfinished gutted part that ended in the new door to the tower. Emily went back to Room 8 and waited. Sometime past midnight, when the light on the staircase was dimmed and the flow of distant traffic muted, she crept out of her bed and tiptoed behind the sheet of plastic that separated the world of the Salvas from that of the Talbots.

At the end of the hall she took hold of the knob of the tower-room door, turned, and pulled. The door wouldn't open. *Damn!* she thought. *Was there a key?* She shined the flashlight on the right stile: no lock. But she discovered a barrel bolt mounted vertically at the top of the stile, with its bolt drawn down. That meant that Maria had gone back and bolted the door since the afternoon. Why? Why have a barrel bolt there in the first place? Emily slid the bolt, opened the door, and went into the tower room on tiptoe—why, she didn't know, since she'd just determined that no one could be in any of the three tower rooms.

Emily was grateful for the full moon; it washed the top floor in pale white light. She was able to make her way without a flashlight to the slant-top desk—the desk that she was absolutely positive stored secrets she should know. The top drawer slid open easily. Holding the tiny flashlight between her teeth, Emily flipped through a pile of papers, then another, and quickly determined that some college kid named Kyle Edwards had used the desk for his own, a generation earlier.

Disappointed, she opened the second drawer and found more term papers and a packet of airmail letters bound by a rotted rubber band. She shined the light on the top blue tissue envelope. It was postmarked Paris, 1972. Flipping through the lot, she found them all addressed, in the same European hand, to Kyle Edwards. She held up the packet to her nose, inhaling the faded fragrance that hinted of words of love. She tossed the packet back into the drawer.

That left the bottom drawer. Heart hammering, Emily pulled it open to find . . . nothing. It had been completely cleared. Yet earlier that afternoon she'd noticed that it had been partly open and stuffed full of papers and bound books or possibly journals. Bitterly disappointed, she slid the drawer back. It resisted. She pulled it open again, carefully, then reached in and back and around, searching for the hindrance. Something was caught between the drawers, and when she removed it, she saw that it was a very old photograph of a family posed in classic formation next to a pedestaled fern: father, mother, son, son, infant in mother's arms.

Emily turned the crumpled photograph over and read "July 1862." In 1862—she did some quick arithmetic—Hessiah Talbot was about a year old. Yes! Her hunch was right! The drawer must have been a treasure trove of Talbot history, and Maria had carted off the contents sometime that afternoon, because—Emily had no idea why, but one way or another she was going to find out. What a lucky break, finding the photograph that was left behind, the photograph . . .

The photograph that had one too many children in it.

Oh, hell, Emily thought, deflated. This is just some family or other from about Hessiah's time period. She stuck the photo in the voluminous pocket of her skirt and removed the drawer altogether, searching with the flashlight for more. But there was nothing. She was in the process of replacing the drawer when she realized that her eyes were smarting and that the overwhelming mustiness of the tower room had turned into another smell altogether.

The smell of smoke.

11

Smoke! It couldn't be happening! Emily jumped to her feet, hitting her head hard on the edge of a marble tabletop. She rubbed the back of her head furiously, willing away the pain, fighting a woozy disorientation. "You have a nose for news, Emily," her mother used to say, "but not for anything else." Her mother was right, she thought, rushing for the door. How had she not smelled smoke? And where was the fire?

She grabbed the doorknob and pushed instead of pulled. Then she pulled. It didn't matter. The door was obviously bolted on the other side. Panicky now, she turned back to the room, looking for another exit. The original door stood across the room, dark and massive in the moonlight. Beyond it must be the crumbling old stairs, situated between the tower and the main house. Emily ran for the door, lifting the folds of her skirt to her mouth, filtering the thickening smoke. She groped at the doorknob, felt a giant key still in the keyhole, turned it, swung the impossibly heavy door inward. She staggered two steps toward the old hall landing. Her foot caught a wire hanger that was on the floor and sent it flying.

Into empty space. There *was* no hall landing, she realized with horror as she peered over the threshold. All she could see was part of a shadowy framework for a stairwell; it would be suicidal to try climbing down it in the dark. She gulped a few mouthfuls of fresh air and tried not to panic. There was no evidence anywhere yet of flames. She could scream for help, here or at the bolted door. Being caught as a snoop was the least of her problems now. She closed the heavy door and made a sprint across the room; she wanted to be at a viable exit.

But the smoke was heavier now, obscuring visibility, making breathing impossible. Emily swung open the first casement window she found and drew in enormous gulps of clean night air. She should cry for help, rouse the neighborhood. But the thought was repugnant to her.

The moon was absolutely brilliant. She couldn't imagine why there wasn't a hook and ladder already on the side lawn. The lack of one infuriated her and at the same time jogged her memory: Mrs. Gibbs had said that the phobic John Talbot had ordered a kind of fire escape cut into the granite walls of the tower. And Emily could see, leading from the casement window to her left, a series of steps carved into the tower, each no more than half a foot wide, zigzagging to ground level.

Without hesitating she ran to the exit window and climbed out onto the sill. Without looking down—if she did that, she would faint from fear—she began backing down the steps of the tower, clinging to the rusted iron handholds that were set every couple of feet in the granite wall, picking her way step by step down the three-story vertical drop. When she was fifteen feet from the ground, she tripped on the hem of her skirt, and the handhold she grabbed gave way completely, making her lose her balance and go flying off the side of the tower like a cat through an unscreened window. She landed on a hedge of boxwood, breaking a few branches, and tumbled onto the lawn more or less in one piece.

God in heaven was the only thought that filled her mind.

But two seconds later she was racing for the front doors, which were already thrown open, and running up to warn Maria, who gave every indication that a fire was in progress. The innkeeper was hurrying the guests out of the house in a surprisingly calm way. When she saw Emily she did a violent double take.

"I banged on your door and no one answered," she managed to say amid the cries and shouts and what's-going-on's of her guests. She turned back to the confusion and counted heads. "That's everyone, then. Everybody out now. Please!"

Trucks were arriving, their sirens wailing, their red lights slashing the length of the entry hall. Emily never got a chance to respond to Maria's challenge; she was gathered up with the rest of the group and herded out by a fire fighter approximately twice her size. They all huddled on the lawn, clinging to themselves not so much with cold as with anxiety, and watched black-slickered men move through the house and grounds with purposeful efficiency.

Maria joined them in a little while and was instantly set upon by her guests while Emily hung back. Maria murmured a few things that Emily couldn't hear, but she had the sense that she was being discussed as the Obvious Suspect. Which was of course crazy. If anything, it was Maria who had some explaining to do.

Why couldn't I get out through the new door?

The closeness of the call began to sink in. She could have died of smoke inhalation. Who would have heard her calls for help? After all, she and Maria hadn't heard the telephone ringing when they were in the tower, nor had they been able to hear Mrs. Gibbs at the front door. Of course, there were the neighbors. Maybe they would have got to her in time; maybe they wouldn't.

Emily walked a little way apart and stood on a grassy knoll that overlooked the orderly chaos taking place alongside the tower. The fire truck was in position, its turntable aligned, its hydraulic lifters sending the ladder skyward. A tiny burst of flame from the tower drew a cry from the crowd on the street and sent a shudder through Emily.

"What is going *on?*" she whispered to herself.

"Ye're a damn fool, that's what."

She turned to see the ghost standing between her and a lilac tree. "Fergus!" She was incredibly relieved to see him.

But Fergus was blistering with anger. "How could ye be so *stupid,* marching into a house of iniquity once I said not to?"

"You didn't tell me not to," she said, taken aback by his fury. "You only said *you* couldn't. I assumed you were barred from entering by some kind of ghost regulations. Or that—well, never mind."

"Jee-sus, woman, that ain't a tearoom ye went into. The house is *empowered.*"

"To do what?" she asked without thinking.

He stood there, dark and shadowy, his anger dissipating into an ominous stillness. "I don't know. I only know that there is a power there. I can sense it."

She shuddered again. "Don't, Fergus. You're frightening me."

His anger erupted anew. "I'd like to shake ye till yer teeth rattle! Don't ye *understand?* Ye could have been killed. I'm *trying* to frighten ye, goddammit!"

"Excellent work, in that case," she said, plunging her hands in her pockets and drawing her arms close to her sides for warmth. "Naturally I know why you're concerned," she added with sullen nonchalance. She was watching the fire fighters go through their paces: Two were inside at windows, and a third was on the ladder, snaking a hose through to one of them. She saw no flames, only small curls of smoke billowing from the open casements. "You're concerned that I won't be around to figure out who killed Hessiah," she said to Fergus. "Because where would that leave you—literally?"

There was an iron garden bench nearby. Emily sat down wearily on it, idly fingering the crumpled photograph still in the pocket of her skirt. Fergus came and took a place beside her; his silence spoke volumes. She knew she shouldn't care whether or why he cared, but she did.

In the pale cast of moonlight he looked truly spectral, as did every other player in the drama that was playing itself out on the stage below them. She stared at the pallor of her own arms in the silver light and thought, *What difference is there between us that a speck of time won't settle?* She felt very alone, and very mortal.

"Fergus . . . I think Maria Salva tried to kill me," she said quietly.

"Ye couldn't get out of the room, I take it."

She shook her head. "If she didn't lock me in, I don't know who did. I suppose it's possible that when I rattled the door in my panic, the bolt on the other side dropped down into place. But I didn't start the fire. It seems too coincidental."

"She may be an instrument. Or she may have had nothing to do with it. The house is empowered," he repeated.

"I won't ask to do what, anymore," Emily said with a short laugh. "I don't want to know." She drew in a deep, deep breath and exhaled, clearing her lungs once and for all, and then forced herself to stand up. "I guess I'll thank my hostess for her hospitality and head home after all. Is there anything," she asked dryly, "you'd like to see while we're still attached to each other in Newarth?"

He thought about it, then shook his head no. " 'Tomorrow is another day,' " he said with an irrepressible look.

She smiled despite herself. *"Gone With the Wind.* Was that on TV, too?"

"TNT," he said at once. "And a glorious film it is."

"So now you're a cinema buff, too. Let's hope you don't get hooked on the daytime soaps."

"Not damn likely," he answered with distaste. "They're too unrealistic."

When Emily arrived at her desk the following morning, the first thing she saw was an open *Newsweek* with the following tidbit highlighted in yellow marker: "There is talk that Massachusetts Senator Lee Alden, whose paranormal pursuits are becoming an open secret with his still-doting voters back home, may be challenged for his Senate seat. Congressman Boyd Strom, who wants to see "dignity and good judgment restored to the office," has been gathering political and financial support for a run in the primary this October."

The second thing she saw was a while-you-were-out message telling her to call about the parakeet, price reduced.

The third thing she saw was a handwritten note from the managing editor, Phil Sparke, telling her to be in his office. Now.

She was dialing the number to Lee Alden's Washington office when Stan Cooper came back to his desk, balancing a cellophaned crumb cake on a cup of vending machine coffee. He gave her a sly and sleepy good morning and said, "Which one are you tackling first: the rumor, the bird, or the boss?" He tore open the crinkly wrapper. "It looks like you're going for the bird."

Emily dropped the phone like a hot brick. "No, it looks like I'm going for the boss."

"A wise choice." He said it casually, brushing crumbs from his seersucker sport coat, but then he caught her look and held it before adding, "Want to talk about it yet?"

"Talk about what, Stan? I'm on to an interesting story, not my usual thing, but a nice summer piece. Light and easy." *Ha.* "When I get a little farther along, I'll clue you in."

"You're in over your head, kiddo," he warned. "National politics is big time."

"Who said anything about national politics? This one's about a little history, a little mystery, that's all."

"Nothing to do with your upcoming interview with Senator Alden?"

"Nothing at all."

Obviously he didn't believe her. "I'm telling you again, you're in over your head."

"Everything's under control, Stan. I gotta run; Phil's waiting."

She walked away with the uneasy sense that Stan was not only professionally jealous but determined to sabotage her interview with Lee Alden in some way, possibly by putting in a bad word with the news editor. Too bad she couldn't just tell Stan that she'd decided to kill the interview. How could she *not* kill it? She'd been to bed with the interviewee, and her emotions were in a state of chaos. The longing she felt over their time together caused her actual physical pain whenever she thought of it, so naturally she tried not to think. She needed desperately to come to terms with that night, but with a ghost running around demanding justice, who had the time?

Not to mention she didn't care to be humiliated about her own work. Originally—it was true—she'd had hopes of getting the senator to embarrass himself. But Fergus had made her a believer and changed all that. Besides, if the *Newsweek* rumor were true, the senator would no doubt play it safe in an interview, and safe wouldn't move her career along at all. No, the best thing she could do would be to let Lee Alden off the hook. In every way. She wondered whether the parakeet call was about the interview. She didn't dare hope it'd be about anything else.

Emily saw the editor through the glass walls of his computer-laden office before he saw her. Phil Sparke looked exactly like his name: a balding, energetic dynamo who liked to clamp cold cigar butts in his teeth while he made reporters' lives hell. So far Emily had managed not to get the cigar butt pointed at her face. Until now.

"What the hell is going on here, Bowditch?" the editor demanded. "I just got a call from Senator Alden's office canceling your interview with him next week."

What nerve! "Did he say why?"

"He's going with Ted Koppel instead."

What nerve! She shrugged and said, "That's it, then, sir. Television. More exposure."

"I don't wanna hear that! You should've had that interview nailed down tight as a drum. What the hell kind of reporter are you? We don't shrug off exclusives around here, Bowditch. Christ, the guy's in *Newsweek,* a campaign fight's brewing—I want that interview!"

Emily stared down the barrel of a cold cigar. "But he canceled," she said in a tiny, fearful voice.

"Well, uncancel him!"

"How?" she asked in a tinier, more fearful voice.

"Call the son of a bitch. There's the phone. Here's the number."

She stared at the slip. It was the number. "Now?"

"Now, goddammit."

As far as Emily could tell, there were only two ways out. She could throw herself through the plate glass window and be carried off bleeding on a stretcher or she could feign a stroke and be carried off unconscious on a stretcher. Phil Sparke would settle for nothing less. She let him hand her the phone while he punched in the number.

This was it, the professional low point of her life. The ditch. The sinkhole. The lowest rung of the limbo pole. Crawling back to a man she hadn't even had the chance to reject, just because another man was standing there telling her to.

"Hello, Senator?" she said faintly at the sound of Lee Alden's voice. "This is Emily Bowditch. I was wondering, Senator. Would you . . . reconsider . . . granting me the interview?"

That was it, her entire speech. It was all her pride would allow. If the result was dismissal and foreclosure on the condo, so be it.

After a brief but agonizing pause the senator said,

"I canceled because I got the distinct impression the other night that the less you saw of me, the better. Was I wrong?"

"In some ways," she said, squirming under Phil's baleful eye.

"You sound like you're not alone. Okay, we'll talk about it later. Actually . . . I'll be in Boston Friday night for a fund-raiser at the Copley Plaza. I'll FedEx a ticket to you. Emily, I've got to free up this line. I'm expecting a call from the White House; they need my vote on a bill, which makes now a good time for some serious horse trading. I'll catch you on Friday night."

Catch me? Does he think I'm falling?

"Well?" asked her boss after she hung up.

"Probably," she answered.

Phil Sparke beamed. "I knew you could do it." Now that he'd got his interview back, he became almost kindly. He asked Emily what project she was working on, and she told him the story of Hessiah Talbot, omitting some things—notably Fergus—and fudging others. He thought the feature had possibilities. He made a suggestion or two, and Emily left him in a very good mood.

For the rest of the day she worked on her consumer complaint column. Every once in a while her glance strayed to the open *Newsweek* still on her desk, but she refused to ask Stan whether he'd put it there. No doubt Stan thought she was the one behind the paranormal rumors. Maybe even Lee Alden thought it—was that why he'd canceled? Still, the truth was it could have been anybody, from Jim Whitewood (an opportunist if ever there was one) to the chatty Mrs. Lividus, Kimberly's mentor.

After work, on a hunch, Emily went back to the Something Old shop on Newbury Street. She was in luck. The Coco Chanel saleswoman was just closing up. Reluctantly the woman let Emily in, but only just inside the door.

Emily apologized profusely and then said, "Do you remember my buying this necklace a couple of weeks ago?"

She'd asked merely as a formality and was astonished when the saleswoman acted unsure. "That isn't at all the kind of thing we carry," the woman said with a sniff.

"I don't have my VISA slip with me," Emily answered, becoming annoyed, "but I assure you it's from here. What I'd like to know—"

The saleswoman glanced at her watch and then at her red fingernails. She was obviously on her way out for the evening, and Emily was holding her up. "What I'd like to know," Emily repeated with a patient smile, "is where this came from. Who owned it before."

Emily might just as well have accused the shop of fencing hot jewelry.

"Well, *really*. Every transaction is perfectly legitimate. But it's impossible to know individual owners. Terri buys from all over the world, usually in odd lots from auctions, estate sales, open markets, whatever. The pieces are itemized, of course, but, well—*really*."

Emily bit back a retort, asked for Terri's business phone, thanked the woman, and left.

When she got back home the television was on, but Fergus was nowhere in sight. Emily turned off *Wheel of Fortune* and said aloud to the empty room, "Fergus, I said to turn off the TV if you're not watching it." She was halfway to the bedroom when she heard Pat Sajak's voice. She came back to the television and turned it off again. It came back on. "How do you do that? I suppose you have a built-in remote." She turned the set off again.

It came back on.

"Dammit, Fergus, I like it quiet after work. I need to wind down. And I've got to use the phone. If you insist on watching, turn it *down* a little. And put on PBS or something. What is it about men and Vanna anyway?" she muttered to herself as she went off to the bedroom to change.

The volume went up.

After she'd changed and eaten a quick meal, she tried calling Terri Simmer on the offhand chance that an independent businesswoman was always available for calls. She was right; Ms. Simmer, who sounded bright, hard, and urban, took the call in her car.

"Yes. I remember the item very well. No, I didn't buy it as part of a lot. I happened to be weekending on the Vineyard and found it at a white elephant sale at the Oak Bluffs Home for the Aged. I doubt that they gave me a receipt. That's all I can tell you."

She probably paid forty-five cents for it, Emily thought as she laid the Princess phone in its cradle. The Yankee in her cringed at the thought of a five-hundred-dollar charge rolling in on next month's VISA statement. Still, she had a promising lead to follow up on, and for now that was all that mattered. The good lead reminded her of the bad one; she'd forgotten all about the photograph that was still in the pocket of the skirt she'd worn at Talbot Manor. It was still in the skirt, lying in a pile bound for the dry cleaners. She pulled out the photo, more crumpled than ever, and took it into the living room.

She turned off the set in the middle of a lurid account of a triple murder being covered on *Hard Copy* and said, "Please show yourself, Fergus. I don't have time to play little games with you." She stepped in front of the television so that the ghost's remote-control power wouldn't work.

But the television behind her came back on anyway, madly flipping through its channel selection. Emily jumped out of the way. "Hey! Don't do that! I want to have children someday!"

Fergus materialized, sprawled on the sofa like any other couch potato. He glanced at the TV, muting it, but he continued to divide his attention between her and the flickering images as he said, "Yeah? What's up?"

"My God," she murmured. "Look at you. Listen to you. You're turning into Bart Simpson."

"Don't have a cow over it," he said in a dead-on mimic that left her speechless. Then he grinned, got the TV to turn itself off, and sat up straight. "Ye'd rather I were Fergus. Fergus it is, then. What's on yer mind?"

His grin was roguish, but there was something dangerous in it, too, and Emily realized that she still had no idea who or even what Fergus O'Malley really was. He had power, undeniably. But whether it was good or evil or some kind of neutral energy, she couldn't say. One thing was sure: His ability to adapt completely to the world he found himself thrown into was unnerving. His approach simply could not be more different from Emily's. Emily had spent all her adult life trying to make the world over to her system of right and wrong: to correct every injustice she happened to come across, and to encourage others to tell her about the ones she hadn't. It was a big job, and it didn't leave time for her to be frivolous. Television was frivolous. Almost as frivolous as dating men.

Looked at a certain way, even sex was frivolous. Sex didn't really *solve* anything. It just complicated matters and knocked you off course. It made you think about it all the time. She knew from the magazines she'd read that men had an entirely different attitude from that of women. Men kept sex in perspective. To them it was a deep, recurring need, like hunger. They acknowledged it; they satisfied it; and that was that—at least until the next time. Somehow she had to become more practical, more like them, in her approach. Somehow she had to put the other night in perspective.

She looked up to see Fergus waving his arms back and forth like a railroad signalman, trying to get her attention. She'd been off in a daze somewhere, just the way she'd been doing ever since the night Lee Alden had made love to her.

"What did ye mean, ye want to have children someday?" he asked her.

She shook off her daydream. "Pardon me?"

"Surely ye're barren," Fergus said, a quizzical look on his face.

"Barren! What put that idea in your head?"

"If ye—" He cleared his throat. "If ye do it with a man, ye will get pregnant by him. It's an old and fairly simple story," he added, finding refuge in irony.

"Birth control, Fergus," she said, smiling at his discomfort. "We have that now. Women don't have to get pregnant unless they want to."

It was a profound revelation to him, she could see that. "It's finally come, then," he said in a strangely melancholy voice. "I can think of some who might've turned out different," he added softly. "I had a sister, she were only fifteen, she died giving birth. Not that she wanted to live. The man never come forward. The neighbors shunned her. Frances hid at home, away from the windows, away from their tongues. She cried all the time. Mum said it was her tears poisoned her. I remember her tears used to fall on the cat, and the cat would lick herself clean. I thought it was strange they never poisoned the cat."

Emily saw that he was somewhere else in time. "Birth control, Frances," he said softly to his sister, wherever she was. "Imagine that."

He pulled himself out of the nineteenth century and came back to the twentieth. "Ye don't have to worry, then," he said to Emily with an inexpressibly tender look. "I would never do anything to hurt yer hopes for a family."

"I know that, Fergus. Not on purpose," she added, because she really did believe that about him now. She sat down beside him, the photograph in her hand.

He was silent a moment, ruminating. "So," he said at last, "who's the father to be?"

"I haven't made any plans, Fergus," she said dryly. "When I do, you'll be the first to know."

"Ye ain't gettin' any younger."

"Thank you for the reminder. Can we talk about something else now?" She held the photograph out in front of him.

"What about that senator fella? He looks able."

"I'll put him on my list," she answered, beating back a furious blush. "Fergus, please. I need your cooperation in this investigation. Do you recognize anyone in this picture? I found it in the tower of Talbot Manor."

He stopped smiling and stared thoughtfully at the family members for a long while, then shook his head. She turned the photograph over. He said, "This was taken in 1862! I was nowhere near Talbot Manor then. In 1862 I was cabin boy on a fishing schooner out of Gloucester. I showed up in Newarth only a few months before Hessiah Talbot was murdered."

"It was a long shot," she admitted. "I thought

maybe the mother in this photo might have reminded you of Hessiah, or the father of her brother Stewart. Sometimes family resemblances run deep."

"It could be anyone—uncles, friends, neighbors. Why do ye think it's the Talbot family? Who's the extra lad, in that case?"

"I don't know; I suppose you're right. This is all that was left in a desk Maria Salva emptied after I started asking questions. One thing I *do* know: Maria knows much more than she's let on about the Talbots. But why keep it so secret?"

"Money or love," Fergus offered. "There are no other motives to speak of, for women."

A vivid picture came to Emily of the mysterious Maria with her vague smile and silky walk. So intense was the memory that Emily forgot to be offended by Fergus O'Malley's chauvinist remark.

"It's not money," she said firmly.

12

Fergus appeared to Emily early the next morning as she was toddling half asleep to the Mr. Coffee machine. It was the first time he'd actually shown up before her morning shower, and being a very private person, Emily didn't take kindly to it.

"Fergus! For Pete's sake, I haven't even brushed my teeth," she said, raking her fingers through her hair and yanking her T-shirt a little closer to her knees.

"I'm only doin' what ye told me, showing meself if I'm in the room," he answered, surprised by her vehemence.

It was true. After her mortification over Lee Alden, she'd made Fergus promise never to observe her unseen in intimate situations. As far as she knew, he'd been as good as his word.

"Sorry. Haven't had my coffee," she mumbled. It was just so weird, having a ghost around in her most unguarded moments. It was like having to adjust to all the disadvantages of marriage with none of the advantages that make it worthwhile.

"I remembered something that might be of some use to ye," Fergus said as she poured herself a cup of coffee. "Yer Mrs. Gibbs just may be right. Once or twice while I lived in Newarth I heard whispers of a curse that lay on the house of Talbot. No one would ever say what the evil was behind the curse. Either they didn't know, or they were too frightened to say. At the time I thought it was just idle gossip, and after the trial, of course, it didn't much matter to me. I believe there was a feeling it had to do with Mrs. Talbot. She were exceeding religious, people said. Who's to say she hadn't got wind of something? Them kind often do."

"But Celeste Talbot must have died fairly young if she was thrown from a horse. Which would mean the evil had happened a whole generation before her daughter was strangled. I don't see the connection, Fergus; that trail is even colder than the one we're on."

But even as Emily said it, an image of moldy, leather-bound journals peeping out from a desk drawer ripped through her thoughts. Who was more likely to keep a diary than a religious woman torn from her homeland and married to a workaholic millowner? She dismissed the thought; it was wildly speculative. Still, the feeling that Maria Salva was hiding Talbot secrets was growing stronger by the minute. "I've got to go back to Talbot Manor," she said, leaning against the counter and sipping her coffee. "Help me think of an excuse."

"Ye cannot go back," Fergus said, incredulous. "I've told ye that."

"For heaven's sake, how am I supposed to get to the bottom of this thing? I'll be careful," she added absently. "I know better now." Her mind was deep in the case.

"I forbid it!" Fergus said angrily. "Get what ye need some other way! Ye claim to be so clever. Show it!"

It was her turn to be surprised. She stared into the angry depths of his green eyes and thought, *Is it possible he cares for my welfare?* But no, she'd been right the day before. If he did care, it was because she was his ticket to eternity. If something happened to her, happened to the necklace, he might be trapped forever in nothingness. "All right, Fergus," she said calmly, not wishing to distress him. "Have it your way. I have another lead I can follow up on for now. Have you ever been to Martha's Vineyard?"

"Never," he said, as if the resort island were somehow beneath contempt. "There's no decent wages to be made on an island."

"Don't worry. I doubt that anyone's going to offer you a job in this economy," she said in a deadpan voice.

He broke into a good-humored grin. "I like that in ye. Ye're a good woman, Emily Bowditch. I begin to believe in ye."

That's my problem, too, she thought. She was pleased at the compliment nonetheless.

Two hours later an express courier handed Emily an envelope with a ticket to a fund-raiser for Senator Lee Alden to be held on Friday at the Copley Plaza. The price for cocktails and a handshake with the senator was five hundred dollars, which basically meant only one thing to Emily: that she couldn't possibly dress as well as the high rollers who were actually paying to get in. It was a silly concern, she knew, but it occupied the better part of her day.

For the first time in her life she wanted to make an

impression. It mattered. She was very aware that she'd never had a bona fide date with Lee Alden, much less bothered to dress up for him—unless she counted her palmist's getup. Nicole Alden, beautiful concert pianist, would've been dazzling at a top-drawer fund-raiser. So would Cara Miles. And so, come hell or high water, would Emily Bowditch.

By the time Friday came Emily had spent several hundred dollars on a complete overhaul (hair, nails, facial) and a silk and beaded dress from an upscale thrift shop in the Back Bay. The dress was a sensational buy, a designer original; she used it to rationalize the extravagant amount she'd forked over without a whimper at Phillip's, the trendy salon on Newbury Street that Cara had recommended.

On Friday evening Emily slipped the dress over her head, stared at herself in the full-length mirror, and decided once again that the crystal necklace she wore was guiding nearly every step of her life. The dress was the perfect choice. It looked as if it were made to accessorize the necklace. The subtle swirl of colors in the patterned silk—mauve and rose and faded pink—perfectly complemented the iridescent hues of the crystal, and the beaded cummerbund offset the heavy costume effect of the chain around her neck. Best of all, the dress fitted like a glove.

Emily ran her fingers through her new, short, sophisticated hair, still a little dazzled by the effect. Phillip, a magician of sorts, had tracked the natural fall of her hair with offhand precision; when he was finished cutting away the excess, all that remained was a soft brown frame that showed her cheekbones to perfection. He'd made a fuss about her cheekbones. She had no idea that her cheekbones were worth fussing over. And now as a bonus her eyes looked larger, her lips fuller, her skin more pale and creamy.

I could get used to this, she thought guiltily, touching up her lip gloss, *to being rich and pampered and dressed to kill.* For now she decided to enjoy the pretense. She'd be turning back into Cinderella soon enough—probably in about twenty-four hours, when her hair needed its first maintenance shampoo. She scooped up the tiny handbag she was carrying for the night and laughed; it was such a useless little thing. *Maybe I should've just donated the cost of this makeover to Lee's campaign; it'd be a heck of a lot more practical.*

When she walked into her living room, Fergus was there, watching the evening news. He was shaking his head in sorrow over the latest shooting of an innocent bystander; she knew that of all the depressing developments in the past century, it was the wholesale arming of the nation that bothered him the most.

"If the Soviets can beat their swords into plowshares," he began, "then I don't see why—"

He stopped in mid-sentence as he beheld her. She saw the pained expression on his face change to stunned surprise, then to a look that she had trouble reading, she who was learning to read him so well. It was a look of admiration, but it was more than that. There was something elemental in it, something that she would not have expected from a ghost. It was very much the look of a man taking the measure of a woman. Yet it was even more than *that.* There was a hint of class warfare in it, as if he were going to have to tip his hat to her and didn't much care for the idea.

Whatever it was, it flustered her. She looked away and said flippantly, "Well, I'm off."

"Ye would do well to go slowly, my friend," he said softly.

She smiled shyly and answered, "I will. Good night, Fergus." She left feeling warm and reassured; it was nice to have a friend.

The Copley Plaza was not quite Emily's cup of tea. The gilding, the marble, the trompe l'oeil paintings but especially the maître d' in turban and tuxedo conspired to make her feel very much like what she was: a tourist sneaking a look into how the other half lived.

No, indeed, Emily thought, surveying the glittering and black-tied group mingling comfortably with their own. *It ain't exactly the rubber-chicken circuit.* For a moment she faltered; the air in the room was rippling with too much money, too much power. She backed into someone—good Lord, the governor's wife—apologized and moved on, searching for the guest of honor. She wished she had Stanley Cooper alongside. She could look terribly amused as he regaled her with too, too delicious gossip about the swells all around her. And she'd have something to do besides juggle a silly little handbag, a napkin, a shrimp, and a glass of champagne.

As it was, there was no one at her side, and she had to fend for herself. She located the senator, engulfed in a tight circle of well-wishers. She saw the back of the top of his head and heard the low murmur of his voice and the instant, inevitable laughter from those around him. It was all pretty much as she'd expected: King Arthur and his minions. The laughter sounded unforced; the minions genuinely liked their king. She tried not to feel depressed about it.

"He has them eating out of his hands, as usual."

She turned to see two women—one blond, one raven, both thin, both tall—comparing notes on the senator. Miss Manners would've told Emily to move politely out of earshot. Miss Manners could jump in the lake. Emily edged a bit closer, hanging on every word.

"Gloria had him to a dinner party last month, paired off with *her.* He had no idea she'd got a divorce since he'd seen her last. I think it was a shabby trick, but Gloria said he was wrapped up in her all evening."

"He couldn't have been too wrapped up; I don't see Gloria here tonight."

"Darling, didn't I say? Gloria lives in D.C. now."

The two women moved closer to the senator's circle, probing for a break in the crowd.

Well, nuts to this, thought Emily. *Let Gloria have him. I'd rather go home and watch* Perfect Strangers *with Fergus.* She was eyeing the door when she was approached by Jim Whitewood, the senator's aide. Had he been there all along?

He was as slippery smooth as ever. "Miss Bowditch! *Quelle surprise!* Let me introduce you to one or two people." He took her by the arm and led her away from the senator's circle and up to a lively group of men and women, all of them younger than she was. It was like being seated at the children's table at Thanksgiving.

"So tell us, Emily," said one of them, a knockdown gorgeous blonde in shrink-wrapped black. "How do *you* know the senator?"

"He's a hard man not to know," Emily answered evasively.

"I just met him and I am in *love,*" the blonde said, followed by an all-too-stagy dip that showed off her thighs.

Another one of the women said, "He belongs to Daddy's club. I've wanted him since I was twelve. He was married then," she said, raising her glass to her date with a seductive smile, "but he isn't now."

"You're trying to make me jealous, Tiff," her young man said. "But it won't work. Besides money, what've you got in common? He reads; you party. He sails; you shop. He thinks the flag's for saluting; you think it's for a jacket lining. He's the jealous type; you like a man on each arm at all times. Get real, Tiff. You'd be bored in a week."

Tiffany was eyeing the senator over Emily's shoulder. "Maybe you're right," she said, sighing. "But what a week."

They fell to chatting about other things, leaving Emily to feign an interest. Since she'd never been spring skiing in Aspen, that was hard to do. Her mind began to wander. It was becoming pretty obvious that to talk to Lee Alden, she'd have to take a number. To go to bed with him would, of course, mean taking another number and probably paying money down. It was amazing. She'd never known a sexual icon before, but as far as she could tell, Lee Alden was right up there with Warren Beatty, Mick Jagger, Paul Newman, and New Kids on the Block. His appeal cut across all ages and all incomes. From Swansea Mall to Copley Plaza, he was the man to beat. His reelection was a shoo-in.

Emily was yanked from her reverie by Heather, of the shrink-wrapped dress. "Oh, *no,*" Heather wailed, "look who my mother's brought. Darryl Douglas. God, I can't stand him. He's, like, *such* a creep."

Emily became very still. Darryl Douglas was one of Boston's most discreet slumlords, hiding modestly behind half a dozen different corporate blinds. After a week of work she'd tracked him down and presented him with a list of complaints from his tenants, who'd come to her in desperation. He threatened to sue her for harassment and threw her out of his offices. The repairs were now being done, but not exactly with enthusiasm.

"I've enjoyed meeting you all. Please excuse me," she said politely, and beat a retreat. It was time to go home. It had been very educational. She wasn't sorry she'd come, but she saw no point in staying. Cinderella had managed to get to the ball, but clearly she would not be dancing with the prince. With a kind of nothing-to-lose recklessness she elbowed her way through the crowd until she caught Lee's eye.

"Senator," she said, extending her hand to him. "Good luck in the campaign."

He held her hand a fraction longer than was necessary. "You look very nice," he said.

Very nice. That's all she'd been able to afford. What did it take to rate a you-look-sensational? A credit line at the Bank of Switzerland?

"Thank you, Senator," she said, and turned to go.

But her luck had run out. She found herself eyeball to eyeball with a complete stranger, a woman older than she but stunningly preserved, who put her hand on Emily's wrist and said, "Darling, it looks *much* better on you than it did on me."

It was like being pinched, hard, by a passerby. It took Emily's breath away. She looked askance at the woman and fled, unsure whether Lee had heard the remark or not. But she did hear his voice before she was out of earshot, saying, "Fiona! You look fantastic."

She should have seen it coming, she told herself over and over in the cab. Buying a designer original at a secondhand shop was the dumbest faux pas in the world. Probably it had appeared—on that woman's body—in every society column in Boston. Dumb, dumb, dumb! Had they been snickering all evening long? She should've shopped at K mart; no danger there of the dress being recognized. Then she remembered that her dress had been displayed in the thrift shop window for all society to remark on: "Oh, look, Fiona's Armani. A really stunning creation. But of course, she's worn it once." Emily buried her head in her hands. She had tried to be someone she was not, and God had punished her. It was as simple as that.

When she got home, Fergus was watching *Wall Street Week.* "Back already?" he said, surprised.

She slumped in the side chair and let the hated little clutch bag drop to the floor. "Yep. Big day tomorrow. We're taking the first ferry out of Woods Hole."

"Fine with me," he said, zapping Louis Rukeyser into oblivion. He turned to her with a friendly smile. "And were ye the belle of the evening?"

"I would have been," she said dryly, "if they'd taken out every other female between twenty and forty and shot her."

"Quite the shindig, then. And the senator? What were his thoughts on it all?"

"You mean, did he break through the admiring throng and take me in his arms? As a matter of fact, he did not."

"What *did* he do?"

"He said, 'You look very nice.' "

"I see." He nodded meditatively. "Well, then." He continued to nod. "Ye had a nice time."

"C'mon, Fergus. Look at me," she said morosely. "Do I look as if I've had a nice time?"

"What ye *look,*" he said in a low voice, "is fair beautiful."

It caught her off guard; she'd been so expecting it from Lee. She stared at her new shoes for a moment, then said awkwardly, "Thanks, Fergus. For trying to cheer me up."

"It's a fact, Emily."

It was the first time he'd ever used her name. She used to wonder why he didn't. Now she was wondering why he did. "I'm being an awful bitch, I know," she said, trying to shift to firmer ground. "I guess it's because I felt so out of my league at the Copley Plaza."

"It's Fiona was the bitch," Fergus said calmly.

"Fiona? Fergus, you were there!" she wailed. Now she *was* mortified.

"Ye forget, I know how it feels," he said. "Anyway, all's well that ends well. Fiona left early with a cigar burn in her hindquarters. At least that's what she thinks it was."

She was scandalized. "Fergus, *don't* tell me—" She caught her lower lip in her teeth, repressing a smile. "This is awful. You're cheering me up."

"That was the intent, ma'am," he drawled.

"Well, I appreciate it." She dragged herself up from the side chair. "Good night again," she said softly. At the door to her bedroom she turned and said, "Fergus? Did she howl?"

"A little," he said with a wink. "Sweet dreams."

Emily had been asleep for a couple of hours when the phone rang. That's how the call about her mother had come, so now whenever she picked up the phone late at night, it was with a fearful, hammering heart.

"Emily? It's Lee. Did I wake you?"

No one was in the hospital, then. She felt relief, then anger. "Yes, you did," she said, annoyed. "It's late."

"I know; I should've waited until morning. But I wanted to know if you got home all right."

"I'm safe," she said ironically. "The cabdriver was a perfect gentleman."

"I mean—well, where the hell did you *go?*" he demanded. "I looked around, and there was no you."

"I decided we should do all our talking by phone. It's easier. And cheaper, I might add."

"I was working my way toward you—"

"I can't believe you even knew I was there."

"Of course I did. Jim dragged you over to Tiffany and her crowd, God knows why."

"Oh." He'd knocked her a little off center with that one. "Tiffany wants to marry you," she said, trying to regain the offensive.

"She's a good kid. A bit of an airhead."

"Gloria wants you, too," she added evilly. "And Heather, whom you met only briefly." Why was she doing this? "And I'm not sure about Fiona, but probably."

"All right, all right. That's what campaigning is about, Emily. I'm sorry if somehow I've offended you, but without contributions there are no reelections, and without pressing the flesh there are no contributions."

"Well, there was plenty of flesh around to press, so you should do just fine," she said coolly.

There was a very cautious-sounding pause at the other end of the line, and then he said, "When do you want to do the interview?"

She sighed. "Soon, I guess. If I want to keep my job."

"I'll be up here this weekend. How about tomorrow morning?"

"No, tomorrow's impossible. I'm going to the Vineyard on—on assignment."

"Before you leave?"

"I'm taking the first ferry."

There was another pause. "All right. Sunday, anytime?"

She'd rather walk on hot coals, but she said, "Sunday at three?"

"That'll be okay. Millie will be in the office. We'll meet there if that's all right."

"Sunday it is, then," she said, ringing off.

Once again he was choosing to meet her in the public arena. Not that she was surprised. After the *Newsweek* rumor Lee Alden obviously was going to play it safe. His days of candor about the paranormal were over, at least until the election. As she drifted off to sleep, she realized that things had come full circle: A few weeks ago he'd been afraid of what she might print about him; now he was afraid of what others might print about *her*.

13

Somewhere around Plymouth it became apparent that they were going to miss the seven-fifteen ferry out of Woods Hole. Between the accident near Braintree and the line for the Egg McMuffin, Emily had used up all the extra time she'd allowed.

"No big deal," Emily told Fergus, who was along for the ride—his first in a horseless carriage. "We'll be there in plenty of time for the eight o'clock," she added, swinging out between two eighteen-wheelers into the passing lane.

Fergus was sitting next to her, his upper body ramrod straight against the back of the seat, his face a study in pale fear. "Ye drive like a madman," he said through gritted teeth.

"I'm only doing sixty," she protested.

"To pass over sixty miles of land in one hour is unnatural."

She hooted. "This, from someone who can zip through time and space in the blink of an eye. How *do* you do that exactly? How did you get back from Talbot Manor on the night of the fire?"

" 'Tisn't a bodily experience. I'm somewhere, and then I'm somewhere else. That's all. It's only when I make the effort to be present in the physical reality that I feel a little of what ye do. At the moment that's a lot."

A red-hot Firebird, weaving in and out of traffic, cut them off ahead. "Another madman!" Fergus said with an oath.

"That's a Pontiac. 'We build excitement'—remember?" she said lightly.

"Aye, well, I'd rather stay home and watch it on TV." His tension was making him irritable. "Could ye not have done yer business with the Home for the Aged by phone?"

"No. They think the necklace belonged to a lady named Hattie Dunbart, but no one seemed very sure. Anyway, Hattie is very old and hard-of-hearing and can't talk on the phone. It seemed simpler to go to her. Besides, Marsalis is playing at the Tabernacle tonight. And it's a lovely day for a ferry ride. All good reasons."

Fergus perked up. "Who is this Marsalis, and what game does he play? Will there be wagers?"

She laughed. "The game he plays is jazz. He—oh, gosh, jazz came after you, I forgot. You're in for a treat, Fergus. The Tabernacle is a lovely place for an outdoor performance. It's in the middle of what used to be a huge camp meeting ground. Church folks from all over the country came to the tents to preach and pray. I'm surprised you never heard of it in your day."

"It sounds like what we used to know as Cottage City. But ye call it Oak Bluffs?"

"Ah, you're right. That name came later. The tents

are long gone, by the way, replaced by tiny gingerbread cottages. It's all very charming now."

"There's no more preaching? No more praying?"

"How can there be? Like it or not, times have changed, Fergus. These are resort properties now. Island real estate is very expensive."

He snorted. "I can't think why. It's damned hard to get to."

"Not the way it once was. Besides all the ferries, there are planes that fly back and forth, at least to the bigger islands."

"Ah, that's right, planes. When will *we* fly the Friendly Skies? That seems to me one hell of a lot safer than this," he said, sticking his head out the window and swearing at a snappy little Celica that was squeezing them.

Emily smiled but did not answer. It was dawning on her that Fergus would probably never know the thrill of air travel. They'd talked about how much time he had, and though he didn't really know, he felt sure it couldn't be that long. It was one of the things she'd worried about the night before: not devoting enough time to Hessiah's murder. She was thinking about taking a temporary leave from her job. But besides jeopardizing her career, she'd certainly be running the risk of foreclosure; her savings were piddling.

But if time ran out—if suddenly Fergus got dragged away—she'd never forgive herself.

"A penny for yer thoughts," Fergus said after a while.

"I wish I could charge more for them," she answered with a sigh. And then they were parking the Corolla in the ferry lot, and she was spared the effort of having to explain. She went in to the ticket office to pay her fare. It was still early in the season and there was no crowd, which she was glad to see. She'd be able to arrange her deck chair away from everyone else and reduce the risk of being seen chatting with air.

Emily turned to leave, but before she got out the door, one of the waiting passengers lowered his newspaper from in front of him and gave her the shock of her life.

"Lee!"

He stood up and folded his paper under his arm. "Mornin'. *Thought* I might run into you."

His smile she recognized, but nothing else. He was wearing well-worn jeans, a bright blue Chicago Cubs baseball jacket, and a black duckbill cap that said "Pennzoil." He looked like many things—Little League coach, True Value store manager, free-lance plumber—but he did not look like a United States senator.

"Nice threads," she remarked, hiding behind irony. Really, it was too much, having him pop up like this. Her heart was still thundering; Fergus himself hadn't given her such a start the first time he'd showed up.

Lee's blue eyes had an ironic cast of their own. "You laugh, but this lets me come and go as I please."

Which must be very important to a hit-and-run type like you, she thought, but she kept it to herself. "Off to the Vineyard?" she asked sweetly. She had no idea why he was following her. If he thought he was going to back her into some pal's cottage for an afternoon quickie, he certainly had another thought coming. She wasn't born yesterday, even if she was born in New Hampshire.

"I have a house on the Vineyard, near West Chop," he said.

Aha!

"Today is my mother's seventy-first birthday, and the family is gathering there to celebrate."

Ah.

"Are you traveling alone?" he asked in the polite tones of someone bumping into an acquaintance on the *QE 2.*

"In a manner of speaking."

"Well, good. We can sit together."

Just like that, "We can sit together." How incredibly presumptuous.

"All right," she answered. (What else could she say? "I can't, the ghost and I have to go over our clues"?)

They walked out of the terminal together and sauntered over to the boarding area, where a dozen passengers had already lined up. The ticket taker took their fares with a big good-morning grin. "Beautiful day, Senator. Goin' sailin'?"

"I'm hoping," he answered pleasantly as they walked on by.

"Real good disguise," she murmured to Lee, smiling in spite of herself.

"Okay, so it's not perfect," he said equably. "Nothing ever is. Speaking of threads," he added, "you look very—"

"I know, nice," she said, wrinkling her nose. She was wearing a pale floral print skirt and a white linen blouse, just the thing for interviewing elderly ladies on the Vineyard. She'd also brought along a cardigan and a straw hat with wide ribbons to protect her from the sun on the ferry ride over.

Lee looked a little puzzled. "Do you have a problem with looking nice?"

God, she was being a boor. She reminded herself of Fiona. "No, of course not," she answered, truly sorry for the prolonged snit she was displaying. It wasn't *his* fault that women up and down the coast were after him.

"Nice will do fine," she answered in a far more gracious voice.

They found two chairs on the foredeck and dragged them a little away from the others. Lee offered to get coffee, Emily accepted, and he went off. While he was gone she remembered—almost as an afterthought—Fergus. Fergus! She jumped up. Where was he? She half expected him to be in the shadow of the bridge deck, sulking. *Don't be stupid, Emily,* she told herself. *Fergus isn't the one with a history of sulking;* you *are.* She sat back down, reassured. "Don't fall overboard, Fergus," she whispered to the air.

Lee returned and presented her with a Saran-wrapped Thing and a cup of coffee, then sat down and stretched his legs out in front of him.

Emily felt the rumble of the *Islander*'s engines beneath her, revving up for departure. Gulls squealed overhead, reeling and diving at the fingertips of a young boy near the rail who was holding up bread crusts for them. The sun was ready to do business with anyone who asked; several day-trippers were frantically positioning their chairs, as if there might not be enough rays to go around. Ahead of them lay the sound—blue, sparkling, enchanting—and beyond that, one of the jewels in New England's crown, Martha's Vineyard.

"It's good to be out here," Lee said in a voice that sounded utterly relieved.

She murmured an agreeable assent. He didn't seem to waste words when he was pleased; she liked that, and it was only later that she realized why.

"I have a confession to make," he said, lifting his cup from the deck and notching a little sipping hole in the plastic cap. "I was here in time for the seven-fifteen."

"And you didn't take it? What were you waiting for?" she asked without thinking. "An in-flight movie?"

He took a tentative sip of the piping hot coffee as he watched the gulls wheel and beg. "Nope."

Her heart poised in anticipation, fluttering in her breast. But then she thought, no. She would not ask, she would not ask. Let him find some other creature to beg him for treats. She let his unspoken compliment drop, like untouched bread. But it was hard.

It was even harder not to look at him, not to drink in the sheer presence of him. In his Pennzoil cap he looked downright fatherly, an all-around guy who by now should have two or three kids. What was he waiting for? There was no one out there who could top Nicole. *Give it up, dope!* she wanted to cry. *Nicole is gone. Settle for someone else! Time's awastin'!*

Time was always awasting.

"So what's the Vineyard assignment?" he asked after a bit. "Or can't you say?"

She had been preparing for the question since his phone call the night before; it was bound to come. There was this vast uncharted territory between them haunted by an impatient ghost, and Emily was only just finding her way around in it. How could she possibly invite Lee in yet? The first time she'd tried, on the night they made love, it ended in their going their separate ways.

She took the plunge anyway and said simply, "Hessiah Talbot."

"Oh. Her," Lee said with a kind of sinking sigh. He looked away, toward the treacherous channel with its tide-bound buoys and swirling eddies. His face became a study in gloom.

"I'm doing a feature for the *Journal* about Newarth, where the murder took place. There's a delightful librarian there who gave me an angle for the story. She says there's a curse on the town because of it, that Newarth's decline began when the girl was strangled."

"So the information you . . . acquired . . . about this girl Hessiah Talbot turned out to be true?"

"Oh, sure," Emily said breezily. "And with the local downturn in the economy, the curse angle fits right in."

His face began to brighten beneath the Pennzoil cap. "In other words, this piece is *really* about the economic decline of a small town, and the Talbot murder's just a convenient hook to hang it on?" In other words, he was saying between the lines, there was no Fergus.

The change in him left Emily stunned. He looked as if a heavy weight had been rolled off his shoulders. His face broke into a broad, captivating grin, followed by an expression so tender, so intense that Emily would have said just about anything to keep it there.

Which is basically what she did. "Yes. There's nothing more to it than that," she said, staring into her coffee. "It's a story of decline."

In that single, bald-faced lie, Emily discovered exactly how far her feelings for Lee had gone. Not only was she willing to take a number for him, but she was also willing to deny the existence of the ghost she knew he'd never be able to see. What else could she do? It was obvious that Fergus stood between them. There were other obstacles, too—Gloria and all the rest—but the big one, the first one, was Fergus. Emily was as committed to helping Fergus as ever, but she saw no real point in saying so to Lee Alden.

There was one thing she did want to say to him, however. "I've never said a word about your coming to my place or about Kimberly or the séance or any of it," she said, glancing around furtively for eavesdroppers.

He took her big straw hat from the back of her chair and placed it gently on her head. "Sun's getting high," he explained with a tender smile. "You're talking about the *Newsweek* bit. Don't worry about it. It comes with the territory. It's nothing new." He laid the ribbons across her shoulders for her to tie. "It never occurred to me to think you were behind that."

She took up the pale green ribbons and tied them under her chin. "Boyd Strom sounds very serious," she said. "But why would he take *you* on? He can't have a chance."

"You flatter me, mademoiselle. Strom will take me on if he thinks he can win. The man plays serious hardball; I have no doubt he'll give me a good run for the money."

Which means one false move from me and down you tumble, she thought with dismay. Her face must have showed her alarm because he smiled and said, "Have I said that you look adorable in that hat?"

"N-n-no," she stammered. "I'm not the adorable type."

"Which makes you all the more adorable. Emily, not to worry. I'll fight the good fight, and with any luck I'll win. I'm not all that concerned," he added seriously. "I have no real skeletons in my closet."

But I've got a real ghost in mine. She should run, not walk, from this man if she really cared for him. Yet she stayed, caught in his spell, snatching these few moments in the sun with him. They talked of innocent things, of family and summer, and all too soon they were rounding the sandy bluffs of West Chop, on their way into the port of Vineyard Haven.

"Why didn't you take the ferry directly to Oak Bluffs?" he asked as they watched the ferry back down smoothly along the pilons.

"This one runs earlier," she answered, intensely aware that his arm was touching hers as they leaned idly against the rail. "I wanted to get my interview done in plenty of time to have supper and see the performance tonight at the Tabernacle."

"You'll never make the last ferry."

"I know. I thought I'd give myself a treat and stay at a bed and breakfast somewhere on the island," she said, holding up her canvas bag.

"But you don't know where?" He frowned, then said, "This is crazy. I have a house with half a dozen guest rooms, and you plan to wander around the island like some carpetbagger. Please. Flag down a cabbie, and come to my place. They all know where it is. I'll leave a light burning."

"Oh, I couldn't," she said, aghast at the thought. "You'll have a house full of family and friends and I'm going to go tapping on strange doors and climbing over sleeping bodies till I find an empty bed? It's an awful intrusion."

"You're right," he said suddenly. "Come to the party instead. It's an informal affair. The kids swim and play ball and end up pitching tents on the lawn, and none of 'em sleep in the house anyway. My mother would love to have your company. And so, needless to say, would I. Come." He tugged gently at the ribbon under her hat, then slid the back of his finger along the line of her chin. "Come."

What an offer: a weekend with the most desirable man she'd ever met, surrounded by a slew of spoiled kids and snobby adults with everything in common except her. Emily teetered, then tottered. "No," she said at last. "It's very kind of you, but I think . . . not."

"Don't think, Emily," he said in a low, compelling voice. "Just come. Wherever you are, whatever the time, just get in the cab and come."

They were in the way now of departing passengers. Emily let herself be nudged into falling in line, and Lee stepped in beside her. At the bottom of the gang-plank she said, "I have some things I have to do"—she meant, solve Hessiah Talbot's murder—"before I can ever come."

"Fine, do them!" he said, brushing her cheek with a kiss. Then they parted, and Emily was left dizzily thinking that she ought to have made herself more clear.

The Oak Bluffs Home for the Aged was a stately Queen Anne with a view across Ocean Park of the Atlantic. Originally it had been a home for retired seamen, but a decade ago it had gone coed. Hattie Dunbart, who was the widow of a merchant mariner, was the first woman ever to hang her hat there. She knew how to play pinochle, and she liked the smell of a pipe, so the men agreed to lower the rope and let her in. After that other women followed, and now the home sheltered seven members of each sex, all of them connected to the sea in some way.

"Hattie's a tough little bird," the director explained to Emily in an affectionate tone as she led her through a series of pleasant and old-fashioned rooms on the ground floor. "She's had a series of strokes which've left her somewhat impaired. But if she wants to, she'll hear you. If she feels like it, she'll answer you. And if she likes you, she'll even tell the truth."

Emily smiled nervously as the director walked up to a tiny woman with a wispy crown of white hair who was seated in a wheelchair facing a spectacular bay-windowed view of the ocean. She wore a dark blue rayon dress with a high ruffled collar and long sleeves, and she had a yellow afghan folded over her knees. Her hands pulled constantly at the edges of the afghan, as if she were afraid it would slip from her lap and leave her in perishing cold.

The director introduced Emily to Hattie and then pointed to the porch, which was wide and white and filled with potted red geraniums. "Would you like us to wheel you out onto the piazza?" she asked loudly.

Hattie waved her away with a withered hand. "Shoo, shoo! What're you thinking of? It's colder'n a witch's tit out there."

The director smiled and shook her finger gently at Hattie and left. Emily took a seat in a Boston rocker whose arms had been rubbed bare of their black paint and said, "This is a wonderful place. You're so near the sea."

"What pony?" Hattie asked with a blank look, picking at her yellow afghan.

"No, I said, 'You're so near the sea.' The *sea,*" Emily repeated, gesturing toward the ocean.

"What about the sea?" Hattie asked at last. "It killed my husband. What do you want? I'm tired. *Shoo.*"

"Oh, Mrs. Dunbart, please don't send me away. I won't take much of your time—"

"How should I know the time?" she snapped. "I don't have a watch."

Emily shook her head. "No, no. I only wanted to ask you about the necklace—"

"Tom wasn't reckless! Everyone says that, but he wasn't!"

"No, wait. Here." Emily lifted her chin and held up the rose crystal away from her throat. "Do you recognize this?"

Hattie squinted in Emily's direction but said nothing. After a minute she said, "What?"

Fearing that she'd be tossed out soon, Emily shouted, *"Did this belong to you?"*

Hattie stared at Emily blankly and then said weakly, "I'm cold. Get out. Shoo."

Emily could see that she was distressing the elderly woman. It was pointless to pursue this. She stood up with a contrite smile on her face. "I'm sorry I troubled you," she said.

And then she noticed the eyeglasses tethered to the side of Hattie's wheelchair. On a hunch she unhooked them from their place and handed them to Hattie, who put them on automatically. Emily leaned over, propping one hand on her knee, and held up the necklace as close to Hattie as she could. *"Was this yours?"* she asked, forming the words carefully with her lips.

Hattie adjusted the spectacles on her small, aquiline nose and peered closely. Then the map of wrinkles that made up her face rearranged themselves into a wonderful, happy grin. "My necklace!" she cried. "I thought it was gone!"

She reached up to tweak her hearing aid and said, "Where did you find it?"

"I bought it," Emily screamed, and poor Hattie clapped her hands over her ears.

"Don't shout! I'm not deaf!" she said, wincing.

Emily lowered her voice to normal and explained how the necklace had ended up with her.

"That's exactly when I was in the hospital," Hattie said, exasperated. "My niece must have sold it at the Penny Sale. What a scatterbrain she is! There was a box in my closet full of things I planned to put out for the sale. But I'm *damned* sure that wasn't in it. Well, I must buy it back. How much did you pay?" She reached under the afghan and with shaking hands brought out a worn leather change purse.

"Oh, dear," Emily said apologetically. "Please, I need the necklace just for a while yet. But when I'm done, I'll bring it back to you. I really do promise." Emily tried not to think about the cost of that promise as she said, "For now can you tell me anything—it's so important—about the necklace?"

Having been reassured that the necklace would soon be hers again, Hattie relaxed, and she and Emily had a nice little chat, helped along by the lemon tea the director herself brought them.

"My uncle discovered that necklace in 1910, the year I was born, hidden between the walls of his house," Hattie began. "Uncle Eric was enlarging a dressing room so that my mother, who was about to have me, could live with his wife and him while my father was at sea. He was a good man, Uncle Eric; my mother always said so. It's just too bad that he lost everything in the Depression."

Hattie took a sip of lemon tea and went on. "He gave my mother the necklace at my baptism. Said if it weren't for me, he'd never have known about it anyway. My mother left it to me when she died fifty years later. And that's all I know about it. Except that it ain't worth nothin'. Jeweler told me that." She gave Emily a look only New England Yankees understand: a little bland, a little sorry, a little shrewd.

"What an interesting story," Emily said, hoping to find out more. "Your uncle sounds like a kind man. How did he lose everything?"

"I told you," Hattie snapped. "In the Depression. It was bound to happen, with or without the crash. Uncle Eric was the kind of man that gave away everything that wasn't nailed down. He and Aunt Alice took in boarders, but half the time nobody paid. It was Uncle Eric's *father* that had all the ambition. That would be Great-uncle Henry. I never knew him myself, but my mother told me she distinctly remembered someone toasting 'the next governor of the state of Massachusetts' at Christmas one year. Course, Great-uncle Henry Abbott never did make it to the governor's office."

Abbott. The remembered name leaped up at Emily from the yellow pages of one of her legal pads. "Henry Abbott? *Mayor* Abbott, could you mean?"

"Oh, yes," said Hattie matter-of-factly, "he was mayor, all right. Mayor of Newarth. Then he got too big for his breeches and ran for governor. Now tell me, who'd elect a small-town mayor to govern a great big state like Massachusetts? But that was Great-uncle Henry all over, my mother used to say. Always wantin' what he couldn't have. Always hobnobbin' with the rich. There never was *that* kind of money in our family, even before the Depression."

Emily was now in overdrive. Mayor Abbott had played cards at Talbot Manor every Thursday night. Fergus had said so. There was no question that he must have known Hessiah Talbot. The question was, where did his son Eric and the necklace fit in? "Did Mayor Abbott ever offer any theory about how the necklace ended up between the walls of his son's house?"

"Great-uncle Henry was long dead by the time I was born," Hattie said. For the first time since Emily had first set eyes on her, the frail old woman seemed uncomfortable. Her head shook slightly as she said almost angrily, "Great-uncle Henry killed himself, the fool. He was forty-five. Wasted half his life. Just threw it away." Hattie shivered and pulled the yellow afghan up higher on her lap.

"Do you remember anything about your uncle Eric's house?" Emily asked softly, partly to change the subject.

"Not much. I was three when we moved away from Newarth, and we never went back. It was a big old house, expensive to heat. Uncle Eric never could have afforded to live there without taking in boarders. I sometimes wonder how Great-uncle Henry managed to keep the place up before he shot himself. Yet they said he lived like royalty."

Emily's eyes opened wide. "Do you mean the necklace was found between the walls of *Mayor Abbott*'s house? That it was *his* house you were born in?"

"Wasn't his house then. It was Uncle Eric's. I told you."

Hattie was tiring, that was obvious. Her head was beginning to droop. She was clearly losing interest in the subject. Emily replaced her china teacup carefully in its saucer and stood up. "I'm very, very grateful to you for seeing me, Mrs. Dunbart," she said. "And I want you to know that I will bring the necklace back to you as soon as I've finished writing the story I'm working on."

"That would be nice," Hattie said wearily. Her head drooped ever closer to the ruffled collar of her dark blue dress. "Now go away . . . shoo . . . I'm cold."

By the time Emily gathered up her canvas bag to leave, Hattie had fallen into a nap. Emily tucked the yellow afghan gently into the sides of the wheelchair and tiptoed away, leaving Hattie like a small, thin bird perched in a thicket, huddled against the coming snow.

14

Emily found a quiet bench nearby in Ocean Park and tried to summon up Fergus. He was a ghost, not a genie in a bottle, she understood that. Nonetheless, she was using up *her* time and *her* money on *his* problem, and it seemed to her that the least he could do was to be there when she called. "Fergus. *Fergus!*" she hissed from her park bench. Three young boys on mountain bikes pedaled past and stared; she heard their snickers as they burned rubber getting away.

She had no idea where she'd lost Fergus. Had he even been on the ferry? Did the forty-five-mile rule really work? Was it all—after all—a dream? She gazed across the dried grass of the treeless park at a benign ocean curling gently on a slender strip of beach. It was a beautiful day for a swim . . . or a sail . . . or a garden party. It was a beautiful day for just about anything except sitting alone and hissing at air.

The heck with him. She whipped out a small notebook and began jotting down details of her interview with Hattie Dunbart before she forgot them. It had been a great day's work. Emily trusted Hattie's memory even if the director didn't. And Hattie had remembered two very critical pieces of information: Mayor Abbott had owned the house where the necklace was eventually found, and Mayor Abbott had committed suicide. Why would someone kill himself? Either he was fatally depressed, or he carried a heavy load of guilt. If only Hattie had known the address. It would have saved Emily the trouble of wading through years of recorded deeds, which was next on her list. Maybe Abbott's descendants still lived in the house; maybe they had even more useful information than Hattie.

Emily closed her notebook, put the cap back on her Bic pen, and put them away. Her chores on the Vineyard were done. Now it was time to do a bit of shopping, and find an inn, and have something to eat before the twilight concert.

"Fergus . . . Fergus, come *on.*"

There was no response. Emily wandered through all the rainy-day shops, priced some rooms, treated herself to clam cakes and an ice-cream cone, and still —still!—there was no Fergus. He was around, she was convinced of it. But it brought home the frightening possibility that at any moment he could be called back to Noplace.

Monday, first thing, Newarth City Hall, she told herself.

But that was Monday, and this was Saturday. It was still a long time until twilight, and Emily was feeling alone and out of sorts. What was the point of planning a day on an island if there was no one to share it with? What was the point of doing *anything,* good or bad, if there was no one to share it with?

Uh-oh. Blame it on Fergus, but this was very new

thinking. *You* like *your singleness,* she reminded herself. *It's efficient. Remember?*

For a moment Emily really did try to remember. Then something snapped, and she hopped into a standing cab. "Lee Alden's place, please. He told me you'll know where it is."

"That I do," the cabbie said as he swung out into traffic.

Emily didn't really come to her senses until the cabbie pulled off State Road onto a narrow lane, and by then, of course, it was too late. The cab stopped in front of a white rose arbor buried under riotous climbing pink roses that nearly knocked her down with their scent. *Fergus would know the name of the rose,* she thought as she paid the cab. Right now she desperately missed him and his common-folk ways.

She paused for courage under the arbor and stared through the full-moon opening at an exquisitely proportioned Greek Revival house, crisp and white and trimmed with black shutters, and set off to perfection by a perennial border bursting with yellows and pinks and whites. A towering oak tree covered the south end of the property with restful shade, and a row of shivering poplars hid the house from its neighbor to the north. It was less than a mansion, much more than a house. It spoke of good taste and sound judgment, and Emily knew that whoever had it built a century and a half ago was a man who knew exactly what he wanted.

Emily lifted the latch on the arbor gate and with a pounding heart started over the flagstone walk. The front door was open and she could see, through its screen, that it lined up with a set of French doors at the back of the house that led onto a lawn where people were gathered. What could have possessed her to think she'd be welcome among them? She decided to cut and run; it wasn't too late. She turned to flee and was startled by two children, a boy and a girl of about eight or nine, popping out from behind a butterfly bush.

"She's here!" the boy cried out to the company, although no one could possibly hear him. "I'll take your bag," he said to Emily, relieving her of the canvas carryall. "Uncle Lee said to be on the lookout for you, and I was!"

"No, *I* saw her first!" the blond girl said, with little hopping jumps in place. "Can I carry your hat? You're Emily," she said, the way she might if Emily were Santa Claus. "And I'm Jane. And my brother isn't Dick; he's Richard. Everyone has to call him Richard or he gets mad. This is so pretty; can I try it on? But I won't try it on if you don't want me to. So if you say no, you don't have to feel bad."

"Jane never stops talking," Richard said with disgust. "If you want to say something, you have to wobble your hands in front of her face, like *this,*" he added, flipping them back and forth in front of his sister the way brothers have a way of doing.

Emily, overwhelmed by the welcoming committee, laughed and said, "I'm pleased to meet you both, and yes, Jane, you may wear the hat, and thank you for the advice, Richard." She wobbled her hands back and forth in front of his eyes. "Did I do it right?" she asked innocently.

Richard stopped in his tracks, gave her a quick and somewhat suspicious appraisal, and then burst into a grin. "Yeah. Like that. I'll take this bag to your room and show you where it is."

"No, *I'll* show her where her room is."

"No, you can show her where to freshen up."

"Okay! No, but first you have to meet everyone," Jane insisted, turning to Emily. "Or would you rather freshen up? Your room almost has its own bathroom. Yours is the best room; you can see Woods Hole from it. Only grown-ups get to use it. Uncle Lee says when I'm fourteen I can sleep in it, but not Richard because he'll always be a pig."

She made an awful face at her brother, and he waved his hands furiously in front of her nose, and before Emily knew it, they were being descended on by half a dozen more children in the two- to six-year-old range, galloping across the rolling lawn. Behind them, at a slower pace, came a slender and still quite beautiful woman leaning gently on the arm of the man who had told Emily, "Don't think. Just come."

She saw at once that Lee Alden was in his element. He seemed neither besieged, as he had at the fund raiser, nor tense, as he had on the ferry. He'd changed from the workaday clothes he'd worn on the ferry to a pair of twill khakis and a white shirt with the sleeves rolled back. His blue tie was loose and flapping uselessly in the sea breeze; his hands were in his pockets. The look in his eyes was filled with satisfaction, the smile on his face relaxed and tender with love for the ones he so obviously held dear.

Emily paused spellbound and waited, her lips parted with a greeting that seemed unnecessary to deliver. The wind whipped her skirt around her legs and blew her big straw hat off little Jane's head; the girl let go of Emily's hand with a laughing screech and raced her brother in hot pursuit of the cartwheeling object. The toddlers followed the example of the rest of the children and cried, "Emly, Emly, Emly" over and over, jerking their short, fat arms excitedly, oblivious to what an "Emly" was but drooling with anticipation anyway.

Emily was surrounded. The kids were everywhere, jumping and tripping and tugging at her skirt, shouting their names—Sarah and Will and Becky and Missy and Rob—and making polite conversation between adults a laughable concept.

"What a wonderful welcome!" Emily cried over the tops of their curly heads.

"That's because I told 'em you were bringing Milky Ways for everyone," Lee said, his eyes dancing with blue light.

Emily looked her dismay, and Lee laughed and said, "Mother, may I present Miss Emily Bowditch," in his best prep school manner. "Emily, this is my mother, Margaret Alden."

Mrs. Alden tapped her son's forearm in tender reproach and extended a firm hand to Emily. "He's an awful tease. Just ignore him; we all do," she said with a warm smile.

Emily nodded, her eyes just catching Lee's in a glance, and said, "Many happy returns, ma'am." She saw in Mrs. Alden's violet-blue gaze the most basic message of all: *Don't be afraid; we will not harm you.* Emily smiled, flushing slightly, and took in the hazy panorama of Vineyard Sound and the bluff-marked islands to the north. "What a magical place this is," she said shyly.

One of the little ones—Becky or Missy—wrapped her arms around Lee's knee and asked plaintively, "Is Emly gon' do magic now?"

Lee looked down at the moppet clinging to his leg and said, "In a little while, sweetheart. Run and show Emily how well you can swing."

The child ran off, accompanied by two or three other little show-offs. "Magic?" Emily repeated as the three adults made their way toward the brick terrace adjoining the house.

"I told them that a beautiful fairy princess named Emily was coming," Lee said as he held out a chair for his mother, "and that she would bring magic with her."

"But I left my wand and stardust in the cab," Emily protested, feigning the dismay she really felt.

"I for one think you're quite charming, even without the wand," interjected Mrs. Alden.

"Which is what I told the kids," Lee agreed. "Come with me, Emily, and we'll scare up my sister. Excuse us, Mother."

Lee took Emily inside the house, fending off little clinging creatures with secret whispered promises that all seemed to end with "later."

When they were alone, Lee turned to her. "I'm glad you came," he said in his quiet way.

"I'm glad you asked me," she answered in kind.

"You look very nice," he said with his gently ironic smile. "Still."

He was giving new meaning to the expression "Less is more." Yet she wouldn't have traded his simple compliments for all the diamonds in Amsterdam. There was something in his voice, something in his eyes. Nine simple words, and they sent a thrill that rolled over her and through her and set her very soul vibrating. Oh, she had it bad, all right. She was just now realizing *how* bad.

She stood there in confusion, wanting him to do something, not quite knowing how to make it happen, stalling for time. "Gee . . . I . . . this . . ."

He brushed her lips with a feather-light kiss. "I know, darling. Me, too." Then he took her hand and said softly, "Come meet the rest of the clan."

They passed through a series of rooms bright with sunlight and chintz and needlepoint rugs scattered on wide-board floors. Fireplaces were everywhere. Even now she smelled the sooty, sweet scent of burned-up pine; apparently nights on the Vineyard were cool. The furnishings, a comfortable blend of Federal and country, were not exactly in museum condition. Everything had been kicked, moved, sat on, stood on, rubbed, polished, pushed, shoved, and rearranged until it fitted the house like an omelet in a pan. There were no hard edges left anywhere, only soft, worn, loved ones.

The kitchen itself was a delight, functional and unadorned, with unmatched pieces of scrubbed pine and a massive butcher-block island. There was a view through six-light windows of an herb garden to the west and the hazy blue sound to the north. The three women who were cleaning up and setting out a birthday cake had obviously done it together before. When Lee and Emily walked through the door, they all looked up as one.

"Just in time!" said the oldest, a plump woman in a housedress and an apron who was lining up cups and saucers on a massive tray. "You carry this right out there, Lee. Your mother likes her coffee *hot,* and you're just dawdlin', I see." She gave Emily a shrewd but not unfriendly look.

The second woman was about Lee's age, beautifully dressed in wrinkle-free linen and quiet gold jewelry. "It's true, Lee. Just because we taxpayers pay you money to sit around and do nothing all week doesn't mean we'll let you get away with it on weekends. You heard Inez. Move along." She gave him a gently ironic look that Emily had seen before, through eyes that matched his shade of blue.

The third woman was in her mid-thirties, dressed in white slacks and a boat-neck striped shirt. Her blond hair was pulled back in a ponytail, and she had an absolutely dazzling smile. "We ran out of pink candles, Lee; I had to add blue. It makes it so obvious that I've gone into a third box," she said, making a funny, guilty face at Emily.

"That's no problem," Lee said, sneaking a bit of frosting from a side flower. "Mother can take it. Emily, I'd like you to meet Inez, the real boss behind our operation, and my sister Grace, and my sister-in-law Hildie. If you're wondering about a pecking order, it goes: Inez, Mother, Grace, and then poor Hildie." He licked the frosting off his finger and wrapped an arm around his sister-in-law and kissed the top of her head. "Hildie's been in the family for only eight years, you see."

Emily shook hands all around and said, "It seems to be a happy arrangement."

Lee seemed almost surprised. "You're right. It is." He gave her another one of those looks, the ones that made her dizzy, and said, "If you want to wash up, I'll rustle up a sandwich for you."

Emily begged off but took him up on his offer of a bathroom. As she walked out of the kitchen and down the hall she heard Hildie whisper, "All in favor? Show of hands."

When she came out, Lee was waiting for her around the corner in the library. It was a man's room, fitted out in tufted leather and smelling faintly of tobacco. On the wall were seascapes in oil and a watercolor by Winslow Homer. Lee was slouched in an easy chair, staring thoughtfully at a cluster of framed photos on a small library table next to him. When he saw Emily, he went to her. "You were a hit," he said, tracing his fingertips across the line of her cheek.

"You folks are easy to please," Emily quipped.

"We're an impulsive bunch, it's true," he said, which is not what she really wanted him to say. He looked at her sideways as they walked out onto the terrace. "But we know what we like."

Two other couples had joined Mrs. Alden on the terrace by now. They were old, old neighbors whose names Emily promptly forgot after being introduced to them. After a minute or two the smaller children began to assemble as if by primal instinct. The French doors were thrown open, and Jane and Richard came through with fierce expressions on their faces, walking in life-or-death synchronism with a blazing sheet cake between them. Somehow they managed to shift the cake from the palms of their hands onto the glass patio table—to a round of relieved applause—and then the birthday song began, cheerful and high-pitched, after which Mrs. Alden and eight little helpers extinguished the flames. There was more applause, and a certain amount of infighting over who got to pull the candles and suck off the frosting. Hildie got it all on video.

The cake was cut and passed around, and the grown-ups chatted easily and amiably over coffee. Emily was neither the focus of the conversation nor ignored. The talk was general enough for her to join in—overdevelopment and the dismal real estate situation, for example—and when it wasn't, someone always made the effort to bring her up to speed. They were, in short, perfectly delightful company, and she wondered why she'd dreaded coming.

After a while Mrs. Alden stood up and said, "Before it gets dark, let me show you the peonies."

It wasn't an invitation so much as a friendly subpoena. Emily saw Lee exchange glances with his sister Grace, and that, more than anything, frightened her. If this was a cross-examination, she'd blow it for sure. She smiled nervously and fell in beside Mrs. Alden, who took her around to the front of the house to view a bed of exotic tree peonies soaking up the last of the day's gold light.

"I do have a favorite, and this is it," Mrs. Alden said as she hovered over an exquisite, subtle flower the color of a Persian Bokhara. "It was here when I was a girl. My grandfather brought it back with him from the Orient."

Emily smiled and murmured something nice, but she was thinking, *My God. Even their flowers have longer bloodlines than I do.* She was afraid to point to any one of the peonies as her own favorite. What if the one she liked was too pink or too common or, God forbid, a recent hybrid? She wanted Fergus and his commonsense approach: If it looked good and smelled good, it must be good.

They walked back and forth a bit, with Emily afraid to have an opinion, until finally Mrs. Alden said, "You know, I've been wondering whether my son would ever bring someone home after, well, Nicole. You do know about Nicole, don't you?"

Emily nodded, and Mrs. Alden went on. "The accident completely shattered Lee. You probably know that he was thinking of resigning his seat in the Senate. We all were so very, very worried about him. He's much more introspective than my other son. Charles is in Europe again this week; he's in sales."

She plucked a brown leaf here and there as she spoke. "But Lee is an idealist, making him perfect for public office but not so very adept at finding, well, someone. You do understand me?"

Emily nodded hesitantly. She had no idea what Mrs. Alden meant. Was she warning Emily away? Was she saying, "Hang in there, he'll come around"? Or was she softening the inevitable blow to come from him?

"I'm glad we had this little chat," Mrs. Alden said

in a kindly way. She reached into the pocket of her challis skirt and took out a pair of pruning shears. "Now. Which ones would you like for your room tonight?"

Emily took a deep breath and pointed to a pale silvery lavender clump, even though she would have preferred the bright crimson ones farther down the line.

"Ah. Mystery. A wise choice," Mrs. Alden said, sounding pleased.

15

When the mosquitoes came out, everyone went in. Inez had set up a small buffet of quiches and cold cuts and crusty French bread. By now all the children were hungry again, and Emily—who was becoming good at moving freely with a small child attached to each leg—helped Hildie and Grace feed their brood. The kids had seized on Emily as one of their own, while Hildie and Grace marveled at the strength of the bond. Emily laughed and said something about being new blood, and Lee came around and made a big thing about biting her on the back of her neck, which made her blush. She saw Hildie and Grace smile at each other, and that made her blush even more.

After the late snack Grace and Hildie began rounding up the littlest ones for bed, but they broke free and ran laughing in jerky, flat-footed steps to Emily, and hid behind her skirt. Very quickly it turned into a game, and the children became more keyed up than ever.

"Hopeless! They're nowhere near ready for sleep," said Hildie to Grace. "We've got to get them out of the living room. All right, you monsters," she said, addressing the horde, "I'm throwing you all in a cage together. Uncle Lee will put a television in your room, and you all can watch videos."

An earsplitting cheer went up, followed by a stampede toward one of the bedrooms. Hildie winked at Emily. "Half of 'em will be asleep before today's tape plays through. We'll peel the bodies off one by one and redistribute them to their own beds later."

"You spoil them, Hildie," said Grace mildly.

But it was clear that Grace was ready for a little peace and quiet and some adult conversation. Emily had learned that Grace's husband, a political consultant, was also away a great deal. Didn't anyone work nine to five for the telephone company anymore? How did these women cope? Obviously, Emily decided, they banded together the way they were doing now. Why not? It worked for the Kennedy family.

Lee stole the nineteen-inch television from the living room and staggered off with it. A moment later Missy—adorable and shy—came out and approached Emily. A couple of the others hung back behind her, peeking from the hall and giggling.

With her thumb hanging comfortably from her lower teeth Missy said, "We want *you* to watch wif us."

Flattered, Emily overrode Grace's objections and Hildie's apologies and let herself be dragged among the bunk beds. Lee was just hooking up the television, and Richard and Jane came in each with an armload of videotapes.

"First we watch the birthday tape," announced Jane with her usual precision. "Then *I* pick the next one. Then Richard picks the next one. Then we go one by one according to age."

Perhaps because Lee was in the room, Richard decided to defend his manhood. "We're twins!" he said. "How come you get to go first if it's according to age?"

"Because I was born twenty-three minutes sooner and because *J* comes before *R*," said Jane. "Uncle Lee, you sit there," she said, pointing to one end of a bunk bed, "because you're biggest. Then Emily sits next to you. Then Will, then Becky, no, Missy, no, wait, then Sarah . . ."

But Richard had jumped the gun and popped in the birthday tape, and all the littlest ones plopped down on the floor in front of the screen except Missy, who climbed onto Emily's lap. "Oh, never mind," said Jane when she saw herself on camera. She fell to her knees in front of the screen and studied her performance with a keen and critical eye.

The tape was a great success. Missy fell asleep in Emily's lap before it was over, and Becky on the floor soon after. Everyone agreed that Grammy did a pretty good job with the candles but that she couldn't have done it alone. But that was true last year, too. Emily was appalled by the number of times she was recorded sneaking looks at Lee—until she saw that the camera had also caught Lee in a long, serene gaze at her while she was talking with Grace.

Sitting on the bunk bed with sweet-smelling Missy in her lap, leaning slightly into Lee's supporting arm behind her, Emily was well aware that she hadn't been so completely, simply happy since before her mother's death. Maybe it was because she'd let herself lose touch with her own family. She hadn't been home to New Hampshire since Christmas. After her mother died, she'd burrowed more deeply into her work and hidden there, like a frightened cub alone in a cave. Today was the first time she'd dared creep a little way out toward the warm sun.

Hildie poked her head in the room just as the tape was finishing. "How did it turn out?" she asked Lee in a hushed voice as she gently lifted up the first fallen soldier she came across.

Lee smiled and said, "Parts of it are downright inspiring." He leaned his arm into Emily's back in a nudging, comical way, sending her to the brink of embarrassed tears.

Hildie shifted the sleepy weight in her arms. "I do possess some small talent, I think. Maybe I'll chuck all this and run away to Hollywood."

"Mom-*mee,*" said Sarah, distressed, "that's not *fun*-ny."

"Oh, Sarah, you know I'd take you with me," Hildie said, smiling. "No one else would keep you."

Jane and Richard were deep in conference behind Hildie, deciding on the next tape. "Let's try," whispered Jane, and Richard slipped the tape into the recorder. It opened on a scene very much like this afternoon's, except that all the characters were dressed in shorts and tank tops and some of them were hot and sweaty. They were split up into teams on either side of a net.

Little Sarah recognized the scene. "Volleyball!" she cried.

Hildie turned around sharply to the television. "Not that one, Dickie," she said coolly. "Eject it."

Richard made a face, either because of the hated nickname or because he'd been the one caught in the deed. Behind her Emily felt Lee's arm stiffen. But he said, "Leave it in, Richard. We haven't seen it for a long time."

"Lee—"

"It's all right, Hildie," Lee said quietly.

Hildie sighed a little nervously, then left with her burden. The tape played on. Emily knew whom she was looking for even before the camera zoomed in on her: a tall, utterly beautiful woman with rich brown hair and a face that could easily force men to their knees. It didn't surprise Emily that Nicole Alden proved to be an inept athlete; concert pianists rarely tried out for the Olympics. When Nicole missed a ball —as she did often—she did it with such good-humored grace and distress that Lee had no choice but to put his arms around her and show her how to shape a fist, and generally act besotted. Who wouldn't? The game ended, and the camera turned to other scenes and other actors.

Hildie came back just as the tape was finishing and asked lightly, "How we doin' here? Can I haul off another one?"

Emily stood up carefully with her own droopy bundle. "I'll give you a hand." She followed Hildie into a bedroom across the hall outfitted with another set of bunk beds and a single. Hildie undressed the sleeping children down to their underwear, and Emily wiped their sticky hands with a warm, damp washcloth. No one spoke until Hildie murmured, "It's the first time he's been able to watch that one through. I hope it wasn't too hard for you."

Really, these people were too unbelievably well bred. What did Emily's feelings have to do with it? Lee Alden had just gone through a traumatic event, and they were worrying whether their guests were comfortable and happy. Emily shrugged helplessly. "Hildie, it hardly matters what I felt."

Hildie gave her a quizzical look, which Emily returned with a tremulous smile. The trouble with the whole bunch was that they were too wound up in one another, she decided. This one-for-all and all-for-one business didn't leave a person any room to hide and sulk.

"I'll go get another one," she whispered to Hildie. But in the hall she ran into Lee.

"Hildie will do just fine on her own," he said. "Let's go outside." He led Emily through the kitchen door and out through the herb garden. The path, a layer of bark mulch, was too narrow to walk side by side, so they walked single file until they came to a wooden bench swing. Even by the dim glow of the path lights she could see that it was thick with generations of green paint. Emily took a seat on one side, and Lee stood facing the structure, setting the swing into gentle motion.

"So. Now you know Nicole," he said quietly. "We played that volleyball game over Labor Day weekend. Then Hildie's camera went on the fritz . . . and the game ended up being the last thing we had of Nicole." He added quietly, "She didn't know she was pregnant then. Anyway . . ." He let the sentence trail off unfinished.

"She was a beautiful woman," Emily said with feeling. "Did she play well?"

He let out a sad little laugh. "She was pathetic; you saw the video."

"No, I meant the piano."

"Ah. Like an angel. She loved Chopin."

And so it went, with Emily leading him step by halting step into a discussion of a woman whose memory she had every reason to fear. She learned that Mrs. Alden had been an early champion of Nicole and that Lee had resisted the match because, among other things, Nicole got deathly seasick on a boat and he could not bear to see her in pain. Eventually Nicole found adequate medication and learned to tolerate, if not enjoy, their outings on water. That was the thing that came through about Nicole: She insisted on trying everything that Lee did. Some things she liked; some she didn't. But she always made herself stick with them.

A cultivated woman with spunk; it was an unbeatable combination. Emily was glad to see that Lee could talk so freely about his wife; it showed he was on the way out of his grief. But she was left with the same old feeling that Nicole had cleared some impossibly high standard that political families held their women to.

"So how're you at volleyball?" Lee asked, almost echoing her thoughts.

"I don't like it," she decided to admit. "I don't think I was meant to be a team player. I'm from New Hampshire, Lee. We're kind of independent. Ask anybody; communes fail there all the time."

His laugh was low and easy. "I admire freethinkers. All right, then. Boats. Where do you stand on sailing?" he asked, not at all put off by her whimsical answer.

"I do love sailing. But if I didn't," she added with a steady look, "I wouldn't put up with nausea just to please my man." She looked away, shocked by her own candor. It wasn't fair to the memory of Nicole. "I'm sorry," she said, rising from the seat. "That was out of line. Please—" She stood on the platform, holding the uprights, wanting to jump off.

But he wrapped his hands around both of hers, pinning them to the uprights and stopping the swing. "It wasn't out of line. It was honest. Why do you try to run from that honesty?"

She hesitated, like a deer before flight. "I suppose . . . I don't think you're ready for it."

"Your honesty is what I like best about you. Don't you see that yet?"

She wanted to believe him, so she hesitated a moment longer. Should she be honest about Fergus? She tried to read his face, so near to hers. No, obviously not. Lee believed that Fergus had been laid to rest. So to speak.

"This is pointless," she said, frustrated by the impasse. She tried to break away, but Lee held her fast.

"No! Stay. Let's have this out. What is it about me that fills you with contempt, goddammit?" It was obvious from his angry bewilderment that he'd never had to ask the question before.

"You mean, besides the power and the money?" she asked dryly. "Besides the fact that everything associated with you has a history or a pedigree or a filigree?"

"Oh, I'm going to have to work my way up to that one," he said. "Where I come from, wealth and success aren't exactly character flaws. No, give me a simpler reason," he said acidly, "something I have a shot at understanding."

She could give him Fergus, but that wouldn't help. She rummaged through her trunkful of reasons, picking out the most likely scrap to fit. "All right. Let's go back to Nicole. Since you ask." She lifted her chin in a dangerous way. "I don't approve of the way you made Nicole bend her will to yours."

"Excuse me?"

"Take sports, for example. If she wasn't any good at them, why not let her be? She could've kept score or read a book or raised pigeons. Why force her to be something she wasn't?"

"I never forced Nicole," he said evenly.

"The pressure must have been there. If not from you, then from all of you."

Even in the dark, she could see that the remark stung. "Is that why you took so well to the kids today?" he asked. "Family pressure?"

"No! I loved being with them," she said quickly. "That's different."

"There's no difference. Nicole did what she did out of love, because she wanted to be with me. Or all of us, depending."

"I don't believe it!" Emily said bluntly. "Why would she let herself look so bad?"

"Hold it, time out!" Lee said, releasing her and shaping his forearms into a *T*. "Nicole never worried about looking bad. Never." For a moment he said nothing. And then: "Are we talking about Nicole—or you?"

Bull's-eye. She didn't realize it until he said it, but it was her own general insecurity she was pinning on Nicole. It had nothing to do with sports. Emily was afraid of not knowing the right people or having the right degree or belonging to the right clubs or wearing the right clothes or saying the right thing. The thought of accompanying Lee to a dinner party at the French Embassy, for example, filled her with terror.

She stepped off the swing and gave it a little push. Without her weight it squeaked on each return swing. "Okay, we *are* talking about me. I don't have Nicole's confidence," she admitted. *Jane Fonda doesn't have that kind of confidence,* she thought with a rueful smile.

"That's crazy," he said, amazed. "You're beautiful, smart, quick-witted, fresh, incorruptible. . . . I can go on like this for a long time, darling," he said, cradling her chin in his hand.

She felt his warm breath on her cheek, heard the heat in his voice. It would have been so easy to drift, spellbound, into his embrace. Yet it was important to her that he understand once and for all that she was not Nicole. She pulled away and threw her shoulders back, as if the chips on them were golden epaulets. "I think you should know that I really am *not* a graceful loser. And that I like to do things my own way. And that I don't like being pushed or cajoled. Into anything."

His hand slid around to the back of her neck, his arm slipped around her waist. "I would never push you into anything, darling," he murmured, nuzzling the nape of her neck. "But I reserve the right to cajole."

He lifted his head and brought his mouth on hers in a long, tonguing kiss of liquefying heat. Maybe it was the night, the stars, the honeysuckle; maybe it was the creaking swing or the cry of an owl nearby. Whether it was one thing or all of them together, Emily never, ever forgot that kiss. It was the kind of kiss that both dreams and memories are made of.

When he released her, he said, "I will come to your room."

She answered simply, "Yes."

16

By midnight the neighbors had gone, the dishes were done, and all the lights were out. Emily stood at the window of her darkened room, staring out at the green and red running lights of ships steaming silently on the sound. Her thoughts were a dim haze of expectations, hardly thoughts at all.

She wanted Lee so much. Sometime in the next little while he would steal into her room and take her in his arms and they would make love. She'd been waiting for this, she realized, since the last time he'd taken her in his arms. And after tonight she would begin to wait for the next time. The thought that she might spend most of the rest of her life waiting filled her with a kind of melancholy panic. She was no longer a whole person; there was a continuing, aching void in her that only Lee Alden could fill.

She sighed deeply. *Okay. He's the cream in my coffee. Now what?* It wasn't as though she had a future with him. It wasn't as though he'd ever said he cared.

She wrapped her arms around herself, trying hard not to care in return.

She wandered over to the nightstand and picked up the ancient tick-tocking clock: one-fifteen. There was a small television on the bureau; she considered turning it on, then rejected the idea as too jarring to her strange and pensive mood. She walked back to the window and let herself become mesmerized by the hypnotic sweep of white light flashing from the lighthouse on Nobska Point across the sound. When the soft rap on the door finally came, Emily stayed where she was, paralyzed by conflicting desires. She heard the door open, and then Lee was behind her, slipping his arms around her, looking over her shoulder at the nighttime traffic on the sea beyond.

"When I was a boy, all I ever wanted to be was a tugboat captain," he murmured, rubbing his cheek on the top of her hair. "It seemed like the perfect life: absolute freedom, my own command, union pay." He laughed ruefully. "I wonder where I went wrong."

"You still get Union pay," she quipped, suddenly, irrationally happy now that he was with her.

"Yeah, but look at the state of the Union; I feel guilty taking money from it." He nuzzled the inside curve of her shoulder, leaving zigzag trails of heat along her bare skin.

"*Your* conscience should be clear," she said, drawing in her breath, forgetting to let it out. "You voted against your last pay raise."

"Uh-oh . . . an informed constituent," he said with a smile buried low in his voice. "Then you know I voted for an increase in your taxes." He began to drop light, skimming kisses on the back of her neck.

"Oh-h-h . . . yes . . . taxes . . ." she murmured, playing along with their teasing chatter, relishing the delay. "They say . . . nothing's . . . more certain than—"

"—an end to this," he said in a husky voice, turning her around and kissing her hard.

Emily's senses were white hot. She'd been waiting for hours, quietly smoldering. In two short minutes Lee had fanned those embers into flames. Whether this kind of fire could cleanse and purify, she had no idea. It almost didn't matter; she had no control over it anyway. She let herself be led to the bed. She let him remove her thin gown. She watched by moonlight as he stripped himself of the slacks and loose shirt he wore. And then, at last, he was in bed with her and his kisses, flame hot, were licking at the edge of her consciousness, threatening meltdown.

"Ah, Lee . . . ah . . . more . . ." she cried in a low moan, knowing full well that she couldn't take much more.

"Darling . . . Emily . . . dearest . . ." Lee was murmuring, his voice hoarse with desire, "Emily, I think I'm fall—"

"Nobody beats Midas! Nobody! Come in tomorrow and save!"

The television was on at full volume, sending Emily's heart pitching through her lungs and Lee rocketing from the bed toward the bureau. He slammed the on-off toggle with his open palm, then switched on the small lamp that stood alongside the set. Wide-eyed, he turned to Emily and whispered, "Good God, we probably woke up half the house!" He picked up the six-inch television by its handle and wiggled it. "What the hell?"

Emily jumped out of bed and threw Lee's pants at him. "Get dressed. Quick!" she cried, perfectly aware of what was happening. "Every set in the house is on!" *Damn Fergus! Damn him, damn him, damn him!*

"What're you talking about? Why would—" Lee cocked his ear toward the door. "My God. You're right."

Above the wail of wakened children they heard several different television programs blaring defiantly. The din was shocking, a horrible, illogical intrusion into the peacefully sleeping house. Emily pulled a T-shirt over a pair of shorts and ran out into the living room, where a color set she hadn't even noticed before was featuring late-night bowling. She rushed to the set and turned it off, watching frantically for other signs of Fergus. If he was capable of such a mean, low deed, he might be capable of much worse.

One by one she heard the other televisions in the house silenced, until there was nothing left but the sleepy whines and whimpers of the youngest children. Grace and Hildie were in the bedrooms, soothing and reassuring them. She had no idea where Lee was. There was nothing left for her to do, so she headed back to her room. Whatever her mood had been, it was decidedly foul now. When Mrs. Alden confronted her in the hall, Emily was hard pressed to sound civil.

"What on earth is going on?" Lee's mother wanted to know.

"What was on *your* TV—Dobie Gillis or Cosby reruns?" Emily asked tersely. Her nerves were completely exposed and raw; at any other time she would have been appalled by her manners.

"There's no television in my room," Mrs. Alden answered, taken aback. "What's happened?" she repeated, gripping Emily's arm. In her pale robe, with her hair unpinned, the elderly woman looked smaller and more fragile somehow. And frightened.

"You needn't worry, Mrs. Alden," Emily answered, forcing herself to calm down. "It's nothing. It was some kind of . . . of power surge, probably. The televisions all malfunctioned."

"Malfunctioned? I never heard of such a thing."

"It's the newer, more electronic ones that do it. Mine at home goes on and off by itself all the time," she said without irony.

"It sounds quite bizarre," Lee's mother said, keeping one ear cocked for danger. Emily continued to stand in the dim hall, smiling inanely, until Mrs. Alden pronounced herself reassured. "Everything seems to have settled down," she whispered at last.

Emily said good night again, but Mrs. Alden seemed to hesitate. "I suppose you think I'm a nervous Nellie," she said. Before Emily could answer, she added, "I'm not. But once, right after Lee was first elected, we had some trouble here. A madman—Lee called him a disenchanted voter—broke into this place and vandalized it. He did terrible things, truly vicious things. . . . Fortunately the house was closed up for the season. But what if the children had been here with only their mothers?"

Mrs. Alden clearly did not expect an answer to her question. She shook her head and smiled sadly, then switched on another wall sconce. "Good night, Emily," she said, and slipped back into her room.

Emily made a decision. She could not stay in the house. The only safe thing was to pack and leave. Immediately. Before Fergus got any other bright ideas. She changed quickly into street clothes and packed her few things into her canvas bag. She was on the telephone trying unsuccessfully to arrange for a ride when Lee knocked and came immediately in.

"Thank you anyway," Emily said, and hung up.

Lee stared at the newly made bed and her packed bag. "What's going on?"

"I wanted to tell you, but I didn't know where you

were." It was the best she could do for an explanation.

"I was taking a quick look around outside. Tell me what?"

"I have to go," she said, lifting her bag from the bed and moving quickly as if she had a plan.

Lee was dumbfounded. "Go where? Why? How?" Automatically his hand reached out for the handle of her bag, to stop her. His uncombed hair, drooping in sandy curls over his forehead, made him look impossibly young and naïve. Yet the look in his eyes, blue and steel, was anything but.

She could see that they had reached a crisis point, but there was no turning back. "I've got to get out of this house, for your sake. For all your sakes." She tried to wrench her bag from his grip, but he held on.

"Emily! What's the *matter* with you?" he said, keeping his voice an undertone. Clearly he didn't want to start another uproar.

She looked away, as if she were being forced to tell him his dog had just been run over. "Don't you understand about the televisions?"

"To be honest, no. Maybe it's the cable hookup."

"Fergus turned them on!" she said impatiently, angry that he refused to see the obvious.

"Oh, not Fergus again," he said wearily, loosening his grip. He walked away from her, running his fingers through his hair, and paused in front of his beloved view of the sound. "What is it with this phantasm—this, this *fantasy* of yours? You're like a kid with a guardian angel—"

"Trust me. Fergus is no angel."

"All right, then," he said, turning around and giving her an even look. "An imaginary playmate. That's okay when you're young and wishing you had a sister, but—"

"How stupid do you think I am?" she asked, her voice rising. He made a shushing motion, and she dropped into a controlled hiss. "If I were making him up, I'd have made him a *her*. What the hell good is another man in my life?"

"He's not a man; he's a figment!"

"That figment scared your family half to death!"

"Come on, Emily. My nieces will survive the Home Shopping Network."

"Don't do that, Lee," she warned. "Don't treat this like a joke."

He sighed in frustration and tried another tack. "Why would he want to scare little kids?"

"He's not really interested in scaring anyone. He just wants to distract you."

"From?"

"Me."

Lee cocked his head and gave her a slant-eyed, quizzical look. "This Fergus . . . this *ghost* . . . is jealous of us together?"

Emily blushed deeply. "I think so. It never would've occurred to me until last night, but the way he looked . . . the things he said . . . yes," she said, her voice dropping to a bare whisper. "I think so."

"Well," Lee said, totally at a loss. He sat down on the edge of the bed, leaning his forearms on his thighs the way he had at the séance. It was as if he were straining to see something that wasn't there. He was so obviously *willing* to see it, but he was so obviously unable to do it. "So Fergus is still in the picture. Somehow, on the ferry, I had the idea that was all over."

"That was my fault. I misled you."

He looked up at her sharply. "Why?"

She was standing next to him, still holding her canvas bag, poised for flight. "Because I thought you wanted to be misled," she admitted. "You weren't exactly thrilled the first time I trotted Fergus out. On the other hand, you sure looked relieved when I said it was over."

He stood up then and took her by the upper arms. His look was intense, searching. "How long did you think you could keep him a secret from me?"

She smiled lamely. "Since you can't see him—for as long as it took."

"Took to solve the crime, you mean." He nodded to himself, as if it all were becoming clearer. "Son of a bitch," he said softly.

He let go of her arms after a gentle, absentminded rub and began to pace the room. Immediately he stopped. "I take it that you've been investigating the murder, then, and not the Newarth economy. So. How's it going? Got your man yet?" He seemed to be listening to himself with amazement. "Son of a bitch," he repeated, shaking his head.

Emily shrugged. "It's going okay. I have a couple of leads." He didn't look fully focused, so she didn't bother going into details. As for the fire, she had no intention of bringing it up; one blistering lecture was enough.

"So. He's back," Lee repeated, staring at the floor. "And he's, what, in love with you now, is that it?"

"I didn't say that," she said quickly, coloring a little. "I think he's maybe just jealous of your, well, *physicality*. He misses sex the way he misses beer and roses."

Lee cocked one eyebrow at Emily. "He treats them all the same?"

"I have no idea," she answered coolly. "It's only a theory."

"What's he like, this Fergus of yours?" Lee asked after a moment. "What kind of man is—was—he?"

Surprised by the thoughtfulness of the question, Emily said, "I think he's hopelessly confused by modern morals—"

"Who isn't?" Lee asked with a soft laugh.

"But I think at bottom he was a good man, caring and sensitive. He was a man of his time, of course; I think he saw women in terms of saints or sinners. But he was the kind of man who loves women, and that's the kind of man women love."

Lee ambled toward her, hands in his pockets. "And what kind of man," he asked, his eyes lit with quiet curiosity, "am I?"

She knew that it wasn't arrogance behind the question. He simply wanted to *know,* the way he'd want to know the type of sparrow if she pointed one out. She lifted her canvas bag to her breast like a shield and wrapped her arms around it.

"You're the kind of man that women love," she said softly, "and that's the kind of man women fear."

He smiled in self-conscious confusion. "Do you have to go to graduate school to understand this stuff?"

That was the thing about him, the frosting on his cake; he simply had no idea how overwhelming he was. Even now, if he took her in his arms, she'd melt like butter in a microwave. She stiffened her resolve by taking one step back as he approached her. It was absolutely time to leave.

Her tiny but determined retreat did not escape him. The light in his eyes seemed to go out and he said, "I don't ever want to see fear in your eyes, Emily—for any reason." She saw the muscles in his jaw working as he said, "If it's your wish, I'll take you into town." He held out his hand to take her bag, and she yielded it.

Lee made a quick call, and they left the house in a whisper and got into a tiny Civic, which Lee explained was the only car that would fit in the tiny downtown.

"Please don't apologize for the car, Lee; I'm very grateful that you're humoring me," Emily said. All the while she was expecting Fergus, wherever he was, to burst out in a Honda commercial.

The trip to town was hideously brief. They said very little, and none of it was about Fergus. Lee was obviously at a loss over how to deal with the whole mess. Emily's heart was disintegrating, like a mound of ashes in a stiff wind.

Here we go again, and it's Fergus's fault. Again. She sighed heavily as Lee pulled up in front of a small guest cottage not far from the ferry landing where the two had parted that morning.

"There's a side entrance; at the top of the landing there'll be a small room with the light on. You'll have to share the bath with two others on the floor, but at this hour that shouldn't be a problem," Lee said in a voice drained of emotion.

"Thank you—for everything," Emily said, in tones equally exhausted. She had her hand on the door handle when she remembered: "The interview!"

"Oh, hell." He snorted derisively. "Well? It's up to you." He stared straight ahead.

"I—I'd like to be heroic and pass, but I can't afford to, Lee. Can you still make our original time and place?"

"Sure," he said through clenched teeth. "No problem."

She swung the door open, but she could not make herself step out of the car, not without some explanation. "If I seemed deluded before, I must seem downright pathetic to you now that I've added a sex angle to this little 'fantasy' of mine. What can I say? He's real. I'm not making it up. But you'd have to have the faith of an apostle to believe me. I know that. Which is why I lied to you on the ferry."

She saw him nod in the darkness. This was new, this cold, hard remoteness. It was understandable; but she was hoping for more. She was hoping for the blind faith that comes from love.

And it just wasn't there. "Good night, Lee," she said, disheartened, and left him.

17

The following morning Emily took the first ferry out of Vineyard Haven. The short trip back to Woods Hole was made under leaden skies that did nothing to dispel her continuing melancholy. It didn't help that Fergus still was not showing himself. *He's probably afraid to come out,* she told herself grimly.

It was almost laughable. She'd managed to drive a full-fledged ghost into hiding and to turn a warm, loving family man into a block of ice. *I was right in the first place. I don't belong in relationships. When and if this comic opera ends, I shall retire to a mountainside and devote myself to the study of Zen Buddhism.*

She had just enough time to shower, change into fresh clothes, and hop a train to Lee's office. At two fifty-nine she found Millie Cusack hard at work at a computer terminal, the remnants of a McDonald's lunch at her right elbow. Not surprisingly for a Sunday, the offices were nearly empty of their dozen or so staffers. From an inner sanctum somewhere she heard a printer spewing out text.

"The senator called from the airport," the secretary explained. "He'll be here any minute. He asked that you kindly wait in his office," she said, holding open Lee's door.

A nice way of letting you get on with your work without any pestering from me, Emily thought, smiling as she was being led through.

The fact was, Millie Cusack was perfectly safe from Emily's scrutiny. Jim Whitewood was safe; their boss was safe; they all were safe. Emily was determined to walk Lee Alden through the easiest interview he'd ever had simply because she owed him, and after that it would be good-bye, Charlie.

She wandered around Lee's office, pausing for a long time before a gallery of framed and signed photographs of movers and shakers in government, some of them taken with Lee aboard a sailboat. A more personal collection of photos was arranged on his desk. The largest among them was a silver-framed family photo. Everyone was in it, including the two traveling husbands, including Nicole. Emily was about to pick it up for a closer look when she noticed, pressed under a glass paperweight, a silk turquoise flower petal. A flower petal from a sham psychic's hat. Jolted, she stared into the paperweight as if it were a crystal ball.

Why had he saved the petal? As a keepsake of their time together? As a trophy of her screwy scheme? On a whim? And did it matter, as long as he saved it at all? She was sitting on the edge of his desk, hovering over the photos and the paperweight, when Lee walked in. Naturally she felt like a spy and began making stupid apologies. But he was the one who seemed embarrassed, and that amazed and pleased her. *It is a keepsake, then,* she thought, her heart lifting.

Or was he just embarrassed by her pushiness? The women in his set probably sat when they were told to sit, whereas here she was, stopping just short of reading his mail. This was hopeless. In matters concerning Lee Alden her moral system was about as clear as peanut butter.

She sat in one of the wing chairs, set up her tape recorder with a "You don't mind, do you?," and took out her notepad. Lee seemed to take his cue from her and sat in the opposite chair, with no attempt at chit-chat. The tension between them was thick enough to slice.

It did not look good. This was about as friendly as an international chess match. *Here goes nothing,* she thought, pressing the start button on her tape recorder.

"Senator, you've decided to run for a third term at a time when the public seems inclined to throw all the rascals out. Would you tell us why?"

"Well, for one thing," he answered with with an utterly charming smile and a disarming shrug, "I ain't a rascal."

Interesting. From stony and remote he went to warm and engaging, all at the touch of a button. *Damn.* How could you ever trust someone this good?

"At the same time," he said in a more serious way, "I don't blame Americans for being fed up. They're not getting their money's worth. Unless we stop bickering and get moving, we deserve to be kicked out of government."

His hands came up in an eloquent stabbing gesture. "There's plenty of good legislation being proposed—on overhauling our health care system, our banking structure, our social services. We just need to pass it. We've *got* to be willing to make hard choices."

"Any suggestions on how to do that?"

"I wish there were a simple answer. We need to free ourselves from pressure by special interests. The average incumbent gets almost half his money from PAC groups. Obviously we need to reform campaign spending. And it's time to limit our terms. We should give governing our best shot and then get out and let someone else try. That's for starters."

Without the benefit of notes he launched into a clear and concise list of proposals to streamline and reform government, backed up by so many statistics that Emily was grateful for the tape recorder winding its accurate way between them.

Good Lord. The man really does know his business, she thought after a very few minutes. And it had nothing to do with the ridiculous, undeniable attraction she was feeling for him. It was more to do with the fact that in an age of bombast and sneering, his was a voice of clear, sweet reason. Lee Alden was neither a knee-jerk liberal nor a pigheaded conservative. He was somewhere in between, and Emily couldn't help thinking that he was exactly what the Founding Fathers had in mind.

We could use ninety-nine more of him, she thought dreamily as he wrapped up a thoughtful and sympathetic response to her question about low-income housing.

He was leaning forward in his chair, driving his point home. "The fact is, residents know and care about the buildings they live in more than government officials do. The resident management experiment has been a success, and it deserves to be expanded."

He waited for the next query. None came. Emily

had worked her way through her list of questions—Stan Cooper would've called them soft lobs—and now she was done. Unless, of course, she was willing to delve into the subject of the paranormal. She was not.

She flipped the cover back over her steno pad and gave him a half-apologetic look. "I'm afraid this is going to read like a paid political endorsement, Senator. That's how impressive a performance it was."

He looked surprisingly confused. "That's it?"

She nodded, but he wasn't satisfied. "No questions about my family, hobbies, favorite junk food, last book read?" He gave her a long, level look. "Nothing about my abiding interest in the otherworldly?"

Remember, keep it light. Keep it easy. "No, sir, no way. I don't even want to know your astrological sign," she said, pressing the stop button on the recorder. She backed up to his challenge and erased it. "Besides, I think the local tabloids have pretty much covered the personal side of your career."

"With a vengeance," he said ironically. He thought about it for a minute. "Thanks for the break," he said, standing and easing into one of his catlike stretches. "Does Stan Cooper know you're waiting in the wings for his job?"

She assumed he was being ironic and shook her head noncommittally.

"Stan and I go back to our childhood together," he added. "Has he ever told you that?"

"No," Emily said, surprised. Tight-lipped Stan had never said a word.

Lee walked over to the gallery of photos. "Yeah. His father was a charter captain on the Vineyard. Here's a picture of my father, my brother, and me aboard the *Snapper Blue*. That's Stan's father at the wheel, and there's Stan sitting on the bait box. We went fishing on the *Blue* every time my dad could get away from the mainland."

Emily came over for a closer look. It was an interesting tableau: the Alden clan, proudly posed with their catches of the day; Captain Cooper, proudly posed at the wheel of his powerboat; and Stan, a sulky look on his face, holding himself aloof from the happy group.

"He never did like the charter business," Lee said thoughtfully. "Too service-oriented, I'd guess. After his father died he sold the *Snapper Blue*, the house, all of it. I haven't seen him on the island in years."

It explained a lot. No, Stan wouldn't have thought much of dispensing bait or serving sandwiches to a couple of preppy teenagers his own age. Young Stan's look said it all too clearly: "Why them and not me?"

Emily shook her head. "I think he can hurt you politically."

"Stan? Why would he want to?"

She tapped the photo. "That's why," she said, and turned away to gather up her things.

But Lee took her by her shoulders and turned her to face him. "Why the concern for my political well-being, Emily? Why this protective surge?" When she said nothing he added, "I could use some answers, kiddo."

He was too near. She'd been careful to keep her distance, to keep the talk on a rational level. But now he'd crossed into the danger zone, the zone of the heart. Alarm bells were going off everywhere. *Intruder alert! Left shoulder! Right shoulder!*

Her hands went up to his. Lifting them gently away, she said in a nearly steady voice, "You're the right man for the job. I don't want to see you blow it."

"Since when? What about the search for extraterrestrial intelligence? What about the séances? I'm a flake, remember?"

"Nah," she answered, confused by his about-face. "I got that part all wrong." Why was he pushing her on this?

"You're patronizing me, Emily," he said in a suddenly dangerous tone. "I won't have it. Those weren't questions; those were cotton balls. I admit I was grateful just now for the reprieve. But I have to be able to face you after you walk out of here."

He went over to her tape recorder and pressed a button. "Ask the hard one. Ask the obvious one. *Do I believe in ghosts?*"

Her head was beginning to spin. What was he after? First he was grateful; now he wasn't. She needed time to think things through, and he wasn't letting her. He was pushing her, prodding her. Why? Why?

She spun on her heel like a cornered thing and faced him. "What are you doing? Why are you forcing this issue? Suppose I do ask you if you believe in ghosts? If you say yes, I'll have to nail you to the wall when I write this up. If you say no, we're back to the I'm-a-nut scenario. Why can't you just leave it alone?" she cried, beyond herself with frustration.

"I will if you will, goddammit!"

They weren't talking about the interview anymore, and she knew it. "I can't! He wouldn't let me if I wanted to!"

In three steps Lee had her in his grip; she'd never seen him so angry before. His breathing was fast, his voice hot and hard. "What would it take to knock you loose from this obsession of yours? What—"

He stopped. Let go. Stared. She turned her head and saw what he saw: The lamp on his desk had begun to brighten and then to blind. Lee squinted and looked away, and so did she, filled with dread for the excruciating pain that was about to follow.

But the pain never came. The light dimmed and then went out. Lee blinked once, twice, and rubbed his eyes, no doubt trying to get the bright spots out from behind his eyelids.

"Give yourself a minute," Emily said. "It goes away." She tried to keep the note of obnoxious triumph from her voice, but it was impossible.

Lee walked over to the lamp and peered over its linen shade. "Bulb's burned out. Must've been a short."

"What! *You're* the nut here! What does it take—"

"Come and look," he said, cutting her off from the road she was headed down. "The bulb's dark on top."

She began stomping toward the lamp but halted dead in her tracks three feet away.

Fergus was standing six inches from the senator.

It was absolutely shocking to her to see the two of them lined up side by side. Fergus was younger, shorter, more sparely built than Lee, but he *was* there, in full view. For a moment she thought quite seriously that she was going to die. Her chest constricted; there was a roaring in her head; her mouth went absolutely dry. She tried to say something but couldn't.

Fergus peered over the lampshade with Lee, then looked up at her with a beatific grin. " 'GE,' " he cried, pointing to the bulb. " 'We bring good things to life!' "

Emily stared wide-eyed at the ghost, then at Lee, who was at first baffled, then alarmed by her behavior. "*What?* Tell me!" he demanded.

He pivoted ninety degrees, putting him face-to-face with Fergus. The scowl on Lee's face was fierce.

Fergus wilted a little before it, but he held his

ground. After a second or two his expression relaxed, then became almost insolent.

But Lee was staring into thin air. "Emily, if there's something here, *describe it to me!*" he implored.

Emily tried desperately to oblige. "He . . . you . . ."

And then she fainted.

That's twice, Emily thought as she came to. She was lying on a small sofa, and her jaw was throbbing. She sat up, rubbing the sore spot. Lee was at his desk, pouring water from a thermal decanter into a glass. He brought it over and sat down beside her.

"Hurts?"

She nodded. "Who took a poke at me, you or him?"

"Go ahead, make jokes. You caught the claw foot of the wing chair when you fainted. Let's have a look." He took her jaw gently between his thumb and index finger and tilted it to one side. "Yep, you'll live. Have you eaten anything today?"

She ignored the question but did drain the glass of half its water. "I take it you didn't see a thing?"

He took the glass she handed to him. "I didn't *see* anything, no."

"But?"

Lee rubbed his eyes, then dragged his fingers down his face, stretching the facial muscles as exhausted people do. She wondered if he'd slept at all. He certainly hadn't shaved.

"*But*. I felt something not unlike the moment of Nicole's death, when I was in the hospital." He was frowning, deep in thought, struggling for the words. "I remember telling you I felt a kind of euphoric joy at the time. That wasn't quite accurate. There was an element of fear in it—fearful joy, if there is such a thing."

He stared at the glass in his hand as if he were wondering how it got there. "But why the fear, I don't know. Was it because I was afraid the moment would end, or was it because I was afraid that I wasn't ready for what was happening to me?

"One thing I do know," he said, placing the glass carefully on a low table as if it were a precious goblet, "is ever since that moment in the hospital I've carried around a nagging feeling of guilt—as if I failed Nicole somehow. As if I'd had the chance to cross over some Rubicon and be with her forever but had chosen to hang back. As if I should have loved her more."

His fingers came up to Emily's jaw, skimming the bruise so lightly that she hardly knew it. "I've never told this to anyone."

Emily wanted to comfort him; he looked so vulnerable. "I don't think you could have loved Nicole more than you did," she said. "I think you feel guilty the way we all feel guilty when we survive the death of someone close. The worst part is, we feel joy that we *are* still alive. And then we feel guilty because we feel that way. We can't help any of it, Lee. We're only human."

"That's how it was with your mother?" he ventured.

"Yes . . . that's how it was."

He twined his fingers through hers. They sat without speaking for a while, and she felt closer to him than she'd ever felt before. But after a bit she became uneasy; what if he felt he'd said too much? She glanced nervously at the door. Millie would realize the interview should've been over by now.

She stood up. "Well!" she said awkwardly, straightening the folds of her cotton skirt. "Your family thinks of me as the guest who wouldn't stay, and now your staff will think of me as the reporter who wouldn't go. I should leave you to your work."

He looked startled by her abrupt move, but he scrambled politely to his feet. The smile on his face was ironic and tender. "My family figures you ran away for a perfectly good reason. But you're right about my staff; they're very schedule-oriented."

"Time to go, in that case." There it was again, that tick-tick-ticking clock. Whenever she was with him, she felt that she was on borrowed time. She scooped up her shoulder bag and began her march out.

"Whoa, hold on!" His arm shot out across her chest like a railroad gate. He was close enough for her to see the golden stubble on his cheeks. "My staff and I don't always agree," he explained, letting his fingertips trail across the top of her breasts before he let his arm fall. "What I'd like to know now is where do we go from here."

She was feeling the heat from his glancing caress, and as usual when he touched her, her body went surging ahead of her brain. He seemed to be waiting for an answer. But what was the question?

Where do we go from here? "I guess you run for Senate and I continue on my way. At least for now."

"Like two ships passing in the night? I don't think so, Emily. Not after this."

"Especially after this, Lee. Face it, you're not positive what happened here. Is there really any point to your getting further involved? The less you know about Fergus, the better. Your press conferences will go a lot more smoothly."

"Look, I'll grant you, I'm still not altogether convinced what it is you're seeing. But it looks more and more like I've fallen for someone with rotten luck and not just a simple crackpot."

"Gee, you know how to make a girl feel good," she

said ironically. But she *was* pleased—her heart was pounding—just because he said he'd "fallen."

"You and your necklaces," he said with a helpless shake of his head. "Me and my séances. What a team."

He made a fist around the crystal of her necklace and drew her gently closer by its chain. Through a haze of longing she saw his mouth, full and skeptical, open slightly for the kiss. A shiver passed through her; she closed her eyes.

And then she remembered. "No!" she cried, pulling her head back. "He might short out every piece of office equipment you have!"

"You can't be serious," Lee said, laughing, holding her close by the chain.

She locked her dark eyes onto his blue gaze. "Put it this way: Can you afford to lose whatever Millie's feeding into her computer right now?"

He thought about it, then released the crystal from his grip. He centered the jewel neatly on her breast. "I don't think I like this Mr. O'Malley of yours," he said, dusting off the crystal with his fingertips.

"What does he care? *He's* not the one running for office," she said impishly.

"Will you tell him for me that I mean him no harm?"

"I think he pretty well knows that." Her voice became more serious. "This conversation seems pretty dumb unless you believe me, Lee. Do you?"

He winced and rubbed the back of his neck as if he'd got a crick there. "It's a pretty stupendous thing, Em, if it's true. Part of me wants to assemble a congressional committee to investigate. Part of me wants to steal that necklace and see for myself."

"Do you?" she repeated doggedly.

"I want to. No one wants to believe you more."

"Do you?"

He leaned his forearms on the back of the wing chair as if he were at the rail of a ship, staring at the horizon. "I wish I had more proof."

Her heart plummeted. Shaking with disappointment and frustration, she walked over to him and put her hand alongside his cheek, turned his face to her, and kissed him long and hard, a mocking, tonguing, daring kiss.

She pulled away abruptly. "Check with Millie in that case," she said, and left.

Emily came to a screeching halt at the curb outside the senator's office building. She could not gather the wit to remember if she'd brought her car or taken the train. In the meantime, rain had begun to fall. She began to storm blindly down Cambridge Street, oblivious to the sky, heading for either the parking garage or the underground rapid transit, she wasn't sure which.

"This is the last straw. This really is," she said in a fury under her breath. "That man will *never* believe me."

"Not if ye try using power ye don't possess."

"Oh. *You,*" she said, throwing her hands up in the air. "Just what I need. Go away, Fergus. I'm not in the mood!"

"What kind of fool stunt was that back there?" he demanded. He was alongside, struggling to keep up with her. "Did ye really believe I'd destroy a piece of the nation's business just to prove a point for ye?"

"The point I was trying to prove, you jerk, was that you exist!"

He flushed angrily. "What the hell do I care if yer boyfriend believes it or not? It would just complicate matters. It would bring the press around in hordes.

Ye couldn't get a goddamned thing done. Not that ye do a hell of a lot anyway. I never saw such a goddamned procrastinator. Why can't ye just get on with the investigation? Why must everything be laid at the feet of this idol like some kind of offering? What's he got to do with my acquittal? When are ye goin' to stop this hemmin' and hawin' and agonizing and *just do it?*"

She stopped and turned the full force of her fury on him, tucking her chin down like a bull before the charge. "You've got a hell of a nerve! I'm trying to fit you in my life the best I can, and you're wrecking it! Do you under*stand?* You're destroying my relationship with this man!"

"Ye wouldn't even know the bastard if it weren't for me!"

"I knew him when you were just a glimmer in Kimberly's eye! And things would've moved right along in a normal way if it weren't for *you!* The least you could've done was prove to him you exist. I mean, this is idiotic! You nearly kill me to show me who and what you are, and all Lee gets is a burned-out light bulb. What am I supposed to do with *that?* I don't blame Lee at all. *I blame you, Fergus.*"

"Fine! Ye want me to go back there and blow Millie's computer records to smithereens? Hey, make my day! What do I care if yer pal never submits another bill to Congress? I'm off to do yer bidding!"

"No! No, no, no," she cried when he disappeared. "Come back here, you! Right now!" she screamed. The rain was streaming down her face; her wet hair clung to her cheeks and neck; and her cotton skirt was plastered against her legs like a big wet washrag. "Right now, I said!" she yelled at the top of her lungs.

There weren't many pedestrians on the street at that hour on a Sunday in the rain. But the ones there were, well dressed and tucked under sturdy black umbrellas, edged closer to the buildings, giving her a wide berth.

Fergus suddenly reappeared, cool, dry, and invincible. "*Now* what?" he sneered. "Ye want me to spell out his name in lights across the downtown sky?"

She stood there in the middle of the sidewalk, looking like a drowned cat. "He's important to me, Fergus. Don't you understand that? Can't you see I'm in love with him?"

She saw him recoil, as if she'd landed a blow to his solar plexus. It was a hit, a palpable hit. He stood there, flushed and oddly appealing, his green eyes intense and stricken. She could hear his agitated breathing, see his chest rise and fall under his brown corduroy vest. For the first time since she'd known him, she forgot completely that he was a phantom.

"What difference can that make?" he said at last. "He's not in love with ye."

Now it was her turn to recoil from the blow. Fergus was a ghost, with knowledge she could never hope to have on earth. He must know if Lee was or wasn't in love or could or couldn't ever get that way.

"If he loved ye he'd believe ye, ye simpleton," Fergus added in a growl. "If ye were mine, I'd accept yer every word as God's own. If ye said the moon was hot, I'd believe ye. If ye said ye could fly, I'd believe ye. If ye said ye could pluck a mountain and drop it in the sea, I'd believe ye. Ye're *not* mine," he added in a voice hoarse with indignation, "and I still believe every blessed word ye say."

The rain was falling more gently now, and it mixed and ran with the tears on her cheeks. "Fergus . . . I'm sorry . . ."

"Nothin' to be sorry over," he said stoically. "The young ones have an expression, don't they? 'Life's a bitch, and then ye die.' As near as I can tell, life's a bitch, and then ye die, and then life seems to be a bitch all over again." He laughed bitterly.

She held out her hand to him, forgetting completely that he couldn't possibly take it. To her astonishment a passerby, an elderly man in a dark green raincoat, pressed a five-dollar bill into her open palm. "Take this, child," he said. "There's a shelter not two miles from here. You can catch the bus at the corner. Never give up hope. Things will get better. There are people all around you who care."

He hurried on his way, and when Emily turned around, Fergus was gone. She felt more destitute than ever.

18

The feeling stayed with Emily through the next morning as she set out early for Newarth City Hall. It didn't help that it was still raining. Rain was depressing. Rain was slow going. The dull slip-slap of the windshield wipers kept time to her mood while she tried to sort things out.

Even though she'd told Fergus she didn't blame Lee for not believing her, she *did* blame Lee. And even though she'd accused Fergus of wrecking her life, Fergus had now become a necessary part of her life. *In other words, I lied. Or I'm hopelessly confused.*

At this point she had no idea where she stood with either Lee or Fergus; her emotional life was truly a shambles. Maybe that's why Hessiah Talbot's murder suddenly looked so appealing; it, at least, was a problem with a solution. Fergus was right. It was time to stop hemming and hawing and trying to work Lee into the equation. It was time to *just do it.*

Emily spent the next hour and a half in the dreary basement of Newarth's City Hall poring over old taxpayer rolls. She had her fingers crossed that Hattie Dunbart's memory was as sharp as her tongue. If Hattie's uncle Eric really had found the necklace in his father's house, then either Mayor Abbott was the murderer, or—less likely—he'd been host to the murderer. Granted, it was circumstantial evidence, but circumstantial evidence was better than no evidence at all.

She ran her finger down the 1892 list of taxpayers: "Abbott, Alfred; Abbott, Carl; Abbott, Francis; *Abbott, Henry*. Here we go," she murmured to herself at the battered oak table she was sharing with a couple of paralegals.

"Oh, no." Henry Abbott's address at the time of his suicide was listed as "Talbot Manor." "Oh, *no*." This was not exactly an interesting twist. This was a cruel and diabolical open end. If Henry Abbott had actually bought and lived in Talbot Manor, then she had not only all the Abbotts to consider—God knows, there were enough of them in the 1892 Newarth directory—but the whole damn Talbot entourage as well.

She remembered from the trial accounts that several Talbot cousins were staying at the manor at the time of the murder, not to mention the usual suspects that Fergus had rounded up for her: the large staff, the itinerant peddlers, even the parish priest who played a game of whist on occasion at the manor. Add to that all the mill employees who must've trafficked through the place . . .

There were thousands of suspects! Ever since she'd interviewed Hattie, she'd pretty much had her mind made up. It was obvious. The mayor did it. Now, who knew? Maybe the darn butler did it. Maybe she'd never know who did it. And where would that leave Fergus? she wondered, beating back the panic that lay so near the surface nowadays.

She left City Hall under a new and blacker cloud than the one dropping steady rain on her. On a whim she drove past Talbot Manor, half intending to pop in on Maria Salva and see how things were going. She rolled toward the manor in first gear, but at the last minute she crept on by. The memory of the recent fire was too fresh. She felt something of Fergus's horror at the place now. In the rain it looked bigger, darker, slicker, altogether forbidding.

Besides, when—and if—she did go, she wanted to have the time and an excuse to stay and snoop. Instead she dropped in at the Newarth Library, which was as empty as ever. She found the energetic Mrs. Gibbs in a tiny cubbyhole just big enough to fit a card table holding a hot plate, some cups and saucers, and a fresh-baked Bundt cake.

The librarian's tired face lit up when she saw Emily. "How nice!" she said, and immediately sat Emily down on a folding chair she produced. "Have a piece of my lemon poppyseed cake. It's the closest thing to sunshine we'll see today."

She poured strong, percolated coffee into a cup and handed it to Emily with a thick wedge of glazed cake. Then she dragged out a second chair and unfolded it. "I don't like to have my coffee in the library," she explained, easing her heavy burden onto the metal seat. "It sets a poor example." Emily had no idea for whom.

So the two of them huddled knee to knee in an oddly cozy way, as if they were sneaking treats, while Mrs. Gibbs plied Emily with questions about her article on Hessiah Talbot.

"I'm pinning my hopes on you, dear," she insisted. "The *Boston Journal* can put Newarth back on the map."

"Mrs. Gibbs! About all this article can do for

Newarth is bring a few curiosity seekers into Talbot Manor."

"If there *is* a Talbot Manor by then," the librarian said darkly. "That fire was so *unnecessary*. The whole place could've burned down. Instead of obsessing on the plumbing, Frank Salva should be fixing up the wiring."

"He *is* a plumber, Mrs. Gibbs," Emily reminded her.

"So what? That's not the reason the tower sits idle. The reason is," she said, lowering her voice, "that Maria won't let Frank touch it. She won't even let him *in* it. I don't like to tell tales out of school, but—well, there's something strange about that woman lately." She put her cup back in its saucer with a decisive little clack.

Emily stabbed the next bite of cake with her fork. "Maria did seem high-strung to me," she ventured casually.

"Overwound and overwrought," Mrs. Gibbs said. "I've known her for only two years, though I've known Frank forever. When Maria came here from France, I thought she was simply shy, you know, because she didn't know anyone. Now I'm not so sure."

"She's not American? She speaks perfect English."

"I think one of her parents was American. Her name is Marie, but Frank likes to call her Maria. It's very hard to get her to talk about her past. Or about anything, for that matter. All I really know about her is that she's intensely religious. I believe she was raised in a convent part of her childhood."

Emily was a little crestfallen. *So much for the young-and-bored-wife theory.* "Well, she's living in the perfect house, then," Emily said lightly. "The main floor is a regular Gothic cathedral."

"Oh, she adores the manor. Frank likes to joke that

she fell in love with the house before she fell in love with him."

"That's interesting; somehow I thought they bought it together."

"Not at all. Frank was doing some contract work for the previous owner, a down-and-out young man who finally gave up and sold it to Frank outright. Maria showed up in Newarth just before the closing. She and Frank were married less than three months later. It was all very romantic. At the time."

"There are no children?"

"Oh, no; I doubt there will be any. Some women are too independent for children, while others are too dependent, if you know what I mean. Maria is one of the latter. She needs to bend her will to someone, and that's not a very good thing to do with children. *You'll* have children, Emily. I've had children. But not Maria, no."

"Does she submit herself so completely to Frank?"

"I'm sure she doesn't. I've never seen any sign that she's devoted to Frank. They kind of go their separate ways. Frank seems puzzled and hurt by it. Well, of course there *is* the age difference. Frank and I grew up together; he's no spring chicken."

"Whom *does* she bend her will to, in that case?"

Mrs. Gibbs laughed, surprised by the naïveté of the question. "Why, I suppose, to God."

Emily nodded. It would explain the faraway look. "But then why did she marry Frank?" she asked, still not convinced.

"That, my dear, is the sixty-four-thousand-dollar question. Another slice? I oughtn't to eat it all myself; the cholesterol is wicked high. The only reason I can think of," she continued, cutting herself another thick wedge, "is the obvious one: She was alone in the States and Frank offered her security. An introspective woman like her would never have many friends. Maybe she realized that about herself."

"There is one other possibility," Emily began, reluctant to admit to such cynicism. "Does Frank have much money?"

"Emily, *really*. Does Maria look like a gold digger to you? Besides, Frank is mortgaged to the hilt. He bought at peak; the place is probably worth less now than it was two years ago. I half expect the Salvas to walk away from the property and let the bank have it."

"Have we figured out yet why Maria is so possessive about the tower?" Emily asked blandly.

"*We* haven't figured out much of anything, dear," the librarian answered in a dry but amused tone. "You're busily pumping me for everything you can get. But I understand. You're a newspaperwoman; you're supposed to do that. Just make sure you write a bang-up story about us."

"I promise. So, are you buying Maria's story about the tower's being too expensive to renovate?"

"Not for a minute," Mrs. Gibbs admitted. She went to the door and peered out into the main room, then came back and sat down. Leaning even closer to Emily, she said, "I suppose I'm a shameless gossip, but . . . about six months ago Maria was out and Frank was in when I went by. He'd just finished tearing down the old stairwell to the tower, and I complained that I'd never seen the inside of it. That's when he told me he hardly ever went in there himself. But there was another door—Maria had insisted he put it in before he took out the original stairs—and Frank let me peek in on the top floor.

"But," she continued, "he was very nervous about it. I stuck my head in and saw an enormous four-poster bed, unmade, *with clean sheets and blankets on it.* Well, you know me. I said, 'For goodness' sake! Are you renting this out?' and Frank seemed mortified. It was only later that I put two and two together: He had no idea that Maria was sleeping in the tower."

"That's crazy. Of course, he'd know!" Emily blurted.

"Oh, he knew she didn't always sleep in their bed. He told me once that Maria was a restless sleeper and sometimes took an available guest room not to disturb him. But I'm positive he didn't know she was spending her nights in the four-poster."

"Hmm."

"That's what I say. *Hmm.*" She pressed her fork into the last few yellow crumbs on her plate to gather them up.

"Well, obviously she's not having an affair," Emily said bluntly. "Their clientele changes daily."

"That's a *scandalous* thought," Mrs. Gibbs said sharply, shocked by Emily's modern candor. "Not what I meant at all. If I was trying to hint at anything, it was that maybe Maria isn't happy with the"—she cleared her throat—"physical side of marriage."

"Well, she's picked a heck of a place to hide out from it. It's almost as if she sees herself as the princess locked in the tower by the cruel king, waiting for her knight in armor to come and rescue her."

Mrs. Gibbs thought about it. She nodded to herself and murmured, "Poor Frank."

"The question is," Emily said softly, "who's the knight?"

Though Emily stayed dutifully poised over the keyboard of her office computer for the entire afternoon, her mind had broken free from her fingertips and was poking around the top floor of the manor's tower. A vivid, relentless picture of Maria—Marie—

fleeing from Frank's bed and crawling into the big four-poster kept blotting out the dull, plodding text on the screen before her.

Why would a poised and well-educated woman steal away periodically to a room filled with cobwebs and mice? Was Frank, with his Sears, Roebuck furniture, really so unbearably mundane? And if Maria was so fascinated by the historic, romantic manor, why did she act as if she knew nothing about it and cared less? A smoke screen? But why? More and more Emily was convinced that Maria held the key to all the secrets of Talbot Manor, past and present.

"Yo! Bowditch!" It was her editor, Phil Sparke, knocking sharply on the side of her desk. "You with us today?" He was the kind of man who treated his female staff exactly the same as he did the men who worked for him, which wasn't very well at all.

"Just barely, chief," she answered truthfully. *Kyle Edwards! That was the name! The name on the packet of envelopes postmarked from France!*

"I really *would* like an answer to my question," Phil said with biting courtesy.

"What was the question?" she asked absently.

"The *interview!* The *goddammed interview!*" he roared.

"Oh. Right. Done. I edited it this morning. Stan has it for review."

"How'd it go?" he demanded, chomping down hard on a cigar butt.

"Very well. I was very impressed." *The envelopes all were postmarked in 1972.*

"Did you nail him on the paranormal shit?"

1972. Were they written in a feminine hand? Definitely. "Uh, not exactly, actually."

" 'Not exactly, actually'? *Yes or no,* Bowditch? Did you bring up the *Newsweek* quote?"

"Newsweek?" *Was Kyle Edwards her knight in shining armor? But how could he be? In 1972 Maria was barely a teenager.*

"What am I, talking to a tape recorder? If you blew the interview, Bowditch, your ass is in a sling. I want a copy on my desk before you leave."

Emily hadn't had her ass put in a sling all that often in life; it was a new and unsettling feeling. She printed a copy of the interview for the managing editor but held on to it while she waited for Stan to return with his opinion. When he did show up, around six, she could see instantly that he was unenthusiastic.

"No good, huh?" she said glumly.

He shrugged. "It's fine, as far as it goes. But here's your competition." He threw a copy of *USA Today* across her desk.

It made the front page: MASS. SENATOR DESPERATELY SEEKING NICOLE.

Pop-eyed with disbelief, Emily read through the piece. "Senator Lee Alden, who is said to have considered resigning his seat after the death of his wife, Nicole, attended a séance in Westford, Mass., last month in an attempt to establish contact with her. Lois Lividus, a Hungarian psychic who manages a channeler known only as Kimberly, invited the senator to the sitting. Several scholars and at least one member of the area press were also present. It is not known whether Senator Alden made contact 'across the veil.' "

"Oh, God. I'm dead." She held her head down with both hands, as if it were going to fall off her shoulders. "What do I do now? My glowing interview just became a joke. I look like Lee Alden's speech writer."

"Worse come to worst, it's a living," Stan said dryly.

She ignored his sarcasm. "Who could've leaked this?"

Stan's lids were half lowered, his thin, long lips curled in an ironic smile. "Maybe it was that member of the 'area press.' "

She shook her head. "No way." She stared at the paper in front of her, still incredulous. "Phil will have my head on a platter for sidestepping this issue. Or worse," she moaned, remembering his threat. "I'll lose my job."

"I doubt it."

Suddenly it dawned on her: "Lee Alden will lose *his* job!"

"That all depends on the voters," Stan said grimly.

And he'll blame me, Emily realized, aghast. It was unbelievable. Through no fault of her own she—and Lee—were going to go down in flames. She sat at her desk, barely acknowledging Stan's amused good night, trying to come up with a way out of the impasse.

At seven o'clock she walked into Phil Sparke's office with a copy of her interview and the *USA Today*. "I'm going to make it easy on you, chief," she said, sighing. "I'm requesting a leave of absence."

Phil yanked the cigar butt from between his teeth. "What the hell you talkin' about?"

"Stan was right; I'm in over my head on the business with Lee Alden. Politics is a big boy's game. My interview reads like something from a high school paper," she said with brutal honesty.

She watched him give his collar a hard yank, always a bad sign. "But that's not the reason I'm asking for some time off. I have some truly pressing, truly urgent personal business to take care of. It's affecting the quality of my work. I simply can't do both anymore. It's a matter, literally, of life and death."

Phil leaned back in his chair and deliberately, slowly read the *USA Today* piece, then skimmed through her interview. It was obvious that he was glancing at her questions, not the senator's answers. Finally he looked up. " 'Life and death' won't cut it. Be specific, Bowditch. Why do you want the time off?"

"I *can't,* Phil. You know that I would never ask for a leave if there were another way. I've never cut out from an assignment, much less from a job, in my life. Begging for this is taking everything I've got," she added with a desperate look at him.

He stuck the two-inch butt in his mouth, then struck a match on the underside of his desk. After two or three deep drags he got the end of the cigar to glow again and, with a deft roll, had it anchored in its usual position on the left side of his mouth. "How long we talkin'?"

She took a deep breath. "A month, more or less. Effective at once."

"Like hell. You'll finish out the week. And you'll check in once a week after that. And what about the historical piece you were doing on that mill family in Newarth?"

"Oh, I'll definitely finish that in the next month," she promised without a trace of irony. "And I have a couple of smaller things I can crank out. One of them is that piece on dangerous summer toys."

He clamped his jaw and ground at the end of his cigar, then pushed her interview and the hated *USA Today* across his desk. "Shitcan this interview. And the paper, too."

Red-faced, she gathered up the papers. "I'm sorry about this, Phil."

"I can't guarantee things will be the same when

you come back," he said calmly. "You're good, I won't deny that. But I can't guarantee."

"I accept that, chief."

She fled feeling empty, frightened, and broke.

The week passed uneventfully. Fergus did one of his disappearing acts, leaving Emily to wonder why. He might have heard her conversation with Phil and was biding his time, or he might have gone into angry hiding after their confrontation in the rain. The only excitement in the week came from a brief statement read by Jim Whitewood, Senator Alden's aide, to the press. The statement confirmed that in accordance with Senator Alden's ongoing interest in the paranormal he had, indeed, attended a channeling the month before. The senator saw nothing to convince him that anything got channeled.

"Ha! Easy for you to say," Emily murmured, watching Whitewood on the Friday evening news.

She was now officially on leave and spent the evening clearing the decks for action: tossing every unread magazine, book, and catalog in her condo. Emptying the top drawer of her file cabinet. Clearing two shelves of her bookcase. Moving her desk to face the wall instead of the view. Formatting a computer disk to hold the mounting volume of information on Hessiah Talbot's murder. Laying in a supply of junk food and index cards.

I'm ready, she decided at midnight. *I'm ready, and I feel good about it.* She really did believe she was the best person to track down Hessiah's murderer. *Lee won't, and Fergus can't. It's as simple as that,* she told herself. She hoped that Fergus would accept her leave of absence as a kind of token of good faith. The look in his eyes, the sound of his voice during their last meeting were still very much with her. He had stirred her soul, and she knew things would never be the same between them again.

"Not that I have a clue what they were in the first place," she mumbled, filling a tea immerser with leaves of Darjeeling.

And then there was Lee Alden, her slightly eccentric, madly handsome, but all too rational . . . ex-lover, would he be? She supposed so. One time—that was all they'd had together. Tears welled in her eyes; she blotted them with her wrists. *Next time fall in love with someone who has a humbler career,* she told herself, sliding the kettle off the burner. *Like an astronaut or a brain surgeon.*

She poured boiling water over the stainless perforated egg and watched it brew. Suddenly she seemed to have time for things like this: for watching the water turn from clear to gold to deep brown. Since she was sixteen, she'd never gone a whole month without working, without a paycheck. It didn't seem possible that she'd be doing it now.

It'd be just my luck to solve the crime tomorrow and have to be back in the office on Monday. And here was another first: She didn't want to. She, the tireless one, was tired of having to be somewhere on Monday. From waiting on tables to selling shoes to investigative reporting, she'd had it with Mondays. "Is that all there is to life?" she whispered. "An endless series of Mondays?

"It's time to get a cat," she said, disgusted by her self-pitying mood. "At least then I won't be talking to myself all the time."

Outside, it was raining—the fourth soaker that week—and inside, it seemed damp and chill, even for late June. Emily pulled her ratty chenille robe around her more tightly and sipped her tea, trying not to think about either Lee or Fergus. She had the Newarth phone book open to the white pages. It was time to think about Kyle Edwards.

19

There were thirteen Edwardses, none of them a Kyle, in the Newarth phone directory, and on Saturday afternoon Emily called them all. The responses ranged from "No Kyle here" to "Who wants to know?" But when she reached Timothy Edwards, she reached pay dirt. Timothy Edwards had a nephew named Kyle who was living in Cambridge—the last anyone heard anyway.

An operator gave Emily a number, and she called it, fingers dancing over the phone with excitement. At the other end a laid-back voice answered. "Yeah, this is Kyle Edwards," he said in a not unfriendly way.

"Mr. Edwards, this is Emily Bowditch. I'm writing a feature story for the *Boston Journal* about Talbot Manor in Newarth. I understand from my research that you had some connection with the place?"

"Hey, no kidding? The manor, huh? I lived there for a couple of years."

Yes, she thought ecstatically, punching a victory fist into thin air. "That's what I thought," she said in a carefully calm voice. "I came across some old term papers of yours there."

"So what's up?" he asked. "Has someone made me their heir? If so, thanks but no thanks. No one needs a white elephant like the manor in their life."

"Well, you can sleep easy, then," she said, laughing. "No one's left it to you. No, I'm just doing profiles of people who've lived there, from the original owners up to the present. I wonder if I could meet with you and get some of your thoughts. It wouldn't take long."

"Sure. What about this afternoon? You in town?"

"I live in Charlestown—"

"Close enough. Can you be in Cambridge tomorrow?"

"Nothing to it; I have to go to the Harvard Coop anyway," she lied. They agreed to meet at the Tangiers coffeehouse in Harvard Square at two in the afternoon. Emily hung up.

That was when she saw Fergus appear alongside her desk. At least, trying to. But his image was indistinct, blurry at the edges. Emily rubbed her eyes; it was as if a film were covering them. She blinked and tried again, but the image remained dim and unfocused. The only thing she could see well were his eyes, which seemed to burn with more indignation than ever. He looked hurt and angry and—something new—anxious.

"Fergus!" she cried, panicky herself now. "You're not coming in clearly!" She jumped up in alarm.

"Mother o' God," he snapped, "I ain't a TV!"

She wanted to run and get him a glass of water, or help him to her bed so that he could lie down, or fan his face with a magazine. Or give him ammonia salts. Or CPR. But there was nothing she could do, nothing. She could only stand by helplessly while he closed his eyes and took on a look of intense concentration that left her feeling weak-kneed.

Whatever it was that Fergus did, it brought him back into sharp focus. The brown of his vest became distinct from the gray of his pants, and the little details, like the four flaps on his vest, became visible once more. But the effort seemed to cost him; he looked exhausted.

"What's happening?" Emily asked faintly, feeling wan and exhausted herself. It was as if they were bound by a common blood supply.

He shook his head. "I don't know; this is new." He made a dismissive gesture, as if he didn't want to talk about it. "Who is this Kyle Edwards?" he asked in a still-unsteady voice.

Emily told him about the bound packet of airmail letters from France that she'd noticed in the drawer of the desk in the tower. "They were written in a young girl's hand, postmarked Paris, and the penmanship was distinctly European. Okay, it's a wild hunch, but I think Maria Salva wrote them to Kyle when she was a teenager."

A tired smile softened the strained features of Fergus's face. "Wild hunch? A flying leap into the great unknown, I'd call it."

"You've got to have more faith in me," she insisted, hurt. A surge of deep emotion for him rippled through her, sending color into her cheeks; she was remembering every word of his impassioned protest of the week before. Obviously, if anyone had faith in her, Fergus did. "That was such a dumb thing for me to say," she admitted.

Fergus was off his feet now, sitting on the floor next to her desk, his head leaning into the wall behind him, his legs stretched out in front of him. The light from her desk lamp was shining on the top of his head, highlighting the shafts of auburn in his hair. His fair skin seemed even more pale than usual. Once again she had an overwhelming urge to reach out and touch him, but she knew, now more than ever, that she'd be crossing the line between two different dimensions. She had to respect that line.

"Are you all right?" she asked, wanting reassurance.

He shrugged. "Time will tell." He meant to sound offhand, but his green eyes were blazing at her from under his brows.

Whenever he'd looked at her that way before, she'd felt either frightened or uncomfortable. But something was different now. This time she didn't look away or try to return the look defiantly. This time she drank it in the way a thirsty child drinks water on a summer day.

"We don't have much more of it—time, I mean," she whispered. "Do we?"

In a voice surprised by its own sadness he said, "Every day I borrow a little more of it." He added with an ironic smile, "Trouble is, no one's told me my credit limit."

"Welcome to the American banking system," she said with an attempt at lightness. But her heart was beginning to crack.

"Emily—"

"Yes?"

"I know this is taking a toll on ye—with yer senator, I mean," he said, his eyes burning with emotion. "I cannot stand to hurt ye."

She leaned her elbows on the desk and propped her chin on her open palms. Emotion was welling up; she was trying very hard not to cry. "That's what friends are for, Fergus," she said with a melancholy smile.

"So it's true. Somewhere along the line we've become friends, ye and me. Real friends." He closed his eyes and leaned his head back. "Oh, brother. This was not part of the plan."

Emily studied him thoughtfully. "Did you actually have a plan?"

"I did, and ye don't want to know it," he said with a grim twist upward of his mouth. "It might strain the friendship."

She lifted her chin from her hands; her eyes became wary. The old tingle rippled down her spine. "You really intended to harm me? Once you got what you needed—"

"Emily, I've told ye before," he interrupted gently, "earthly notions of right and wrong do not carry over to the state of nothingness."

"But it was an earthly wrong that put you there in the first place," she argued, distressed. "Are you saying that if there are other astral beings trapped as you are in that state, they'll do whatever they have to do to break out of it? Whether it's right or wrong? They don't have to go by any rules of conduct?"

"I know only about myself," he said wearily.

"But there must be other beings like you. What about Talbot Manor, in fact? If there *is* a power of some kind there, it could be trapped the same way you are." He shrugged, and she said, "It could be trying to break out of its nothingness the same way you are. And it could be prepared to do whatever it takes, the same way you were. Of course!"

She jumped up, jittery with nervous energy and resolve, and trekked over to the Mr. Coffee machine to set up the last thing she needed, a pot of caffeine. "I've been assuming that the only thing haunting Talbot Manor was Maria Salva—or, at worst, some poltergeist that she was creating. That's Lee's fault; he's the one who got me going on poltergeists as projections of psychic disturbances—because I do believe that Maria is disturbed. But now I see a simpler explanation."

She dumped a good part of a bag of ground A&P coffee into the pleated filter and slid the drip tray back into the machine. Instantly it began to glub and hiss, an evil, manipulative sound to her ears. She turned around to Fergus, gripping the counter's edge behind her.

"It's my belief that the manor is possessed by Hessiah Talbot's murderer," she said with almost lurid intensity.

Fergus was seated sideways on the sofa, his legs folded in front of him like a Buddha's. "Ye sound like them Basil Rathbone Sherlocks I been watchin'," he said, chuckling despite himself. "Let me see if I have this correct. Ye think that the murderer is itching to break out of his entrapped state—"

"Yes!"

"So that he—or she—can rush headlong into his—or her—punishment."

"Oh." She chewed on the inside of her cheek while she stared at the thin brown stream of liquid filling the glass decanter. "I suppose it's true; he doesn't have as much to gain as you do. *But,"* she said, pulling out a mug from the rack, "you said yourself you'd rather exist in someplace like hell than not exist at all. Why couldn't the murderer feel that way, too?"

"If it *is* the murderer we're even talking about," Fergus added, slipping back into melancholy. "This is too damn fanciful for me. I need some facts."

"Then tag along with me to Cambridge tomorrow," Emily answered, filled with confidence enough for both of them. "I'll give you facts enough to fill a barn."

* * *

That night Emily slept poorly, probably because she'd overdosed on caffeine. Sometime before dawn she was troubled by a tremendous awareness that she was not alone in the room. Fretful and anxious but still half asleep, she opened one eye slightly and was able to make out Fergus standing at the foot of her bed, arms folded across his chest. The sense that it was the last time she'd ever see him cut through her like a bolt of lightning.

"Fergus!" she cried, her voice ripping through the night's stillness.

He was absolutely silent: unwilling, or unable, to answer her.

"Don't leave me," she moaned in sleep-shattered confusion. "You always do that . . . so don't . . . anymore . . . please . . . I don't want you to go. . . ."

He remained there silently, a look of intense emotion on his face, and eventually Emily, confused and disoriented, fell back asleep. In the morning she couldn't remember the incident with any clarity at all.

The Tangiers coffeehouse, tucked in a small alley behind the Harvard Coop, was one of many intimate gathering spots that make up the lifeblood of Harvard Square. Subterranean and dimly lit, it had a reputation for attracting aging hippies and unorthodox intellectuals. Emily asked for and left her name with a waitress named Laura and was led to a small round table in the corner. The brick floor, bentwood chairs, and Bob Dylan sound track lent a certain earnest ambience to the place. Kyle Edwards, seated at the corner table, fitted right in.

He was a big man, gray-bearded and balding and

gone a little to seed. Emily introduced herself, and he put out his cigarette at once, shuffling to his feet with a bulky man's awkwardness. The hand he extended was surprisingly soft.

They sat down together and talked a little about Cambridge. Emily learned that Kyle had dropped out of Harvard Business School to protest the war in Vietnam. He'd never gone back and was casually vague about what he did for a living.

"For the past twenty years I've dealt in a little of this, a little of that," he said amiably, lighting up another cigarette. "D'you mind?" he asked as an afterthought.

"Not at all," Emily replied stoically.

He sent a stream of smoke scudding through the side of his mouth. "So tell me about Talbot Manor. Is it the same pile of rubble it was when we lived there in the early seventies?"

"I wanted to ask you who all was there," she asked after filling him in about the renovations.

"Gawd, that's hard to say. We came and went. I mean, someone'd crash there for a few days or weeks and then move on. You know how it was." He sized up her youth with a grimace and a sigh. "Or maybe you don't."

"I have a pretty good picture," she said. "So you were in a commune. Was there anything special that bound you to one another—the antiwar movement, the Whole Earth thing, something like that?" What she really wanted was to know whether he was part of a religious or drug cult of any kind.

"Nah. Everyone was into, y'know, something, but we weren't all into the same thing. One of the women used to tie-dye shirts and sell 'em on the corner. Then there was Varuna. She worked with clay and kept a pet chicken. She had a potter's wheel up on the top floor of that tower—jeez, we had to haul that concrete kick wheel up there for her, must've weighed a coupla hundred pounds. Some of the stairs actually collapsed under us, but we managed to save the wheel. Course, Bill—Bill something—did break a leg. I can't believe I've forgotten his last name."

He took a deep drag of his cigarette, held in the smoke reflectively, then sent it off like a missile. "Yeah, those were the days."

Emily was busy scratching down the memories of the shaggy leftover from Woodstock. A pet chicken in the tower; at least now she had a good idea where the small bones had come from. "So you had a kind of arts and crafts commune, would you say?"

He flicked an ash into an empty saucer. "Well, no one took the trouble to apply for a retail tax number or anything, if that's what you mean," he said dryly. "Like I said, we did a little of this, a little of that. Whatever it took to get by."

The Bob Dylan album launched into the plaintive "Tomorrow Is a Long Time," and Kyle became thoughtful. He had the look of a man who'd been hurt by a woman a long time ago. Still, after a moment he shook himself free of the memory with a lame smile —Emily suspected he was the kind who got emotionally sideswiped often—and returned to the conversation.

With his elbows propped on the black tabletop, one hand folded loosely over the other, a plume of smoke snaking from the cigarette he held, he looked attractively sinister. "Now. What is it you *really* want to know?" he asked with a flash of sudden, shrewd intelligence.

"Since you ask," she said with a level look, "what was your connection with Maria Salva? You'd have known her by the name Marie. She lived in France and sent you quite a few letters at one time." It was pretty brazen bluffing, considering Emily hadn't had the wits to look at the return addresses on the other sides of the envelopes when she was in the tower.

For a long while—too long—Kyle looked puzzled, struggling with the information. Finally he put it together. "Marie . . . right! The kid who got thrown in a convent! How do you know about her?"

"I'll tell you after you tell me," Emily answered lightly.

"Isn't much to tell. It's probably been fifteen years or more since I've thought about her. I remember how it started. Varuna came into my room one day with a letter addressed to the caretaker of Talbot Manor. No one wanted to bother with it, and I had nothing to do, so I thought what the hell. The letter was one of those teenage ramblings, you know how kids are—all earnestness and naïve sincerity."

He motioned the waitress for a refill on his coffee. "Apparently the kid had journals or something of ancestors who were supposed to have lived in Talbot Manor; maybe they were Talbots, maybe not, I don't remember. So she was on this *Roots* kick, you know? Where you want to trace your lineage? Only she seemed *really* into it; she yearned to walk the halls, feel the pain, that kind of thing. She seemed a little around the, uh, bend, you know what I mean? A little *too* intense, even for a teenage girl. I should know; I've got one of my own now. Somewhere."

Emily nodded sympathetically, noting that Kyle was taking some kind of emotional hit even as he spoke.

But just as quickly he recovered. "So I sent off some nice little answer about, yeah, how the place reeks of history, figuring that would be that. No such luck. Every two weeks I got another letter and more questions. She wanted room-by-room descriptions. She wanted to know every piece of furniture. She wanted *photographs*, for Pete's sake. Yeah, I remember now. As a kind of joke we all got in front of a tripod one night—we were zonked—and sent off a group photo. I seem to remember it was a pretty funky shot."

He shook his head, chuckling at the memory. "Next thing I know, I get a letter from her parents threatening me with the Mann Act if I go near their daughter. She's in Paris, I'm in Newarth, but never mind. They said she was being shipped off to a convent, just to make sure. Grissette. That was her name. Marie Grissette." Pleased that at least part of his memory was still intact, Kyle leaned back in his chair.

"And you never heard from her again?"

"Not a word. If there were any more letters, I never got them; I moved on."

"What did the parents seem like? Could you tell?"

"Well educated. Articulate. Uptight. Marie was their only kid, I think. I suppose it was the photo that freaked them out. A bunch of long-haired hippies in tie-dyed rags lying on top of one another—it was a joke, but I could see where a parent might not think it was all that funny. Poor Marie. I wonder where she ended up." He gave Emily another shrewd look. "I take it you know?"

"Coincidentally, Marie's living in Talbot Manor," Emily answered with a bland face. She took another sip of thick French brew. "She's married to the present owner."

"Whoa," Kyle said softly. "That's pretty heavy." He took out his Camels and tapped the packet across the edge of the table. "Still, it doesn't surprise me. Her letters were loaded with talk of kismet and karma.

Strange kid. I'll have to go around there one of these days and say hi."

He stuck a cigarette in his mouth and began patting his pockets for matches. "Or not," he said between compressed lips. "Newarth's always depressed me. I'm not sure why."

But Emily knew. "Because there's a curse on the town, that's why."

They parted amicably a few minutes later. The afternoon was warm and pleasant, and since Emily had just about had her fill of living like a cave dweller, she strolled the half dozen blocks over to the Longfellow House to take advantage of the outdoor concert series there. She found a quiet spot on the side grounds of the historic yellow house—where George and Martha Washington had spent their seventeenth anniversary—and settled in for an hour or so of classical guitar and violin.

The crowd of a hundred was friendly and evenly split among the old, the middle-aged, and the young. Several couples came with infants packed neatly in carriers. Nearby a pretty woman with flame red hair rocked her baby to the soothing sounds of a baroque sonata while her husband sipped bottled lemonade. A black Labrador with a red kerchief tied around its neck worked the edges of the crowd, panhandling for sandwich scraps, then lay down obediently next to its master, a John Lennon look-alike with steel-rimmed glasses.

These are very nice people, she thought, pleased that she'd come. *The music is wonderful. The sun is shining. And it's free.*

And she was alone. Her thoughts drifted inevitably to Fergus, who could be there just like that if he wanted to be. Under her breath she whispered his name, though she'd never yet succeeded in making him show.

Fergus—for once, for one wonderful once—appeared alongside her, his legs pulled up in front of him, leaning back on his hands.

"I love this," he said happily. "When I was a boy, I worked in a stable near a concert hall. Me dad knew the rear doorman, who used to let me sneak in backstage. The music's eighteenth-century, right? Ye're a wonderful woman, Emily Bowditch." He turned to her with a look that took her breath away. "I will not forget this." For the first time, ever, he reached his hand out to her, as if he wanted to stroke her hair. "If only I—

"Anyway," he said, turning back to the performance, his jaw set resolutely. "Ye're a wonderful woman, Emily Bowditch."

Emily listened to the rest of the performance in a state of exaltation, because the music was expressing exactly what she was feeling. The low strains of the guitar moved some unknown part of her soul, and the violin answered in an anguished, tremulous voice that exactly matched her thoughts.

But Emily wasn't a composer; she couldn't analyze her feelings for Fergus in musical terms. All she had were words, and words weren't enough. How did she feel about him? What *could* she feel about him? Every once in a while she'd turn to look at him, and he'd return her look. They were sharing something very deep, very real, for the first time.

The final rondo wound to a lively close, and everyone applauded. The concert was over. Emily turned, and Fergus was gone. People began to gather up their blankets and babies and backpacks. The Labrador made one last pass through the crowd and came back with a pork chop bone; for some reason it chose to drop down next to Emily to gnaw on its spoils. It was a friendly Lab and submitted with grace to Emily's pats on its head.

"Hey, boy," she murmured, scratching its ears. "You made out pretty well this afternoon." She thought about Kyle Edwards and Marie Grissette, and then she thought about Fergus. She was aware of a rush of pleasure passing all through her.

"And so did I."

20

The next time Emily saw Lee Alden she was sitting in —of all places—a bar, and he was on television.

The bar was near the Newarth Library, and the $3.99 supper special seemed too good to be true. As it turned out, the Reuben was a rip-off (soggy bread, rubbery corned beef) and the draft brew tasted more like a near beer. Still, if Emily hadn't ducked into the place, she'd never have known that Lee Alden was the featured guest on *Bay State Live,* a local interview and call-in show.

Emily's table wasn't really close enough to hear the TV, perched high above the far end of the bar. *Fine with me,* she decided initially. She had no interest in tracking the perils of Lee's career. She had plenty of other perils to track.

And wasn't it just like him to turn up on a five o'clock show—when women were in their kitchens, making supper with their small TVs on? Oh, he knew where and when to reach his voters, all right. And how *annoying* that he was so photogenic.

She sneaked a second look, then a third. By the time the waitress came by with her after-meal coffee, Emily had thrown up her hands emotionally. She pointed to the television and said, "Would you mind turning it up a bit?"

"Sure, honey," the waitress answered, shifting her gum over to her right molars. "Ain't he a doll? Hey, Jack. Kick it up a little, will ya?"

The bartender didn't think much of the idea. "How about you bring your coffee over here instead?" he said to Emily.

So she took her cup and settled in at the empty bar with the waitress and Jack while the only other customers, three men and a woman, hovered around a video game near the other end.

"You been followin' this guy?" Jack asked Emily. "He's some hot ticket. Never saw anyone so dead set on getting voted outta office. It's like he's got some kinda suicide wish."

"Baloney," the waitress said. "He ain't afraid to say what he feels, that's all. Which is more than I can say about the rest of them jerks in Washington. What d'*you* think, honey? What's wrong with a guy believing in ghosts?"

"Well-l-l, I'm not exactly sure he does believe in them," Emily answered carefully. She glanced cautiously at the light fixtures. *Stay out of this, Fergus,* she prayed.

"The heck he don't!" the waitress shot back. "The *Enquirer* says he's living with the ghost of his wife on some uninhabited island off the coast of Massachusetts."

"What?"

"I got out my atlas; I figure it has to be one of the Elizabeth Islands," she said, tearing off Emily's check from a pad and slapping it on the bar. "Where else could it be?"

"Brenda's a stickler for detail," the bartender offered dryly. "Bren, I told you once, I told you a thousand times. Don't ever, never believe what you read in the papers. Right, miss?"

Emily cleared her throat. "Absolutely." She moved over to the next barstool, closer to the television. "Let's hear what the senator has to say for himself," she suggested, desperate to know what was going on.

They'd missed the whole beginning. At the moment the program's host was summing up the senator's record in Congress, toting up the legislation he'd proposed that had or had not passed. Put that way, it did sound dry.

"Bor-rring," said Brenda. "Switch to *Cheers*."

"And that brings us, Senator, to a subject that's been much in the news of late: your interest in the paranormal."

"Wait!" cried Brenda and Emily together.

Jack put the remote back on the bar. "That's it; he's dead meat now," he said, looking forward to the kill.

In his blazer, striped tie, and gray flannels Lee looked typically at ease, as though being asked about ghosts were an everyday thing for a senator.

Emily had never watched the program before, probably because she'd never been out of work so early on a weeknight before. She had no idea of the host's political bias, but he seemed to her a fair man.

"You've admitted attending a séance recently in an attempt to establish contact with your wife, who died two years ago," the host elaborated.

"That's not quite accurate, Jim," Lee said amiably. "I'd read an interesting piece in a magazine about poltergeists, and the house I visited had had on-and-off reports of some kind of disturbances within."

"You mean the house was haunted?"

Lee weighed the question. "I don't know. Apparently some of its owners thought so."

"And what did you think?"

"I thought it looked like an old house that needed work."

"What about this Kimberly, this channeler?"

"I'd rather not say too much about her because I understand she's just gone back to her parents to live."

"You mean she's had a change of heart? She doesn't want to do séances anymore?"

"I can't say that she ever wanted to channel. I think she was willing to give it a try, and it didn't work out for her. Historically such people have been sensitive and high-strung in the extreme. Whatever it is they do, it seems to be a demanding, exhausting effort."

"You sound like you believe in these so-called clairvoyants, Senator."

"I'd like to," he admitted. "I think we all would. I think that people who *do* have the ability to believe are in general happier than the skeptics."

"I'd love to ask you more, Senator, but I think I'll throw the phones open and let our viewers have the chance now. Yes," the host said into a mike. "You're on the air. Go ahead."

The voice that came on was sweet, young, and timid. "I wanted to know, Senator, if you've ever seen your wife in any way or at any time after she passed away?"

The bartender chuckled maliciously. "That's cutting to the chase."

Emily watched with trepidation. How would Lee get out of that one?

"After she passed away? No," Lee answered after a pause.

"Oh." The caller was obviously disappointed. "Then you're not—"

"Living on a deserted island with my wife's ghost? Nope."

"That's too bad," said the caller, and she really meant it. "It would've been such a romantic story."

"That it would," said Lee with a half nod and a smile that made Brenda sigh.

Another caller, this time a man. "Senator, if you don't mind my saying so, this is horse manure. No one much cares what you do with your spare time, as long as it doesn't cost anything. But I don't mind telling you, I resent any more money for SETI. Let's put the Search for Extraterrestrial Intelligence on a back burner for now. We've got other fish to fry up front. Well?"

"You have a point, sir," said Lee. "There'll have to be cuts, and SETI is one of them. I don't like it, but it'd be unconscionable to go forward with an ambitious program until we've paid our bills and taken care of the many who're going down for the third time."

Jack snorted. "See that? Backpedaling. I knew he would."

Another caller, another man. "I've voted for you in the past, Senator, but I've never felt too comfortable about it. Now, with all these rumors flying right and left, well, I wanted you to know that I'm voting for Congressman Strom in the primary, and so are the guys I play poker with. I don't exactly trust the fella, but like I said, we don't go much for this supernatural stuff. We all believe you shouldn't be poking around in it, even as a hobby."

In a carefully patient voice Lee said something

about keeping an open mind, but the rest of his remark was drowned out by Jack. "Oh, yeah, that's how this one's gonna go," the bartender decided. "Gals for him, guys for Strom. That's because men vote with their heads, women with their hearts."

"Men vote with their heads?" cried Brenda. "Who you kidding? Men never bother to think; they just vote a straight ticket."

They were off and running on a track they seemed to have covered before—politics. High-spirited and noisy, the two of them easily shouted down Lee and his call-in viewers. Emily was reduced to trying to read Lee's lips. All things considered, she preferred not to concentrate there; the memories of his kisses were still too painful.

A customer came in, forcing an end to Jack's lively defense of his sex and allowing Emily to hear a voice say over the rolling credits, "Portions of this program will be rebroadcast on Sunday morning at nine-thirty on *Bay State Week in Review.*"

She tried to forget the announcement she'd just heard, dropped a five-dollar bill on the counter, and went away more frustrated than not. She realized now that the day of her interview had been a turning point in their relationship. She'd watched Lee walk a fence between faith and skepticism, and then she'd watched him trip and fall on the wrong damn side. How painfully ironic that he was being skewered for being a believer.

In the last half hour it had also become obvious that forgetting him was bound to be an uphill battle. The trick was to avoid being reminded of him. In some ways that wouldn't be hard. It wasn't as though she had a photo album of their time together, or love letters from him, or a song they'd shared, or even some dried corsage to mope over. On the other hand, the senator did have a distressing habit of popping up in newspapers, in magazines, and now on television.

And with a primary coming up, he was bound to be popping up more and more. Just that morning she'd read that he'd hired a campaign manager (not Cara Miles—praise the Lord—but some heavy hitter who'd run the last New York senatorial campaign). That person was being paid ten thousand dollars a month to keep Lee Alden's face in front of Emily at all times.

But. If he *did* lose the primary race—and for the first time Emily was beginning to believe that could happen—he'd probably leave politics to become senior partner in some high-powered law firm. He'd drop out of the public eye. And out of sight, after all, was out of mind.

Gee, Em, why stop there? she asked herself caustically. *Why not hope that he gets kidnapped by an adoring constituent and locked away in her basement? Wouldn't that be helpful?*

Emily squared her shoulders. Getting over the man was going to be a long, hard battle. If it wasn't for Fergus O'Malley, she wasn't certain she'd be up to it.

On Sunday morning Emily and Fergus were sifting for clues in the rubble of debris that she'd dragged home after a week of research. Fergus, thinking he was doing Emily a kindness, zapped on *Bay State Week in Review.* Lee Alden's chiseled face was being featured in close-up.

She protested, then went over to the television to turn it off. But she didn't, or couldn't, and ended up standing next to the tube with her hand on the button —ready, willing, but not quite able to switch Lee Alden out of her life. She was painfully aware that he'd made no attempt to see her since the interview. Granted, Congress was still in session, but she knew full well that the senator had been spending weekends in Massachusetts on damage control.

"The bloke's under siege," Fergus said thoughtfully as he studied the senator's image flickering on the screen. "Ye think he'll pull through in one piece?"

"It doesn't look good," Emily admitted. "Stan Cooper's roughing him up pretty badly in my paper. And Stan's not the only one."

"Aye. They travel in a pack, them press people—present company excepted, o' course. Times haven't changed much that way. It's funny, though. The man don't even believe."

"Ah, but he's admitted he'd *like* to believe, and that's enough for most of them."

The program ended; Emily turned it off with a funny little sound, as if she were straining to move a heavy piece of furniture.

"I'd vote for him," Fergus admitted. "It does puzzle me why some folks want him brought down. He's quick, honest, smart—"

"Three good reasons, my friend," Emily said tersely. "Can we talk about something else now?"

"I understand," Fergus said.

He did understand. Lately the two of them seemed to operate on exactly the same wavelength; Emily could hardly remember their last sharp exchange. Despite the fact that they were divided by sex, status, education, even the centuries themselves, they were completely in tune. When Emily bothered to wonder why, she always came to the same conclusion: Each of them had decided to trust the other because neither of them had anything to lose. That just wasn't true between Lee Alden and her.

Perhaps more important, Fergus and Emily shared the same obsession: solving Hessiah Talbot's murder. Ironically it was the shrewd Mrs. Gibbs who'd pointed Emily to her most interesting find recently. On Wednesday the librarian had called Emily at home. "Are you aware," she had asked, "that the *Newarth Sentinel* has complete archives of all the newspapers it's published—"

"Sure, that's standard practice," Emily, puzzled by the call, had told her.

"—and that the *Sentinel* also keeps copies of pieces that were written up but never published?"

"I didn't know that! As far back as 1887?"

"Well, maybe the records aren't complete, but it's worth a look."

"I'll go there tomorrow," Emily had answered.

On Thursday Emily had called the *Sentinel* and got permission to go through its library. On Friday she'd spent the day carefully sifting through crumbling copy that had never made the leap to the printed page. The archives seemed almost maniacally in order; some old New England newspapers were like that.

She'd managed to pan out one gold nugget: a column, written by what passed for a society columnist back then, that covered what had to be the last ball in Hessiah Talbot's life. It seemed to Emily that the account of the ball must have become suddenly awkward after the murder of its most prominent guest and been pulled at the last minute.

It was written in the typically breathless, gushing voice of the society writer and described the guests, their clothes, the decorative theme (silver and gold), and the designated charity (local soup kitchen). It was a fascinating piece, filled with small and telling details. When Emily returned to her condo that night, she called Mrs. Gibbs and thanked her profusely.

Now for the tenth time she was reading the column back to Fergus.

"Okay, let's see what we've got," she said, between spoons of oat bran cereal. "We've got Mrs. William Wellington the Fourth. She sounds like an enormous woman, or she'd never have been able to wear a gown with 'a thousand golden roses sewn into its folds.' Would her husband Will, the 'prominent physican,' still find her attractive? Dr. Wellington must have hobnobbed with the Talbot family. Could he ever have treated Hessiah Talbot? Known something about her? Could she have known something about him?"

"Can't answer ye," said Fergus steadfastly, sitting opposite her at the kitchen table. "Never saw a physician in me life, either professionally or socially."

She killed the last of her orange juice. "All right. Next. Jeremiah Blood. Obviously a *nouveau riche*. Proprietor of a string of liveries and smithies in the area. A bachelor, but clearly would be looking for a wife. Think, Fergus. Could he have loved Hessiah from afar? Shod her favorite horse before he worked his way up the ladder and became a parvenu?"

"Will ye drop that foreign talk, woman?" he groused. "I have trouble enough with modern English."

"Okay, okay; I'm just being snotty about this ball. It's so easy for me to picture it. Small town, not enough bluebloods for a quorum, they're forced to let in the upstarts, all in the name of charity. I can imagine the sniping and the put-downs all evening long. C'mon, Fergus." She gave him a dangerously tender smile. "Don't be mad at me."

He returned her look with a slant-eyed, half-mocking one of his own, and they were friends again. Emily ran down the rest of the list, which included the local priest whose soup kitchen was benefiting from the charity ball.

"It bothers me that Father O'Neil keeps popping up in this investigation," she admitted. "You've said that he played whist regularly at the manor, that he was close friends with Hessiah's mother before she died, that—"

"What's yer point?" Fergus interrupted, more shocked than angry. "Ye think a man of the cloth, a Catholic priest, actually strangled this innocent young woman?"

"It sounds unbelievable, I grant you. I'm just trying to be thorough. Anyway, since when is Hessiah Talbot an 'innocent young woman'? You once called her a bitch, remember?"

"That's because I was remembering the way she ordered me hauled off to Father O'Brien's mission. I didn't really mean it," he said, a little sullenly.

"But was she really all that innocent? Listen to this again: 'Miss Hessiah Talbot, whose late arrival only heightened the effect of her entrance, was quickly acclaimed by all to be the belle of the event. Miss Talbot was a vision of pure loveliness in a Paris gown of silver taffeta trimmed in exquisite French braid. Her ensemble was crowned by an extraordinary jewel that had the entire company, especially *les débutantes charmantes,* remarking on its striking size and color. Very soon it became apparent to all and sundry that her dance card was quite full, and it was even whispered that Lieutenant Dale Culver had earlier torn away an inscribed sheet and commanded those dances for himself, on the quite justifiable ground that he was beginning a tour of duty the following day. The gay and dashing lieutenant shall be sorely missed by many of the company and is wished godspeed.'

"Well?"

"Ye're reading more between them lines than ever was intended."

"Not at all," she said, taking a shovelful of by now soggy cereal. "I think it was the Silver and Gold Ball that was the ball alluded to during the trial, the ball Hessiah Talbot attended on the night of her death. It explains why the society column was never printed."

"Why didn't they call it a Silver and Gold Ball at my trial, then? All they said was she was wearing a linen nightdress after some ball she'd attended."

"To them it wasn't important which ball. Besides, the trial coverage was bizarrely erratic by modern standards. The reporters were more concerned about the shocking effects of the murder on Hessiah's family and friends."

"And crying out for my death," he added grimly.

Emily bit her lip. "That, too."

"Say it was the Silver and Gold Ball she went to before she was strangled. What makes you so convinced that the 'extraordinary jewel' she wore was the necklace? It could've been an emerald coronet. It could've been a diamond brooch. The description's altogether too vague."

"You might be right, but I don't think so. When a guest is wearing the real thing—say, a pearl choker—this writer spells it out in fawning detail. But all the writer dares say about Hessiah's jewel is that it was 'extraordinary' and that everyone talked about its 'striking size and color.' It could've been a lump of anthracite. This writer is hedging, Fergus; he's being ironic."

"Ye'd know more about such things than I. But why would the wealthiest woman in town wear a piece of junk like that to a fancy ball?"

"Oh, for love, unquestionably. It was a present, I'm sure of that. If only we knew from whom."

"And why would she be wearing it over a nightdress?"

"Also for love. Don't you understand women at all?"

"No. I don't," he said, flushing. "For one thing, ye don't *know* that she was wearing the necklace when she was strangled. Maybe someone picked it up from her dressing table and wrapped it around her neck. And here's another thing, this Lieutenant Culver. Nobody ever mentioned him at my trial. Shouldn't I be bothered by that?" he demanded.

"Good question. It's too convenient that Lieutenant Culver was scheduled to leave Newarth the day after the Silver and Gold Ball. I doubt if the police ever bothered to track him down and question him. It sounds like half—I assume, the female half—of Newarth society was willing to vouch for the lieutenant in any case. As you said yourself, the police weren't very motivated to look any farther than you."

"Will ye be the one who finally runs him to ground, then?"

"I don't see how, Fergus; we don't know a thing about him except his name and rank. It's not as if we can subpoena the man," she said, uneasy about Fergus's spiraling confidence in her.

Fergus jumped up from the table and began to pace the length of the apartment. "We can't just let him go! All yer speculating about the necklace and the ball may or may not be, but the one thing we do know is that this military bloke—Gawd, they go for the uniform every time, don't they?—tore up the lady's dance card and waltzed away the night with her."

"That was the *rumor*. And even if it were true, we don't know whether she was taken with him."

"She danced with the bastard, didn't she? If ye're correct and this is a *crime de passion,"* he said, per-

fectly mimicking her use of the phrase, "then we'd damn well better hunt him down."

He was so relentlessly logical, almost primitive in his responses. The two of them may have been simpatico lately, but their styles were completely at odds. Emily liked to approach a problem the way she would an onion, peeling away its complications layer by layer. Fergus grabbed the first sharp knife at hand and brought it down hard, chopping the thing in half.

21

As far as Emily could tell, neither Lee Alden's campaign to get reelected nor her campaign to pinpoint Lieutenant Culver's historic whereabouts went forward in the next week. When she ran into the military, she ran into a brick wall. The archives of the Newarth Library and the *Sentinel* were one thing; the archives of the United States Navy were something else altogether. Around and around and around Emily went, alternately calling Boston, Annapolis, and Washington. It got to the point where she seriously considered installing a WATS line on her phone.

Lee Alden's week wasn't going so well either. It started off with a debate against Boyd Strom. Boyd Strom was a rough-and-tumble self-made man, a street fighter with no compunctions about playing dirty. He never once bothered to address an issue. Instead, he needled Lee about his wealth, promised everyone everything, vowed never in his life to raise a single tax, and generally stuck to the low road. The debate was too carefully structured to squeeze in any digs about Lee's interest in the paranormal, but Boyd Strom was obviously biding his time; there would be another debate.

When it was over, Emily switched on the vacuum cleaner and went back to her rugs. "There was no comparison between them," she said above the roar of the Hoover. "Lee blew him out of the water."

"What, are ye nuts?" Fergus answered in a voice just as loud. "It's Strom who talks people's language."

"Strom was pious and self-serving!"

"So what? He tells 'em what they want to hear. Ye don't know a damn thing about politics!"

Emily banged the big Hoover into the sofa. "You're not for Boyd Strom; you're just against Lee Alden!"

"I'm not for either one of 'em, ye twit! *I won't be voting!*"

Stung, Emily stopped and turned off the machine. "I'm sorry. I forgot again," she said, distressed. "It's so hard to believe you might not be around for the primary. Who'll watch the returns with me after all this?" she asked in a plaintive voice.

"Probably me," he said grimly. "If ye can't find that damn lieutenant, I might be around till doomsday."

"Would that be so bad?" she asked with a sad little smile. "Think of the times we'd have."

"True. I could take a hell of an accurate exit poll for yer paper."

They shared a quiet, conspiratorial laugh. Emily hid her dismay over the thought of losing him by making a production of wrapping the extension cord around the upright handle of the Hoover.

So this is what it's come to, she thought. *From trying like crazy to bump him out of my life to simple panic at the thought that I might succeed.*

She leaned both hands on the vacuum handle as if it were a high-tech walking stick. Her back was to Fergus; she simply could not direct the question to his face. "Fergus? Do you really have to go?" she whispered.

There was no response from him, and in the meantime, tears had started to roll. She brushed them away quickly, feeling unbearably self-conscious. When she finally found the courage to turn around, Fergus was standing very close, looking very serious. His mouth was without a flicker of animation; his eyes had a depth that was profound.

"What's happening between us is impossible, ye know that," he said in a voice weighed down by pain.

"N-no, I don't know that," she argued, unable to look at him. "Just about everything that's happened so far is impossible. Why should this be any different?"

"Well, for one thing there's nothing, absolutely nothing, that I can do for . . . to . . . with . . . ye," he said with a self-conscious sound deep in his throat.

"Naturally not," she said, coloring. "But that's not all there is to a relationship."

"Nowadays it seems to be," he said tersely.

"No, no. It really isn't important to me. Not at all. There's a trend nowadays toward abstinence. Really. You've read those magazines. Sex is just too . . . complicated."

Yet even as she said it, she was aware that the most natural, logical, desirable thing in the world would be for him to take her in his arms.

Fergus saw the frustration she was feeling. He must have, because he answered in a husky voice, "Why are we doing this to ourselves?"

His image seemed to waver and soften around the

edges into transparent light, and then he was gone. The effect on Emily was devastating; he'd never disappeared in quite that way before. She had no idea what it meant; the rules seemed to evolve and change as time went on.

Oh, God, she thought wearily, falling onto the sofa in a trembling heap. It was all too much. Lee Alden had done his level best to bat her emotions right out of the park, and now Fergus, a great outfielder if ever there was one, had leaped high, high in the air with his glove and caught them.

When the call came from the Oak Bluffs Home for the Aged, Emily was folding three weeks' worth of laundry and was in a subdued mood; heat waves and Laundromats did that to her. She let the answering machine kick in, partly because she hadn't been calling the newsroom as she had promised she would. But as soon as she heard the director's voice recording a message, she knew something was wrong. She rang back the number immediately; the director answered.

Emily apologized for not having been quicker to pick up the phone, and the director said, "I'm afraid I have bad news. Hattie Dunbart passed away in her sleep last week. It was a very peaceful end and not unexpected. But we'll all miss her terribly."

It was an awful shock, like the crack of ice on a pond giving way underfoot. For all her frailness, Hattie Dunbart seemed like the kind of woman who could will herself to live forever, and Emily said so.

"She was determined. Incidentally, Hattie was very taken with you. She mentioned you several times after you left, and that's why I'm calling. She wanted you to keep the necklace. Her exact words were 'What the hell am I going to do with it? I have a neck like a chicken.' "

Emily smiled, picturing the gaudy crystal around Hattie's thin and wrinkled neck. "It'll always remind me of her. But Hattie has a niece; shouldn't I hand it over to her?" She did not add "eventually."

"Not at all. And I nearly forgot. Hattie was pleased with the research you were doing into her family history. We were going through her things—her niece wanted none of it—and found a box of, oh, letters and memorabilia, some of it dating back a way. Would you have any interest in it?"

"I'm sure I would," Emily answered, although it seemed to her that Hattie would have mentioned anything relevant to Talbot Manor.

So they struck a deal whereby Emily would go through the papers and return anything specifically dealing with the history of Martha's Vineyard. It was a long shot that Talbot Manor would be involved, but the next morning Emily was on an early ferry out of Woods Hole. This time there was no Lee Alden in a Cubs jacket and Pennzoil cap to greet her, just a crush of hot and sweaty tourists wanting to get away from the mainland. Nor was there any sign of Fergus. Emily wondered if he'd ever show himself to her again after their mutual declaration of frustration.

She stood at the rail while the ferry sliced through a dull, flat sea hazed over with the sticky stillness of summer. It seemed a lifetime ago that Emily and Lee had sat and talked on the foredeck. At the time all she could think of was the fact that she'd made passionate love with the man. The funny thing was that even without him next to her on the foredeck, it was all she could think of.

This is not good, Emily Bowditch. Your emotions are all over the map. Try to make up your mind who or what it is you want in life, will you? She watched idly as a teenage passenger held up a potato chip to a flock of circling gulls. One of them broke away from the pack, swooped down in a precision strike, and flew off with the chip in its beak.

That was the kind of certainty she wanted.

By the time she shook hands with the director of the Home for the Aged, Emily was limp from the heat. She wasn't the only one; in the sitting rooms and on the veranda the elderly residents of the home were scattered about like water lilies, neither toiling nor spinning, speaking very little and then without much energy. When she and the director paused for a moment at the bay window with the view where Emily had spoken with Hattie, the only sound she heard was of the ticking wall clock.

Hattie's room, pleasant with cabbage rose wallpaper and sheer curtains, was nonetheless empty of the photos and sweaters and fuzzy slippers by the bed that mark a place as home. Hattie had come, and Hattie had gone, and now all that was left for anyone to know her by was a large seaman's trunk of battered pine with sisal handles that stood in the middle of the floor, waiting to be hauled away.

Emily lifted the lid and saw hundreds of letters, newspaper clippings, photos, and odd papers heaped in a jumbled mess. It wasn't Hattie's style; Emily remembered the precise little motion Hattie had used to take out her change purse and the particular way she had laid her yellow afghan across her withered knees.

"You're quite right," said the director in a tone of annoyance when Emily made some remark. "Hattie's niece rummaged through it when she came to clear away her aunt's things, and this is how she left everything."

"I didn't realize there was so much," Emily admitted, daunted by the prospect of going through it all with one eye open for Fergus and the other for the Martha's Vineyard Historical Society. This would be a time-consuming detour. "I don't have a car with me."

"Don't worry about that. I'll have someone help you get it to the ferry, and you'll have plenty of help at Woods Hole to get the trunk in your car; islanders are like that."

Ten minutes later the home's handyman was putting a couple of half hitches around rope ties on the trunk and lifting it onto his back like a block of ice. With a stevedore's nonchalance he loaded it into the back of the director's wagon, drove Emily and his cargo to Vineyard Haven, and unloaded them both at the ferry landing. Emily could see the ferry approaching on the other side of the stone breakwater; in minutes the black and white behemoth was backing down smartly while deckhands dropped the spliced eyes of its massive dock lines onto pylons.

The midmorning ferry was usually the most crowded of the day, and this one was no exception. The crowd was lined up at the ferry's gate, impatient to get ashore. The most impatient one of all turned out to be Becky Alden, Hildie Alden's oldest child, who burst out of the gate like a greyhound at the track. At the bottom of the ramp Becky fetched up on the other side of the rope that separated Emily from off-loading passengers and cried, "I know you! Emily! You're Uncle Lee's girlfriend!"

"Hi, Becky," Emily answered, laughing despite the stab of embarrassment she felt. "Don't tell me you're all by yourself?"

"No, but my cousin Jane went on the ferry alone when she was only seven! Here comes Rob, and I don't see Sarah and Mom yet. Aren't you staying with us again?"

Emily explained that she was not, and Becky demanded to know the reason why. By the time Hildie came along with Sarah clutching her hand, Rob and Becky had pulled Emily out of the line and were holding her more or less captive for their mother's arrival.

Hildie, who with her blond hair and white sundress looked sunshine bright, beamed when she saw Emily. "This is great! I'm all alone at the house. Have lunch with us; there'll be another ferry." No mention of Emily's nighttime escape; just a friendly, open invitation to share a sandwich and iced tea.

Emily explained that she was traveling with a trunk. Hildie, taking that to mean yes, had a couple of beach boy types load it into the back of a Buick wagon that Lee's housekeeper, Inez, had left in the parking lot by arrangement. The kids piled in and immediately began assembling large kites they'd brought with them from the mainland.

"The to-ing–and–fro-ing is the worst part, isn't it?" Hildie remarked as she shifted the car into gear. "Too bad islands come surrounded by water."

Oh, right, Emily found herself thinking. *This is really rough.* But she contented herself with saying, "You seem to have a system pretty well worked out."

"I know what you're thinking," Hildie said with a sideways glance at Emily. "But I'm *not* a poor little rich girl. I worked on the Vineyard during my college summers. After my last year, but before I began teaching, I took a job as nanny for Grace's kids—she used to stay here all summer long—and then I met Charles, fell in love, and the rest, as they say, is history."

"Hildie, you don't have to apologize for it—least of

all to me," Emily said, embarrassed. She added, "Do I sound that much like a Communist?"

Hildie laughed. "I'm not usually like this. But I'll be the first to admit there's a difference between them and me—my dad was an insurance salesman—that's impossible to ignore." She added shrewdly, "I thought I noticed a little of that in you on Grammy's birthday."

"Uh-oh," Emily said jokingly. "You mean you saw me make a fist every time someone talked about cutting the capital gains tax?"

"Something like that," Hildie said, chuckling.

"I suppose you can admit that the difference exists, as long as you don't feel defeated by it," Emily allowed.

They pulled into the driveway, where they could see Inez behind the house taking down dry linens from a clothesline. From out of the blue Emily had an intense, vivid image of her mother gathering billowing white sheets and burying her nose in them, swearing that there wasn't a softener in the world that could take the place of sunshine. The memory rolled in on a wave of pure love; for the first time since her mother's death there was no pain.

Lunch was very pleasant. Inez sat with them and gave them a capsule biography of Lee Alden's youth, and afterward they all went outside and tried to fly really big kites in two knots of wind. Little Sarah was the first to become bored and sleepy, then Rob, then Becky. Hildie spread out a blanket under the oak tree, and the children stretched out for their naps there.

"Just like cod fillets at the fish counter," said Inez. She went inside, and Hildie and Emily chatted in hushed tones in lawn chairs nearby. After a while

Emily was forced to admit that it was time to face up to the ferry ride home.

But Hildie was having none of it. "Stay, at least overnight," she begged. "We have everything you need here. You're my size; I have clothes that would fit. This way you'll have time to sort through Hattie's trunk real quick and leave the irrelevant stuff behind. Why drag it all back and forth?"

It was tempting. But. "I'd feel very awkward staying," Emily blurted. "You do realize that Lee and I aren't seeing each other anymore?"

"You mean, because you were at the séance with him? But that's just politics. After Lee's reelected, you can take each other up again," Hildie said serenely. "Anyway, Lee's not due here until next week."

So. They knew about the séance, but they did not know about Fergus. Obviously Lee had offered the only explanation that a politically minded family would understand. All in all, Lee had opted for the chivalrous way out.

"So, will you stay?"

Emily bit on her lip, considering the offer. "I'd be an awful guest. That trunk is crammed full. I'm very directed when I research anything. The kids would feel slighted."

"Not at all. They're going to a birthday party later this afternoon, and I have a dinner engagement tonight. We'll stay completely out of your way."

Sitting there sipping mineral water, watching cottony sails dotting the blue horizon, cooled by the faintest of ocean breezes, Emily realized she was being made an offer she couldn't rationally refuse.

The two women manhandled the trunk into what everyone insisted on calling Emily's old bedroom, even though she'd spent exactly two hours there, neither of them in bed. Hildie went out and came back with some clothes for Emily, who immediately changed from her skirt and blouse to shorts and a tank top. In the meantime, Hildie had thrown open the single, multipaned door and was standing outside on a tiny brick terrace enfolded in heady midseason roses, all pinks and creams and yellows.

Emily went out to join Hildie. "This place is too enchanted to be true," she said, gazing at the ocean. A desultory sea breeze had begun to fill in, bathing her cheek in cool, slightly damp air.

"I keep forgetting how perfectly placed this room is," Hildie admitted. "I never use it because all my things are set up in the bedroom near the kids. And it's too small for Lee; his room has a massive desk that came down from his grandfather's law firm. His mother doesn't care for it because it doesn't have its own bath. So there you are. The best room in the house, and nobody wants it. Well, cheerio. You know where the kitchen is."

She left, and Emily had to force herself just to come in from the view. *How will I ever get anything done?* she wondered, pleasantly dismayed. Still, without either Lee or Fergus it was altogether possible that she'd be able to concentrate. After clearing away a chair or two and rolling up a small but exquisite serape from the foot of the rope-twist spindle bed, Emily got down to business.

She began pulling out papers, photos, and clippings one armful at a time and heaping them on a ladder-back chair. Then she sorted them according to time and place. A good deal of the material related to the Vineyard, but it was nothing that couldn't also be found in various island archives: clippings from the *Vineyard Gazette;* old church bulletins; commemorative menus and programs from social gatherings. These she tossed. There were also dozens and dozens of greeting cards. Hattie seemed to have saved every birthday, get-well, and anniversary card she'd ever got; it was interesting and a little sad to see that there were no Mother's Day cards. With some regret Emily had to toss the cards as well.

There were photographs, two shoeboxes' worth, that had tumbled out from their cardboard containers and were becoming bent and ruined in the jumble. Emily began to stack them carefully, out of respect, even though the people captured in them neither knew nor cared that the photos existed. She could no more throw them out than she could toss a litter of newborn kittens. They'd have to go back to the director.

And there were letters, hundreds of letters, some of them dating back to the twenties and before. Most of them weren't addressed to Hattie, but whether they belonged to other residents at the home or to Hattie's relations, it was impossible to tell. She'd have to take them all and read them all, not because she thought they'd help her but because she'd promised the director.

By seven or so Emily had succeeded in completely carpeting the wide-board floor of her room with neat, compulsive stacks of history. She stood up and stretched. A streak of pain went rippling through her spine; she'd been bent over for hours. The household had been true to Hildie's word and left her unmolested, and as a result, Emily had no idea what the feeding arrangements were. She made her way timidly to the kitchen, where Inez was emptying the dishwasher.

"Ah, there you are," the housekeeper said. "I wanted to bring you a supper tray, but Hildie said to leave you alone under pain of death. That wouldn't be your stomach grumbling, would it?" Inez asked cheerfully.

Emily nodded sheepishly, and Inez sat her down on a high chair at the butcher-block island dominating the center of the room. "I'll make you an omelet, dear," she said. "While we talk."

"Are the kids all asleep already?" Emily asked, surprised.

"Lord, yes. It was an exhausting day. Pony rides, sack races, they did it all." The housekeeper chopped some onions into a pat of butter sizzling in an omelet pan. "Especially that Becky; she runs everyone ragged. But I'll tell you a secret: She's my favorite. Smart as a whip. She does have a tendency to sass, but then again she usually feels awful about it later and brings me treats."

Inez cracked two eggs into a bowl, whisked them around briefly, and dumped them in the pan. "I think Lee is partial to Becky as well. He likes the way she speaks her mind. I suppose that's what happens when you're surrounded by yes-men all day long." She looked up pointedly at Emily. "Isn't that your impression, dear?"

"Oh, definitely," Emily said, to be polite. In general it was true. In the matter of Fergus it was not true.

Inez laid out a plate of French bread and a beautifully browned omelet smothered in a cheese sauce and then excused herself, leaving Emily to enjoy a view of the herb garden at twilight. When she was finished she rinsed out her dishes and left them in the rack, boiled herself a cup of tea, and went back to what was no longer a fun or even an interesting task. It was too irrelevant, too distracting from the business at hand. And it was too hot to work.

Back in her room she took one last tour of the rose terrace before darkness set in. The fragrance was even more pronounced at night; she went around and smelled every plant, wondering if Fergus was around to enjoy her enjoyment. After a few minutes she went back inside and scooped up yet another armful of Hattie's mementos. As before, she pulled out the photos first to spare them further bending and mutilating.

And then, quite simply, her heart stood still. In her hand she held a sepia-toned studio photograph that was a variant of the one she had found stuck in the drawer of the desk in the tower of Talbot Manor. Same fern, same family, different pose. In this shot both parents were looking adoringly at the infant in the mother's arms; the father's face was obscured. One of the boys was smiling tentatively, and one remained formal and impassive.

Emily turned the photo over. Her hand began to shake. The names of the subjects were written clearly in a woman's hand on the back: John Talbot, Celeste Talbot, Hessiah, Stewart, and—a complete surprise—James. So! She'd been right all along, and the first feeling that roared through her was one of triumph. But little James with his timid smile was a puzzle. There was no mention of him in Celeste Talbot's obituary. Was he even her child? Had he already succumbed, as so many children of the period did, to fever and disease?

In a blaze of enthusiasm Emily dove back into the trunk for another armful of memorabilia. If there was one photo, there must be others. She shuffled through the photographs feverishly, looking for more evidence of the Talbots. Before very long she sat back on her heels.

Waitaminnit. Hattie Dunbart should link back to Mayor Henry Abbott, not to the Talbots. So why was the Talbots' photo among the Abbotts' keepsakes? It's not as if they were family. Would a bridge partner ask for and keep so personal an item as this?

Oh, hell's bells, she thought, dazed and confused. It was like unwinding a coil of hopelessly tangled line. *This is what happens when you rush a job,* she thought, illogically annoyed with Hildie. *I should've gone home with the trunk.*

She was still sitting back on her heels, staring blankly into space and trying to remember what was in her computer, when the door was swung open with no warning.

"My God. You *are* here."

22

Emily jumped up in panic, sending papers flying in every direction. She felt as if she'd been caught breaking and entering. Like a fool, she instantly blurted, "Hildie said I could stay."

Lee Alden's grin lit up his eyes, lit up the room, lit up every one of her nerve endings. "If Hildie says so, then I guess it must be all right," he said with good-humored irony. "Hi."

"We thought you weren't going to be here," she added. That, of course, explained everything.

Lee was leaning against the doorframe now, arms folded across his chest, completely filling the doorway. He was wearing a navy polo shirt; she could see damp circles under the sleeves, as if he'd been running.

"I see my sister-in-law has clothed you," he said, casting an attentive eye over Hildie's shorts and scanty tank top. "But has she taken the trouble to feed you?"

"Oh. Yes. Sure. Inez made an omelet," Emily said

in a rush, then fell to her knees and began haphazardly scooping the stacks of papers back into a common pile much the way Hattie's niece would've done. "I'm so embarrassed about this, Lee," she said, hardly daring to look at him. "It seemed like such a good idea at the time. I had no idea you might be dropping in—"

"Dope. *You're* the reason I'm 'dropping in,'" he said, unfolding himself from the doorway. "I called a little while ago, and Inez told me you were here." He came into the room and crouched down in a catcher's pose, facing her. "So I hopped a flight with a pal to the Edgartown Air Park, then forced him practically at gunpoint to drive me across the island."

"Gee, you didn't have to do that," she said without looking at him, hurriedly unsorting her sorted piles. "Your silver would've been safe from me."

"Yeah, but would it have been safe from Fergus?" he asked, casually plucking out a photo, then tossing it back on the pile.

Her head came up; a dangerous flush tramped across her cheeks. "We've been around this block before, Lee." She threw an armful of mementos into the trunk and gathered up another. "So leave Fergus out of it."

Lee grabbed both her wrists, flattening her hands over the pile of papers that fell from her arms. "Emily, please. Stop. Wait. *Listen.*"

"You sound like a crossing guard," she said, feeling the anger rise in her gorge. "Let go of me."

His blue eyes were inches from her face; his forehead was damp with sweat. The veins in his temple were working overtime; she'd seen the look before. "I asked you nice," he said. "Now I'll try another way. Shut up for a minute. I have something to say."

She made a sudden hostile motion, trying to whip her hands free, but he held them fast. It was bizarre—the two of them, kneeling on a pile of old pictures and mail, locked in physical combat.

"*What?* What can you possibly have to say to me that you haven't said before? That after the elections we can try again? That you didn't realize until now that I really, really wasn't fooling about Fergus? That you've thought it over and you'll give me thirty days to solve the murder and get him out of here? That—"

Lee brought his hand up and clamped it over her mouth. "I *can't* shut you up," he said, almost in wonder. "There's no way to shut you up. How can I get a word in edgewise? How can—"

He took her face in both his hands and kissed her, a hard, uncompromising kiss, hot and deep and tonguing, in every way a match for the kiss she'd given him before she marched out of his office and out of his life. Emily had thrown down the gauntlet that day in his office; now he was picking it up. She didn't expect this, couldn't imagine that he'd throw off his instinctive caution and claim her this way.

"I . . . I don't . . . understand," she said, reeling under his assault. She staggered to her feet.

But he was right there, quick and relentless. "Does this explain it?" He kissed her again, harder, hotter, then broke it off suddenly. *"I love you, Sherlock,"* he said, taking her by her shoulders, giving her an almost symbolic shake. "Don't you get it? You get everything else—can't you get this one simple thing?"

She stared at him, still in shock, her body trembling in the aftermath of their encounter. She'd spent weeks backing away from him emotionally, telling herself that her interest in him was academic, even accepting Hildie's invitation just to prove the fact. And now Lee Alden had come flying back into her life on the wings of some twin-engine plane, kissing her until she begged for mercy, insisting that he loved her. It took her breath away.

"What about Fergus?" she whispered, because she knew that when everything was said and done, it all came down to Fergus.

She expected Lee to recoil under the blow, but if anything, he became more animated. "Fergus. Okay; Fergus. I've been thinking about that, pretty much night and day."

He began to pace, then looked down and realized that the floor was carpeted with papers; he stopped abruptly and dropped into the wicker chair near the door. "He's a project you're working on," he said, his agitation barely under control. "I accept that. You see him; I don't. You hear him; I can't. So what?"

He leaped up from the chair, as if a shot had been fired in the darkness somewhere. "Some of the profoundest thinkers in history have heard and seen things the rest of us haven't—from Dionysius to Nostradamus. Should we have locked them up, shunned them, because we were too caught up in the noise and clatter of everyday life to hear what they heard? I don't think so. I don't think so."

He began to pace again, remembered the papers again, stopped again. He was next to her, and almost as an afterthought, he kissed her—gently this time, as if her lips were flower petals. "You've found something that I've been searching for for years," he said in a voice blended of envy and awe. "What right do I have to insist you're wrong?"

She was reeling again, this time from the strength of his conversion. "When—when did you decide this?"

He laughed softly. "The day you first told me about Fergus, I suppose. I fought it, of course. It was too wildly illogical. How could a woman as rational as you have the ability to see into another dimension? Let's face it, darling," he said, caressing her cheek with his hand, "you don't fit the profile of a mystic."

He slipped his arms around her waist. "But when Inez mentioned that you were here, that's when it all fell into place for me. You were *here.* That's all that mattered. There's plenty of space, literally and figuratively, for Fergus. He can have this room," Lee added, bringing his mouth down on Emily's in a kiss of surpassing tenderness, "and we'll take the master."

Lee was keeping it light, but she could tell from the suppressed excitement in his voice that he was dead serious about Fergus. One way or another, Lee was willing to move over and make room for her convictions. She was intensely moved by his act of faith. And then, of course, there was the fact that she was in his arms, and his warm cheek was pressing hers, and his voice, low and persuasive, was telling her what she'd been waiting a short lifetime to hear.

She closed her eyes and savored the moment. Lee Alden, the very first man she'd ever loved, was very much here and now, while Fergus was—somewhere, sometime. Emily took a great swallow of air, then let out a shuddering sigh.

Lee held her away at arm's length and lowered his head to meet her averted eyes. "Emily? Did I just make a royal ass of myself? Was I so busy with my speech that I didn't understand the sound of your silence?"

When she said nothing, his breathing became very controlled, very deliberate, as if he were replaying the scene in his mind. "My God," he murmured. "I was wrong. You're not in love—"

Now it was her turn to clamp her hand over his

mouth. "That's not true!" she said passionately. "If you knew how I've been waiting for you . . ."

She released her hand, and then they kissed again, deep, hungry kisses. She had the sense that they'd been in an impenetrable forest, and then they'd become separated, and now they'd found each other again. For the moment it didn't matter that they didn't know how to get out; it mattered only that they were together again.

"Will you let me make love to you?" he whispered.

For her answer Emily reached over to turn off the bright reading light that she'd been using to study. In the golden glimmer of a small Chinese lamp they removed what little they were wearing, and then, wrapped only in the night's sultry heat, they pulled back the bedcovers together. For one wild second Emily wondered whether the television would stay off this time; and then she forgot about the television, and Fergus, and what Lee had called the noise and clatter of everyday life, because she was in his arms again.

"I fell apart when you walked out on me," he confessed, burying his face in the curve of her throat. "They had to glue me back together. Please, darling, don't ever," he begged between kisses, "do that . . . to me . . . again."

"No . . . no, how could I?" she murmured. "Everything's different now . . . night-and-day different. . . ."

"What's different, for pity's sake? Any fool could see he's loved ye all along."

Of all the voices in the world—this world or any other—*that* voice was the one voice Emily was not prepared to hear. She shut her eyes; she became stiff as a barn board.

Lee pulled away. "Emily? What's wrong?"

"Tell him, Em," she heard Fergus prod. "Test his faith."

"Oh, God," Emily whispered, afraid to open her eyes. "Not *now*. How could you?"

"Emily, are you serious?" Lee demanded, his voice shaky with frustrated passion.

"Yes. No—I don't mean the sex. Is that what you're thinking of?" she asked Lee, bolting upright and looking around the room frantically.

"At this minute? Yes," Lee confessed in a wondering voice.

"He's not kidding, ye know." Fergus, standing with his arms crossed at the foot of the bed, was perusing Lee with a kind of good-natured leer.

"Oh! How *could* you?" Emily wailed to Fergus, pulling a sheet up over her breasts. "We're not even dressed!"

"Darling, that's the general idea," Lee said in hapless confusion.

But Emily, wide-eyed, didn't respond. Lee waved his hand in front of the fixed expression on her face, then said in an instantly more serious tone, "He's here, isn't he?"

Somehow that got through to her. She gave the faintest of nods and whispered, "This is the most—the most *unacceptable* moment of my life." Tears of mortification rolled down her cheeks.

"Don't cry, dammit to hell," growled Fergus. "It's yer own damn fault. Did ye think I could stand by idly and watch ye give yerself to this—this hunk? I like him well enough," he added, "but not enough to share ye with 'im."

Emily pulled the sheet up with both hands to her mouth to stifle a scream of frustration. This was it, the point at which she might well tip over into madness. She closed her eyes and bit on the cloth, summoning every fiber of self-control she possessed. When she opened her eyes, Fergus was still there and Lee was standing alongside the bed, hauling his pants up over his nakedness. It all seemed very funny. She let out a high-pitched yelp of sheer nervous energy. The sound of it frightened her; she bit the inside of her lip so hard that she tasted blood.

Lee came around to her side of the bed and sat there, his thigh touching hers, his hands gripping her shoulders. Emily searched his face for signs of fear and revulsion, but all she found was a kind of overwhelming humanity. "We'll walk through it together, darling; it's all right." He turned around and looked right through Fergus, then turned back to her. "Will he tolerate my being here with you?"

Her face became ashen. Fergus could destroy Lee in one blinding flash. She'd been so caught up in her own embarrassment that she'd forgotten the ghost's power. She shook her head bleakly, incapable of putting together a coherent explanation of the danger.

"Ah, hell, let 'im stay," Fergus said with a magnanimous wave of his hand.

Emily gazed over Lee's shoulder into the green, dancing eyes of the ghost. She saw a cat, ready to pounce. "He says you can stay," she repeated to Lee, feeling foolish and fearful.

Lee seemed to relax. "Well, that's a start, then. Where exactly is he?"

"He's standing at the foot of the bed," she answered, gathering courage. "With his arms crossed and a snotty expression on his face," she added angrily.

Lee said calmly, "I take it he doesn't approve of what we are—were—doing?"

She shook her head and said through clenched teeth, "He doesn't seem to want to share me."

"Ye don't have to bloody well tell him *everything,*" Fergus interrupted, flushing deeply.

"You're the one who has the advantage in this little dynamic," she shot back at him. "All the power, all the knowledge!"

The ghost looked surprised, then looked at Lee's broad, rippling back, and an expression of torment twisted the features of his face. "Ye haven't heard anything I've said if that's what ye believe," he said in a voice cut low by her anger.

Lee was watching Emily's reactions carefully; he saw the stricken look on her face. When she had no answer for Fergus, he said simply, "He's hurt you."

But Emily shook her head, deeply distressed. "No, I'm the one who's hurt him." Hildie's little tank top was on the nightstand; Emily picked it up and pulled it over her head, not because she felt particularly modest, but because she didn't want anyone to want her anymore. Maybe that was the definition of modesty; she didn't know.

"Oh, no, ye don't," Fergus said, in a lightning shift of mood. "Don't ye be layin' any guilt trip on *me.* I watch Donahue. I watch Oprah. I watch *Geraldo,* for God's sake. I know everything there is to know about manipulation. Unh-unh. Take that little thing off. Go back to yer business. I'll just wait outside. From what I seen," he added with a sly and jealous glance at the senator, "ye'll only be a minute."

Lee had been tracing the play of emotions on Emily's face. "Now what?" he asked her.

Emily turned defiant, folding her arms across her chest. "He wants us to resume," she explained with fine outrage, her foot tapping thin air under the sheet. "He promises not to look."

Lee burst out in a laugh. "Does he say *why* he wants us to resume?"

"He doesn't want to feel guilty."

"Guilty! What does a ghost know about guilt?"

"He watches all the talk shows."

"Ah. Of course. Well. This really is . . . unbelievable," Lee said softly, shaking his head.

"Don't say 'unbelievable,'" Emily moaned. "Or we'll be back where we started."

"Wrong word," Lee said, kissing the top of her hair. "I meant 'weird.'"

She was dismayed to see Lee stand up and approach the spot where Fergus was standing. The ghost remained where he was, arms akimbo now, watching Lee with a narrow, calculating expression. Emily was reminded again of her cat. Her heart began to pound as Lee paused, stared, moved to another angle, and repeated the pattern. Fergus said nothing; only his eyes, glittering and attentive, conveyed any sense of danger. Lee brought one arm up and very calmly, very deliberately began to cut a swath through the air.

Right through Fergus. Emily cried, "Don't!" at the same time that she saw both Fergus's image and Lee's broad, bare arm occupying the same space. The hair on the back of her neck stood up. In one fell swoop Lee had violated a taboo that Emily had been extremely careful to honor. For an instant Fergus looked stunned. Then the light began: blinding, terrifying, and focused completely on Lee.

"Fergus, don't!" Emily cried out. "He didn't mean it! Stop it!" she commanded in a shrill voice.

"Keep him away from me," Fergus growled, and then he disappeared. Instantly the light subsided, although random shafts of brightness continued to play around the room, the way thunder rolls after the initial crack of lightning. Lee, who hadn't been seriously hurt, looked dazed.

"What was *that* all about?" he asked in a voice that wasn't quite steady.

Emily had climbed back out of bed and dressed. "You offended him, Lee," she said, zipping up her shorts. She looked at him across the bed—unoccupied, yet again—and said with a sigh, "He wants desperately to be a human being again, and you made it really clear that he's not."

"For that he was going to annihilate me?"

"I don't know what he was going to do. He's been very tense lately."

Lee pulled his blue Izod shirt back over his head and said in a voice muffled by fabric, "I can't believe we're having this conversation." When his head popped through, he gave Emily a look that was both ironic and apologetic. *"But* . . . I do believe everything else." He came over to Emily and locked his arms around the small of her back, holding her close. "I love you, darling. I love you. But I've got to admit, this guy is formidable competition."

Emily laid her cheek against his chest and said in a low, confused voice, "He'll probably be glad to hear that."

They had coffee in the kitchen after that, even though it was late. Lee rummaged around for something sweet and came up with a still-warm carrot cake with cream cheese frosting. They left the kitchen lights low and spoke in undertones about Hessiah Talbot's murder. As it turned out, Lee *had* read the notebooks she'd left on the desk in her condo that first night; he was more informed than she'd thought.

"Anyway, now that I've found the photograph and identified the family as the Talbots, I feel a lot more motivated about searching that pile of memorabilia in the bedroom. I think there's a significant connection between the mayor and them," she said. "If I can't find it in that pile, I'm going back to Talbot Manor for those diaries."

"Not without telling me first," he urged. "Maria Salva sounds more dangerous than Fergus."

Emily agreed to keep him posted. "This is crazy, Lee," she said, sliding her hand around the back of his neck. "Somehow I thought that if you believed me, everything else would fall into place—including us, right into each other's arms." She drew his face closer to hers and, moved by an overwhelming feeling of tenderness toward him, kissed him.

Lee answered the kiss in kind, holding himself in check. But the kiss turned deeper; a low sound escaped from his throat. "Unless you want to be carried off to bed, this is not a good idea." His smile was taut.

"No," she said, sighing. "You're right. I want to, but—" She laughed softly and shook her head. "It'd have to be in a lead-lined room. You do understand, don't you?" she asked, tracing her finger over the fullness of his lips. "I don't want to hurt Fergus. I'm not sure I can actually help him, but I can't—I won't—hurt him.

"And besides, you have a primary race to run," she said, changing the subject.

But Lee didn't want to talk about the primary. "You're pretty serious about this fellow, aren't you? Should I be jealous?"

"Not in any normal sense of the word," she said, coloring a little.

"Heck, if he were normal we could duke it out behind the barn, winner take all—with your permission, of course," he added gallantly.

"Lee, I'm serious about the primary," she said, switching the subject again. "For all we know there's a reporter from the *Washington Post* hiding in your front bushes right now. Even putting the subject of

Fergus's hostility to you aside, we don't dare be seen together until the primary next month—until after the election, I mean," she corrected.

Lee's playful mood evaporated. His brow became furrowed and his blue eyes went gray. "I hate to say this. But I'm in trouble, Emily. I haven't let on to my family yet, but I'm hanging by a thread. The projections don't look good. Strom is picking up speed while I'm dropping back fast."

"But it's early days yet," she argued. "This is politics. Anything can happen."

"Yeah. Maybe you can talk Fergus into haunting Strom instead," he quipped. "Come on, I'll see you safely to your bedroom door." He pointed a finger heavenward. "You owe me for this, Fergus."

23

Emily found the mayor's letter the next morning right after breakfast, long after Lee had left for the mainland. She'd focused her search on anything written in an old-school style, and she wasn't disappointed. The letter was written on heavy official paper in a man's hand and undated. What caught Emily's eye was the salutation: "Dearest H."

Dearest H,

Let me say at once that I am discouraged by the position you have taken regarding your cousin. He has brought forth his suit in a most seemly way, and my only regret is that John Talbot is not alive to give him the support and encouragement you so perversely withhold. What can be your possible objection to the man? He is well provided and of impeccable character and manners. Most important, his family are your own. I do not accept your frivolous lament to your brother that Thomas Dayton lacks color. You are not in search of a rainbow; you are in desperate need of a husband.

Stewart has led me to understand that Thomas is in the process of angrily packing his portmanteau, not so much because you will not take him as because you will not take him seriously. Your brother seems to find your irresponsible manner amusing —I believe he encourages you—but I confess I find it incomprehensible and infuriating. While I am on the subject, I also have had reason to believe that yet another officer has caught your fancy. This I find truly insupportable. Must I remind you that the only reason any man joins the military is that he possesses neither a decent fortune nor a steadfast heart? It is all very well for a debutante to be dazzled by the shine of gold braid. But has it occurred to you that at the age of twenty-six you are no longer an ingenue? I have no choice

And there the letter ended. Emily searched long and hard for page two but came up empty. There was nothing else in the same hand or on the same stationery. There was nothing, really, to prove that it *was* Mayor Abbott who was venting his fury at Hessiah, except for the fact that the single sheet of paper was embossed with the seal of the mayor's office.

"Still, that's good enough for me," Emily murmured, satisfied. As always, she wanted to share the news. "Fergus?"

He appeared at once, seated in the wicker chair with his legs stretched out in front of him, his elbows resting on the arms of the chair, his hands tipped against his mouth in a prayerful pose. He looked both wary and hopeful. "This had better be good, girl."

"I think it is, Fergus," Emily answered with an awkward, contrite smile. She still hadn't come up with a decent method for smoothing over their fallings-out. Lee was right. It'd be a lot easier if you could just stand there and duke it out. The trouble was, one minute Fergus was there, and then, just as you were working up a smart answer, he was gone.

"Look what I've found." She waved the letter in front of him and then read it aloud, relieved that Hildie and the children were in town and Inez had the day off.

Fergus leaped up and reread the mayor's angry diatribe over her shoulder. "God in heaven!" he said when he was done. "It sounds like any one of them could've done it! But the letter's undated. Are we certain the military man *is* Lieutenant Culver? And why should the mayor take Hessiah's flirting so personal?

"That's the real question here. I don't think the mayor could ever have been her lover. He might've been more like a kindly Dutch uncle who agreed to watch over Hessiah after her father died."

"Ha! He never seemed all that kindly to me."

"No, you're probably right," she admitted. "If Hattie Dunbart's stories are accurate, the mayor was blindly ambitious. But then why make such a fuss over Hessiah? She was nothing to him." Emily puzzled over that for a moment. "Unless—"

"He was her real father, say. Bejesus, now ye have *me* thinking the way ye do."

Their eyes met; they were again in perfect harmony.

"Why not?" she said excitedly. "You once told me there was talk of a secret affair. Maybe it had nothing to do with Hessiah but with her mother. When Celeste Talbot died after being thrown from her horse, Hessiah was still a baby. Celeste was young, passionate, beautiful. Now I ask you, whom would she be more attracted to: a charismatic up-and-coming politician or a dour, workaholic millowner?"

"Well, but folks claimed she was religious," Fergus said reluctantly. Clearly he wanted to believe the scenario. "Ye're a female; could she have been tempted into a romance?"

"Sometimes there's a thin line between religion and romance," Emily answered cryptically. "And remember," she added, "Mayor Abbott had one of the Talbot family photos in his possession. To me it's interesting that the face of John Talbot is obscured in it. Hold it. All we're doing is eliminating the mayor as a suspect. He wouldn't have murdered his own daughter."

"If he was in a rage? He might have," Fergus said, driving the argument home. "Here he was, trying his best to arrange a decent marriage for this love child of his, and here the little brat was, doing something stupid like taking up with a ne'er-do-well. It's also a fact that the mayor eventually shot himself to death. *Some*thing must've been bothering him," Fergus summed up in a dry voice.

Emily frowned. "A father strangle his own daughter? It's too inconceivable," she said, dismissing the notion. "*And* in the meantime, we now have Cousin Thomas. I never thought about him, although he was mentioned in the accounts of the trial. So the whispers you once heard about a scorned suitor must have been true. Which means Thomas Dayton has motive. Which means Thomas Dayton has opportunity. Perfect," she said wearily. "Add Thomas Dayton to the list."

"Sure. I'll pencil him in right after Lieutenant Culver, who *still* is nowhere to be found." Fergus was back in the chair, looking disgusted. He stared at the letter Emily was holding in her hand. "What if the mayor didn't even write that? What if someone else was really in love with Hessiah all along, and *he* wrote it on official paper? Maybe a deputy mayor or a clerk . . ."

Emily waved the suggestions away. "Enough! With any luck I'll be able to compare the handwriting to Mayor Abbott's signature on some city document. Unfortunately that means more boring searches through more moldy records."

She began loading some of the stacks of memorabilia back into the trunk. "The next time I solve a murder," she mused, "I'd like it to be in the twentieth century. I'd like a real body, and real eyewitnesses, and a real police report. I'd like hair, blood, and DNA samples, and it would be nice if it all took place on a resort island."

She sat back on the heels of her feet. "I'd like to be Jessica Fletcher," she said, sighing. "Jessica Fletcher never has to go to City Hall."

Nevertheless, that's where Emily ended up two days later. It was no real challenge to locate a sample of Mayor Henry Abbott's handwriting; during his term of office he was constantly signing proclamations of something or other. If the document was not an official welcome of an important guest, it was likely to be an official observation of an important day. The mayor had seemed quite determined to put Newarth on the map; he would've been crushed to see how thoroughly he'd failed.

In any case, the handwriting matched. It was small comfort. Although she now had suspects to spare, Emily was no closer to solving the murder of Hessiah Talbot. Worst of all—and she took this very personally—Emily had not yet figured out who had given Hessiah Talbot the necklace. It seemed to her that if she knew that, she might know who had murdered Hessiah. The question was who would have given Hessiah such a cheap and tasteless piece of jewelry. Surely the most likely one was Lieutenant Culver. Yet they still knew nothing about him, not even if he'd had a wife.

Frustrated, Emily drove from City Hall to the Newarth Library. She thought she'd just say hello to Mrs. Gibbs, then poke around a little more through old *Sentinels*. She was hoping to find something connecting the mayor and Celeste Talbot, and so far she hadn't bothered to pay much attention to the early years of Hessiah's life.

She found Mrs. Gibbs presiding over a plate of frosted brownies. "I'm so glad you've come," Mrs. Gibbs said almost wistfully. "No one else has all day. Even Mr. Bireth isn't around to snore over his morning paper; he's visiting his children on the Jersey shore. And it's too hot to garden. I have nothing to do."

She cut Emily a brownie the size of a small backyard and added, "So you've been busy finding out things. What are they? Is there anything I can do to help?"

Emily brought her up-to-date—omitting, as always, all mention of Fergus—and announced her plan to find something, anything, in the time period of the early 1860s. They went down to the basement together, Emily following slowly behind Mrs. Gibbs's halting, arthritic descent. They dragged out two big volumes of *Sentinels* and sat at each end of the battered library table, carefully turning crumbling pages, searching for evidence of a liaison between the mayor and Celeste Talbot—or anything else scandalous and indecent.

The afternoon passed with very few interruptions upstairs and not much in the way of discoveries downstairs. But just before closing time Mrs. Gibbs murmured across the table, "This is very strange. Did you know that the Talbots had a son who died?"

Emily's head shot up. "Is his name James?"

"That's right. Listen to this: 'In a tragic mishap at Talbot Manor, James Talbot, the younger son of John and Celeste Talbot, fell down a well adjacent to the formal gardens. Rescuers were unable to reach the boy in time to prevent his drowning. The boy, who with his sister and brother was in the care of a young governess at the time of his death, was said to have been fetching a drink of water for his baby sister. Further details are unknown at this time. Funeral arrangements have yet to be announced.'

"And that's it," Mrs. Gibbs said, stunned. "Page three, at the bottom. The younger son of the town scion dies, and it's tucked on page three. At the bottom."

Emily was standing next to her now, turning the paper back to page one. "The paper's dated July 1863. James couldn't have been more than four years old. Hessiah was two years old in 1863; her brother Stewart must've been five or six."

"What a terrible thing for them to live with," Mrs. Gibbs said, holding her hand to her cheek in an old-fashioned way.

"Hessiah wouldn't remember that, would she? At two?"

"She easily could have," Mrs. Gibbs said, shaking her head and tsking like the grandmother she was. "But why wasn't this mentioned at the time of the trial? I'm sure I would have remembered reading about it. Of course, my research was never so thorough as yours, dear. Do you remember anything about this?"

"There *wasn't* anything about this," Emily said, every instinct on the alert for a cover-up. "We'll have to go through the next issues with a fine-tooth comb."

They searched through 1865, but all poor James ever rated in the *Sentinel* was the one mention at the bottom of page three.

"For whatever reason, the *Sentinel* shied away from this story," Emily said to Mrs. Gibbs. "I remember your saying that John Talbot was close friends with the publisher; there must have been an understanding. This is interesting. Was Celeste racked by shame? What happened to their governess? Was she some romantic, silly young thing? Who hired her anyway?"

"We're supposed to be answering questions, dear, not asking them," Mrs. Gibbs said pragmatically. "Now that we know James existed we can at least verify his birth and death dates. Would it be a help if I did that?"

The librarian wanted very much to be a part of things, and Emily was glad to have her help; it would save her the drive back to Newarth. Besides, the Toyota had been making eerie strangling noises lately, and Emily was petrified at the thought of having to roll it in for repairs.

That night as Emily lay in bed, hot and uncomfortable, she began to suspect that information had begun flowing almost too quickly. It was as if some hand were guiding her through a tortuous maze of characters and events to some fated conclusion. She didn't like it. If she didn't know better, she'd say it was a trap. The question was who had set it.

Surely not Fergus. The suspicion came and went, like a shooting star in the night sky, and there was nothing Emily could do to unthink it. After all, Fergus *was* the logical, obvious suspect in the murder. It was fair to say that Emily knew nothing about how astral spirits were assigned their destinies. What if Fergus could successfully pin the rap on someone else? It happened in court all the time. If Emily were really a detective, then no one would be above suspicion.

Not even Fergus, she thought, restlessly throwing off the sheets from her body.

The next day Emily got two phone calls. The first was in the morning, and it was from Mrs. Gibbs, verifying the obvious: that Hessiah was two years old, James was four, and Stewart six at the time of the drowning. "Thank you, Dr. Watson," Emily had said, and the librarian laughed and hung up, pleased.

The second call was in the afternoon, from someone who very definitely did not wish to be identified, and it had nothing at all to do with the ongoing investigation. That was the bad news. The good news was that it had everything to do with destroying Lee Alden's primary opponent, Boyd Strom. Emily was being given a hot, hot tip, so hot that the phone she held felt like a charcoal ember.

"Boyd Strom is up to his neck in toxic waste. I want him to be up to his eyeballs," the caller said in a growl. "He's a partner in Rondale Associates; they own some land on Rondale Road in Scanset, in the northwest part of the state. It ain't a town, more like an intersection. Ever heard of it?"

"No—"

"It's there. Trust me. Check it out; he's been dumping PCBs illegally there for years. There's a guy named Sid willing to talk from Wally's Hauling out of Winslow. But you got to ask him first."

Click.

Emily grabbed a pencil and wrote first, thought later. She got out a map, verified the town's location, made herself a cup of tea. *A toxic dump.* If the caller was on the level, Boyd Strom wouldn't be running for anything except possibly his life in a federal prison. *If* the caller was on the level. The first thing tomorrow, she'd see what she could find out at the office—

Or not. After all, she'd just declared herself on leave from this kind of investigation. She'd have to do it on her own time, then. Except that it was too big a story, too big an investigation, for her to pursue alone. She didn't have the resources, and she wasn't even sure she had the courage; a trail of PCBs could lead to some pretty rough characters.

But it was an explosive story; she couldn't just sit on it. The next day she called Stanley Cooper. After a little backing and filling in the way of pleasantries, Emily gave him a verbatim account of the anonymous tipster. Predictably Stan listened quietly, then fired both barrels simultaneously. "The story's bullshit. There's nothing you can do anymore to put Lee Alden on top in the primary, Emily. Give it up."

"I'm *not* trying to put anyone on top," she said, blushing irrationally at the image. "Someone called me with a tip. I think the paper should check it out. That's all there is to it, Stan. Dammit!"

"I'm not allocating resources to this story," Stan said flatly. "I've heard it before. It's bullshit. Strom's a lot of things, but he's not connected. Nice try."

"I *told* you, Stan—oh, forget it." She slammed the receiver down, furious with him for suspecting her motives. Granted, it was a fantastic window of opportunity for Lee. But it was a genuinely newsworthy story as well. She tried not to think of the enormous conflict of interest the story represented for her as she punched in Lee's phone number. She'd made him promise not to call her, so he sounded surprised and—she had to admit—extremely pleased to hear from her.

She brought him up-to-date on her progress in the case, then said, "I'm not sure I'm doing the right thing here, Lee. I think this violates the Hippocratic oath or something. But I got an anonymous tip last night, and I don't know what to do with it. I can't follow it up myself, and Stan told me flat out that it's an old rumor and untrue. But I just have this feeling—"

"My Emily of the Hunches," Lee said in a slightly doting voice. "Okay. What now? Shoot. Who's your latest suspect?"

"Oh, this isn't about Hessiah." She told him exactly what the caller had said about Boyd Strom's toxic dump. Lee listened in absolute silence. When she was done, he said, "I see."

"I don't know what you can do with it. The guy called me at home, and I wasn't on the payroll at the time, and anyway, the *Journal* has turned it down, so—"

"So you wrapped it up in a big red ribbon and gave it to me. Thanks," he said dryly.

"Well, for goodness' sake, the primary is less than a month away, everyone says the second debate ended in a draw, and you're running out of options, mister. If Boyd Strom doesn't make a real boner in that last debate, if he doesn't say that Poland is the capital of Iraq or something, then— Do you *want* to lose?"

"Doesn't what you're saying leave you with just a little bit of a bad taste in your mouth?" he asked her quietly.

She felt the heat fire up in her cheeks, then burst into flame. It was the first time in her life that anyone had even *hinted* she might be doing something unethical. Especially when she wasn't quite sure that it wasn't.

"It doesn't leave as bad a taste in my mouth as—as

what *you're* saying," she said petulantly. And then she placed the receiver very gently, very precisely in its cradle.

When she turned around Fergus was there, shaking his head. "What a world," he said sympathetically. "What's a toxic dump anyway?"

She told him, but he was puzzled. "Poison has to go somewhere. Here's a man willing to pile it up on his own land. Why would that stop him from getting elected in the primary?"

"Because he's not going to tell anyone about it," Emily said impatiently. "He's going to sell the land for a school or a playground or to some unsuspecting home builders. And in the meantime the stuff is going to leach into the groundwater or nearby streams—well, never mind. You couldn't possibly imagine what we've done to our environment, Fergus. I can't begin to explain it."

"If it's so bad, why's the senator miffed with ye?"

"I suppose," she said with a sigh, "because I've thrown all the dirt in his lap. He has to decide whether he wants to brush it off or make it into a mud pie and sling it at Boyd Strom."

"I see yer point. Better to have someone else sling it for ye." He wandered over to the window and stared, as he often did, into the hot summer night. "Ye two seem to be having a hell of a time working things out."

"I know," she said sadly, shutting down her computer for the evening. "If it's not one damn thing, it's another."

"Without me ye'd have all the time ye need to give over to this toxic business." He threw his head back slightly and closed his eyes. "Am I right?"

It gave her pleasure to watch him unobserved. It evened things out somehow. Besides, there was something about him that held her in thrall. It was as if she'd pulled aside a veil and was able to see how angels moved.

"It's more complicated than that, Fergus," she said softly, addressing his question at last. "It has to do with priorities. With you it's a matter of life and death, not just of political survival. I love you, Fergus," she said, surprised by how easily the words came flowing out. "I'll always be here for you."

He came over to the desk, splayed the palms of his hands on its surface, and leaned toward her, his green eyes glittering with emotion. "This isn't the way it was supposed to be, dear one. I never meant to mess up yer life this way. I thought I'd be in and out of it, and that would be that."

He reached his hand out to touch her hair. She held her breath, but she could not feel his touch, only a kind of soft and pleasurable charge. He drew his hand away. She knew instinctively that for him to dare caress her would be fatal, yet right now she was willing to take the chance.

"I've got into yer life now," he added hoarsely, "and now I don't want to get out."

"But you can't stay . . . I can't let you take that risk . . . I have to keep going, or—"

"Or what?" he asked with a bleak smile. "Either way I die."

24

Emily had her key in the lock and was sliding the dead bolt into place when she heard the phone ring inside her condo. She swore under her breath and ran back over her steps, catching the phone just as the answering machine kicked in. "Wait!" she shouted over the recorded message and Lee's voice. She began madly punching buttons, unsure which one stopped the machine. There was a screech and a howling sound, and the beast came grudgingly to rest at her fingertips.

"Sorry about that," she said, breathless from the effort. "I was on my way out."

"I'm glad I caught you, then," Lee answered in a relieved voice. "Emily, I'm sorry about the other day. I'd given my staff standing orders to turn aside anonymous tips; when you and I spoke, I was acting from reflex. During campaigns we get besieged with 'helpful' information."

"Really."

"No kidding. Just today Jim Whitewood told me

that the friend of an ex-girlfriend of a second cousin of Boyd Strom's called with what she claimed was the Scout's honor truth about Strom: When he was a kid, he stole crayons from the dime store and sold them to his classmates at a discount. She claimed it was an indication of his character. Maybe he did, and maybe it is," Lee added, "but it's not the way we do business."

"I see," she said, unmollified. "Toxic waste equals stolen crayons."

"Okay, that wasn't a great example. We've heard far worse, but I'm not about to jump into the rumor maelstrom and repeat them. Emily, please, I know your motives are snow-white. But I can't use it," he argued. "Don't you see that?"

"I don't know," she admitted.

"I miss your voice," he murmured with a weary sigh. "You're the champagne in my campaign, and lately I've been living on bread and water. I have half an hour before I leave for a Kiwanis speech. Am I making you late for anything?"

"I'm on my way to Talbot Manor," she said offhandedly. "But I can go anytime." *Take that, Senator.*

There was an extra beat or two of silence. Then: "Do you think that's wise? As I recall, you said Fergus had a healthy fear of the place."

"Fergus can't stop me," she said, sounding more reckless than she felt. "No one can," she added, just to be ornery.

"Of course not. You're a grown-up," he said in his beautifully deadpan way. "You don't want to hear this from me, Emily," he said much more seriously, "but I think you're losing your perspective. You've romanticized this whole event and all the people in it, past and present. You're so hell-bent on solving this thing that you're forgetting your justifiable fears about Maria—"

"I can handle Maria," she interrupted.

"—and whatever it is in there that Fergus refuses to face."

"I can handle that, too," she said defiantly. She was behaving like an absolute witch, and she knew the reason why: because her feelings were still hurting from the day she'd called him about the toxic dump tip.

"Look, at least promise me you'll wait until the weekend. I'll be free early Saturday; we both can—"

"Oh, right!" she crowed. "What could be more discreet than my showing up with a six-foot-two-inch celebrity senator on one arm, in a house that might be haunted, that rents beds for the night? If your opponent ever found that out, he'd think he'd died and gone to heaven."

"Don't worry about my opponent; worry about yourself. I'm serious about this, Emily. Don't go."

" 'Don't go'? Is that an order?"

"Have you ever followed an order in your life? If you have, then it is."

"I think you know the answer to that one, Senator. Gosh! Look at the time; the Kiwanis will be getting restless." She was about to hang up when she added nervously, "Call me again when you get a chance, Lee?" Then she hung up.

Emily drove in deepening twilight to Newarth, her Toyota moaning and groaning all the way. By the time she reached the Bourbon roses that graced the massive iron gates of Talbot Manor, it was dark—dark and oppressively hot, with the first stirrings of wind. The air was very heavy, very charged. A thunderstorm was imminent. That was fine with her; it'd be a distraction to the people inside Talbot Manor.

Still, Emily hoped the storm would hold off until she'd climbed the granite steps carved into the side of the tower; she had no great desire to go hurtling through space into the bushes again. She crept around to the tower, located the foot of the granite escape, and aimed her flashlight at the window at the top of the steps.

It was boarded shut with plywood.

Nuts. Now what? Maybe the tower was so fire-damaged that Maria hadn't bothered moving the papers and diaries back into the desk drawer. Emily hadn't considered that, although Fergus might have. She should've mentioned her plan to him, *but no-o-o*, she had to decide to spare him any distress.

She went back to the front and hovered in the dark near the huge double doors, trying to figure out which room she should break into on the main floor. As she stood there the doors swung open and two couples, laughing and talking restaurants, stepped out onto the sandstone steps. Acting on impulse Emily said, "Good evening," and walked through the door being held open for her by one of the men.

She ducked into a side receiving room and peeked around the corner. The front desk, thank God, was unattended. Emily knew from Mrs. Gibbs that Frank was out of town; that left only Maria, presumably watching television in her private sitting room. Emily tiptoed past the desk on cat feet, her heart lodged firmly in her throat, and up the stairs leading to the guest rooms. There was no one in sight. If August was considered high season at Talbot Manor, she'd hate to own the place in the off season.

On the third floor the smell of smoke seemed to permeate everything, no doubt including all the beige drapes and all the beige carpets; the fire must have been a bitter blow to poor Frank's plans. Emily paused just long enough in the dimly lit hall to fling back the bolt on the new door into the tower. When she stepped inside she had to switch on the flashlight she carried; there was no moon to light up the room this time. Except for the acrid smell the tower seemed much the same, at least by flashlight. Emily shined her beam on the four-poster and saw different sheets, this time in a rich paisley pattern. So her hunch had been right. Not even the fire had been enough to drive Maria away.

There was a kerosene lamp on the floor next to the bed, and matches. Emily decided to take the risk of lighting the lamp; the room was too pitch-black to move around with any ease. In the dim cast of yellow light she made her way to the desk behind the tall Oriental screen and pulled open the middle drawer. Maria had brought everything back—the diaries, the photos, the letters.

Emily went straight for the diaries. They all were bound in leather with tiny brass locks but were of varying styles and sizes. The first one was locked. That threw Emily for a loop, but the second snapped open nicely. The bookplate inside was inscribed in a neat but childish hand, "*Mon Livre.* Celeste de la Croix." Emily flipped through the pages. It was in French, every blessed word.

She was able to figure out that "*1 janvier 1852*" meant that Celeste was about thirteen when she wrote it, but for anything more than that she'd need a French dictionary. She put the diary down and picked up another: also in French, written by Celeste two years later. And another, still in French, three years after that. But by 1863, the date inscribed in the next diary, Celeste had become confident enough to write in her naturalized tongue, English. By 1863 Hessiah had been born and James had drowned;

surely Celeste would have had been moved to write about it all. With a prayer of gratitude Emily held the diary close to her breast.

Immediately she felt the heat. Her thumb, which had been resting on the brass plate of the locking mechanism, might just as well have been resting on a hot iron. Shocked and in pain, she dropped her flashlight and the diary at the same time. In the dark she could see the diary's brass plate, glowing red.

"Oh, God." She snatched up the diary and stumbled with it across the room to one of the casements, opened it, and dropped the diary onto the lawn thirty-five feet below her. She watched in horror as the little brass plate continued to glow, a small and evil eye staring back up at her.

This was not Fergus.

For a small eternity she stood at the casement, paralyzed with fear and indecision. Whatever it was, whoever it was, understood completely that she was an enemy force come to do battle over the diaries. Whatever was in those books, they were meant to stay in the manor. And now without thinking, Emily had violated that territorial imperative. She could still retrieve the book, throw it back through an open window, and flee, leaving the evil in the house to reign freely, with the beautiful and bizarre descendant of Celeste de la Croix Talbot in devoted attendance.

But what about Fergus?

Emily closed her eyes and took a deep breath, then blew it out and went back to the desk. There were six diaries in the drawer: the locked one, the three in French, the one she had thrown out the window, and one other. Calmly, deliberately, she picked up the first and jimmied open the lock with her Swiss army knife. It was in French and dated 1849, when Celeste was ten. Emily tested it by holding it to her breast, laying it over the crystal just as she had done before. Nothing happened.

She put it back and repeated the gesture with each of the others she'd looked at. The diaries remained cool and inert. That left the sixth one. She picked it up and flashed her light over the first page. It was in English, dated 1867, the year Celeste was thrown from her horse. The last entry was in July.

> Every day it becomes more apparent to me, though no one else seems to see it. Yesterday he flew into a rage after Hessiah went up to Chef and presented him with her "dear 'ittle kittycat" in exchange for a piece of marzipan. Everyone else was amused—the girl is charming in an outrageous way—but now this evening the gardener has found the kitten in back with its neck twisted. The presumption is that a vagrant with a grievance against Chef was to blame. But I do not believe it.

Emily flipped through the pages feverishly, scanning for other telling passages, but it was hard to read by flashlight, and she was too much in a hurry. She found nothing specific, nothing incriminating. Her eye fell on several expressions of unhappiness with John Talbot—Celeste thought her husband was "relentless" and "sharp" and "intolerant"—but there was nothing about the mayor, nothing that jumped out anyway. Still, she'd been right about the Talbots' marriage being loveless. If that was true, then anything was possible.

Slowly, fearfully, she brought the diary up to her breast and tested it against the necklace. The heat came at once, of such burning ferocity that she felt the crystal searing her flesh. She let out a scream of pain and hurled the diary across the room. The leather cover, dry and brittle with years, glowed red hot in the dim room, then erupted spontaneously into flame. Horrified, Emily stumbled toward the bed and yanked the coverlet from it, then ran to throw it over the burning book, knocking down chairs and small tables in her panic. She grabbed a broom and stomped the coverlet repeatedly, fiercely, as if a deadly snake were writhing underneath it.

Now the coverlet was on fire, smoking at first, and then bursting with small, wicked spikes of flame. Too late she remembered the fire extinguisher in the third-floor hall. She ran through the door she'd left open, ripped the heavy red cylinder from its bracket, and ran back to the coverlet, pulling the pin and spraying the coverlet with almost maniacal zeal. When the flames were quelled she kept on spraying anyway, until the cylinder was emptied. Exhausted and dripping with sweat, she let the extinguisher fall to the floor and cautiously, gingerly crouched down and lifted the coverlet to see if there was anything to salvage.

The diary was a charred, misshapen lump. Emily unfolded her knife and poked it into its edge, to see if any of the text had survived. Suddenly the lump exploded into flames again, one of them licking Emily's hair with a kind of evil deliberation. With a cry of pain she threw the coverlet down and jumped back, her nostrils filling with the sickening stench of burning hair and skin. Tendrils of black smoke began to crawl out from under the sodden coverlet, snaking toward her.

She took one step back, then two. "Don't you dare," she whispered faintly. "Don't you dare . . ."

She didn't know what was there anymore; she knew only that it lay writhing and curling between her and the door. There wasn't a doubt in her mind that she'd never make it past the incinerated diary. The exit window was boarded up, and the original door led to nowhere. This was it, then. She was going to die. She looked down and saw a sharply defined, very black needle of smoke encircling her blue jeans.

"No!" she cried, outraged. *"I'm not finished yet!"*

But her knees had turned to jelly. She collapsed to the floor, overcome by a hideous, indescribable pain, as if the oxygen were being sucked from her chest. She wanted desperately to black out and be done with it, but she was being tortured with continuing consciousness. She tried to think of what she'd done to deserve this, but she could not, and that made her think of Fergus, hanging from a rope that should never have been looped around his neck. "Fergus . . . oh, Fergus." It came out in a dizzying whimper.

When the room began flooding with light her first thought was that Fergus should not have come, that the house was empowered. But her second thought was one of almost sublime elation. He *had* come; he *would* prevail. Even now the pain inside her seemed to subside to something bearable. But she couldn't possibly stand, much less run from the tower. She was caught between two equal and opposing forces of heat and light, and there was nothing she could do but watch and pray.

Yet there was little to see, because she was blinded by the light, and little to do, because she was powerless. She felt a great pulsing and shifting of energy back and forth through her, as if the cosmos were expanding and contracting. Even in her brutalized, victimized state she felt a sense of awe for the sheer power of the forces involved. Wave after wave advanced through her, then retreated, until finally she felt that she had been broken down into the smallest possible particles, like sand on a beach. Then, gradually, the fury began to subside. It was over.

And she knew that Fergus had won, because she was able to breathe again, and stand up again, and swallow without pain. But at what cost to him? "Fergus," she said in a frightened, tentative voice. "Fergus?"

But he did not answer. When Emily turned around she realized that although Fergus had destroyed something terrible, he'd left intact the handmaiden to that terror: Marie Grissette. She was standing in the open doorway, tall and thin and poised, surveying the destruction that had gone before. Behind her—unless he was an apparition—stood Lee Alden, alert, watchful, calm.

The three of them stood frozen in an eerie, silent tableau for what seemed like a small eternity. To break the spell, Emily suddenly lifted the blanket and flipped it aside, revealing the burned lump that was all that remained of the last year of Celeste Talbot's life.

Maria understood instantly what had happened. Emily was prepared for just about anything, but not for the speed of the horrifying transformation in the woman. Maria let out a scream that was not of this world and charged at Emily, her arms outstretched before her, her fingers curled into talons. Her face was stripped free of its serenity, twisted with rage and pain.

She clawed at Emily and began pulling her down, but Lee jumped between them, using all his considerable strength to drag the madwoman away. Emily had all the fight of a rag doll left in her; when Maria let her go she fell hard into the corner of a nearby dresser. And then everything went much blacker than it had ever gone before.

* * *

When she regained consciousness, she was being loaded into an ambulance, and Lee was alongside, getting directions from the driver to the hospital.

"Wait . . . wait," she said rather stupidly, trying to sit up. "I'm fine. And I left my bag." She was thinking of the diary, lying in the wet grass somewhere next to the knapsack she'd left there. "Let me up. Right now, please. I must insist."

"Easy does it, Emily," Lee said with a shaky laugh. "These guys are bigger than you are; don't give 'em any trouble. I'll get your bag for you and bring it along. Where'd you leave it?"

"In the grass, by the tower." She grabbed the lapel of Lee's suit and pulled him close. "There's a diary somewhere around it," she whispered loudly in his ear. "Bring it. I don't think it can hurt you. It should be cool by now. If it's not, leave it. I know who it was anyway."

Lee gave her a baffled look, and dopey but pleased with the presence of mind she was showing, she fell back on the stretcher. The paramedics lifted it to the floor of the ambulance. "Wait . . . wait," she cried again.

Lee murmured something to the driver and in a voice of gentle reason asked Emily, "What is it now, darling?"

"Maria—where is she?"

The interior lights of the ambulance threw a ghastly pallor over Lee's face. "She's inside," he said tersely. "They're with her now."

He refused to say any more than that. Before she could question him further, Emily was being whisked away to New Bedford General, the sounds of sirens screaming directly over her head. Once or twice she said Fergus's name, with no response. She was still a little groggy—but not, as the paramedics speculated, because of a possible concussion. "It's been a rough night," she said with an apologetic smile to the paramedic beside her. Another thought occurred to her. "Is there a BMW following us?"

The paramedic looked out the rear window and came back to her. "Yeah, he's right behind us." He sat silently for a little while, then looked out the window again. "Still coming. Right through the red light. I guess he can get a ticket fixed easy enough," he added, chuckling.

Emily smiled gamely, but she wasn't about to let him engage her in chitchat over the senator. She closed her eyes and played dead until they wheeled her into the emergency room. When she got there she was examined by a staff physician who checked her out and said, "How do you feel?"

"Fine. I'm a little tired, but otherwise I'm fine," Emily answered.

He smiled in a kindly way and said, "Good. Someone will fix up that burn for you." Then he left her for a while, and when he came back he had her knapsack with him. Emily tore it open and saw that the diary was inside, completely soaked—it must've rained while she was in the tower—but still in one piece.

"I think we're going to keep you overnight for observation," the physician said. "You got conked pretty good."

"What? No. I can't. It's out of the question. I feel perfect. You can't make me stay, can you? No. Really. I can't." She looked around, distracted, fully intending to run for it if she had to. "Is the—the man who gave you this still around?" she asked.

"He's very definitely still around, which is one reason you're staying, young lady. Do you think I want to butt heads with a United States senator?"

"May I speak with him for just a moment, please?" she asked, clutching her knapsack.

In two minutes a nurse ushered Lee into the examining room, and they were alone. Emily was a mess, with her patched-up chest and her burned-out hair, but she tried to put on a bright face. "Hi!" she said in an absurdly chipper voice. "I hear you're trying to have me locked up."

Lee didn't smile at all. He looked haggard, in fact, which made her feel a little better. At least he wasn't any more presentable than she was. "Give it a rest, Emily," he said. "For once in your life, stop seeing every little thing as a battle of wills."

"That's not it at all," she lied. "I know you're concerned, but I really am fine. I want to go home."

"What happened in the tower?" Lee asked. "Did he show up after all?"

"He was there," she said, less chipper now. "I'm not sure what happened, but I know the house has been purged. There's nothing there anymore. I—I don't think I'll be seeing Fergus again," she added, her voice catching in her throat. "I think whatever force he had, whatever energy—he used it up fighting the horror that was in there. And it was my fault, Lee," she said mournfully. "He warned me away from Talbot Manor. Now I don't know what's happened to him." The tears began to roll freely; she did nothing to stop them.

"Hey, hey, he's come and gone before. Wait and see, darling," Lee said, cradling her in his arms. "Wait and see."

25

Eventually they let her go. After a little kicking and screaming Emily was turned over to Lee's care with the proviso that she call an ambulance immediately if she ran into a severe headache or loss of motor function in the next twenty-four hours. In exchange she agreed to let Lee drive her home and have one of his staff members hand-deliver her Toyota the next day.

"You drive a hard bargain, Senator," she said, handing over the keys to her car. The funny thing was she meant it.

They left the hospital at midnight and drove through rain-slicked streets littered with downed tree limbs. The thunderstorm had been extraordinarily violent, with sixty-mile winds and a ferocious display of lightning; Emily hadn't been aware of any of it. She wasn't very clear on what she'd experienced in the tower, and after a halfhearted attempt to explain it she gave it up and closed her eyes. She needed desperately to sleep.

The next thing she knew, Lee was shaking her

gently awake. "We're home," he murmured in a low voice.

She sat up and rubbed her eyes drowsily. "Lee, the media are going to have a field day over tonight. What will you do?"

His arm was on the seat behind her; he looked calm, almost cavalier, considering his career was officially in a shambles. "I dunno. Punt, I guess."

She laughed sadly and shook her head, wincing from even that small effort. "Boy. You must curse the day you took me to that séance."

"Nope. I still bless the day I found you."

She thought he was being ironic, but in the darkened car there was no way to be sure. It was impossible to tell him how grateful she was that he tracked her down to the tower. She sighed and said, "I have to admit, Maria gives new meaning to the concept of ancestor worship. She could have killed me, Lee," she added. "You saved my life."

"Yeah, but did you notice? I had to take a number to do it," he said with an ironic smile. "You had a hell of a guardian angel in there."

"So to speak," she said with a bleak smile. "What's going to happen to Maria?"

"I expect they'll keep her for observation. The husband's been contacted; apparently there's a history of schizophrenia in her family."

Lee began to get out of the car, but she didn't want him to see her to her door; she wasn't sure why.

"Get some sleep," he said, brushing her lips gently with his. "I'll call you tomorrow."

Once Emily had cleaned herself up and got into her pajamas, sleep became just another enemy to have to fight. She popped the soggy 1863 diary into an oven set on low and began monitoring it carefully while she made a pot of double-strength tea. Then, while the diary was drying and the tea was brewing, she turned her computer on. The screen, pale and blank and endlessly patient, stared back at her.

Somehow this wasn't the way it was supposed to be. She'd always assumed that when the time came, Fergus would be looking over her shoulder and she'd be having a beer and he'd be putting in his two cents' worth. But he wasn't over her shoulder; after tonight he might not be anywhere. It was a dismal thought. How could she write the story without him?

And if he *was* around, but just not showing himself? Then she didn't want to write the damn story anyway, because once the story was published he'd leave her forever, and that was an even worse thought.

"My God, Fergus," she cried, tipping her chair back on its hind legs. "I'm paralyzed. What if I have writer's block? Wouldn't *that* be a kick in the pants?"

She laughed softly to herself, glancing at the sofa, half expecting to see Fergus appear there, and at the television, half expecting it to turn on by itself. She got up and poured herself a cup of tea and went over and opened a window and felt cool, clean air wash over her aching burns. She went back to her computer. And looked at the sofa and then at the television. It had begun to sink in. Her time with Fergus was over.

There was nothing left now but to free him once and for all. Blinking back tears, washing down the lump in her throat with hot Darjeeling, Emily began to type out her best guess about who murdered Hessiah Talbot.

Newarth, Massachusetts, is a town that time would like to forget. We can't let that happen. We can't, because a hundred years ago its citizens played fast and loose with an innocent man's life. It's time to set the record straight.

Emily Bowditch had given Fergus O'Malley her word; now she was putting it down in writing. The words, once begun, came in a rush; before long she had the broad strokes of the trial and the hanging laid out. Unaware that it was now the middle of the night, she began to stitch together the few facts she had into a patchwork quilt of Hessiah Talbot's life.

Just before dawn Emily was ready to lay down what she knew, and what she'd deduced, about the night of Hessiah's murder:

When Hessiah Talbot arrived home after the Silver and Gold Ball, she was in high spirits. The handsome and dashing lieutenant had danced nearly every dance with her, and together they'd sent the rest of the company into fits of gossip. The younger women were jealous, but the older men were relieved: Their daughters were safe, at least for the night, from Lieutenant Dale Culver's charms.

The crystal necklace that Hessiah wore to the ball was a gaudy, impossible trinket, just the thing a flashy military man might pick up in a bazaar on his travels overseas. Even after she had changed out of her ball gown into her dressing gown, Hessiah kept on wearing the necklace. It was so like Dale Culver, who after all was so unlike the rest of the stuffy, boring men in Newarth.

Men like Thomas Dayton, her cousin. Hessiah found Tom as dull as toast. For as long as she could remember, Tom Dayton had been part of the scenery—solid and efficient, like the gateposts in front of the manor. She wondered again why Henry Abbott was pressing her to reconsider her rejection of Tom's proposal.

Granted, Henry Abbott, an old friend of her father's, had always taken a special interest in her welfare. But she couldn't understand why he'd push her into a marriage that had nothing to recommend it but money. Money wasn't everything to her. The mayor, who'd been a charmer in his own day, ought to have known that. Besides, Hessiah had all the money she needed; her brother Stewart gave it to her.

No, Hessiah much preferred someone who could make her laugh, and Lieutenant Culver was very good at that. They'd laughed together over the fuss poor Cousin Tom made when she turned him down. And they'd laughed over the temper tantrum Henry Abbott threw when he learned that she'd turned aside a stodgy provider for a penniless charmer. It *was* funny, as far as Hessiah was concerned. Besides, who said the mayor could run her life?

That was her brother's job. And Stewart did it well. All her life.

Emily stopped and went over to the oven where she slipped a hot mitt over her hand and took out the diary. Two hundred degrees seemed about right; the pages were drying out slowly, from the outside in. She was able to catch a dry edge and peel each page carefully back, but it hardly mattered. The ink had run in random squiggles all over the place. The secrets of 1863 were as safe now as the secrets of 1867.

Fire and water. It seemed almost mystical, yet Emily believed more than ever that there was nothing mystical about the diaries. They'd been written by a woman who had been horribly unlucky in love—as a wife, a mother, and a lover. Celeste de la Croix had married a man who was cold and driven, then had a baby by another who was hot-blooded and driven. Two of her children were murdered.

And the third got away with the crimes.

All her life Stewart had been obsessive about Hessiah. In his aloof and cynical way he doted on his sister. He wanted her for himself, this charming, saucy moppet wrapped in ruffles and with ice in her veins. Unquestionably they were kindred spirits, very much like their father. The difference was that John Talbot's obsession, the textile mill, was socially acceptable, whereas a brother who wanted nothing more than to keep his sister in his thrall—that presented a series of problems.

The first of them was James Talbot. Alone among the children, James must have been much like his mother Celeste. With his gentle, sweet face and big brown eyes, James was the sensitive one. To him his baby sister was a fragile, adorable creature. He liked to do things for her, like bringing cool drinks to her in the summer. Every time he did such a thing he ran a risk. One summer day not too far into his life, his luck ran out. It was nothing at all for six-year-old Stewart to shove him down the well.

If his parents suspected anything—and Celeste undoubtedly did, because the matter was kept out of the local newspaper—they kept it to themselves. Stewart was left to kill again another day. When he twisted the neck of Hessiah's kitten, which she had offered—not even in affection—to a member of the staff, Stewart never thought twice about it. The kitten was just another obstacle, with neither less nor more significance than his brother James.

There were other obstacles, of course. The only daughter of the richest man in town was bound to be harassed with proposals of marriage. Stewart was surprisingly successful in fending them off, convincing Hessiah to turn away suitors, encouraging her in her many pointless infatuations. (He also bribed her shamelessly to stay at home. There was enough money to keep her amused, although after John Talbot's death it began to slip away at an alarming rate.)

But Lieutenant Dale Culver was another matter. To Stewart, of course, he was just another pretty face. All things considered, Stewart preferred military men to court his sister; they tended to move on before things could get too serious. But this time something went awry. Maybe it was because Hessiah was aware that her debutante years were behind her. (Certainly Henry Abbott didn't mind reminding her; no doubt there were whispers behind her back as well.)

Or maybe it was because Hessiah Talbot had fallen in love for the first time in her empty, frivolous life. Probably the handsome lieutenant never looked back once he'd left Newarth the morning after the ball. But Hessiah took him for the real thing. That's why she wore his bauble to the Silver and Gold Ball; that's why she kept on wearing the necklace after she had tossed her expensive gown aside for the night. Her maid might have noticed the new sparkle in her mistress, but her maid had been dismissed the day before, the latest in a long line of servants who'd come and gone through Hessiah's dressing room. There were no witnesses to the argument that ended Hessiah Talbot's life.

Emily shook herself free of her self-induced trance. She was aware of a crick in her neck and of increasing pain from the burns. Her head ached from a dizzying lack of sleep, but she wanted desperately to finish the story. Then, in the morning, she could rush it to Phil, who fortunately was suffering from a summertime shortage of copy.

So she took two aspirin and did a few stretches and made another pot of tea. Somehow the sleeve of her pajama hooked on the spout of the ceramic pot, pulling it off the Formica counter. It fell to the floor with a crash, breaking into a dozen pieces. The teapot had been a pretty thing, bright yellow, with cobalt flowers in an oriental design. Emily stared at the fragments—and broke into uncontrollable sobs.

For the next ten minutes she cried, not for the broken teapot but for the night of fear and agony she'd just lived through. Afterward, when she felt calmer, she sat down at her computer to finish the story.

> At first it wasn't even an argument. Her brother dropped by her bedroom, as he always did after Hessiah returned from an evening out. Stewart had been at the ball only briefly, but he'd seen enough. "What a little idiot you are, darling," he'd told her with a charming smile. At any other time, over any other man, Hessiah would have laughed and traded insults with her brother. But tonight she was still walking on clouds, and Stewart's cynical affection was unacceptable. Her retort was angry, cruel, and defiant.
>
> But Stewart decided that he'd had enough of his increasingly hard-to-manage sister. She was costing him far too much: in money, in devotion, in heartbreak. When he pulled the heavy chain sharply around her neck, it wasn't even in anger.

He had simply had enough. His one emotional indulgence was to take the hated trinket from her neck and hide it away in the house. After that he continued on his way to a card game with the rascally set he sometimes visited. And after *that,* Fergus O'Malley came creeping into the house, bent on thievery.

But nothing else.

It was done. Whether she was right or wrong was for other powers to decide. All that remained for Emily was to print the story out and see that it was published. With a pounding head and a heavy heart she dragged herself off to bed and didn't awake until the doorbell sounded off like a fire alarm in the morning. She tripped and staggered to the buzzer and a minute later opened the door to a young and earnest aide of Senator Alden's.

"Oh, cripes, I came too early." The aide, no older than a college freshman, was clearly embarrassed. "Your car's parked up the block. Here are the keys."

"Wha—what time is it?" she asked him woozily, holding out her hand for the keys. She was having a tremendous problem focusing.

"It's not eight yet. But the senator said he wanted the car here early for you. I guess I got a little gung ho," he added with a loopy grin.

It looked loopy to Emily anyway. She took the keys but then promptly dropped them on the floor.

When she bent over to pick them up, she went tumbling head over heels.

By the time they rushed her to Mass General, Emily was barely conscious. Her thoughts came and went in bits and pieces. She tried several times to speak, but the best she could do was to mumble, "Have the publish . . . paper . . . now."

The surgeon on duty had been told that Emily was a journalist. "Don't worry, Emily; you have lots of publishing left in you," he said, shining a tiny flashlight into each of her eyes.

He turned and gave some instructions to a nurse to call in a neurosurgeon while Emily was put on an IV solution and her vital signs were monitored. A few minutes after that she heard the neurosurgeon order an emergency CAT scan.

She didn't like the sound of things at all. By now she could barely open her eyes. She tried to ask questions, but all that came out was a jumble of syllables. The neurosurgeon was hovering over her; his voice was crisp, urgent. "We may have to evacuate the hematoma," he said. It sounded like a military maneuver. She became frightened, far more frightened than she'd ever been in Talbot Manor.

After that she was wheeled here and then there on the gurney, presumably for the CAT scan. By now she couldn't speak at all, couldn't open her eyes. All she knew was what she heard, and all she heard were things she didn't understand. She felt trapped in her own dream, yet it seemed to her that she'd gone a long time without sleep. She thought about letting herself nod off for a while.

But then someone said, "Prep her for surgery," and that sent her into a silent panic. She didn't want surgery. She didn't need surgery. Surgery was for the old and middle-aged, for the gunshot and the cancer victim, not for someone who'd hit her head on a stupid table. She tried desperately to object, but no one heard her. Yet she could hear everyone else with clarity.

"Have you got a consent yet?"

"Not yet, Doctor; I've faxed the forms to her father in New Hampshire."

No! Don't tell my dad! You'll just upset him. He has a bad heart. You can't—

"We can't wait. Come on; let's go."

After that they put a mask over her face, just the way they'd done for her tonsillectomy. *This is silly,* she thought. *I had more fight in me when I was five than I do now.* She tried to lift her hands, to pull the mask away and breathe clear air. But her arms wouldn't lift when she willed them to.

Ah, the hell with it, she thought tiredly. *I'll take that nap after all.*

26

Comatose. Emily heard the word distinctly. At first she assumed she was still caught in the same boring dream, the one in which she was going around endlessly, trying to get someone to hear her.

But it wasn't a dream.

"Dr. Redd, my sister's been this way for over twenty-four hours now! How much longer will we have to wait?"

Gerry? How did you get here? Who's minding the shop? You can't afford to—

"I understand your concern, Mr. Bowditch. And again I'll tell you not to worry unduly. It's perfectly normal for Emily to be in a state of coma at this point. But we've relieved the pressure from the hematoma that was threatening her. Now it's just a matter of time."

"But she looks so—oh, God. What am I supposed to tell my father? Is she really out of danger? Can you guarantee that?"

Didn't you hear the man? "It's just a matter of time." Don't be such a worrywart.

"Well, *guarantee* is a word we don't like to use around here. This isn't an auto shop, Mr. Bowditch. I wish it were. It would be nice to think that if we just threw enough skill and spare parts at a problem, we could fix it. Let me just say, I see no obvious reason for Emily not to recover fully."

But no guarantees?

"Yeah, sure, I understand. I don't mean to ride you on this, but she's the baby of the family. There's us four guys, and there's Emily, who has more guts than the rest of us put together—and that includes a cop and a Gulf vet. The thing is, we were always tough on her for being a girl. And that made her play harder, work longer, study more. Y'know? Because she was a girl. If it's our fault she's like this . . ."

"Nonsense. You can't go blaming yourself. Emily ran into some bad company, that's all. She's lucky she was able to get away in one piece."

"Thanks to the senator, yeah. You know she never told us a thing about him? We're a pretty tight family; she calls her dad once a week. Yet all we know about the other night is what we read in *USA Today*. It's—"

"Yes, well. I see the head nurse glaring at us. The limit in the ICU is ten minutes. Maybe we should take this outside."

Stay! Dammit, stay! How could she possibly learn anything if they took things outside? If she were more like Fergus, well, that'd be one thing. She could hop around from room to room. But apparently comas didn't give you that kind of flexibility; now she couldn't hear anything except the hum of the monitors next to her bed.

Don't panic. She focused on what Dr. Redd—or was it Wred?—had just told Gerry: "It's just a matter of time." *God. If that isn't the story of my life lately.* She tried to laugh, but no sound came, not even a snicker.

Comatose. The panic roared in anyway, despite her effort to stay calm. She tried desperately to get out of bed. Within seconds someone was in the room with her, making calming sounds but holding her firmly. After that she felt sticky things being placed back on her chest while a hand—a nurse's hand, surely—patted her cheek and gave her a little squeeze of reassurance. Emily began breathing more easily. Just a matter of time.

After that Emily drifted off, she wasn't sure where. The next thing she realized was pain; someone was sticking her thigh with a pin. "She's fairly deep," he said in a businesslike voice. The pin hurt; she wanted to stick him back. But even before they left the room, Emily went drifting off again.

Eventually she heard voices.

"Does she answer to her name?"

"Not as far as I can tell."

Ben? You're here, too? I meant to tell you, I need more Mace. I can't seem to go anywhere anymore without needing Mace. . . .

"Emily? Honey? It's Benjamin. Hey, kiddo. It's time to wake up. You know how you hate to oversleep . . . wake up, kiddo. We miss you . . ."

I miss you, too, Ben. I miss all of you.

"You poor little kid, you poor—" She heard a catch in Ben's voice, and then she heard him break down. He was squeezing her hand in his huge paw and sobbing. She'd heard him cry only once before, this tough cop brother of hers, and that was at their mother's funeral.

I'm not dead yet! Don't cry. Don't, don't cry, Ben. It scares me.

Gerry eased Ben out of the room, and then she was alone again, alone and floating between life and not-life. It seemed to her that she stayed there for a long, long time, floating back every once in a while to check on things, and then away again, she wasn't sure where. She felt like a plastic cup on Cape Cod Bay, ebbing back and forth with the tide.

Whenever she heard her name, she tried to make her way back, but if the seas were running, or the wind was blowing, there was nothing she could do, because she was only a styrofoam cup.

"Emily, hi, darlin'. I'm back."

Lee.

"So. What have you been up to? I know, bad joke. It looks like the burned part of your hair's growing out nicely. So's the shaved part. After this, let your hair grow long. I said you looked nice at that Copley Plaza fund-raiser, but I lied. I liked your hair better before you got it cut."

Lee.

"The first time I saw you—in that hilarious palmist's getup—it was all I could do not to run my fingers through it. You were on the floor, madly plucking flower petals. . . ."

Lee.

"I know you can hear me, darling . . . I can tell from the monitor . . . I got a crash course in reading EEGs from the head nurse."

Lee was holding her hand in both of his now; she felt his heat wrap around her coolness, insulating her. "I like your brothers," he said. "Both of 'em. Too bad Gerry had to go back to New Hampshire. I guess your sister-in-law's due any day now. Gerry was pretty torn up about which hospital to park himself in. Of course, you still have Ben camping out weekends in the waiting room outside the ICU.

"Ben stays with a cop buddy here in Boston—Tim Reilly. You may remember Tim; he said he met you at the policemen's picnic back home in Manchester a few years ago. Big guy, built like a tank? Tim came around to say hi last week. We had coffee downstairs together. He remembers you well. No question, I was jealous, darlin'."

Lee knew Gerry and Ben and Tim? Lee, a coffee klatcher? Lee?

She felt her hand being lifted to his lips. "I have to leave you now. I ran into Cara Miles in the lobby. We negotiated: I took seven of the minutes; she got three. There she is, tapping on the windows as I speak. I'll try to sneak in again after hours, but I'm not sure how much clout a lame-duck senator can wield. I'll be back, Emily. I love you."

She tried desperately to will herself into consciousness. She was still struggling when she felt Cara's cool, made-up cheek press close to hers.

Cara's voice was a discreet whisper, as if she were afraid of waking Emily. "Poor darling. The senator said I should talk to you just as if you were alive—or whatever; that's not how he said it—but . . .

"I mean, I could probably talk to a doorknob for three minutes if I had to, so . . . By the way, you *did* pick the world's worst time to do this; you've missed all the excitement. There was an uproar after that awful business with that Maria person. Someone, I think one of the paramedics, leaked what they saw to the press, and that was *it*. They've been all over the senator ever since. There's a pack of reporters in the lobby right now.

"Not that they have a prayer of making it up here. I've never seen such tight security. *I* almost didn't get to see you. I suppose I should've brought a *People* magazine to read to you. They say that's good for comas. But I didn't, so-o-o I'd better run. Take care, darling. You look much better than I thought you would. Hurry up and come out of this. You're taking a lot longer than they said."

Emily felt Cara's smooth cheek glancing over hers again, and then Cara, too, was gone.

After Cara left, Emily seemed to ebb farther than ever from wakefulness. In her drifting, dreamlike state she became convinced that there was a full moon, cold and white and serene, pulling the ocean away from the shore, dragging her farther and farther out to sea. No longer could she hear voices on the shore, even distant ones.

The tide will rise, and I will be able to float nearer to shore again. I will wait for the tide to rise.

And it did. When Stanley Cooper came in, she was near enough to the shore to smell his cigarette-smoked clothing. She heard his raspy voice with perfect clarity. It filled her with hope that she was on her way back.

"Well, you've done it this time, kid," she heard him say in his familiar, sardonic tone. "You've gone a step too far. You couldn't just stick to rent control violations. You had to go for the big story."

The big story is stuck in my computer, Stan.

"You vowed to take His Highness down a peg, and by golly, you did."

I never said that! If I did, I didn't mean it!

"The irony is, you're in here while we're all busy mining your mother lode."

The mother lode is stuck in my computer, Stan.

"I've heard that you shouldn't say bad things to comatose patients; they'll hate you later and not know why. I wish I was optimistic enough to believe that. But the idea's hooey, and it's not going to stop me from making a little confession: I'm the one who leaked the story of your going to the séance with Lee Alden.

Impossible . . . I never said a word to you.

"I'll tell you how I found out. Mrs. Lividus called the newsroom, wanting to talk to you. I chatted her up—I admit, I have a way with older women—and she was very forthcoming. By the way, she's convinced Kimberly produced something that night. The girl thought so, anyway, and was scared half to death. That's why she took down her shingle and went back home to California.

"And I guess I'll tell you something else. I'm not sure how I feel about having been instrumental in Lee Alden's political death. It was a little too much like shooting fish in a barrel.

"Well, that's pretty much what I came to say. If you do pull out of this and you end up with an urge to slap me every time you see me, I promise to explain the reason why."

Emily heard him shuffle to his feet slowly, and then she felt her head being patted clumsily.

"It'd be a small price for me to pay," Stan added. "Hang in there, kid. The newsroom's not the same without you." He left, leaving the smell of tobacco lingering in the room for a long time.

I can smell his cigarettes. I must not be dead, because I can smell Stanley's god-awful cigarettes. I remember that Fergus wasn't able to smell the Bourbon roses near the gates of Talbot Manor. But I'm alive. If I want to be. Is this what I want?

Emily drifted away again, farther from the shore than ever before. She knew nothing, felt nothing, thought nothing. Once she was vaguely aware of a cluster of medical people around her, murmuring. It fascinated her. For the first time she realized she was closer to death than to life. And then they, too, left.

"Oh, Mother of God! You poor, poor child—it's me, Loretta Gibbs. Can you hear me? They said maybe you could hear me. Oh, this is awful. What have they done to you . . . these tubes . . . going in, going out . . . and your lips, so dry . . . oh, this is terrible. I'll be back."

Mrs. Gibbs, please don't go. It's so good to hear your voice, to hear any voice. I thought I was gone. . . .

"Here you go, poor dear, some water. There, isn't that better? There, there . . ."

Emily felt a small wet sponge being pressed gently to her lips. It seemed to her a long, long time since there'd been anything cool and damp on her lips.

"Yes, that's better; just like a Popsicle, isn't it, dear? And before you know it, you'll be drinking from a cup, and we'll be having coffee at the library. I'll make those double-fudge brownies you like. I've been so busy, you know. The maple leaves have started to fall, and I'm trying to keep up with the raking as best I can. Most of the roses are still blooming, especially the floribundas. We're having a wonderful Indian summer."

It seemed to Emily that Mrs. Gibbs stayed a long time, pouring pleasant, simple thoughts into her ear and pressing the cool, damp sponge repeatedly to her lips. Emily let herself be lulled into a kind of nap and never heard the old woman leave.

Sometime after that Emily dreamed that it was winter and she was walking, half frozen, through waist-high snow. In her dream there was a coat lying on the snow ahead of her, but she couldn't reach it because the snow was too deep. Every step forward was an exhausting effort. But no matter how hard she pressed on, the coat was always lying just out of reach. Finally she got close, close enough to see that it wasn't really a coat; it was a brown corduroy vest with four flaps on it.

"Hey, darlin'. I've got news: Stan Cooper broke the toxic dump story this morning, and broke it in a big way. He had to have been working flat-out to turn it around this fast. Names, dates, associates—they're all there. You were wrong about him, Em. If he has a grudge against me, he has a funny way of showing it. They had a call-in poll on Channel Seven tonight. Seventy-one percent of the respondents think Strom should withdraw. He won't, of course, but things look a little less bleak.

"And here's more news for you: Your office has retrieved the Hessiah Talbot story out of your computer. Phil's read it, and he loves it; I talked with him myself. The *Journal* plans to go with a big spread in the Sunday magazine section. I've seen some of the preliminary artwork. They're doing a beautiful job with it.

"Hey. Emily. I'm watching the monitor, sweetheart. I don't see a whole lot of excitement. Darling, this is what you fought for so long and hard. This is what Fergus has been waiting for. Before long that story will be rolling off the press and Fergus will be free. That's what he wanted, Emily. Even if it isn't . . . you know he has no choice.

"Emily . . . you have to let him go. I know how much it hurts; I do. Letting go is the hardest thing there is. I've been there. Listen to me. After Nicole died, I didn't want to go on any longer. I'm ashamed to admit it, but . . . I, ah, toyed with the notion of suicide.

"Oh, it was nothing overt, like holding a gun to my head or dumping arsenic in my brandy. But I began to do stupid things, like dashing against the lights in rush hour. And taking my boat out alone in wild weather. And bridges, they began to fascinate me. I'd slow down on them, wondering if I could make it out of the car and over the side before someone stopped me.

"I don't really know why I kept on living. Habit? Fear? Maybe I just wanted to finish out my term. And then . . . I met you.

"I don't have all the pieces fitted together yet. For one thing, you don't seem all that keen on my declarations of love, not if that monitor is any guide. And of course, you never did say you loved me, Em. I'm painfully aware of that.

"But to me these are all details. Because I *know* how right we are for each other, Emily. I know what you feel like in my arms and how I feel when you're not around, as if half of me were missing. I know exactly how the sun hits your cheek and lights up your hair, and I can hear your laugh as clearly as if I had it at home on a compact disk. I know every smile and every scowl and every single shade you've ever blushed.

"I even know why you're hanging back now, and I can't blame you for it. Whatever I saw when I was in the hospital, whatever I felt, it was enough to lead me on a search that lasted years. Yet it was nothing—*nothing*—compared with what you've seen and felt.

"I can't make you come back, Emily. I want to, more than anything else I've ever wanted in my life—more than I wanted Nicole. But I couldn't make Nicole come back, and I can't—

"God. What is it I'm trying to tell you? Listen to me, Emily. There's a Tibetan saying: Learn to die, and you will learn to live. Somehow I think you're struggling with that right now. I wish I could help you, but all I can do is wait. Here. On this side. Because life goes on. I just want it to go on with you. I love you, Emily."

Learn to die, and you will learn to live . . . to die . . . to live.

For what seemed like infinity Emily clung to a great, cosmic pendulum, swinging in a slow arc through space: To die . . . to live . . . to die . . . to live.

And then, at last, Emily saw a great, shining light beckoning at the end of a long pathway, and she just let go. She let herself be drawn willingly into the radiance. It seemed to her that there was a sound, not music exactly, but a sound, unbearably poignant, and that she herself felt an extraordinary lightness of being. She began to feel almost impossibly happy, without knowing why. And then she saw that Fergus was ahead of her on the shining path. He seemed to be waiting for her, even though the light continued beyond him.

As she drew nearer, he lifted his arms to her, and that made her want to run to him. But she was aware that she could no more run than she could pinch herself, that it was joy that was transporting her. It seemed odd, too, that she didn't cry out Fergus's name, and that Fergus had no more need to speak than she did.

When she was closer to Fergus, she saw him in a new dimension. Once she would have been able to see a flush under his cheeks or the play of muscle in his jaw. Now he was transcendently beautiful, part of another plane of existence, and she felt humbled to be in his presence. She understood full well that she was seeing into his soul, yet the yearning to be one with him was overwhelming. He was part of all the joy and all the love in the universe, and if she were with him, she could be part of it too. She lifted her arms to him, to Fergus—and to the universe beyond.

In his face, transfigured by light and love, she saw a flash of his old grin: He'd made it, and he loved her beyond anything she could hope to hear expressed in words. When she drew nearer, she moved, quite simply, into his soul. And for one blink in the universe of time, Emily ceased to exist. There was only joy. And a great, abiding love. And peace.

"Dr. Redd, come quickly! I think the patient's coming around."

Emily winced, as though she'd been splashed with ice water, and groaned.

"There you go, honey . . . take it slow . . . shh . . . the doctor'll be right here. . . ."

Emily's eyelids fluttered, then opened sleepily. "I . . . oh-h-h . . . what's happening?" she said in a dry whisper.

She was staring at a nurse with a grin as big as Texas. "You're coming out of a coma that's gone on way too long, honey. And I can name a lot of people who're going to line up to give you a piece of their mind."

For a long moment Emily just stared at the nurse. Her mind was an absolute blank. Coma? The last thing she remembered was crawling into bed exhausted after an all-night session at her computer. Hessiah Talbot's murderer. Yes. Her brother Stewart did it. Yes. Emily was quite sure. And just as soon as she handed over the story to be published, then Fergus—

Fergus. She'd been with Fergus. Just now . . . Suddenly she became very still. She closed her eyes, focusing every atom of her being inward.

"She's slipping back."

She'd been with Fergus, been with him in a way

she never knew existed. That much she knew. But she couldn't remember the experience; it was all hidden behind a veil. She drew her brows together, concentrating fiercely.

"Emily, Emily, don't go back." It was Dr. Redd's voice. "We're just about to call your family. Don't you want to see them? Come on, girl, stay with us. You can do it."

Her hand went up to hold the crystal, to summon Fergus, but the necklace was gone. "My necklace . . ." she moaned, opening her eyes again. The doctor standing next to the nurse looked startled, then pleased at her alertness.

"Don't worry at all about it. It's perfectly safe. We had to cut it off with snips; no one could figure out how it opened. Don't worry. Any goldsmith—"

"No, you don't understand . . . how could you . . . how could you?" she said, scandalized.

"You're getting upset, honey," said the nurse, "and all for nothing. Now, how were we supposed to bathe you with that old thing around your neck, hmm?"

Emily closed her eyes again, shutting up the tears behind her lids. "Never mind . . . you couldn't have known."

The nurse smiled and said, "That's better. Look, I'll tell you what. Senator Alden is holding the necklace for you. Do you want me to call him right now?"

"No . . . no, you'd better not." She put her hand to her head wearily and was amazed to feel that her hair was both longer and shorter than she'd had it before the hospital. "Can you tell me the date, please?"

"October third, dear, believe it or not."

"There's nothing I don't believe anymore," Emily answered with a tired, limp smile.

27

When it was over Emily went home, home to New Hampshire. After the good wishes and hugs from the hospital staff, after the happy embraces of her co-workers and friends, after a brief statement to the relentless press, after the roses and the cards and the calls, Emily went back to where she'd begun.

She couldn't face the condo. Not yet, and maybe not ever. She got Ben's wife Sarah to empty her drawers and much of her closet into a couple of trunks for her, and together they made the trip north in companionable silence. The car was filled with the smell of roses, roses she couldn't very well leave behind since everyone knew the card had been signed with Lee's name. She'd taken the roses, but she'd had to leave Lee. There was no other way. After her transcendent moment with Fergus, Emily felt that anything less than a complete break with Lee would be dishonest.

And Lee had made it easy for her. Emily learned from Sarah that he'd hung back deliberately from the well-wishers, not wishing to intrude among family. Both Ben and Sarah had encouraged him to intrude to his heart's content, but he'd just smiled and said it was enough to know that Emily had pulled through.

Afterward Ben had shaken his head, baffled. "The man checks in like clockwork every day, then takes off when she finally comes to. It's not like he's shy, so what goes on?"

Sarah had told her husband, "Leave him alone. And leave your sister alone."

Emily spent the first week with Gerry and Jean, helping her sister-in-law with her newborn. After that she went on to her father's ramshackle farmhouse, where she divided her time between listening to her father reminisce and scraping the peeling clapboard under the roof of the wraparound porch. The weather was very fine for doing both.

As usual after his one o'clock nap, her father came out to chat with her while she worked. Emily was sharpening the scraper blade with a file, aware that for as long as she could remember the house had needed paint on one side or another.

"Have you decided on a color yet, Dad?"

"Any color, as long as it's white," her father grumped, rubbing the sleep from his eyes.

She looked up from her sharpening with a wry smile. "Still as flexible as ever, I see."

"What's right is right," he answered stolidly.

He grabbed hold of the arms of the ladder-back rocker that was a permanent fixture on the porch and eased himself into it. The afternoon sun, October low, threw him in golden relief, softening the stark whiteness of his hair and the craggy, weathered lines of his face. She was reminded of a night more than a decade ago when—no longer young, even then—her father had sat in the same rocker on the same porch with the same righteous look on his face, waiting for her to come home from a date in a car that had broken down three different ways in three hours.

George Bowditch had tried hard to raise good people; he'd tried hardest of all with Emily. Now, with his Agnes gone and his children all grown, it was obvious that his house was too big, the burden of maintaining it too great. Obvious, that is, to everyone but him.

"Don't you wish you'd sold this old place a couple of years back, when Boston yuppies were snapping up anything with a gable and a frieze?"

"Them damn fools? They'd be pickin' out the trim in designer teal and brick red and settin' up the cordwood all picturesque on the porch where the termites could step nicely into the parlor, thank you very much. No. I ain't sorry."

"The gutter's bad on the west side, Dad. The trim underneath here is pretty punky. I don't think it'll hold paint."

"Sure, I know it. Ben's promised to fix it first thing. Just do the best you can. And, Emily?"

Emily dragged the scraper across a long stretch of peeling paint, bringing down a rain of flakes into her hair. "Yeah, Dad?"

"I suppose you know I'm pleased to have you here," he said gruffly.

"Yeah, Dad," she said, smiling. "I know."

One day rolled into another, with the two of them falling into an easy, predictable routine: an early-morning walk in the woods, followed by a meat and eggs breakfast, after which Emily scraped and primed a section of the porch while her father puttered inside. Then they had lunch, and while he napped she put on the finish coat. She was rushing the work, but she had no choice; the weather could turn any day. Besides, it was time to return to her job. Bankruptcy was imminent.

Still, being an obsessive type, Emily wanted at *least* to finish the porch, and that included 122 peely balusters. She was on her knees, working on number 83, when one of the loaner clunkers Gerry kept handy at his garage pulled into the gravel drive. She waved her paintbrush at the big yellow Ford Fairlane, glad of her brother's company, and went back to painting.

But it wasn't Gerry who got out. When she looked up again, Emily was face-to-face with the man she'd fled, face-to-face with the emotions she thought she'd put to rest.

"Lee. This is a surprise," she said, her voice unnaturally calm. *Oh, no! I'm a disaster! My hair's sticking out like a punk rocker's; I'm dressed in salvage from an all-male rag box. Where can I run? Where can I hide?*

Lee, not surprisingly, was impeccably casual in oxford shirt and khakis. "Hello," he said, shifting a large paper-wrapped parcel from his right arm to his left.

"*Please* don't say I look very nice," she warned, standing up and wiping her paint-stained fingers on her brother's worn-out fatigues. She was blushing to the core.

Lee's smile was tentative, as if someone were giving him directions and he wasn't exactly sure which way north was. "You look very . . . independent," he ventured.

She laughed and said breezily, "Hey, you've seen our license plates: 'Live Free or Die.' What brings you to this neck of the woods, anyway—in that hulk?"

He had one foot on the bottom step, but he declined to come up farther, and Emily's mind was somewhere else than on her manners. So they stood there in a kind of New Hampshire standoff, with him not pressing and her not inviting.

"I'm here for a couple of reasons, actually. Sarah and Ben invited me up for the night—"

"*My* sister-in-law?"

"—and on the way up my car developed a funny knock. Gerry insisted on taking a look at it and gave me the loaner—"

"*My* brother?"

"—so that I could still make my lunch date with Jean and the new baby—"

"*My* niece?"

"—Katherine. Yes. She's a doll."

Emily didn't know what to say. Here he was, lock, stock, and barrel, settled in snugly with her family. She had a passing sense of déjà vu, but she couldn't imagine where she'd learned about it.

"Katherine weighed eight pounds nine ounces," she said with startling irrelevance.

Lee smiled, shifted feet, shifted the package. "I think Jean mentioned that on the phone."

There was a pause, and then Emily said rather defiantly, "Are you just passing by, then?"

For an answer he held up the package, the size of a framed poster, to her. "This is from Helen."

Helen was one of the illustrators at the *Boston Journal*. Emily checked to see that her hands were dry and accepted the parcel from him, then tore off the brown paper. It was the original artwork for her piece on Fergus and Hessiah Talbot, beautifully framed and matted. Emily had steadfastly refused to open the *Journal* magazine section that she knew Sarah had packed along with her things. And now, just when she'd least expected it—bang! Ambushed.

"It—it's beautifully done," she said, her voice

catching in her throat. She stared at the artist's rendering of the principal players in the drama: Hessiah herself, not really pretty but somehow intriguing; Mayor Abbott, dashing and driven; the handsome Lieutenant Culver; Hessiah's brother Stewart, aloof and dangerous; and, of course, Fergus O'Malley. The artist caught *him* perfectly, from his finely cut features to his flashing green eyes. "It looks very like him," she whispered.

"I recognized him right away," Lee agreed.

"I . . . well, thank you for bringing this," she said, holding up the frame a little in acknowledgment. "You shouldn't have gone out of your way. I'll be heading back to my job sometime next week."

He looked up quickly, then turned casual again. "Phil will be glad to hear it."

So he knew Phil didn't know. "Phil's not the reason I'm going back," she said, rather perversely. "I've got a mortgage to pay." Not that Lee would know what a mortgage was.

He nodded sympathetically, then glanced around the crisp white porch. "This is nice work. Have you considered exterior painting as an alternate career?" he asked in a friendly, teasing way.

She allowed herself a small, wry smile. "Probably not. The pay's not great, the commute's too long, and my father stifles creativity. Speaking of careers, congratulations on holding on to yours. I read Stanley's exposé. It was devastating. If I were Strom, I'd have run for the hills instead of sticking out the primary."

"I supposed he figured what the hell, he had as good a chance as I did of winning."

"You're too hard on yourself, Lee," she said in a softer voice than she'd intended. "People are a lot more afraid of toxins than ghosts."

Their polite standoff ended when Emily's father harrumphed his way onto the porch behind her.

"Dad!" she said, surprised to see him up early from his nap. She felt exactly the way she'd felt at fifteen, when he wandered out one evening right into the middle of her first kiss with a boy named Tommy Betts. "Dad, this is Sen—Lee Alden," she said, confused about the proper protocol. "My father, George Bowditch," she added to Lee.

"Mr. Bowditch, pleased to meet you, sir," Lee said, extending his hand.

Emily's father took it, saying, "My boys been tellin' me about you, Mr. Alden. Come in. Emily, you'll be wanting to clean yourself up now."

"I'm not finished yet, Dad," Emily said through a tight smile.

"Tomorrow's supposed to be a good drying day. C'mon, c'mon," he added, which had the immediate effect of driving Emily's blood pressure up ten points.

She stood her ground, more to resist the littlest-kid syndrome than anything else. "Mr. Alden is on his way to visit Ben and Sarah, Dad. I don't think we should keep him."

"Oh, pshaw. I'll take care of Ben. 'Tisn't every day I have a Democrat under my roof," he said with a sly glance at Lee. "How do you take your coffee, sir?"

Emily rolled her eyes and left Lee at the mercy of her father. Upstairs she scrubbed the latex paint from her hands and arms as well as she could and slipped into a pair of stone-washed jeans and a clean white shirt. Her hair, with the shaved part growing out, was in that indeterminate stage between avant-garde and normal. She combed it through, flopped it around a little, and gave up. As for makeup, she didn't need any; her cheeks were ruddy from the outside work. She hesitated over her tiny bottle of Joy perfume, then purposely dabbed a little scent behind each ear, just to prove she didn't care either way.

When she returned to the old-fashioned bay-windowed parlor, she found Lee Alden in her father's BarcaLounger—a rare concession by her father to any guest—flipping slowly through a photo album while her father kept up a running commentary on family history from a Hiscock chair alongside.

Lee tried to stand up when she entered the room, but her father said, "Sit, sit," and flipped the next page for him. "This is her at a school play, I forget which grade. She was Mr. Frog. I remember the day the assignments were made; minute she steps off the bus, she starts wailing over the cruelty of it."

"Dad, Lee doesn't want to hear that old—"

"But I think she looked real cute, don't you? Her mom taped those frog lips across her cheeks; how they flapped when she done her lines! How'd they go again, Em? 'Sittin' on a rock, just takin' stock, that's what I do, the whole day through, 'cause I'm Mr. Frog.' She wanted to be *Ms.* Frog, if you please, but the song needed two syllables before 'Frog.' "

"Dad!" she said, her eyes wide with reproach.

"It sounds like your father's a big fan, Emily," Lee said politely. She wasn't fooled; his blue eyes were howling with laughter.

"Dad, if you're going to put me through the bear-skin rug routine, then I'd just as soon go outside and paint."

"No, no," he said, waving the idea away. "Not now that you're all cleaned up." He looked up from the album at his daughter. "You *did* change, didn't you?" he asked suspiciously.

Emily said, "Very funny," and he turned to Lee with a shake of his head and said, "You clean 'em, you clothe 'em, and this is how they turn out. Her mother, now, she wouldn't have been caught dead in dungarees. Whenever *I* came courtin', Agnes'd be waitin' in a nice floral dress."

Emily went faint with embarrassment. Her father had never been one to mince words. It was one reason she'd never dated much, one reason she'd moved out as soon as she could. Her brothers had never minded the teasing, but of course, they were boys. She sat stonily silent, staring out the window. Let *them* come up with the damn small talk.

"Uh-oh, I went too far," said her father with a wink at Lee. "Em, I'm sorry," he said candidly, rubbing his knees in an almost distressed way. "I can't get it out of my head that you're not my little girl anymore. Y'see, Senator, with my boys it was different. They all grew up in the normal way: got married, had kids—"

"I *believe* it's time I started dinner," Emily said, slicing through her father's good intentions.

"It's chops, tonight, isn't it? For three, Em."

"Oh, but the senator—"

"Is staying. He didn't want to, but I prevailed."

On what possible pretext? she wanted to ask. She turned and headed for the kitchen without further comment. Behind her she heard her father whisper, "Here's a cute one. Look at her at fourteen, her first date. She's half a foot taller than the little feller. . . ."

In the kitchen Emily slammed each chop into a bowl of beaten eggs, then into one with breadcrumbs. *He can't stay. I can see why he stopped by—to see that I was alive and functional, to satisfy his curiosity. But he can't stay. Dad shouldn't have put him on the spot like that. Sarah shouldn't have asked him up in the first place. And Gerry shouldn't have gotten in on the act. What is this, a conspiracy?*

She hauled out a cast-iron frying pan, then poured

oil over the bottom and turned the heat on high. Moving around the kitchen in a state of maximum distress, she began assembling a meal that was neither imaginative nor healthy, just her father's favorite: fried pork chops, mashed potatoes, and canned peas. (Her father had never farmed his five acres—he'd worked for the railroad all his life—so the charm of fresh vegetables had pretty much eluded him.)

Why couldn't Lee have dropped in yesterday for the trout meunière instead?

She was opening the second can of peas when Lee walked in, without his host.

"Where's my dad?" she asked. She glanced at the wall clock, then answered her own question. "Oh. *Wheel of Fortune.*"

"My mother's addicted to it, too," Lee said. "Need any help in here?"

"No, really . . . I'm sorry, I haven't offered you a drink. Would you like anything?"

"I'll pass," he said, lifting himself up onto a high wood stool.

"I'm afraid we're not an aperitif kind of family," she said coolly.

His eyebrows lifted. "It's good to see you completely recovered."

She knew exactly what he meant. "Okay, I'm being defensive. You caught me by surprise; I wasn't expecting you."

"I didn't assume your family would keep my coming a secret."

"Oh, I'm sure they have some stupid idea in their heads that—well, you know what I mean. You heard my father out there."

"And *you* heard my mother when you were at my place. I doubt that she sounded much different. That's how parents are with unattached kids."

Emily thought of Margaret Alden by her peonies. No, it wasn't quite the same.

Lee picked up on her hesitation instantly. "Are you suggesting my mother didn't approve of you?"

Emily shrugged and dumped the peas into a saucepan. "I don't really know how she felt about me."

"She felt strongly enough to visit you at the hospital. As did Hildie. And the kids. And Grace."

"They *did?* I didn't know that. I—I do remember some visits. I know I remember Mrs. Gibbs . . . but mostly it's a blur."

"Do you remember mine?"

It seemed to her that it cost him something to ask her that. She heard it in his voice, in the way he kept it low and controlled.

"Yes," she answered quietly. She walked away, to the refrigerator, which she opened and stared into blankly. *Why am I here?* She had no idea.

She closed it carefully, as if she were closing a door to a chamber of her heart, and without turning around, said, "I remember one time . . . I don't remember your words, but I remember the sense of them . . . that you were calling me back. . . ."

"And you *came* back—"

"No, that's just it, I didn't."

28

"Don't you understand, Lee? I *didn't* come back," she repeated, staring straight ahead. "Not voluntarily. I kept right on going . . . something drew me . . . irresistibly . . . an indescribable feeling of joy . . . I had no intentions of coming back." It was the most painful thing she'd ever said, to him or anyone else.

With a deep sigh she turned around to face him. "I don't know what happened at the end," she said with a helpless look. "I think I got tossed back—rejected—as if I were undersize or something." She tried to smile and make light of it, but it was the first time she'd spoken of her near-death experience, and the smile seemed to be trapped in the lump in her throat.

"I vowed I wouldn't tell this to anyone," she added. "And yet here I am, chatting all about it over pork chops—"

As if to demonstrate how bad her timing was, the smoke alarm went off from the smoking oil. The piercing squeal brought George Bowditch thundering into the kitchen. "Holy hell, who put the battery back in?"

Rattled, Emily switched on the stove exhaust and turned down the flame. "*I* did, and it *stays* in. There, it's stopped already. Lee, set the table. Dad, finish your program. We eat in five minutes. Dammit, anyway!"

The two men exchanged glances. Her father shrugged and left the room. Lee scanned the glass-fronted cabinets and took down dishes for the meal. It was impossible for Emily to read his thoughts as he set the table for her in silence. Was he shocked by her admission that she'd wanted to die? Annoyed that he'd let himself wander into this loony bin? Wishing she were more like Sarah or Jean? Or was he just being a good Samaritan and counting the minutes until supper was up?

The strained silence as they sat down to eat didn't last long. Emily's father, a true native of the Granite State, was an expert on politics. Everyone in New Hampshire knew why Lee had almost lost the Massachusetts primary, and everyone knew why Lee had pulled through by the skin of his teeth.

"I'm so glad it was Stanley," Emily said during a lull in the conversation. She had a flashback of Stan sitting beside her hospital bed and a sharp sense that she'd felt great affection for him. "You must have been stunned when you picked up the *Journal* the day the story broke," she said to Lee.

"I had advance word, actually. Stan sent me a copy of the story along with a note apologizing for being so slow out of the gate."

That tidbit was meant entirely for Emily, to let her know that whatever problems Stan had had about Lee, he was trying to put them behind him. "I really *am* glad," she said, and she meant it.

The three of them lingered over dessert—leftover blueberry cobbler—talking more politics. In fact it was Emily's father who did most of the talking, with Lee an attentive audience. Politics had never been Emily's strong suit, so she was just as happy to sit back and watch the arch-Republican spar with the lifelong Democrat.

There's something about the way men argue, she mused. *They don't pull their punches or second-guess. They're blunt; heck, they're brutal. Yet at the end they can shake hands with no hard feelings.* Was there a lesson in here somewhere?

Lee caught her thoughtful look; she saw the color creep up from his neck as he cleared his throat and became particularly engrossed in her father's comments. George Bowditch carried on a little while longer about the need for a strong defense budget, and then he looked from his daughter to his visitor to his daughter again.

"Time for the news," he said, rising abruptly from the dining table. "I'll have my decaf out there, Em."

Lee stacked the dishes on the counter while Emily scraped them clean for the dishwasher. They chatted about the new bay Gerry was adding to his service station—a nice, safe topic guaranteed to get them through a moment alone. When they rejoined Emily's father, he looked surprised, almost annoyed, to see them pop out from the kitchen so soon.

Admit it, Emily told herself. *You're afraid to be alone with the man. He's entitled to an explanation, and you're too cowardly to give him one. How do you say, "I passed you up for a ghost, sorry about that"?* When she did try, the smoke alarm went off. Surely that was a sign of some kind.

The three of them sat awkwardly through the rest of the news and then the entire MacNeil/Lehrer report. Clearly her father had decided that he'd had enough of one or both of them; he seemed to ignore their presence altogether. Probably it was because he was used to living alone now. Whenever the family piled in on him for the day and stayed too long, he never felt any qualms about throwing them out.

At the end of the news analysis her father ejected himself from his BarcaLounger and said, "It's late. I'm turning in. Good night."

"It's only eight-thirty, Dad," she said, looking up in surprise.

"Best put out an extra blanket for Lee. It's supposed to go down tonight."

Emily whipped her head around. "You're staying the *night?*" she asked Lee, amazed. Her father hated having any overnight guest who hadn't actually been born in the house.

"Didn't I mention that?" her father asked blandly. "Come get the blanket out of my room."

Upstairs her father took a wool Hudson's Bay blanket from the shelf in his closet and handed it to his daughter. "This makes us even for the time I walked in on you and the Betts boy," he said with a wry smile.

And then he turned off his hearing aid.

When Emily came back downstairs, still in a state of shock, Lee was standing with his back to her, hands in his pockets, looking at a cheap little print of *Whistler's Mother* that had been hanging on the wall behind the sofa for as long as she could remember.

At least it's not Elvis on velvet. But she became suddenly aware of the crazy mix of Yankee carpentry and discount furniture that filled the rooms of her father's house. There was no rhyme or reason or color scheme. The place had evolved, just like Lee's house on the Vineyard, except without taste. Out of the blue she had an image of her father having high tea with Lee's mother. *Ha!* was her first reaction. Her second was, *Dad could hold his own. We all could.* It was a revelation.

Lee turned around, and she found herself looking into his eyes, seeing her smile reflected in them. "He's great," Lee said simply, mirroring her thoughts about her father.

"I'm not sure I even knew it, not until tonight," she admitted.

"Emily . . . I didn't mean to put you through this. I don't plan to stay—"

"But you've got to stay!" she said in a knee-jerk panic. "This isn't like at your house. If you walked out, my dad would expect to know why. His feelings might be hurt. He might be afraid he'd been rude, which, of course, he *has* been, only he doesn't really mean it. It's just his way."

"So I'm . . . staying?" Lee ventured, confused.

"Yes," she said, humbled by the sound of her own babble. "If you would."

He was standing very near her. She caught herself sneaking a lungful of air, as if she were about to take a deep plunge into a depth of some kind, she didn't know what.

"Emily, the reason I'm here . . . it seemed absurd to try to mail this to you . . . and I didn't know whether you wanted your family to know about it. . . ." He took his hand from his pocket and came out with the rose-colored crystal, still on its chain, now with two of its links cut through and twisted, and offered it to her.

"Oh. That's why you came?" she asked, crestfallen. So it wasn't out of either morbid curiosity or a sense of unrequited love? It was just from simple courtesy?

She looked down at the pale gem lying in the palm

of her hand. The chain seemed less weighty somehow; the crystal, less mysterious. It looked like just another gaudy trinket, the kind you found in the jewelry counters of secondhand stores everywhere. Fifteen dollars. You could get it for twelve.

When she looked up her cheeks were stained with tears.

"I'll get my duffel bag from my car. Will you tell me which is my room?" he asked in a strained voice.

Was it all a dream, then, after all? Fergus never was? And Lee was never to be? Stricken and confused, she looked up at Lee and whispered, "Your room . . . yes . . . it's upstairs . . . to the left."

She waited until he'd finished in the only bathroom and settled in the bedroom next to hers before she ventured out in her pajamas to wash up. When she returned to her room, which looked out on the back, she tucked herself into the rocker at the window and stared at the same stars she'd wished on as a child.

Is it possible he doesn't care anymore? All evening long she'd been trying to avoid him. It never occurred to her that he might have been trying to avoid *her.* Yet he had driven up here, hadn't he? *Ah. To return the necklace.* But he had blushed and stammered once or twice tonight, hadn't he? *Ah. Because he was afraid she might be getting the wrong idea.*

Emily had been assuming he'd stayed away after she awoke from her coma because he cared too much. But what if he just hadn't cared *enough?* As for her suspicion that he was warming up to Ben and Sarah and to Jean and Gerry just to get closer to her —it was insulting to her family *and* to Lee. The more she thought about it, the more she was staggered by her sense of her own importance.

She jumped up from the chair, incapable suddenly of sitting still, and began to pace the room. Her eye fell on the necklace lying on the dresser. She picked it up, fingered it idly, tossed it back. *This has to be resolved. Tonight.*

There was a door joining the two rooms; Lee's had been a sewing room in days gone by. Nothing separated them now but a thin wall. *It's always something. Money. Family. Status. Fergus. A coma, for Pete's sake. And now lath and plaster.* Unwilling to put up with it anymore, she marched up to the door and banged on it. She heard him say, "Come in." And that's what she did.

He was in his pajama bottoms, sitting in a chair facing the same starry view that she had, with his legs outstretched and his feet perched on the inside windowsill. The window was ajar. There were no lamps on in his room, only a shaft of light that poured in from hers. It fell across his chest, which was bare, but left his face in relative darkness.

He said nothing. He didn't move. She seized on the sound of the hissing radiator as her excuse for exploding into his privacy. "I was wondering . . . it's too hot for you, isn't it? My father keeps it unbearable. Just turn the knob clockwise on the radiator."

Still, he said nothing. "Unless you'd rather just leave the window open."

Nothing. Still. "Dammit, Lee! I need an answer!"

"What was the question?" he asked in a voice devoid of emotion.

"The question? The *question? Do* you love me or *don't* you?"

"Gee." He laughed under his breath. "Let me think."

She stood there, panting and frightened, like a small bird that alights on a sailboat a hundred miles from shore and clings to the rigging, hoping it won't be shooed away. *Don't say no,* she begged. *If you say no, I'll die.* Suddenly it was as simple as that. Crystal clear, and as simple as that.

He stood up from his chair and walked over to her. "Do I love you?" he repeated in a voice drawn bow tight. "I love you enough not to make you think you love me."

She wanted a yes, was dreading a no—but this?

He saw her confusion. "Let me put it another way," he said, taking her by her shoulders. He brought his mouth down on hers in a kiss of such deep, searing intensity that it took away her breath, took away speech, took away choice.

He's right, she thought dizzily. *When he takes me in his arms, he can make me do whatever he wants.* She was awed by it, this ability he had to electrify her and make her feel powerless at the same time.

He let her go gently, gradually, as if he didn't want her to fall and be hurt. "I need more than that from you, Emily. Once it would have been enough, but not now."

"How much more can there be?" she asked weakly, collapsing wobble-kneed on the side of his bed.

He towered over her, hands on his hips, in a pose of classic confrontation. "There can be a *lot* more," he said impatiently, almost angrily. "There can be a wedding. Anniversaries. Kids. Little League. Shopping. Biking. Disneyland."

He sat on the bed next to her and took her hand in his, dropping a sudden, wistful kiss in her open palm. "There can be Trivial Pursuit . . . picnics . . . birthdays . . . tomato plants . . . grandkids." He cradled her face in his hands. "There can be a whole long life together. I love sharing your bed, Emily. But it's not enough. I need to share your life."

"Is that what this is?" she whispered. "A *proposal?*"

"I know it's mundane," he said. "You've been through an unbelievable time, gone wandering through the stars, experienced incredible things. But this is all I am, Emily. This is all I have."

A tear of joy rolled down her cheek, and then another. She said, "You're everything to me. Don't you know that? I do love you—before, during, after the kiss. It's true, I did go wandering through the stars. But then I fell back to earth. And when I realized you might not be there to pick me up—don't you see? That's why I'm here. That's why I barged into your room in a panic."

He broke into a sudden, broad grin of relief and wrapped his arms around her waist. "I thought it was to turn down the heat," he quipped, nuzzling her neck inside her pajama collar.

"No, sir," she murmured with a crazy kind of glee, arching her neck to his kisses. "It was to turn it up."

After that he wanted her to stay the night with him, but only after whispering in her ear, "Would your father be upset if he found out?"

Emily laughed low in her throat, a laugh that was wise in half a dozen new ways. "He owes me for Tommy," she whispered back, and Lee knew enough not to ask who Tommy was.

"I love you," he murmured in a voice hazy with pleasure, drawing her down on top of him. She pulled back, bracing herself on her hands and hovering above him, the better to see him, to drink in the wonder of him.

Slowly his fingers opened each of the buttons of her pajama tops; carefully he pulled them aside, exposing her breasts. His fingers strayed lightly over the pink tips with a conjurer's touch, deliberate and magical. Robbed of strength and resolve, she found herself lowering down on top of him, her soft flesh pressing the hard, muscled surface of his chest, their lower torsos separated by two thin barricades of cotton.

"It's been a long, long time," he said in something close to a groan. "Probably you can tell."

She laughed wickedly and pressed herself to him. "Ah, *time.*" She rolled the word luxuriously over her lips, savoring the taste of it. "It's something we'll have so much of from now on."

"Which reminds me, darlin'," he said, sliding his hands around her buttocks, holding her close. "Was that a yes to Trivial Pursuit?"

She teased him mercilessly, her lips playing over his, her tongue testing and tasting his. "Hmm, didn't I say?" she asked, catching his lips lightly in her teeth, holding them with taunting good humor.

He waited until she released him. Then he brought his hand quickly behind her head and held her mouth to his in a kiss of instant, annihilating eroticism.

"Ah, Lee," she said when at last he let her speak. "Isn't it obvious? I'd rather pursue trivia with you than with anyone else on earth. Yes. I'll marry you. *Yes.*"

Epilogue

"So what do you think? Will we make a sailor of him?"

Emily took her husband's hand and laid it over her swollen belly. "Feel that? She's loving every minute of it," she answered, grinning.

Lee laughed, then drew his hand across Emily's cheek in a loving caress. "How about you, kiddo? No nausea?"

"Not a bit. What's to be nauseated about? The weather's perfect; the sea's quiet; your boat moves like a dream. And have I mentioned I'm starving to death?"

He looked startled, as if hunger were a concept untested at sea. "Really? Great," he said, rubbing his hands together. "I'd love a sandwich myself," he said, handing over the tiller to her and diving down the companionway in search of forage.

"Don't forget chips!" she yelled down after him. "And a pickle! Two pickles!"

She sucked in a huge lungful of clean sea air,

happy to be alive, happier still to be alive for two. "This is bliss," she whispered to the elements. She knocked on wood, easy to do on a wood sailboat, and gave silent thanks to the gods who'd presented her with a man so considerate that he'd go without food before running the risk of making his wife seasick by eating in front of her.

Considerate, and knock-down sexy. When he popped out of the cabin a few minutes later with a pickle-filled plastic bag in his teeth, clutching an egg salad sandwich in each hand, with a diet Coke tucked under each armpit, she went absolutely giddy with desire.

"Thanks, Senator," she said, relieving him of a sandwich and the pickles. "Any chance of getting you in the sack when we reach Hadley Harbor?"

"Oh, ye of insatiable appetite!"

"Appe*tites*."

"Yeah," he said, kissing her, "I'd say there's a pretty good chance."

He scooted her over and took the tiller, steering with his foot while he packed away his huge sandwich, and half of Emily's, in very short order. They were sitting on the low side of the cockpit, making it easier for Lee to see the trim of the jib. Every once in a while the boat took a gust of wind, sending it heeling on its side, its leeward gunnels awash; Emily trailed her hand overboard, watching the small but perfect diamond on her finger glittering through the water.

Lee had his arm around her waist. "You'd better be careful, girl. Some fish comes along and chomps off your ring finger, there'll be hell to pay back home."

She whipped her hand out of the water, then blushed when he laughed at her gullibility. "Still, it *was* a touching gesture on your mother's part to give me her own ring," she said. "I can't believe it didn't go to Grace or Hildie," she also ventured, for the first time.

"Too small a stone for Grace, too late for Hildie's engagement in Europe. It was you or never," he said mischievously. "And of course, my mother does happen to adore you," he added when Emily looked crestfallen. "Gosh, woman, will you *ever* feel confident among our tribe?"

"I'm making *great* strides," she insisted. "*Who* had the courage to decline a calligrapher and address her own wedding invitations?"

"You did."

"And *who* served meat loaf when your mother and Inez visited last week, instead of working myself into a frenzy trying to impress them both?"

"You're a model of courage for us all. Kiss me and take the helm again. I'm about to risk my life going forward to drop the jib; who knows if I'll come back?" he said gaily.

She put her hand over his mouth. "Not funny. Don't say that," she begged in a soft, stricken voice.

Instantly the expression on his face changed. "You're right," he said, taking her hand from his mouth, kissing her tenderly. "I can't think of anything less funny. I love you, Emily, mother of my child." He leaned over and kissed her belly. "I love you both."

Just as instantly his expression changed again, from somber to deadpan. "What I will do is, I will wrap a line around my waist and secure it to a cleat. Then I will crawl forward on all fours, even though the wind is blowing only seven knots, and after I douse the sail, I will crawl back again. To the absolute, impenetrable safety of your arms."

She pulled off her visor and whacked him with it.

* * *

At sundown Lee had a drink in the cockpit while Emily heated up homemade chili on the tiny two-burner stove in the yacht's scaled-down galley. Because the galley was tucked under the companionway, it was easy for them to chat back and forth while Emily put together a salad.

"Looks like a front to our southwest," he said lazily. "We may get some thunderstorms later. I hope I got that leak fixed okay."

"Which leak?" she asked absently, slicing tomatoes.

"The one above your half of the berth."

She looked up with a sly smile. "We'll both stay on your side again, that's all."

"That's all? That's heaven."

They ate dinner in the cockpit, and then Lee offered to clean up belowdecks. Emily had her tea in the cockpit while he did so, enjoying the last perfect moments of a perfect summer's day. This was her special time, supper tea, and Lee made a point of letting her savor her solitude, often in the garden somewhere. She saw a light go on in the berth up forward; Lee had two more chapters to go in a Tom Clancy novel.

A half-moon began its steady climb from the southeast among a few bright stars, while to the southwest Emily saw occasional, spectacular streaks of lightning. It was an extraordinarily beautiful sky, bizarre and exciting at the same time, split evenly between the serene and the diabolical. She thought of calling Lee away from his thriller, but she didn't have the heart. There were very few boats anchored in the nearly landlocked harbor, and the stillness was absolute. There was no sound except of an occasional fish jumping. It was all so new, so different, not like any night she had ever known. Her senses were absolutely alive.

Emily sat with her legs folded under her, sipping the last of her tea, wondering which would prevail: the lightning, or the moon. Suddenly a loud hiss sounded practically under her elbow; she jumped so high the tea spilled over the edge of her mug. She peered over the cockpit coaming, and in the combatant light of the night sky she saw it: an enormous swan, his neck arched to the height of the cockpit itself, obviously begging for food, just as a family of geese and goslings had done earlier.

"Oh," she said breathlessly, "wait right here." She dashed down below and rummaged in the cupboard for the last of their bakery bread and a box of oat crackers. "There's a huge swan swimming alongside, Lee; you really should come out and see it."

"Hmm? That's nice," he answered, completely lost in his book.

Outside, she tore off hunks of bread and held them up for the swan to take from her hand. She had no idea how he was able to see the food; despite the moon, despite the lightning, it was an inky night. From the west she was able to see black clouds headed for a mixup with the lightning and after that, the moon.

"Where's your mate?" she whispered to the swan, feeding him the last of the bread.

Hiss-s-s-s-s.

He floated alongside, waiting, and then began to leave—in anger, it seemed to her. She opened the box of oat crackers quickly, and at the first crinkle sound of the plastic liner the swan returned. He took an oat cracker from her, then dropped it in the water. He would not take another.

"Picky," she murmured.

Hiss-s-s-s-s.

He circled once, twice, then glided off. It depressed her somehow, as if she'd failed him. She remembered a bran muffin she was saving for her breakfast and ran below to fetch it, on the chance that the swan might come back. For ten minutes she sat alone, holding her muffin in her lap, waiting.

He was no ordinary swan, of that she was sure. He was too big, too powerful, too vocal. Lee had told her that all the waterfowl around here panhandled: the ducks, the geese, the sea gulls. They brought their young; generations, he said, had done it. But he'd said nothing about a swan, a swan without a mate.

Hiss-s-s-s-s.

He was back! On the other side of the boat! Delighted, Emily broke off a chunk of muffin and tried feeding it to him. He accepted it with an offhand arrogance that Emily had run into only once before in her life. She caught her breath.

"Fergus?" she whispered, faint with wonder.

Hiss-s-s-s-s.

The moon and lightning lit up the sky, lit up the nearly uninhabited shoreline, lit up the great white swan. In six swipes at her fingers the muffin was gone. She had nothing more to give him. He circled alongside, imperial and impatient. "That's all there is," she said sadly.

The swan paused and circled, then swung away from the boat and struck out for the entrance to the harbor. Emily could see him in the moonlight for perhaps a thousand feet or so. And then the first of the black clouds from the west passed over the moon, and the great white swan was swallowed up in darkness.

But then a tremendous bolt of lightning ripped the sky open. In its flash she saw the swan one last time.

After that the lightning moved off, and the rest of the black clouds moved in, and darkness reigned. It was over.

"Good-bye, Fergus," she whispered, a tear breaking through and rolling down her cheek. "Good-bye."

When she went below again, Lee was just closing *The Hunt for Red October*. "Great read," he said, reaching up one arm behind him and catching her in his embrace. "They always are. What've you been up to?" he said, pulling her toward him for an upside-down kiss.

She let herself test the novelty of his mouth from the new position and said, "Just saying good-bye to a friend."

"Same old friend?" he asked in a quiet, thoughtful way.

"Yes," she said, smiling. "He was just passing through."